Bewitching Hawthorn Lane

Tales From Hawthorn Lane

~Libris One~

Kristina Schram

Mischief Maker Media

Published by Mischief Maker Media (USA)

First printing: February, 2017

Copyright © 2017 by Kristina Schram

All rights reserved.

This is a work of fiction. Names, characters, places, and incidents are products of the author's imagination or are used fictitiously and should not be construed as real. Any resemblance to actual events, locales, organizations or persons, living or dead, is entirely coincidental.

No part of this book may be used or reproduced in any manner whatsoever without written permission, except in the case of brief quotations embodied in critical articles and reviews. For more information e-mail all inquiries to: info@KristinaSchram.com

Cover Design, Interior, and Technical Expertise: GorKee

Cover Photo: Young Woman and Castle from iStockPhoto

ISBN: 978-1-939397-27-0

Visit Kristina Schram at: www.KristinaSchram.com

Acknowledgements

The idea for this book came to me as most my ideas do—by slowly making its way down a long, dark hallway. Some days I feel like most things come to me that way, but that's okay. I rather like long, dark hallways.

Now, at last, this book has reached the end of that hallway, and made it into the light of day, and that's thanks to my beta readers: Elizabeth Schram, Dan Unzen, Ian More, and Heather Duane. Your comments and support kept me in the light long enough to get the job done.

Thank you!

I also want to thank all my fervent supporters over the years, who've bought my books, sent me inspiring comments, who've taken the time to leave a review or share my book links with others. Dear readers, you keep me going on those days when the dark clouds threaten to blot out the sunshine.

You are a warm light at the end of that long, dark hallway.

⚡

...I dedicate this book to those who believe...

Chapter One

A sharp rap on the door echoed through the small cottage, and the fire, which had been dying down after an evening of frenzied burning, suddenly roared back to life, snapping and hissing like a live creature. The knock heralded the arrival of a visitor I'd been expecting to show at any moment, though I'd received no warning of her coming.

Pushing myself to my feet, I crossed the cool, oaken planks on tiptoe, then leaned against the door, arms crossed to ward off the chill.

Knock...knock...knock.

With each decisive strike on the thick wood, my grip on my biceps tightened, turning my fingertips white with anticipation. At the last bang, I shivered, unable to stop Shakespeare's infamous words from entering my mind: "By the pricking of my thumbs, something wicked this way comes." But then, something wicked was always coming to Hawthorn Lane. This place attracted the illicit like a vampire to blood.

"Lorelle?" a low voice called my name in a seductive purr. "I know you're in there. Open up, you elusive brat. It's raining cats and dogs out here and I've brought you something!" Silence. "Something tasty. So *very* tasty." Blast her, my visitor was telling the truth. I knew from past experience that what Avice Montrose had in her possession was something so tantalizing I could actually taste it simply by hearing her luscious voice.

Well, she'd already had me at *so very tasty*, so I opened the door a smidgeon and poked my face through the crack. Misty air greeted me softly as a kiss, leaving behind a fine layer of water droplets on my skin.

"What do you want, Avice? I was just off to bed." That was very close to the truth. I was already in my thin white nightgown, which did little to warm me in this damp weather, and my long, black hair had been released from its confining bun.

Avice grinned at me, knowing she'd won half the battle simply by getting me to open the door. Leaning forward and exposing a vast amount of cleavage, pale and soft as bread dough, she thrust a bottle at me. A dark bottle full of dark spirits.

In fact, that was the name of the drink...*Dark Spirits*. My favorite liquorous potation, and a load of trouble, to boot. I took the bottle from her, opened the door to let her in, peeked out to see her carriage waiting outside the gate, then closed the door behind me.

I turned to face the lovely Avice, who knew her beauty as sure as she knew her name. She'd brought the cool smell of spring rain in with her, along with her own private sultry scent of sandalwood and peony. I was careful not to breathe in too deeply. Avice is a hard woman to resist, which is why I shouldn't have let her in when my defenses were down.

But here she was, along with my favorite indulgence, and I thought I might as well make the best of it. To be on the safe side, I wouldn't touch a drop with Avice here. A self-proclaimed equal-opportunity seductress, she was a temptress of all kinds, and it was best to keep a clear head around her.

Avice had already made herself at home, pulling off her wet cape and leaving it to puddle on the floor before draping herself along the worn chaise longue that fronted my fireplace. It was my favorite place to read, and was, in fact, where I'd been sitting, wrapped in a spider silk shawl and reading *My Wicked Ways*, when she'd knocked.

Her cherry red lips parted as she smiled at me, revealing the tip of her pink, no doubt agile, tongue. I tried not to stare at it. I knew why she was here; she had come looking for answers about a strange occurrence that had happened late last night, when darkness was mistress and only those touched in the head roamed freely about. But she wouldn't get much from me. I saw most everything going on about Hawthorn Lane; I heard most everything, too. Though what I saw and what I heard was nobody's business but my own.

Mostly my own, that is.

Miss 'Busybody' Montrose failed to grasp that concept. She believed everyone's business was hers, too.

"It's awfully early to be nipping off to bed with the intention to sleep. Only nine bells? What are you? An old woman?"

"I didn't sleep well last night."

Of course she already knew that. She patted a spot next to her, her smile triumphant. "Do come sit down, Lorelle. This rain has driven the heat right out of me, and you look so very warm. Like a portable pot of fire."

"Fire burns," I reminded her.

Her eyelids lowered invitingly. "I don't mind." Avice patted the seat again. "Sit." This time it was a command. I knew well enough to go along with her simple requests. Obeying made my life easier and saved my energy for defying her *less* simple requests. My bare feet crossed the old wood planks, worn by the tired boots and heels of countless folk who'd inhabited this space over the several hundred years of its existence, and I sat down in the tiny spot she'd left me, barely big enough for my backside, which wasn't very big. "Do relax," she ordered. "You're stiff as a board."

I considered making some snide comment to the effect that she likely preferred a little stiffness, at least in her dealings with men, but I kept my words to myself. I wasn't a man, and besides that, I didn't want to encourage her flirtations.

Following orders, I let my shoulders droop slightly, and in doing so my elbow nudged her soft breast. She gave an ecstatic sigh and let her eyelids flutter. "That's better," she moaned, and I swallowed hard. Avice was in fine form tonight. I stared longingly at the black bottle clasped in my hands.

Just a sip to take the edge off?

I shook my head. Many a fool had passed down that road, never to return. I would not be that fool.

"To what do I owe the pleasure of your company, Avice?" I asked.

"No need to be cheeky, you impudent wench. You know what I want."

"Information," I replied, because it was, after all, what I did. Gather it, that is. Part of what I did around here, anyway.

"Of course." She laid a hand on my arm, then began to stroke up and down, her skin warm as liquid flame through the thin fabric of my gown, forcing me to relax even further so that soon I was nearly melting against her soft fullness. "We all felt the breach," she breathed into my ear. "So tell me what it means. No one seems to know, nor was anyone especially up to finding out."

I straightened up, a tad reluctantly, I do admit. "You needn't use your wiles on me, harlot."

I glanced back to see her saucy grin. "Oh, but I enjoy it, Lorelle. You're such a prickly pear, and I long to bite into what I'm quite positive must be sweet, tender flesh beneath those pesky thorns."

A deep breath was in order, and I didn't care that she saw me take it. For what came next I needed a clear head, not one fogged by the promise of sensual pleasures I had not experienced from another in many years...beyond Avice's seduction attempts whenever she tried to get information out of me.

"You want to know what happened, I suppose."

She leaned forward, pushing her breasts against me. "I do."

"And you think I know?" I asked breathily.

"You know everything, Lorelle. You have a gift for perception."

"You know very well that all it takes are brains and the desire to know."

"Desire. Ummm…" She stretched languorously, shifting beneath me. "I do so like that word."

"Isn't it your middle name?"

She laughed, a deep chuckle that vibrated through me, from her full chest to my less well-endowed one. I bit my lip and pulled myself away from temptation once more. "Desiree, to be exact. I chose the name myself. Very apt, isn't it?"

"Very."

"Now I know you're tired, luv, so do be a dear and share. I had a busy time of it last night." No doubt a part of that busy time had been spent with the Damnay twins. "A doubleheader, you could say," she went on. *Definitely* the Damnay twins. Recently turned twenty, delicately handsome, and new to Hawthorn Lane, those boys hadn't stood a chance with Avice. "It was Beltane, after all, and we all know what that means. It's bloody good fun, but rather tiring." As if to prove her point, Avice yawned, and I took the opportunity to stand. She looked up at me lazily as I faced her. "Well?"

"The Van der Daarkes," I announced dramatically, "have returned to Hawthorn Lane."

She gasped, both in shock and excitement, and sat up, her large blue eyes already narrowing in calculation as she processed what this could mean for her. This was big news in our little village, in more ways than one. For a century, Daarke Castle had stood empty on its mountain perch, looking down on us all with silent disdain. A shroud of mystery cloaked the Daarke family's departure, and continued absence, though plenty of rumors abounded, ranging from the mundane (they'd gotten bored of Hawthorn Lane and wanted to see the world) to the outrageous (virgin sacrifices and cold-blooded murder). Someone in the village must know the real reason for their flight, though the rest of us remained ignorant.

Including myself, which annoyed me to no end.

I had not existed a hundred years ago, not even close, being only twenty-four years of age. Only six of those spent here in Hawthorn Lane, I possessed no first-hand knowledge of the scandalous affair. I'd tried to find out more—believe me—but I could not track down the truth. My failure bothered me dearly.

"Why have they come?" Avice paused. "And why now?"

I shrugged. While I had given her information, it was only a small bit of what I'd learned, and only what she'd find out soon enough. But I knew more. "You were raised here, so I thought *you* might know something."

Her twilight blue eyes blinked lazily. "No more than you. There are rumors, of course."

"Yes, I've heard them."

"But nobody knows the truth, do they?" She leaned forward avidly, offering me yet another generous view of her busty landscape. A red curl rested on the white expanse, rising and falling with each exhilarated breath she took.

My eyes escaped to the relative peace of the snapping fire. "I've tried to find out…"

"I'm sure you have."

"Lady Faylan is tight-lipped."

"You don't know the half of it," Avice grumpily agreed. Lady Faylan was one of the few residents of Hawthorn Lane who could resist Avice's charms. She was also one of the oldest, having been around when the Van der Daarkes had left, and who knew how long before that.

"You could try again," I urged, more because it would distract her than from any real belief she could find anything out from Lady Faylan.

"Or I could pay a visit to the castle."

"You could do that," I said slowly, remembering what I'd seen, what I'd heard. "But I would be very careful. The Van der Daarkes are not to be trifled with."

Avice reached down to pick up her cloak, then in one smooth movement rose and came to me. She stood so close that I could feel her warm breath on my cheek, her heart beating against my still arm. She blinked slowly at me. "How sweet that you care about my welfare, Lorelle."

"Hawthorn Lane wouldn't be the same without you." Which was true, though whether for the better or worse I wasn't quite sure.

She laughed, reading my mind. "You'd miss me, admit it."

"I would." As much as Avice aggravated me with her faux seductions, I would not like our little world without her. "Which is why I'm warning you about the Van der Daarkes. Something's not right with them."

She leaned forward and pressed her warm, soft lips against mine. My eyelids fluttered closed. "I shall be careful, luv."

With a soft laugh and a whirl, she was gone, leaving me standing with my eyes closed, the memory of another's lips touching mine stirring within me…

Someone I had once loved and would never see again.

Chapter Two

I'm not sure how I managed to hear it over the rain, but the insistent tapping woke me from a deep sleep. I sat up, rubbed my gritty eyes, and glared in the general direction from whence the annoying racket came. On such a damp and dreary day I did not want to leave the comfort of my cozy bed nook with its warm downy quilts and soft pillows.

The tapping came again, louder this time. It was my door knocker, a vicious little gargoyle that always looked as though he'd rather bite your hand clean off than let it touch his precious, knobbly head.

"Hello?" a tentative voice called. It sounded very young, and carried the whispery burden of a slight lisp. "Is, like, anyone home?"

I groaned, then rolled out of my nook, and with quick jerks drew on my red, embroidered dragon robe. I made my stumbling way to the loft railing in time to see the cast-iron handle lift as though someone was trying to open the door. The door was locked, though, so whoever it was wasn't getting in.

It wasn't Avice. She might be a lot of things, but subtlety wasn't one of her limited virtues, as evidenced by her visit the night before. She'd come searching for information and had made no secret of it. I, on the other hand, am sneaky. When talking to her, I'd held back because that's what I did, and also because I'd yet to make sense of what I'd seen and heard the night of Beltane.

I remembered everything clearly, as though watching a scene playing out on stage. I'd been working in Fell Forest, the ancient stand of conifers that covered Savage Mountain, collecting mushrooms and snails by the light of the full moon. Working close to the main road, I'd just spotted the elusive Black Murder Mushroom, a favorite amongst the more affluent residents of Hawthorn Lane, when I heard something coming. Soon I could see it—a carriage blacker than night and moving at a fast clip as though the hounds of hell were after it. I ducked behind the wide trunk of a Black Pine and watched the coach pass, feeling with each pounding hoof a growing sense of unease, thick and oily in my veins. Here was the culprit who'd triggered the breach, and I was the lone witness to it.

Everyone else was enjoying the revelry of Beltane still going on down below in the village. I had not joined in; I never did, as this time of year was the best for collecting a particularly elusive truffle. Though I did participate in the day's earlier activities. I would not miss out on the early morning dew ceremony, not wanting to forego any potential help the dew might provide my complexion and/or visage, plus it was the best time to collect it. Nor would I miss the laying of flowers at midday or the indulgent feasting as the sun went down.

But when the bonfires reached their peak, I left the confines of the village with basket in hand. I not only gather information, I collect delectables—various foods, herbs, and fungi I found or grew and prepared to sell to various shop owners in the village.

Yesterday, the day after Beltane, our little village had been quiet except for the violent cracks of thunder and vindictive gusts of wind from a storm that had followed in on the coach's spinning wheels. The wild storm, along with a merry night, was why Avice had come so late yesterday evening. Normally when a breach is felt, curiosity runs high, with messengers flying here and there to disseminate news and rumors. But the Van der Daarkes had planned their arrival wisely, coming at a time when most of the villagers would be occupied with revelries of some sort or another, and likely soused, to boot. We Hawthornites treasure our celebrations and carry them out with great enthusiasm. They help us to forget.

The knocking came again and I made my way down the ladder, grumbling to myself about unwanted visitors and their obnoxious rapping at my chamber door.

"Who's there?" I called as I crossed the floor.

"Please let me in!" The childish voice grew suddenly frantic. "It's an emergency!"

Typically not easily startled, this time I couldn't help but be surprised. I unlocked the door and pulled it open, warily but quickly. Before me stood a young girl, about fifteen years of age, shivering in the cool May air. She wore jeans that tapered at the ankles and a red hooded pullover with the words, *Go Big or Go Home*, on it. She was too thin, and even under the rain-darkened hood, I could see her long blond hair needed a good wash.

"What's the matter?" I looked past her, but saw nothing threatening. I lived on the outskirts of Hawthorn Lane, but close enough to the village that if I required assistance, I need only holler. Not that I ever had, or would, if I could help it.

"Please help me!" she begged, bouncing up and down on her red-sneakered tiptoes and looking over her shoulder every few seconds. "He's going to catch me, and if he does, I'm totally screwed!"

Her voice sounded vaguely familiar, and besides that, I knew I could handle her if she tried anything—I outweighed her by a good twenty pounds. "You'd better come in then." I pulled the door open and ushered her and a rush of cold, wet air inside, wondering what the hell I was getting myself into.

Before I could see who was coming after her, she pushed past me, grabbed my arm and pulled me away from the door, then slammed it shut and shoved home the lock. Turning about, she fell dramatically against the door, panting wildly.

"You saved my life!" She rushed toward me and enveloped me in her skinny arms.

Not being the comforting type, when she relaxed slightly, I pulled back and grabbed hold of her damp sleeves. I held her away from me and examined her closely. She had dark circles under her wide blue, bloodshot eyes, and her little, round nose was running. Probably because she was soaked through.

"Who's chasing you, and why?"

"He's trying to make me live with him. *Here*. In this awful place!" Her body shuddered violently, and to my dismay, she started to cry, her upper lip rising to reveal two slightly prominent front teeth that were surely the cause of her lisp.

"There, there," I soothed awkwardly. "Just calm down. Come on." I pushed her onto my chaise longue. "Sit here. I'm going to make you some tea."

The kitchen, tiny and cozy, was only a few steps away, and I stirred the dying embers in the cast-iron stove before adding a few pieces of kindling. When they caught, I placed a kettle on the burner, then added a few pieces of wood and peat to the dying coals in the cave-like fireplace to help warm my visitor, who was shivering convulsively.

Modern conveniences do exist in Hawthorn Lane, but they come at a cost, both monetarily and to one's pride. I preferred to do most things the old-fashioned way, as it kept me from becoming too reliant on soft living. Even so, my cottage wasn't entirely devoid of amenities. I had plumbing, and a back-up heat source in the case of an unusually hard winter. Unfortunately this past winter had been one of the rough ones and I'd been forced to use up a great amount of my stores. Using backup was expensive and I avoided doing so as much as possible. Saved currency gave me more time to do the things I liked, such as reading my beloved penny dreadfuls and gothic novels, tending to my gardens, and playing my clariflute. But this season had forced me to blow through much of my savings simply trying to keep the pipes from freezing. I was now short on Goldenars and wasn't sure how I was going to pay for the damage the deep cold had done to the cottage's foundation.

A brief peek showed my visitor still shaking, her eyes closed and her hands clasped tight. I didn't bother speaking to her or introducing myself. She looked wrung-out and I figured all that could wait until she had something warm inside her.

The kettle whistled imperiously and I prepared us limoney tea and slices of warm wild blueberry bread and clover honey. I placed our repast on a dinged-up, but well-polished pewter tray, and set it on the small table in front of the chaise longue. Then I sat next to the girl's frail frame and poured us each a cup of fragrant brew, its citrusy scent conjuring up spring right before us.

The girl helped herself to the bread and gobbled it down so quickly that I ended up giving her my own helping. I would get more for myself later. For now, I was glad to see that she ate normally. Had her pursuer starved her? Was that why she'd run away? If that were the case, she would not be going back to him. I would take her to Lady Faylan, the matriarch and overseer of the village. While she wasn't the warmest soul I'd ever met, all my dealings with her had convinced me she was a prudent and respectable woman. Still, I wouldn't dare cross her.

"I think you need to get out of those wet clothes," I told the girl when she'd drunk two cups of tea and was now dotting up any remaining breadcrumbs with her finger. "I've a dress you can wear, though it'd be a bit big on you." I was slender myself, but she was built like a stick.

She waved my suggestion away with a fluttering hand. "Oh, no. I couldn't. I'm fine now."

"You smell of wet clothes. You could do with a wash, too."

She winced and her sunken cheeks flamed red. "I don't usually look like this, you know. It's just that, well, since it happened… Well, I haven't felt safe enough to do much of anything. And now I'm here, in this strange place, and it's raining…" She gulped down a sob.

"You'd feel better if you were warm and dry."

"I'm sure I would, but like I told you, he's *coming*."

"When?" I asked, though really I wanted to know *who*.

Her bony shoulders lifted and dropped. "I don't know exactly because I snuck out. But he'll figure it out soon. I didn't go down to breakfast when he called."

"Did he kidnap you?"

She gave a brief shake of her head. "But he brought me here against my will."

Weren't the two one and the same? "Why will he come here, to my place?"

"Because he will *know*."

Suddenly I remembered where I'd heard her voice. After I'd spotted the carriage, I followed it up the hillside to Daarke Castle—a castle that had stood empty for a hundred years and was now lit up like a macabre birthday cake. The village coach was moving fast, but I possess a speed and stamina that would have stood me well as a messenger back in the old days. Even so, I was glad the castle wasn't too far from where I'd been gathering.

The carriage passed beneath the gateway's fang-like portcullis and when I reached the opening, I ducked out of sight to watch. Seconds after the coach pulled to a stop in front of the main entrance, three dark figures exited the vehicle. Two moved quickly and freely, though the third hesitated.

"Come along." The speaker sounded tired, but in command, his British accent clipped and sure. "There's much to do, and it's late."

"I really don't want to stay here," a small voice complained—the same voice as the girl now sitting beside me. She was not British, but American like myself.

"We've discussed this, Ilia. It's our only option right now."

"My mother wouldn't want me to stay *here*." She waved a hand at the foreboding building.

"Your mother no longer has any say in the matter."

A ragged sob echoed through the courtyard. "You're so mean!"

"I'll be whatever I have to be to follow through on my duties."

"I want to go home!"

"You have no home," the man responded brutally, and I took an immediate dislike to him.

At that moment, a loud banging rattled the door, and we both jumped. Ilia, as I now remembered she was called, started to shake, her young eyes widening in fright. The sound reverberated through the small cottage like a summons to war, and we turned toward the door in unison.

"Ilia Elizabeth," the same commanding voice from last night pierced the thick door, "you're to quit this place at once!"

"I will not!" she cried, a bit of rebellion hardening her delicate jaw.

"You'll do what I tell you!"

Ilia launched herself into my arms. "Don't let him take me!"

I slowly peeled her wet, shivering form off me. "I don't plan on letting him. Go to the loft." I nodded at the ladder. She was quick, picking up on my meaning and scurrying up the steps swift as a squirrel. I stood, grabbed the diamond willow staff I kept for such purposes, and marched toward the door, my black hair streaming behind me like a witch's cape. "You are not welcome here," I shouted boldly, a strange sense of sympathy for the girl stirring within me. "Now go!"

But my words were for naught, and I watched in dismay as the lock slowly slid back and the door blew open.

Chapter Three

A crack of thunder shook the cottage, and I blinked in shock as the dark outline of a massive man filled the doorway. How had he opened my door?

The stranger ducked low to enter and before I could react, he was inside my cottage with the door shut behind him. The air all around me crackled with electricity, as though he'd brought the storm in with him, and my heart began to beat a little harder.

He stepped forward and I swung the staff at him as hard as I could. I was hoping to buy some time, not to mention wanting to get out of this alive, and my fear whipped the staff through the air with great speed. He nimbly avoided getting hit, then reached down, grabbed the staff, and pulled hard. As I was still hanging onto it, he was able to drag me to him with one strong jerk. In a startlingly short time the staff was yanked from my hands to land on the floor, and I was held captive in his arms. An electric shock shot through me, setting off tingles all over my body and making my hair lift. It was like he'd absorbed the storm and was now spreading its power to everything he touched, which, right now, was me.

"Let me go!" I stomped hard on his riding boot, but my bare foot made no impact. He spun me about and lifted me into the air, as easily as though I were a sack of feathers. The shock pulsing between us grew in intensity, and I felt weak as my feet dangled helplessly a foot above the floor. *It's harmless,* I assured myself. *Simply static electricity from the storm, nothing more.* But I didn't really believe it.

For several long moments my hazy senses could only take in the heady scent of damp leather and fresh rain, the scratch of wet wool on my bare neck, the strength in the arms of my captor. Finally it occurred to my dazed brain that I must fight if I wanted to break free of the lunatic holding me tightly to his heaving chest.

I started to struggle when I thought, *Wait a second...heaving chest?* Had he run here? The distance from the castle was more than a mile, and rough terrain at that. Why not take a horse? *Because he doesn't want anyone to know he's here...*

Despite what this might mean to my future safety, I smiled. It was knowledge I could use to my advantage...if he didn't kill me first.

"I told you to let me go," I repeated, after realizing my attempts to escape were getting me nowhere.

"I'll let you go when you return what's mine," he answered, his tone imperious.

"I don't know what you're talking about."

"I know Ilia is here."

"Of course you do. She yelled at you and you answered back. But what you don't seem to understand is that she's not *yours*. She's her own person."

He snorted. "I'm quite aware of that. But she belongs to me."

"You bought her? She's your slave? That's against the law, you know, not to mention plain wrong."

"You're being deliberately contrary."

I was. I didn't appreciate his highhanded manner, like he was lord of all he surveyed and I his lowly serving wench. I'd heard that the Van der Daarkes had been huge snobs, and it seemed the stories were true. My fingers curled into fists. I hated snobs. Growing up, they'd made my life miserable simply because I was poor and they were not. "She came to me for haven, and I cannot deny her that. You should understand that better than most who come here."

He hitched me up higher and tightened his grip just below my ribcage, making it hard to breathe. "You have the advantage of me," he whispered in my ear, and I could smell the scent of cloves carried along on his warm, demanding breath.

"Do I?" I gasped. "Yet here I'm the one dangling two feet off the floor."

Without warning, he let go and I dropped like a brick. If he hadn't grabbed me as soon as my feet hit the floor, I'd have fallen hard. But I wasn't grateful for his intervention. Oh, no. I'd rather have a bruise or two as evidence of his barbaric behavior. They'd make a good bargaining tool…if he were the type to care about that sort of thing. Somehow I didn't think he was. But I'd been wrong about men before, and my inexperience had cost me dearly. Best not to make assumptions.

I shook off his hands and turned on him, relieved to discover the electrical current zapping through me, while not altogether unpleasant, had dissipated. His black, voluminous hood, pearls of water beading up on its impenetrable surface, hid his features, and I pointed to it. "Take that off." I'd learned early on in life that being able to see your adversary's expression gives one a distinct advantage.

"I don't have time for this," he growled.

"I feel like I'm being held up by a rogue monk," I jested. He didn't move. "Take it off, and we'll talk," I promised.

He paused for a moment, then yanked off the hood, his expression cross as a wet cat as he turned his dark, heavy-lidded eyes on me. Veiled as they were, I could see secrets in their depths. Here was a man who'd witnessed awful things and had kept the experience to himself. I wondered if he saw the same trait in me.

"Who are you?" he demanded, and I took a moment to look him over before answering. He was a brawny man, a bit on the rugged side despite his expensively cut hair, its color black as a shadow. His strong jaw, clean-shaven even this early, looked as though it could take a pounding and ask for more. He was tall, over six four, and broad in the shoulder. Beyond that I couldn't tell what lay beneath his dark cloak, though he carried himself as one used to running things. I had the feeling he was a proud man, and that his hubris had done him harm.

Good.

"My name is Lorelle Gragan, thank you for asking," I answered when I'd taken in as much information as he was willing to reveal. "And who might you be? I only ask since you've barged into my home, uninvited, and demanded I return a girl who's obviously frightened by you. And no wonder," I added, unable to resist throwing a barb at his ego to see what would happen. His dark eyebrows drew together as though seeking comfort from each other, and he opened his mouth to protest. The barb had hit its mark.

Then, as though thinking better of it, he straightened his shoulders and bowed deeply, ingrained manners kicking in despite his pricked pride. "Kyran Van der Daarke, and the girl has no reason to be frightened by me. I'm her uncle."

Ah. This was unexpected news, but although their relation was a complication, it was not an obstacle. "You might be her uncle, but she *is* frightened of you. You're behaving like a prison warden *and* a bully."

His mouth tightened, whitening a small scar riding his upper lip. "I don't have time to be chasing after a moody teenager. There's too much work to be done."

"I imagine there is. It's been a long time since anyone lived in the castle."

He pulled back, an assessing gleam in his perceptive eyes as he looked down on me. "You seem to be quite knowledgeable about our business. What has Ilia told you?"

"I didn't tell her anything!" Ilia yelled from the loft. He made to go after her, but I put a hand to his chest to stop him. It was a pitiful attempt to hold him back, though for some reason it worked. He stopped.

"She's telling the truth, Mr. Van der Daarke." I kept my hand on his chest, liking how powerful the action made me feel, though the current that had passed between us earlier returned, sending pulses through my veins. Oddly enough, he made no attempt to remove my hand, though he eyed it thoughtfully. "She only told me that she'd run away and that you were coming after her."

"She makes it sound as though I'm her enemy when in fact I'm merely her guardian."

"I don't know all the facts. I only know that she's afraid."

His eyes simmered as they met mine. "What are you suggesting?"

What was I suggesting? "Let her stay with me," I ventured. "Just for a short while. So she can adjust to being in this world, and so I can assure myself that you mean her no harm."

Ah, yes. That should work.

His dark eyes widened. "Are you mad?"

"I don't think so. In fact," I paused and pretended to ponder, "I'm feeling only mildly upset."

"She can't stay *here*," he ignored my little quip.

I dropped my hand from his chest. "What's wrong with my cottage?"

He lifted his chin. "First of all, I know nothing about you, and second, it simply isn't done. She's a Van der Daarke; she must stay at the castle."

"Really? Even though your family hasn't lived there for a century?"

"Ha!" Ilia leaned over the loft's railing. "She's got you on that one, Uncle."

He aimed a cold look at her. "She's *got* me on nothing, Ilia. Now stop acting like a child and come down here at once. I'm doing this for your protection. Nothing more."

"You do understand," I interrupted, "that what's happening here—or some version of it—is going to be all over the village before you step out that door?"

"It will not," he protested, though his tone was hesitant.

"Yes, it will. And you don't want to add fuel to the fire when they see you dragging Ilia from here, kicking and screaming all the way." I paused to let that little nugget soak in. Judging by the pursing of his contemptuous lips, it had soaked in. "All I ask is that you give Ilia some time to adjust. I know you brought her from across the border, and I know this place will seem very strange to her."

Hawthorn Lane should seem very strange to him, too. As far as I knew, he hadn't ever lived here, or even visited. If he had, *someone* would have mentioned it. That someone being Avice. Kyran Van der Daarke was exactly the type of man she coveted, and no way could she stay quiet about him.

His secretive eyes narrowed to suspicious slits. "Why do you care about someone you don't know?"

"Because someone once offered me sanctuary here and it saved my life."

He dismissed this with a wave of his gloved hand. "Ilia's life is not in danger."

"Maybe not, but her relationship with you is."

A shadow crossed his face, like a cloud passing over the moon. My comment had certainly struck a nerve. Seconds passed in silence, with only the rain pattering on the roof to fill it. Kyran's expression as he stared at me was hard to read, but it wasn't kindly, that much I could ascertain.

Finally he spoke. "You have twenty-four hours," he called up to Ilia. "Make the most of them. I'll be back for you."

She peeked down at him and nodded, not daring to say a word.

He turned to me, and I quickly hid my shock at his acquiescence. "She's now your responsibility, Miss Gragan. Keep her safe. If she's harmed, you'll have me to answer to." He gave a curt nod, then strode toward the door. When he reached it, he turned back. "I'll pay you, of course, for any expense."

"That would be lovely," I replied, knowing full well he thought I'd demur.

"Oh. Yes, well, we can come to terms when I return."

"Naturally. Good day, Mr. Van der Daarke. Good luck with your settling in."

He paused, his haughty features grim as he considered whether or not to ask me the question so obviously perched on the tip of his tongue. Finally, common sense won out. "Would there be anyone in the village interested in working at the castle? Someone I could trust?"

He was asking me? Someone he barely knew? Of course, he *was* leaving his niece in my care, so I suppressed my surprise. "Lady Faylan would know best."

He grimaced, then rubbed a hand over his face to hide it. Was there something not quite right between the Van der Daarkes and Lady Faylan? It was possible, being that she'd been here when they had. Maybe she knew something damning about the family. "But do *you* know of anyone, Miss Gragan?"

It had been fun toying with him, but I was hungry and I had things to do. "The Fiersen family is loyal, and while vociferous, they can keep their mouths shut if commanded. They live up the road from me, on the edge of the woods. Their home is quite large, to accommodate their brood of twelve, and a hideous green, pink, and orange affair. You can't miss it, nor could anyone, even from distant planets. See if you can convince them to tone it down, will you?"

The whole time I'd been talking he'd been frowning, but this last part served to widen his eyes in affront. "I shall be sending a representative," he managed, "and while I might share your sentiments, I'm quite sure that would be a terrible way to begin my acquaintance with the Fiersen family."

Despite myself, I laughed. "Probably. They're loyal even to the color of their house."

"I shall return tomorrow to fetch Ilia."

"Not a representative?"

His mouth quirked. "Two difficult tasks in such a short space of time could be the undoing of the man." He bowed, then disappeared out the door, taking his haughty personality with him.

Ilia poked her head down. "He's gone?"

"Yes," I assured her. "Now why don't you come take a hot bath so you can change into something warm and dry."

"I am feeling a bit chafed," she admitted.

And when you're warm and comfortable, Miss Ilia Van der Daarke, I shall set about determining the real reason you're here in my cottage, and the real reason behind what drove the Van der Daarke family back to a world they'd long since fled.

Naturally I did not speak this last part out loud.

Chapter Four

When I had told Kyran Van der Daarke that someone had once taken me in, thus saving my life, I'd been speaking the truth. My savior brought me to Hawthorn Lane when I was eighteen, and I've been here ever since.

It's an appropriate place for those who seek sanctuary, as it serves as a haven, and has for centuries. It's a place for those in need of respite from the real world, also known around here as the Alterworld. Lying just beyond the border, somewhere between hither and yon, Hawthorn Lane is a dark and wild place accessible only to a few odd types. Some come by invitation, as I did, some stumble across the place, but all of us are drawn by a need for refuge. We have found some measure of safety here, but really, I have to wonder, who is truly safe in a world populated by magical beings?

Unfortunately, I was an exception to the magical being bit, not bearing an ounce of fey or magic in blood or bones, a fact I've yet to share with anyone here. I work hard to make up for my deficiency through brains and determination, but my lack of fey concerns me more often than I care to admit. The feeling that one day I would be found out by the others and driven away, back to a world where I had no place, where I had nothing left, haunted me. I didn't want to go back.

In fact, I find it hard to believe I've only lived in Hawthorn Lane for six years, when it feels as though I've been here all my life. From the beginning, the villagers' archaic speech charmed me, and the moment I crossed the border, their patois came naturally to my lips. I readily, even happily, wore the whirling cloaks and long gowns, kept my ways simple, and learned the skill of gathering as well as the rituals of a time long passed. I was quite pleased to discover it wasn't hard for me to become a part of this world even though I wasn't a true fey. But I was a Hawthornite through and through now, and nothing could ever convince me to return to the twenty-first century life of the Alterworld from which I'd fled.

While Ilia took a hot bath, singing a pop tune all the while—a bit taxing on the ears, I must admit—I slipped out to feed my chickens, then fixed myself breakfast. After quickly washing the dishes, I dressed in a midnight blue gown, skirt to my ankles, neckline just high enough above my breasts to cover a birthmark. The small red blemish looked like two halves of a broken heart, and served as a reminder of the heartache I'd suffered. Every time I undressed I wished desperately that the mark didn't exist, or at the very least that it wasn't so easily seen. I pulled my waist-length, wavy black hair into a bun, then donned a death's head necklace and matching ring, both of which had a convenient secret compartment for poison. Last came my baby spider earrings, after which I attached my reticule to hang at my waist. A sheath housing my favorite dagger strapped just above my calf-high leather boots completed my outfit.

When Ilia was dressed—I'd set out an older gown on the bed and left her to it—I led her to the little conservatory on the south side of the cottage and my favorite room. At the moment, rain streaked down the leaded glass windows, but on sunny days it was the warmest place in the cottage even though any sunlight shining in was muted by the numerous plants and trees that grew thick as an ancient forest throughout the cramped space. The multitude of greenery grew in pots of varying colors, sizes, and shapes—a mutant frog, a giant mushroom—and the decorations ranged from Roman and Greek deities to hideous gargoyles.

A multitude of gears attached to crankshafts near the ceiling made it possible to open windows when it grew too hot, and a red pump speckled with rust spots provided water for the thirsty little demons. All year round, in here and out in my garden during the summer months, I grew a variety of herbs and plants, both for healing, as well as for other, less compassionate, applications. Their dried ancestors hung in my kitchen, and covering one wall, hand-made shelves harbored vials and jars containing strange elixirs, the result of hours of mixing and experimenting. I'd learned all my concoction skills from Missy Thornback, an old witch now retired and living in a tree house in Wuthering Wood.

Miniature orange, lemon, and lime trees provided fruit for those bleak winter days when I craved a little sunshine, while several Venus flytraps and other equally fascinating carnivorous plants kept the insect population low. Thick, juicy succulents were easy to grow, including a massive, thorny one that often scratched me whenever I went to water it. Despite its cruelty, I kept it because I liked its potential as a weapon if anyone ever were to set upon me while I was working in the conservatory.

I settled Ilia on a soft, cushy loveseat, then sat down next to her. Avice had discarded the cozy couch last year after deciding to re-do her flat (which she did every odd year). To be on the safe side—who knew what sort of activities had taken place on it—I'd reupholstered it in a lovely moss green velvet material *Fawn's Fashions* had marked way down. It fit in well, I found, with all my other green friends.

"Now, Ilia," I said gently, deceptively. "Is there something I need to know about your uncle? I couldn't live with myself if I let him take you home and something bad happened."

"Oh, he wouldn't hurt me," she was quick to assure me in her sweet, lispy voice. "It's just that…well, he wants me to get married, and I totally don't think I'm ready for that."

"Get married?" I practically choked on the word. "But you're only a child!"

She looked appalled. "A child? But I'm eighteen and two *months*!"

My eyes roamed over her skinny frame and young face. "Sorry, but you don't look it."

"Well, I am. My mother looked young, too. It's a family gift, I guess. Though it doesn't feel like one," she grumbled, "when everyone thinks you're still in middle school."

"Then your Uncle Kyran, who looks thirty, must actually be fifty." I gave her a little smile to show I was joking.

She didn't return it. "He *is* thirty. My mother's older than him, and she had me when she was my age." Her lips scrunched up and she began to sniffle. "It's hard to believe she's dead, and that I'm here in this weird place with an uncle who barely speaks and a cousin who won't leave me be." Her shoulders shook with self-pity.

I patted her awkwardly on the back as she sagged heavily against me. I must admit I was not used to comforting others. It seemed a strange thing to do, the patting, but as with babies and overexcited dogs, it worked with Ilia. Sitting up, she stopped crying and wiped her nose on the sleeve of her dress. I was glad I hadn't given her one of my better gowns.

"I'm sorry about your mother," I said after a moment. She nodded jerkily, but didn't respond, leaving me stranded. Searching for something else to say, I latched on to what she'd mentioned before. "So why does your uncle want you to get married?"

"Probably because then he won't have to worry about me anymore."

"Can't you go to college when you graduate? Like other kids your age?"

She shrugged. "I was never very good at school. Didn't do better than C's most of the time. Except in art. I like drawing."

"Ah, well. We can't all be good students." I, myself, hadn't gone to college. There weren't any in Hawthorn Lane, and if there were, they'd be teaching Magic 101, not Computer Programming. "Well, there must be something you can do. No one should have to get married if they don't want to!" This last bit came out rather loudly, and Ilia glanced at me, her mouth slightly open in surprise. This was obviously a bit of a hot spot for me. "Sorry," I said in what I hoped was a calmer voice. "But it's just not right."

"I wouldn't mind so much, actually. But I'm supposed to be marrying our cousin…many times removed, but still… *Gross.*" Her little button nose wrinkled in disgust.

I had wanted to ask her more about the cousin who wouldn't leave her alone, but it was much better that she'd volunteered the information. He must be the third figure I'd seen getting out of the coach. "Does your cousin want to marry you?"

She gave me an incredulous look. "What do you think?"

I thought she had an overinflated sense of her attractiveness, but then again I had no idea what her cousin looked like. "So can you tell me what happened? From the beginning?"

"I don't know if I should. Uncle—"

The door to my cottage flew open for the second time in the space of an hour and I turned toward it. Who the hell was it now? Was I really going to have to start locking the door while I was home? What a pain that would be.

But it wasn't Kyran Van der Daarke or one of his minions. It was Avice. Probably looking to drag me with her to visit the castle. Little did she know the castle had come to me.

She slammed the door behind her, then stopped, her perfect nose sniffing at the air. "Where is he?" she demanded, striding toward me determinedly.

"Where's who?" I parried, not sure how she'd already managed to find out about my visitor. While I hadn't especially liked Mr. High and Mighty Van der Daarke, I wasn't quite ready to let him go. I had information to pry out of him.

"The love of my life!" she cried dramatically. At the threshold of the conservatory, she spotted Ilia and paused, running her eyes up and down the startled girl. "What do we have here?"

I sighed. "It's a long story, Avice."

"They always are, you old dog. I thought you weren't into the fairer sex." She nodded at Ilia. Though her tone was teasing, her brow had wrinkled up in annoyance. I'm not sure why she was annoyed. I was the one she was interrupting.

"I'm not." Upon first meeting Avice in the village, she'd come on to me quite strongly, and having heard the stories about her, I'd firmly told her that I didn't swing that way. She replied, in typical Avice fashion, "Luv, sooner or later, *everyone* swings my way."

She was probably right. There'd been moments of temptation, especially after a glass or two of *Dark Spirits* on a particularly trying day. A warm body is a warm body, after all, and a girl has desires. The other villagers might accept me, some were even friendly, but they sensed something different about me. They didn't know what it was—thank goodness—but they knew it wasn't normal, and its intangible presence placed a barrier between us. Avice was the only person who didn't seem to care that I was different. We'd been friends for years now, and while it hasn't ever been easy, I would hate to lose her friendship.

"Oh, sure. Just a friend, then?" Her tone was deceptively light, though her eyes were hot with vexation.

"Actually, Avice, this is Ilia Van der Daarke."

At the name Van der Daarke, Avice's disgruntled expression altered to one of avarice, which I've always suspected is her full name. "Van der Daarke? Now why does that name ring a bell?" She pulled off her damp cloak and handed it to me. "Hang that up for me, luv."

I knew exactly what she was doing, but I decided to go along with it, standing and taking her cloak from her outstretched hand. Getting further information out of Ilia would have to wait. The moment I turned my back, I knew Avice had taken my place next to Ilia and was leaning toward her confidentially.

"Tell me everything," she coaxed.

Turning from hanging Avice's cloak near the fireplace, I caught Ilia's trapped expression. "Leave the poor girl alone," I admonished Avice as I sat down on a purple footstool. "She looks like a mouse caught in a hawk's beak."

Avice patted Ilia on the arm, then looped hers through it. Ilia, seeming to crave close contact, leaned into Avice, already won over by her charm. "She does not. In fact, I have the feeling we're going to be the best of friends."

Not if Kyran Van der Daarke has anything to say about it, I thought with a private smile.

"Do you live here?" Ilia asked Avice. "In this place?" Her wide eyes roved about the cottage.

Avice threw back her head and laughed, revealing a dune-like expanse of jiggling bosom. While Avice's gowns were made from the finest material and expensively cut and draped, she often reminded me of a tavern wench…always exposing her goods in the hope of luring in the next big thing. You'd think that would cheapen her or sully her appeal, but it didn't.

I sighed at myself. I really needed to bed someone, and soon.

"Darling, I have my own flat, of course. You're welcome to visit. Any time."

"Oh, well, thank you. But I meant in this village. What's it called again?"

"Hawthorn Lane," I told her.

"And didn't you tell my uncle it was a sanctuary?"

"I did."

Ilia shivered. "Well, it doesn't feel like one."

Avice slid her arm around Ilia's thin shoulders and threw me a conspiratorial glance. "You poor thing. You must be frightened out of your mind. Why don't you tell me everything and I'll see what I can do. Perhaps I can convince your mean old uncle to let you stay with me." She looked around. "Lorelle's cottage is quaint, but tiny as a snail shell. Right, Lorelle?"

"It's not much smaller than your flat, you know, and Ilia's not leaving. I told her uncle that I'd look after her until he returned."

"And when would that be?"

Ilia was about to answer, but I cut her off. "When he can. In the meantime, while I think it's important to make Ilia feel welcome, we don't want to overwhelm her with our, um, *hospitality*." Ilia was staring helplessly into Avice's cleavage. It really was hard to look away, like when you pass by a car accident or see a charging rhino running straight at you.

"Do you like to shop?" Avice asked Ilia, completely ignoring everything I'd just said...or tried to say.

Ilia's face lit up. "Do I? Oh my gosh, it's, like, my favorite thing to do in the whole world!"

"Then we should go shopping! So you can see that Hawthorn Lane really is a lovely place. Quite friendly, in fact. My driver dropped me off, so we can walk. The fresh air will do you good."

I stifled an exasperated snort. "It's raining out, Avice, and Ilia is tired from her journey. I think it best that she stay here and rest."

Avice looked up through the conservatory's mottled glass ceiling. My bad luck, a ray of sun beamed down on her at that moment like a benediction from the sun god, Helios. "Why, I do believe it's stopped. What do you say I take you shopping, my little amour? My treat."

Ilia blinked nervously. "I don't know... My uncle probably wouldn't like it."

"Leave me to deal with him."

"Well... If you think he'd be okay with it..."

Avice patted her hand. "He'll not only be okay with it, he'll be thrilled. Trust me, sweetie."

"Avice!"

But it was too late. She had risen to her feet and was pulling Ilia along with her, bolting for her cloak and then the door like an escaping convict. Damn that self-absorbed trollop, I had no choice but to follow.

Chapter Five

Avice and Ilia marched toward the village, arm in arm as though they'd been best friends for ages. Not for the first time I wished I had magic powers so that I could knock Avice unconscious and steal Ilia back to my cottage where I could continue my interrogation.

I also found it most irritating that the skies were indeed clearing and rays of sun were slipping through the heavy cloud cover. It seemed that, for the moment, the light was winning out over the dark.

Twisted hawthorn trees on the verge of flowering lined the cobblestone road leading into the village. Accompanying them were solid stone walls, which ran alongside the road, and old-fashioned lampposts that lit up the lane like a scene from Victorian London. Stones still slick from the rain made walking a bit precarious, and while I had to focus my attention on the road or risk falling, Ilia and Avice skipped blithely along.

Luckily the way to the village was short. Soon we would meet up with the tiny shops, eateries, and pubs that lined the main thoroughfare—Vildrey Boulevard—its offshoots, or wynds, also packed with more shops and flats. Most of the villagers, like Avice, chose to live in the heart of the village, where something was always going on; others, like myself, preferred the outskirts, close by but not overly involved in the never-ending drama. The few exceptions were the Van der Daarkes, with their Gothic castle up on the mountainside, Lady Faylan and her dark Victorian manor, and the Iverich family, who lived in an extensive mansion that never seemed to be finished. The latter two buildings were situated on the opposite side of the village near Haunted Hollow. The Fiersens, with their multi-level hodgepodge of an abode on the edge of Fell Forest, were also set apart, probably because nobody wanted to live by a clown house. In addition to these well-established families, numerous fey took up residence in Fell Forest, which covered the mountain, or in Wuthering Wood, where Missy Thornback now lived, and which lay on the other side of the Wold, a gloriously wild stretch of moorland and home to our very own standing stones, Netherton Menhir.

As we walked, ravens and falcons flew overhead, dotting the sky with scraps of black and brown. The irritated squawks of the ravens competed against the slightly more majestic falcon shrieks, and all were doing a brisk business, flying up and down the boulevard and in and out amongst the side streets, delivering messages and gossip. Spotting Ilia, several of the messenger birds circled above her for a few moments, then took off, wings flapping like mad.

My fingers curled into fists. Damn Avice. We'd been spotted. Kyran Van der Daarke was not going to like this one bit. It was bad enough that most of the village probably already knew that Ilia had come to my cottage. But now here she was, parading about the village like Miss Paranormica, an easy target for speculation and insinuation.

I caught up to the two new besties just as we passed *Puck's Pub*, an Irish bar that served pretty much anything of Celtic origin, as long as it was green. "Listen, Avice. Can we keep this on the lowdown?"

She flapped an elegant hand at me, making the enormous ruby on her finger flash in the sunlight. "Oh, luv. You know that'd be impossible for me. Besides, trying to keep this news quiet is like shutting the barn door after the cow has flown the coop. Word is already out." She gave a 'royal wave' to the remaining ravens and falcons and they cried back with great enthusiasm. Avice was something of a celebrity here in Hawthorn Lane, as evidenced by how much attention she drew everywhere she went. For someone like myself, who liked to keep a low profile for many reasons, being her friend was challenging.

I tried to appeal to Ilia. "Are you sure you want to do this? I know this place feels a bit odd to you." I wondered how much she actually knew about Hawthorn Lane's true nature. Our little village seemed to make her nervous, yet she'd never been here before so had no reason to be afraid. Had her uncle told her about us? Had stories been passed down from generation to generation? What exactly were those stories? I was itching to find out, but Avice was getting in my way. She had her own agenda, as usual. "You can always go shopping with Avice another time," I tried again, "when you've settled in."

"Actually"—Ilia's childish face lit up—"I feel like I'm already settling in."

I cocked my head. Had she taken on the Hawthorn Lane dialect? The accent, a changeable blend of British, French, and Russian, was unique to this place, as were the archaic words often used. I decided that she had. *I wonder who's responsible for that*, I thought sarcastically, aiming daggers at Avice. Sadly, only with my eyes.

Avice patted my arm. "Stop frowning, Lorelle. It'll give you wrinkles, and besides, you know just the hint of a squabble between us would make good copy for Berenea." Berenea Battle ran *Thorny Issues*, the local rag, which came out three times a week, and she was not averse to committing murder if there were ever a slow news day. "That hag would exploit a child and think nothing of it."

Avice was right on both counts, and I fought to bring my scowl under control. It wasn't easy, but I managed. I had, after all, been well-schooled in hiding my feelings.

"Well, let's at least make it more difficult for the messengers to track us. Shall we try *Fawn's Fashions*? A person could get lost in that place." It wasn't a large building, yet inside it gave off the impression of being massive. Filled with the latest European and New York haute couture and vintage selections dating as far back as Cleopatra, it was *the* place to shop for your wardrobe, and while I couldn't afford the prices, I still liked looking.

"It's too early for them," Avice said regretfully. "Too early for me, too. I am hungry, though. I was hoping to lose a speck of weight…my clothes are getting a bit tight." She tugged ineffectually at her bodice, which was always a bit tight. "But I'm already regretting that idea. Let's go to *Devil's Cakes*. They serve the most scrumptious cream tea."

"I'm hungry, too," Ilia admitted, though I wasn't sure how she could be after eating most of a loaf of bread. "But I don't have any money."

Avice bestowed upon her a gracious smile. "It's on me, luv." I knew that smile. It meant she expected something in return. Of course, Avice always expected something in return, which might be why she was always smiling that smile.

"I'll take care of it, Ilia," I interrupted. "Your uncle is, after all, paying for you to stay with me."

"Oh, yeah!" She brightened. "Thanks anyway, Avice."

Avice's plump lower lip jutted out at me. "Spoiler."

"Oh, just come on." I led the way into the warm little bakery and we placed our orders with Jacques, the impossibly skinny warlock who ran the place. *Impossibly* skinny, being that the food here was sinfully scrumptious. Even the air tasted sweet. I couldn't imagine how he stayed so trim. If I worked here I'd be massive as a potbelly pig.

I paid for Ilia and myself and Avice put hers on account, as she always did. I'm not sure how she made her money to pay off her accounts, though I had my suspicions and they weren't very nice.

Placing the tray on our table, Jacques bowed without a word and left us, though he did look Ilia over with a practiced eye, of which he had only one—the other had been mysteriously lost and was now covered with a patch. At any rate, for hardly ever speaking, Jacques was very good at spreading gossip, though I think he simply told his wife, Killew, everything and she was the one to pass it on.

The queen of tittle-tattle, Killew held court in a small, dark room at the back of the bakery, which she'd converted into a welcoming niche resembling a Victorian courtesan's boudoir. Rumors abounded that she never left the room because she could no longer fit through the door, and I half believed those rumors. I'd met Killew a few times and found her large beyond belief, and terribly perverse, with a droll sense of humor. It would be exactly like her to settle into a room and never leave it, just to spite life...and maybe her husband, too.

Avice launched into her scone and soon lush cream and ripe red strawberry juice covered her mouth. The tip of her tongue slowly traveled the expanse of her full lips as she licked them clean. Out of the corner of my eye, I could see Jacques staring at her. I wasn't sure if his interest was because of Avice's seductive charm—she made eating look like an invitation to paradise—or if he was simply hungry. Probably a bit of both.

"So who's this uncle Lorelle mentioned?" Avice asked Ilia around a mouthful of pastry.

"He's my guardian," Ilia answered, starting on her third scone. Really, where did that girl put it all?

"Oh, yes? Old, I suppose?"

"Ancient," Ilia replied wholeheartedly, and I did nothing to correct what to her was very likely the absolute truth. Though it would have been quite amusing to casually mention that he was nearly the same age as Avice. Well, the age Avice claimed to be, which was a perpetual twenty-nine. In a place like Hawthorn Lane, who knew how old the residents actually were? Lady Faylan had been around a century ago and didn't look a day over thirty-five.

"So what brought the Van der Daarkes back to Hawthorn Lane after all this time?" Avice asked the question I'd been dying to know the answer to. Ilia shrugged, suddenly uncommunicative. "Oh, you can tell me, luv. Mum's the word." She placed a finger on her lips, got some cream on it, and casually licked it off.

Ilia glanced at me and I nodded, not because she could count on Avice to keep her mouth shut, but because I wanted to know, too.

"My mother died a couple weeks ago"—heavy sigh—"and my uncle needed to get away, so he brought me here."

Avice leaned forward, her eyes sparkling. "Why did he have to get away?"

"Avice!" I cried, though a darker part of me hadn't wanted to interrupt, being just as interested in Ilia's answer. I was no saint, but I also wasn't like the Desolates that supposedly inhabited Haunted Hollow. I'd yet to come across one there, and based on the stories, hoped I never would. Part of why they're called Desolates is because if they get their hands on you, they'd make you regret you'd ever been born, and I fancy I'm a bit nicer than that.

Avice looked surprised at my tone. "What?"

"Ilia just told you her mother died. Show a little sensitivity."

Avice's beautiful face puckered up sympathetically. "Oh, luv! So sorry. Sometimes my mouth works faster than my brain." She pushed the last scone toward Ilia. "Here, take this."

"No probs," Ilia mumbled around the scone she'd already shoved into her mouth. "She was kind of bossy anyway." Her eyes slid over to me. "She's the one who wanted me to get married."

"Married?" Avice exploded, echoing my earlier sentiment on the subject. "Absolutely do not head down that rocky road." She punctuated each syllable with a shake of her finger. "Or your life will soon be filled with snotty noses, dirty nappies, and deadly dull boredom. Marriage is for fools!"

I thought I heard a distant, "hear, hear" to that, but when I glanced back at Jacques he was busy wiping down the counter. His stiff movements, however, told me he was listening to our every word. Luckily, at that moment, Killew called to him from the back room and he reluctantly went to her, his gaunt face drooping with disappointment.

"It's what my mother wanted," Ilia sighed when he was gone, "and since he is my guardian, I imagine Uncle feels obligated to heed her wishes."

"But you're eighteen," I argued. "Legally he can't make you do anything."

"But I told you," she grumbled. "I can't really *do* anything. How am I supposed to live?"

"By your wits," I replied unsympathetically, hardly able to believe a girl in this day and age—an American one at that—still believed marriage was the answer to all her troubles.

"I don't have much of those."

"But you've got your health," Avice spoke up. Eying Ilia's skinny frame and finding it wanting, Avice shook her head and held up her glass of *Bloodagne*, a concoction of champagne, black cherry juice, and a secret ingredient I suspected was an aphrodisiac, like she needed more of that. "So that's something!" Neither Ilia nor I, with our melted chocos, joined in the toast and Avice, unabashed, swallowed up the remaining bubbly liquid. "Oh, that really hit the spot. Now I'm ready to shop, darlings."

I glanced at Ilia, who was looking at me nervously. Well, not *at* me, actually, over my shoulder. Curious, I swiveled about. The door was opening, as though of its own accord, and in strode a man. I'd never seen him before, though dressed as he was in tails and a top hat, which he removed as he crossed the threshold, he fit right in to Hawthorn Lane. He was boyishly handsome, and his curly brown hair, which fell to his chin, was a mess, but endearingly so, inviting you to run your hands through it in an attempt to smooth it down.

Just so you could mess it up later in a wild and passionate lovemaking session.

I cleared my throat, hoping to re-direct my thought processes toward more important and less Avice-like matters.

The stranger pointed an ebony cane at Ilia. "I thought I saw you come in here!"

His grin was charming, but Ilia only blushed to her roots and turned toward me, her eyes desperate. "That's my cousin!" she hissed. "You have to save me from him."

"Oh, Ilia," he cooed, approaching the table, his shining eyes on Ilia and Ilia alone. Avice noticed his lack of attention and her cross expression told me what she thought of it. "You are looking exceptionally lovely today. I don't think I've ever seen you in a dress. It suits you. Do my new threads suit me?" He indicated his outfit, then brushed at a speck on his lapel. "I found this hanging in the wardrobe in my room, looking practically brand new." He peered down into her frightened eyes and held out his arm. "Aren't you the rabbit today. Come. Let us make the most of this beautiful weather."

I stood up. "I'm afraid Ilia has other plans for today, Mister…"

The man started, as though he hadn't seen me sitting a mere two feet away, and spun about. With a bow, he introduced himself. "Renwick Van der Daarke, at your service." His voice was familiar, and I knew I'd heard it before—on the night of Beltane up at the castle. His golden-brown eyes looked playfully wicked as he reached for my hand and brought it to his mouth, his full, sensual lips nearly as red as Avice's strawberries, and as they brushed my skin, my heart beat a little harder.

The ruddy bounder!

"A pleasure, Mr. Van der Daarke," I said as politely as I could, being that I think he'd just licked my hand.

His lids lowered slightly, hooding his dark eyes seductively, eyes just like Kyran's. "I like being a pleasure, Miss…"

"Gragan," I supplied. "I'm currently looking after Ilia. Her uncle left her in my charge."

"Did he now?" Renwick looked mildly amused at this news.

"He did. Now, if you will be so kind as to return my hand to me, we must be on our way. We have errands to run." He squeezed my fingers suggestively, then reluctantly freed them.

Ruddy bounder, indeed.

"Might I join you?" he asked. "I'd like to get to know the village better."

Ilia's eyes were wide as she mouthed, *No, no, no!*

But Avice had had enough. "Mr. Van der Daarke…" She held out her hand to him. A perfect gentleman, he took it and bowed over it. No kissing or licking involved, I noted…perhaps a shade triumphantly.

"This is Miss Avice Montrose," I introduced.

He turned to me, letting go of her hand. "Do you not have a first name, Miss Gragan? I apologize, but your surname sounds a bit terrifying, like hearing a death threat from a troll."

"That sounds exactly like me," I said dryly, and his golden-brown eyes twinkled with amusement.

Avice stood up, her eyes *blazing*. She was not used to being ignored. Ever. In fact, I suspect she kept us all under her spell, literally, by using some sort of enhancer charm. Yet Renwick Van der Daarke had not succumbed to it. Interesting.

"Join us, Mr. Van der Daarke," she ordered and Ilia's shoulders slumped. "We can give you a tour."

"I thought we were going shopping," Ilia bleated.

"We can do that another day. As Mr. Van der Daarke remarked, such glorious weather deserves to be enjoyed. After all, it has worked so hard to put on its finest show for us."

"I would be honored," Renwick said, and Avice smiled triumphantly.

Then he turned to me and offered his arm. "Shall we?"

If looks could kill, I'm sure he and I would be dead on the spot.

Chapter Six

Hawthorn Lane reminds me of an old European city with its dark, narrow streets and high, intricately carved stone walls. Peculiar statues, ropy vines, and unique architecture complete the vision. There's even a tower—Yeats Thoor—where a sage elf, Professor Ballylee, lives and works. Some buildings are painted in bright, bold colors; others remain tucked into themselves, shadowed and mysterious. A definite duality exists here, and there are times when I feel that everything in this village is involved in a constant battle between light and dark.

Embraced by the tall firs and twisted cedars of Fell Forest on one side and the ancient elms, rowans, and oaks of Wuthering Wood on the other, the village gives one the illusion of safety. Under the watchful eye of Savage Mountain, the inhabitants of Hawthorn Lane go about their everyday business, which often includes intrigue of some sort. Hawthorn Lane might serve as a sanctuary, but that did not make its residents saints. Far from it. The beings who live here possess many secrets, and work to either hide their skeletons or dig them out of other people's closets.

Being a gatherer by trade, I know a lot about the residents, but even I don't know the full truth of things. There are so many versions here, and while my talent is the ability to sort out the truth amongst the detritus, even so, I can never be quite sure what's real and what isn't. Take Jacques and his wife, Killew. A number of stories about the two of them circulate throughout the village, but no one story holds more weight than any other. I have my theories, and feel pretty confident in them, but still, I can never be quite certain, and so I keep my mouth shut.

I also keep my mouth shut because it drives the other Hawthornites mad, especially Berenea Battle, who, rumor has it, is not averse to using torture to extract information for a story. Besides, my knowledge is my one bit of power in a world populated by very powerful creatures, and I intend to hang onto it with both hands. Though it isn't easy. Berenea is pigheaded to the extreme, and that's putting it nicely.

Avice, also not being the type to give up easily, grabbed Renwick's other arm, leaving Ilia to trail along behind us as we began our tour. I took over as guide, as I had a plan concerning Ilia's unwanted cousin. I steered us toward Dullahan Bridge, which crossed the Brook of Bones, so named because of the strangely shaped rocks that littered its bottom. Some hypothesized that the stones were the fossilized bones of unfortunate fey killed in the War of Immolation. Others thought they came from numerous poor souls who'd been turned to stone by a mad witch in the 10th century. Those events had taken place before Hawthorn Lane became a sanctuary, so they certainly could have happened. *Never rule out the possibility of anything* is a good motto to abide by here in Hawthorn Lane.

The brook, which is actually more like a large stream, runs behind my cottage and also powers the Fiersen's water wheel, used to grind the honey wheat and sugar corn they grow in the fields near their house. In exchange for the flour they produce, I give them herbal remedies, and it's worth the extra work. Madera Fiersen is a big believer in dosing her elfin children with nourishing tonics, so she keeps me busy. Maybe she's in the right—her children, all with hair in varying shades of red, are a hardy lot.

"So, Ren... May I call you Ren?" Avice asked, trying her utmost to look endearingly innocent.

"It's what my friends call me, so of course, Ms. Montrose."

"Well, then, if we are to be friends, you must call me Avice."

"It would be a pleasure." She simpered. "Though I still don't know the first name of our elusive Miss Gragan," he went on, and the simper dried up in the heat of her displeasure. Leaning against the bridge's railing, Renwick stared down at the loudly babbling brook, unaware of, or unconcerned about, her reaction. "*Gragan.*" With all the recent rain and from the spring run-off, he had to raise his voice to be heard. "How appropriate to be speaking such a name as we cross a bridge. Should I be looking for billy goats?" He winked at me.

I didn't return his flirtation with so much as a smile, as he surely expected. He struck me as a person much like Avice—used to everyone succumbing to his charm. But I wasn't taken in. He was up to something, I could tell. Ilia obviously didn't like him, and was way too young for him. So why pursue her? Did a marriage with her give him an in with the family? He was their cousin, so he already had a connection, though the relation was apparently slight. So perhaps his branch of the family had little money, and Renwick knew a potential cash cow in Ilia when he saw one. It was obvious that her guardian, Kyran, looking to hire workers and to occupy a building ruinous to most people from heating costs alone, was possessed of a substantial income.

"I'm not sure why you feel the need to know my first name," I said primly. I found the schoolmarm attitude was often helpful in deterring unwanted attention, not that I got much of that in Hawthorn Lane, or before I'd come here, either. My mother was fond of telling me that my mopey face scared people away, prompting me to spend hours in front of the mirror trying to exchange it for a provocative Mona Lisa smile. Judging from my lack of suitors here, I'd failed in my endeavor. "Unless you plan on staying long in Hawthorn Lane, there'll not be the time to develop the sort of relationship I feel is necessary to put us on a first-name basis."

A nervous giggle erupted behind us...Ilia expressing her approval, I hoped.

We had passed to the other side of the arched bridge and were now heading toward Haunted Hollow. Filled with shadowy mists and deadly silence, the ravine was not the most inviting of places. Blackthorn trees surrounded the sunken area, their twisted trunks and thorny branches keeping most intruders away. Despite the rumors about Desolates, who supposedly reside in the Hollow, it was one of my favorite places to visit, especially when I didn't want to be found or needed quiet. Often the only sounds were that of the youngsters in nearby Watery Grave Pond dunking each other, playing the Lady of Shalott, or frightening each other with their best dead-man's float.

Renwick—I refused to think of him as Ren—laughed. "Is she always this friendly?" he asked Avice.

She sniffed in annoyance. "Lorelle has *standards*, which is probably why she hasn't bedded anyone since her arrival." Bloody hell. Whenever Avice felt like someone was stealing her spotlight—attention was like oxygen to her—she went on the attack. First she found your weak spot, then she ripped off your defensive bandages, exposing your wounds to the world. So perhaps I had more to blame for my lack of suitors than my mopey face.

"And Avice," I responded in kind, "with her lack of standards, has bedded everyone."

"Aha! I now know your first name," Renwick triumphed, turning his back on Avice. "Much prettier than Gragan." His eyes twinkled, inviting me to join in his amusement.

"I prefer being thought of as a troll."

He tapped the ground with his cane. "Impossible."

I could practically feel Avice seething on the other side of him. "We're approaching Haunted Hollow," I announced. "Where you'll find that being a troll is preferable."

"I'm not going in there, Lorelle!" Avice protested. "Even with the sun out, there's still fog over it." She shuddered. "It's never free of the bloody stuff."

"How fascinating." Renwick's expression was curious. "Let's go in."

Avice pouted. "It'll ruin my hair."

"Nothing can ruin your hair, Avice," I said, feeling conciliatory. "You're always gorgeous."

"Yes, well, I suppose that's true," she conceded, looking pleased. "But still... Haunted Hollow, Lorelle! How can you stand that place?"

"It speaks to me."

She gave a bitter laugh. "Well, you always did have a dark side to you."

"Nothing wrong with a little darkness," Renwick said. "For how else can you appreciate the light?" With his cane he indicated a shaft of sunlight at our feet, brighter for its proximity to the dark cloud it had pierced.

"Very poetic," Avice remarked appreciatively. "Unlike that place." She nodded at the Hollow.

"Come on, Avice," Renwick cajoled. "Let's be adventurers."

"I didn't say I wouldn't do it," she answered lightly, smiling now.

"I don't want to go in there," Ilia said from behind us. I pulled myself from Renwick's tight grasp and went to her. "I have a bad feeling about it." Her arms were wrapped around her skinny frame and she was shivering.

"Would you like to go home?" I asked her.

"We'll only be a moment, Ilia," Renwick chided. When she didn't move, he sighed. "Fine. Wait here for me, and when I come out, we'll go somewhere more cheerful."

"I'll stay with her," I volunteered, though really I was just baiting the hook.

"No!" Avice cried. "You're the only one of us who knows your way about. It's treacherous in there," she told Renwick. "Giant boulders, slippery moss, fog everywhere. On a dare I went in there as a child and got lost. It was the worst experience of my life." She shuddered delicately, and hugged his arm tighter. "I always felt like someone was watching me, following my every move. It was horrid." I'd always felt the same thing, but hadn't found it horrid. No, the effect simply made me curious, and I kept my eyes open, but I'd never once found any sign of a watcher.

"Then maybe *you* should stay with Ilia," Renwick suggested.

Avice's eyes flashed. "And miss out on our adventure? I think not!"

"I'll be fine," Ilia said softly, her gaze focused on the ground. "Take your time."

I didn't feel good about leaving her alone, but I felt even less good about leaving Avice with Renwick. She'd soon have him spilling everything about himself and the Van der Daarke family, either by using her feminine wiles or magic, and I'd hear nothing. I couldn't have her spoiling my plan. "Don't wander about," I told Ilia. "It's easy to get lost around here. We'll be back soon."

She didn't respond, merely kicked miserably at the dirt with the toe of her red sneaker, its casual air childishly at odds with her formal gown. I vowed that as soon as we came back out, I'd take her home. I was feeling rather chilled myself, as though something evil was approaching on stealthy feet, with only the click of claws on stone to mark its presence, and if I were to turn around, it would leap for my throat.

"Let's go," I said, leading the way at a brisk pace. Avice and Renwick followed after me, Avice still holding onto Renwick's arm for dear life. I found the narrow opening amidst the tightly packed blackthorn trees and slipped through. On the other side a jagged ledge overlooked the deep chasm, and if you didn't know where you were going, you could easily fall and break your neck. "Apparently this place has been like this for centuries," I told Renwick as we descended a set of crooked stairs carved out of the ravine's stone walls. With each treacherous step, the mist grew thicker, wrapping around our ankles, tugging at our hair and clothes. "Dating back to before Hawthorn Lane became a village."

We reached the ravine floor and I stopped, pointing to the monoliths covered in a rash of moss. "Some say these boulders are giant warriors under a spell and someday the spell will be broken. When that happens, they'll awaken, revenge on their minds."

"Oh, Lorelle!" Avice cried. "Did you have to bring that up?"

"I find it interesting." Renwick's smile was amused, and I had the impression he was going out of his way to be contrary to Avice.

"But they aren't the worst part," I went on as I wove in and out amongst the stones. I wanted to frighten Renwick, shake that aura of supreme self-confidence he had about him. I barely knew him, but he reminded me of someone I didn't want to think about, and he was going to suffer for that. "The Desolates haunt this place. They're all that remains of the poor souls who've died of broken hearts. That doesn't sound very scary," I went on in a macabre voice, "until you realize that they're willing to do anything to rid themselves of their painful burdens. When Desolates find a victim, they'll rip the heart right out of his chest. Still beating, of course, and use it for their own."

I smiled at Renwick and he smiled back, not the least bit disturbed.

Damn.

"Lorelle!" Avice looked about nervously. "You know that's just a story. Now stop talking at once and get us out of here."

I quickly slipped behind a nearby boulder, disappearing from sight. It was my favorite haunt, as it was the tallest and relatively easy to climb. I quickly made my way to the top and eased down onto my stomach, giving me a perfect view of my victim. "Avice Montrose…" I moaned. "Leave this place!"

She screeched and spun about blindly. "Who's there?"

I stifled a laugh. "Leave…this…place!"

Her scream echoed off the stones. She tried to drag Renwick with her, but he wasn't having it so she pushed him away and took off, racing toward the exit. In the fog, one could barely make it out, and I was glad she could still see it. I wanted her out of here so I could interrogate Renwick on my own.

I scrambled down the steps and stood behind him as he stared after her, finally a little disconcerted. "Why did your family return?" I whispered to him.

He jumped and spun around. "Was that you?"

"Of course it was. I owed Avice for her snotty remark."

Fine pearls of mist coated his autumn hair; their watery weight not enough to tame his curls. He took a step toward me. "Was it true, what she said?"

"The truth is that Avice is jealous," I replied calmly, dodging the question.

"I think you might be right about that. So, if I answer your question, will you answer mine—was it true what she said?" So I hadn't dodged it after all.

I bit my lower lip. It was a high price to pay. "All right," I answered quickly. I was used to paying high prices. "You first."

He took another step forward and I could smell the wet wool of his coat. "My cousin Kyran felt the need to escape the real world for a while. That's why we came here."

"Escape? That sounds intriguing."

"His life was being threatened."

"Threatened? Even better. Why?"

His expression was calm, his eyes bland. "Beats me. That's all I know."

"So why are you marrying Ilia?" I fired at him, knowing I had a small window to get the information I wanted.

"Who said I was?"

"She did."

"She's rather young for me, don't you think? Though I'm glad the possibility bothers you." His smile was smug. "Now, your turn to answer my question. Was what Avice said true?"

I thrust my chin into the air. "It doesn't bother me in the least who you marry, as long as it's not me, and I'm not ashamed of my past."

"I'll take that as a yes."

Bastard.

He reached out a hand to expel a water droplet from my cheek, but before he could touch me, a scream breached the tense air between us. "Lorelle, come quick!"

"That was Avice. Come on!"

We raced toward the steps, pounding up them as fast as we could. I slipped and nearly fell, but Renwick's hand caught my arm, keeping me upright. We burst through the gap in the blackthorn trees, out into the bright sunlight to find Avice whirling about distractedly.

"She's gone," she cried when she saw us. "Ilia's gone!"

Chapter Seven

Avice clapped her hands to her heaving bosom. "A Desolate must have taken her!"

"Calm down, Avice," I warned, as inward-sucking whistles coming from her chest signaled an imminent spiral into hysteria, "or I'll be forced to slap you."

She laughed breathily. "I might like that."

"What exactly happened?" I demanded when she stopped wheezing. "Did you see Ilia run off?"

"She was gone when I got here."

"Your scream might have frightened her off," Renwick surmised, his expression wry.

"Or Lorelle's stupid trick!" Avice turned on me. "I figured out it was you."

I smiled. "You know I owed you one."

"I suppose you did," she admitted. "Touché, Lorelle." She gave me a provocative wink, all forgiven. That was Avice—quick to take offense, quick to let it go.

"Well, she can't have gotten far," Renwick offered. I noticed he didn't look all that concerned. Apparently he hadn't heard the stories about Hawthorn Lane, or the bad ones, anyway.

"She probably followed the road. Come on." I went on ahead, dashing across the bridge without bothering to look back. Renwick could take care of himself, and Avice avoided running like she avoided self-improvement. Besides that, those ridiculous cloven heels she insisted on wearing would slow her down. Served her right for starting this whole mess in the first place.

At the village center, which featured a fountain, a crowd had gathered—a jumble of dark-cloaked witches and warlocks, brightly adorned faeries, and a few elves clad in leather and wool. I noted a dryad in the mix, along with a handful of pixies. The dwarves would already be working in the silver and gold mines of Savage Mountain, though typically Gorn, an elderly busybody, stuck around to stir up trouble.

Ah, there he was, standing on the edge of the fountain's pool for a better view, his magic monocle, which allowed him to see far more than he should, clenched firmly in one droopy eye.

"What's going on?" I called out, more as a distraction than with any hope they'd tell me. The streets had been empty when we entered the village—most fey preferred late hours—so it was unusual to see so many of them out and about this early. No doubt word had gotten out about our unusual little menagerie, and the one thing fey cannot resist is a dramatic moment.

The crowd, strangely silent and watchful, parted for me, and there I found Ilia, backed up to the lip of the pool surrounding the fountain, her eyes wide with fright. Behind her, water spewed from a werewolf's decapitated head, held aloft by a majestic fray elf, Arius Vildrey, whose pointy-toed boot pressed down on the neck of a fanged villain. The macabre statue serves as a reminder that while Hawthorn Lane is a place of fey, it's reserved only for a certain kind. Any creature that must be changed over to become fey, and who also has to feed on other beings to survive, is not welcome here. That means no werewolves, and certainly no vampires. That's not to say that a few haven't tried their luck, and will likely continue to do so. It's no secret that fey blood is the best tasting blood there is. Powerful, too.

Renwick pushed his way toward us. "Are you all right, Ilia?"

"Something bad is coming," she said and the crowd gasped. I had a feeling she'd already said this, or something similar—why else would they be so quiet when typically they loved to hear themselves prattle on? The fey placed great faith in prophecy, as evidenced by the awed looks they were aiming at Ilia. "Something very bad."

I stepped forward, and after a moment's hesitation, placed a hand on Ilia's thin, shaking arm. She looked up at me gratefully. "Did you feel something? Back at Haunted Hollow?"

I caught the worried glances passing amongst those in the crowd, especially the elders. A threat to Hawthorn Lane always existed, either from banished fey, from non-fey, or from pursuers certain residents were avoiding. But sometimes the threat was even bigger. And those were the times to really worry.

Avice pushed her way through the crowd, panting hard. I stared at her in shock. "You actually ran?"

She nodded, her cheeks flushed, her eyes bright. "You think I'd miss out on this?" She gestured with the hand holding her heels. Her bare toes peeked out from beneath her skirt and the sight of her perfect little piggies, not to mention her heaving bosom, momentarily distracted numerous villagers from the drama of the moment.

"I'd have told you about it."

Her lips twisted into a disbelieving smirk. "Sure you would've."

"I would have…eventually." I turned to the rest of the crowd. "No need to worry. The girl simply got frightened. She's new here, as you probably already know, and finds our world a bit unsettling." There were a few understanding chuckles. "So let's leave her be, all right?" The crowd started to protest, as I knew they would. The fey were a querulous bunch.

"But she's prophesizing!" Gorn declared, his voice deep and guttural. Whenever I heard a dwarf speak, I imagined their voices scrambling to get around a handful of rocks lodged in their throats, a hazardous outcome of breaking the mountain into pieces in their obsessive search for precious metals. "We've a right to hear more!"

"She was frightened by the Hollow," I repeated, "and now you lot are surrounding her like a bunch of gorms, frightening her even further."

"Lorelle is speaking good sense," a carrying voice rang out. The crowd reluctantly parted for Lady Faylan, the village overseer, and she strode on long legs toward Ilia, placing herself in front of the girl. I joined her, and between the two of us, it was hard for the others to see Ilia. "Go back to your business and let me take care of things, as I've always done and always will. I'll determine whether or not there's reason to be worried and will let you know accordingly."

The crowd hesitated, unwilling to walk away from such a spectacle. But it was hard to disobey Lady Faylan. One, because in her black, severely cut dress and matching hat, she made a formidable figure, much like a Victorian governess or a prison warden. And two, because she'd find a way to punish you if you didn't do as she said. Pretty much all of us at one time or another have been on the receiving end of Lady Faylan's wrath, so we choose to obey. I was punished only once, but that had been enough to see me through this lifetime, and probably a few after that.

Realizing that nothing else was going to happen, or be allowed to with Lady Faylan there, the others began to disperse, talking amongst themselves and aiming looks at us over their shoulders.

When there was only myself, Avice, Ilia, and Lady Faylan remaining, she turned to me. "Why in the name of Grim's Keep did you let that girl leave your cottage, Lorelle?"

I shouldn't have been surprised to hear she'd known I was involved with Ilia. Not only involved, but responsible for the girl. "Lady Faylan. This is Ilia Van der Daarke."

"I know who she is," she snapped, not looking at the girl.

Of course she did.

"The Van der Daarkes have returned…" I began again.

"Obviously."

I wasn't doing well, but Lady Faylan made me nervous…for many reasons, not the least being that she reminded me of a hawk perched on the branch of a dead tree, looking down on the rest of us as prey, and only because she isn't hungry at the moment are we spared. As I've said, I respect Lady Faylan, but she scares the bejeebers out of me.

It was tempting to throw Avice to the lions, or the hawk, as the case may be, but I didn't do it. There was enough rancor between the two of them as it was. "I thought she might like to get to know the village a little better. She's frightened of this place—"

"As she should be," Lady Faylan sniffed.

"Any particular reason?" I ventured.

Her cool gray eyes narrowed. "We all will do well to be afraid." She was dodging the question. She knew it, Avice and I knew it, even Ilia had likely picked up on it. But would we challenge her on it? Absolutely not. I would have to find a sneakier way of learning what I wanted to know.

Speaking of sneaky, I realized Renwick had gone missing. Where had he got himself off to, I wondered, and why had he disappeared the moment Lady Faylan had shown up?

Mysteries. Always mysteries in this place. I smiled.

"Do not wish for trouble, Lorelle," Lady Faylan cautioned, noting my expression. "It will find you all too easily on its own." I peered up at her, but not before straightening my features into a more suitable solemnity. It was quite a ways to look up. Lady Faylan is very tall for a woman, probably over six feet, and dresses as plainly as a servant in her dark Victorian gown, belted at the waist, a chatelaine her only decoration, her reddish-brown hair pulled tightly back into a bun. No *Fawn's Fashions* for her. No cream tea at *Devil's Cakes*, either. Ramrod straight and slender as a young girl, this woman was the epitome of discipline. Not even the various accoutrements hanging from her chatelaine dared to rattle when she moved. I wondered how she could stand living in Hawthorn Lane, a place out of control with all its decadence and drama. What keeps her here?

"Shall I take Ilia home?" I asked, unsure under her unwavering glare what she wanted me to do.

Through all this, Avice had stayed quiet. Though she often played the featherbrained role, she wasn't stupid. She knew Lady Faylan tolerated her…barely. And since she wanted to hear what was going on, she kept her mouth shut. Ilia was watching us, too, her expression curious despite the fear in her eyes.

Lady Faylan noticed their attention and grabbed my arm, pulling me out of earshot. "Keep an eye on the Van der Daarkes, Lorelle. Invent excuses to visit the castle. Do whatever it takes to learn their every move. They've brought change to our little world, and I'm inclined to believe it comes on an ill wind. I have a feeling the Van der Daarkes are the 'something bad' Ilia warned us about, and I'm not sure they should be allowed to stay here."

"All right," I readily agreed, giddy that I'd been granted permission to snoop. "What shall I say to Mr. Van der Daarke? I mean, what excuse would I give?"

She slowly blinked her uncompromising eyes at me. "I imagine you'll think of something. And it's *Count* Van der Daarke, not mister." My eyes widened. *Count?* Why hadn't I heard that Kyran was a Count?

"Got it."

"Keep her away from Haunted Hollow," she ordered, nodding at Ilia. "And keep that other one from interfering again."

Ah. So she'd known Avice's part in this all along. Lady Faylan's falcon, Bowie, which she actually resembled quite closely—similar noses, same steely eyes, same regal bearing—had probably brought her the news.

"I'll try," I promised, though short of locking Avice in a dungeon I wasn't sure how I was going to accomplish such a monumental task.

Judging from Lady Faylan's skeptical look, she wasn't sure, either. "Send me an air post when you have something. Mind you, I want to hear any news sooner rather than later."

I nodded, and she swung about, her black skirt barely flaring—it didn't dare—and strode away. I looked around, noted all the slightly parted curtains, cracked shutters, and peeking eyes, then went to Ilia.

"I'm sorry you were frightened back at the Hollow," I told her. "I was only playing a joke on Avice."

"I heard that," Ilia said, her eyes darting about. "But that's not what frightened me."

Avice and I both stared at her, and I felt a tug of anticipation. "What do you mean?"

"I heard everything you said when you were in the Hollow, Lorelle. It was that thing you talked about. A Desolate. It came to me, and it…" She paused, swallowed hard. "It wanted my heart."

Chapter Eight

A heavy silence weighted the air as I tried to take in what Ilia had told us.

"All that Desolate silliness is just a story," Avice rushed to assure the girl, then looked my way, nodding at me to confirm her words.

"Exactly, Ilia," I agreed heartily. "It's a scary story we like to tell around the fire. You know, like they do at camp back in the Alterworld…"

Ilia shook her head in denial. "You don't get it. I *saw* a Desolate. At first it looked like a shadow stepping out of the fog, then it floated toward me, its horrible hands reaching out. It said it wanted my *heart*." She pressed her fists against her stomach, looking as though she wanted to be sick. "That's when I ran."

"All your imagination, luv," Avice said with determination, though doubt darkened her eyes. "That's what that place does to a person… makes you see things that aren't there." She wrapped her arms around herself and shivered. "It's what makes the Hollow so scary."

Ilia's pointy chin jutted out defiantly. "I know what I saw."

"Why don't we go back to my place," I suggested, "and I'll fix you something to eat."

"I'm not hungry," she declared stoutly, which was a little worrisome. Ilia's appetite had seemed unappeasable.

"Then we'll drink tea." I paused. "You know, one good thing came out of this…your cousin scarpered."

Ilia glanced around and her thin face relaxed slightly. "You're right. That is a good thing."

"I'm coming with you." Avice thrust out her chest determinedly. "I don't want to be alone right now."

"Fine," I agreed, because really I was feeling a bit spooked myself and there's safety in numbers, especially when one of those numbers is a mage.

Our walk back to the cottage was quiet except for the squawks and shrieks of the messenger birds flying overhead. They kept their distance, though I had a feeling that before long we could expect a visit from our local paparazzi, Berenea. She would want to know the details of what had happened, and she could be relentless in getting them. I reminded myself to lock the door, not that doing so would keep her out, the sneaky witch.

Once inside the cottage, I hastened to stir up the fire. A bank of dark clouds had smothered the sun, which had been trying valiantly to shine all morning. Thunder rumbled and a crackly tension electrified the air. At times the weather in Hawthorn Lane functioned like a mood ring for the village—sunny and bright when all was going well, but quick to darken the moment anything went awry. Typically I rather liked that, but with the events of today, another storm seemed a sinister sign of bad things yet to come.

Just as Ilia had warned.

She and Avice took the chaise longue in front of the fire, and after making a pot of chamomile and lemon tea, I sat nearby in an ancient rocking chair and sipped from my steaming cup. After a few moments, I turned to Ilia. "Better now?"

She nodded over her cup. "A little." She took a sip. "So who was that woman at the fountain?"

"That was Lady Faylan. She's the village overseer, meaning she's in charge of keeping Hawthorn Lane safe. She's lived here a long time."

"She gives me the creeps."

I struggled to keep from laughing. "Well, she is rather intimidating, I agree, but she has to be. This is not an easy place to run."

"I suppose." She paused. "Not that I care what happens to him, but where do you think my cousin went?"

"Probably got scared and ran, crying wee, wee, wee all the way home."

She giggled. "Probably."

I wasn't so sure that's what he'd done, but my little joke had the desired effect of bringing a smile to Ilia's pinched face. The true story likely had more to do with the fact that Renwick hadn't wanted to be seen. But by whom? Did he know the village better than I thought he did? Or maybe he was tracking someone who lived here and had spotted him in the crowd. Or what if he wasn't a Van der Daarke, after all, but some sort of spy? It was certainly possible in this place, and I determined to keep a close eye on him, preferably without him knowing. If he caught me watching him, he'd think I was interested in his lean good looks and bedroom eyes, when really, I'd hardly noticed either.

"So why was your mother so keen on you marrying, and Renwick Van der Daarke, of all people?" I asked. "He doesn't strike me as the most stable guy."

She made a little face. "I suppose she thought I couldn't handle myself out in the real world." A forlorn sigh dropped her bony shoulders. "She's probably right. Back home I couldn't even remember to charge my cell phone and that thing was my *life*."

"Your life?" I found that hard to believe.

"It's how I talked to my best friend, Tiffany, made plans to meet her, posted selfies. You know…got involved in the world."

It sounded a bit odd to me, but then I'd never been allowed to have a cell phone, and when I'd lived in the Alterworld, cell phones and social media weren't that big a deal yet. I'd heard that everyone had a cell phone now, and if you weren't on Chatterbox, or whatever it's called, your life was basically pointless.

Personally I prefer to keep my life private and would not have wanted to participate in such nonsense. Then again, a resource like that would make snooping into other people's lives a lot easier. I'd heard that people in the Alterworld shared *everything* about themselves on these sites, including pictures of their *thighs*. I wasn't sure if this was done to attract a mate, or if they were trying to make others jealous of their sculpted musculature. Possibly both. Or maybe they simply wanted people to say, "Your thighs aren't huge at all. No, they're perfectly lovely." Because don't we all want to hear that?

"You must miss having it," Avice sympathized, already looking pleasantly buzzed. She never drank tea without adding a bit of a kick to it from her flask, and usually in the form of *Lightning*, her favorite liquorous beverage. "I wish we could have them here."

That would never happen. In Hawthorn Lane modern innovations seem to have an adverse effect on fey. While they aren't a problem back in the Alterworld, here they drain your magic. So gadgets, anything that runs on fossil fuels, and GMO foods, of all things, are banned here.

Yet deadly nightshade is still allowed. Go figure.

That doesn't mean we go without, of course. Grim forbid we make sacrifices (and yes, I'm including myself in this snide remark). Once a month we have Ware-Port Day, when we send and receive goods to and from the Alterworld and other villages like our own. We can make or spell most things, but some we either can't produce, or don't care to. Sometimes it's simply that we want something new and exotic, such as the novels I like to read.

But as I said, we don't suffer. Our homes are heated and lit using candles, pine oil lanterns, and peat or wood, or with Effervescence, an expensive, but amazing, energy source created by the Iveriches, a powerful and ancient faerie family. They'd also virtually cornered the market on food production with a particular proliferation spell they'd invented and sell at an exorbitant price, which is why I'm glad for my outdoor garden and brood of Galykin chickens, both of which provide me with most of the food I need. I had the feeling the Iverich family lived in Hawthorn Lane, not for safety reasons, but because they like being big fish in a small pond, and because living here makes them stinking rich.

There is a downside to residing in Hawthorn Lane. Being seen to rely too much on outside power sources is looked down upon. To the fey, showing you need help running your life is basically admitting that your powers are weak. That being so, you'd think the Hawthornites would flaunt their magical abilities all the time. But they don't. I don't often see magic being done, and what I do see, seems to be fairly innocuous, even simple. Perhaps, like me, the fey want others to underestimate their powers, rewriting the old saw to say, "What you don't know *can* hurt you."

Since I don't have any magical ability, I don't feel the least bit guilty about using Effervescence to heat my water. My nightly hot baths are a weakness, and I don't care who knows it. I like my rose-petal and myrrh oil soaks immensely and would give them up for neither queen nor country.

"I don't miss cell phones," I said firmly. "We have enough rumor-mongering around here as it is."

"People can be so hateful," Ilia agreed, staring into the fire. "One girl, who was supposed to be my friend, told everyone I was hooking up with Jake Howard, this guy I met in the town where I go to school, even though I wasn't, and she called me a whore, too. Then she took a picture of me at a dance, captioned it, 'Slut' and posted it right on her page. And people liked it and shared it! Even though it isn't true!" She slouched miserably.

"I hate to say it, Ilia, but that sort of thing goes on here, too."

"I suppose," she sighed, "but at least what happens here won't get spread all over the world, and last forever and ever."

I wasn't so sure about that, as the rumors around here seemed to persist despite evidence to the contrary, but Ilia had experienced enough bad things lately. Best to keep that detail to myself.

I decided to return to an issue that really stuck in my craw, determined to gather as much ammunition as I could to confront Kyran on the subject when I next saw him. "Speaking of forever and ever, I can't get over that your uncle is forcing you to marry your cousin."

She hunched her shoulders, looking a little guilty. "Well, actually, he's not really *forcing* me. I mean, I guess I just thought he'd do what my mother wanted, because everyone always does what my mother wants. *Did*, I mean," she corrected, cringing as though expecting to be chastised.

Well, that put a different slant on things. "So he doesn't want you to marry your cousin?"

"I don't know what he wants. He keeps everything to himself. The reason I ran away is because he won't answer my questions or tell me why we had to come to this awful place—" Her eyes widened. "I keep saying that."

"Don't worry about it. It can be a little scary." As much as I love Hawthorn Lane, it definitely has a dark side. "So he might actually not want it at all?"

She shrugged. "Maybe. But no way am I talking to him about it. He kind of scares me. Not in a bad way," she rushed to assure me. "It's just hard to talk to someone who stares at you like he sees every bad thing you've ever done."

Had he stared at me like that? I couldn't recall, so probably not. Though I rather hoped he might give it a try.

"I'll tell you what…I'll talk to him," I promised. "When he comes back for you." I was careful to keep the time vague in case Avice was listening more carefully than her closed eyes would suggest. Knowing her, just as he walked in the door she'd show up to 'borrow a cup of blossom sugar' even though she hadn't baked so much as a macaroon in her life.

Ilia perked up. "You would?" For the first time since I'd met her, she looked rather pretty. Maybe her misery soured her looks, though I suppose the same could be said of all of us. Except Avice, of course. I don't know how she did it, but petulance made her *more* attractive.

"Tell me what you know about your cousin Renwick," I asked, changing the subject.

Avice's eyes sprung open, her attention caught.

Ilia's prettiness disappeared as her mouth turned down at the corners. "I don't know much about him. He knew my mother, though I'm not sure how or how long. I think maybe he was her assistant. Before her funeral I only met him a few times because I was away at boarding school. Not long after my mother was buried, my uncle brought me here. Renwick came with us, though I don't know why. I'm not even sure why I'm here. I was right in the middle of an art project." She frowned unhappily. "And now I won't even get to graduate."

"Oh, luv, graduation is way overrated." Avice patted her hand, though I'm not entirely sure she understood the concept. Like college, they didn't exactly have graduations in Hawthorn Lane. "Especially when there are more important things to talk about. Now tell me, does your cousin have money?" I glared at Avice and she returned the look with an innocent, "What did I say?" expression.

Ilia shrugged. "I don't know."

"Do you have any idea why your uncle came back here?" I asked a more pertinent question, one that seemed quite adept at remaining unanswered. "I know you mentioned he had to get away, and Renwick said it had something to do with his life being threatened."

Ilia straightened up, looking worried. "Threatened? I hadn't heard that. Something was going on with him, I know that for sure, so I guess it would make sense. While driving here he kept looking at the rearview mirror as though watching for someone. And then I fell asleep, and the next thing I know we're in a horse carriage, which is weird, cause how did we end up there? And we were racing down the road like something was chasing us." She shivered. "It was horrible."

I remembered seeing the carriage, how fast it had been going, like the proverbial bat out of hell. I remembered something else, as well. It was after the Van der Daarkes had all gone inside the castle. I was about to take my leave when Kyran and Renwick returned to the carriage to fetch the luggage.

"Do you think this place is safe for you?" Renwick had asked Kyran.

"I can only hope so. Though from the stories I've heard, I'm not entirely sure. Unfortunately, it's the only place I can think of to go."

"It is a bit gloomy looking," Renwick observed, looking about.

"It suits my mood," Kyran answered shortly.

"Ah, yes. Sorry. I imagine you miss your sister."

"As much as she would miss me." At the time it had seemed a harmless remark, and one I'd interpreted to mean they'd been close. Now, after hearing what Ilia had said about her mother, I had to reconsider what Kyran might have meant.

"But *I'm* here," Renwick said heartily.

"Yes, you are." Kyran's tone had been bland, but I wondered if there'd been a cynical note in his voice. Having met Renwick, I thought there might have been. Did Kyran not trust his own cousin? I know I didn't trust the man, and I barely knew him.

They had gone inside after that, and I'd hurried home with my basket. Their driver had been Josepha Isola, an enterprising young wood elf without ties or family here, and I thought perhaps he had overheard the conversation inside the coach—elves, of course, have fantastic hearing. Josepha might be willing to barter information for some of my elderberry tarts. He very much likes tarts, which could be why he and Avice get along so well.

"I want to go home," Ilia sighed, then took a sip of tea.

"To the castle?"

"*No.*" She shivered. "Back to Burten Academy. I'm not good at school stuff, like I said, but I want to finish my art project, and I wouldn't mind graduating so at least I can say I have my high school diploma. I don't want to be a *total* failure."

I felt sorry for the girl. I knew what it was like to have family dictate what you did. My mother had kept a tight rein over my sister and myself and it had been awful, and also one of the reasons why I'd run away.

"Well, that can still happen. This move might only be temporary." Then I remembered that Kyran had wanted to engage the Fiersen family to work at the castle and revised my opinion. That didn't sound short-term to me. It did, however, give me a clue as to where Renwick had disappeared. He must be Kyran's 'representative,' the one who'd be doing any busywork beneath Kyran, like engaging the Fiersens. Knowing Renwick now, I had to smile. By making his cousin his assistant, Kyran was either lording it over him because that's what he did, or he was putting him in his place because he didn't especially like the guy.

I didn't know which it was nor did I understand why Renwick had deserted us, leaving his 'beloved' Ilia to fend for herself. If he truly wanted to marry the girl, why act so hot and cold with her? When he'd first come into *Devil's Cakes*, he'd only had eyes for her. Then he'd latched onto me, pretty much ignoring Avice and not paying much attention to Ilia after that, either.

I would love to believe my irresistible good looks and charming personality had lured him in, but I knew better. I was attractive enough not to crack a mirror when I looked into it and could hold my own in conversation, but I also knew I was not at Avice's level, looks or station-wise. So my guess is that he wanted something from me other than my virtue.

But what?

Chapter Nine

Rousing herself, Avice signaled to her raven, Eros, to send around her barouche. He was perched on a small post on the conservatory's roof, where he kept watch while waiting for her. Soon after, the carriage arrived and she left us. I had turned the conversation to art, a topic I figured Ilia would like, and knew Avice would not. She claimed all paintings looked the same to her. Well, all those that didn't showcase her as the subject. Decorating the walls of her flat were at least seven portraits of her, all by different artists and all with her in various states of undress. No doubt there were numerous others in the village, either ostentatiously displayed or tucked away to be drooled over when no one was around to witness such lecherous behavior.

I had wanted Avice to leave for a few different reasons, but mainly it was about to storm again and from the looks of it, the rain wasn't going to depart any time soon. That meant Avice would want to spend the night and I wasn't about to give up my bed for *her*. I'm not being entirely selfish here, as it was either give up my bed or share it with her, and from past experience I knew how the latter would go down. Even in her sleep Avice is predatory. The one time I'd made that mistake, it had been a long night, with very little sleep gained on my part. We both awoke grumpy, me from not catching enough z's, her from not catching her intended quarry.

As the day went on, I began to like Ilia more and her mother, who sounded a lot like my own, less. We did some painting together and I discovered that Ilia was quite talented. Hearing my praise, which is not something I give out easily, seemed to buoy her and the thin, pinched look to her face grew less pronounced as she worked on her painting, which was reminiscent of Salvador Dalí's work.

I taught her a little about my plants and she sketched a few, including Mr. Prickly, my thorny succulent. She wasn't as dumb as she seemed to think, learning the names and their uses quickly. While she drew, Ilia confided that her mother was either constantly telling her she was inadequate, or would send her away on the spur of the moment, conveying the less than subtle message that she found her daughter tiresome. Her current school, Burten Academy, was the last of a long line, though this one Ilia had actually liked, mainly because she had a good friend there and the art department was 'awesome.'

"I didn't actually want my mother to die," Ilia confessed as we prepared a simple supper—chicken noodle soup using my own vegetables, herbs, and chicken (poor old Squawk hadn't been long for this world anyway), warm slices of cinnamon rhubarb bread, and spiced hot apple cider. "But I'm not sorry she's gone."

"My mother was the same way. Is," I corrected. "As far as I know she's still alive, though I haven't seen her in six years." It was the most I'd told anyone about my previous life, including Avice. She and I shared subjects related to Hawthorn Lane, and Hawthorn Lane only. Admittedly it was not all that much to give Ilia, but I felt she deserved a little tit for tat.

"Why so long?" she asked as she set the table with mismatched silver, a pair of mushroom mugs, and two skull bowls.

"She tried to make me do something I didn't want to do. I had to get away."

"That sounds just like me," Ilia breathed in awe. "Maybe that's why I came to your cottage. Maybe I sensed we had a connection, and it drew me here."

I shrugged and ladled the steaming soup into our bowls. "I wouldn't doubt it, being what this place is."

"Is it...? Well, are the people here...?" Ilia couldn't quite get the question out and I couldn't blame her. This was a strange world and a bit hard to believe in at first. While I'd adjusted fairly quickly, those early days had been a bit daunting. Elves? Faeries? Dwarves? All here, walking about the village as though it were perfectly normal. Then there are the centaurs and nymphs, griffins and shape-shifters, specters and elementals, not to mention the elusive unicorns and doppelgangers populating Fey Forest and Wuthering Wood. Like my beloved Narnia, many of the animals supposedly could even talk.

However, I'd yet to encounter any of the woodland fey up close, which didn't exactly break my heart as the tales I'd heard condemned them as irrational at best, murderous at worst. I didn't entirely believe the stories, but I wasn't taking any chances, sticking only to the heavily worn paths of Fell Forest and avoiding Wuthering Wood as much as possible, regretting that Missy Thornback had moved there. Each time I went to visit her, I felt watching eyes, and it was enough to keep my visits short, rare, and only when the weather was fine. I wasn't scared of the wood dwellers, but I had this awful feeling that they would know I wasn't fey, and I couldn't take the risk of being found out.

"They're fey, if that's what you want to know," I told her. *And you must be, too, if you're a Van der Daarke.* I didn't say this last part out loud. If she didn't know yet, it wasn't for me to tell her. I was to regret this omission later, when everything came to a head, but for the moment I merely thought I was protecting her. "That means they have something magical about them, and that they're not human."

"Wow," she breathed, her eyes sparkling. "Wait 'til I tell Tiffany about this place. She loves that fantasy stuff. Obsessed with it, actually. All she draws are mythical creatures…faeries, elves, unicorns, stuff like that."

"I'm not sure telling Tiffany is a good idea," I cautioned. "Since Hawthorn Lane is a sanctuary, we do our best to keep it hidden. Plus, if you were to tell someone, well, something bad could happen to you." I wasn't sure what that 'something bad' was exactly, but it had been imparted to me that whatever it was would be pretty horrible. Worse than death, was how I think Lady Faylan worded it.

"Oh." She looked a little downcast. "Oh, well. I probably won't see her again anyway." She sat still for a moment, though her mouth continued chewing. "Hey," she went on after she swallowed, "you think that's why Uncle Kyran came here? Because it's a sanctuary and he was being threatened?"

"It would make sense. Did you know about this place before coming here?"

She shook her head. "I didn't know anything. On the drive, Renwick told me we used to live here. I didn't realize it was like this, though, you know…" She waggled her hand back and forth. "He said our family had to leave because something bad happened, and that no one has returned for a long, long time."

"A hundred years," I confirmed, wondering why she wasn't making the connection between her family living here and herself being fey. Maybe she didn't want to see it.

"That's a *long* time," she acknowledged. "But now we're back."

"What changed, I wonder?"

She thought for a moment, then shook her head and ladled a spoonful of soup into her mouth. Her eyes closed in bliss. "This is *really* good soup, Lorelle. I could eat it all day. I'm always hungry. My mother, she said nobody would want me if I was fat, so I tried to stay thin for her, and…well, because I wouldn't have minded having a boyfriend. Now that she's dead, I can eat what I want. Right? I don't care if I don't get a boyfriend. I'm sick of being hungry all the time."

Her eyes, innocent pools of blue, glanced up at me, begging me to agree. "Absolutely," I answered. "Boyfriends are overrated, and besides, if you're hungry all the time, how would you ever enjoy being with anyone? At some point, your body will figure out what it needs and you won't feel so desperate to stuff yourself."

"But I'll enjoy myself while it figures it out, eh?" She grinned and I smiled back. She was already picking up on our lingo, like she'd been here for years.

Watching Ilia eat, my smile soon evaporated. Hawthorn Lane was not a good place for her right now. That she thought she'd seen a Desolate disturbed me. Because if she truly had, then something was stirring—something old and wicked and filled with malevolent intentions, and it was after her.

⚡

I made Ilia take my bed. She protested, but after a long, hot bath, a relaxant tisane, and a half hour of my determined ministrations to comb out her rat nest of hair, which turned out to be a lovely golden color, and another half hour to smooth her ragged fingernails, she didn't have much left in her to argue. I tucked her under my thick quilts, and she was asleep before I even left the loft.

Before going to bed myself, I drank a cup of choco and read on the chaise in front of the crackling fire, the sound of thunder and billowing wind punctuating the stillness of the cottage at random intervals, sometimes making me jump. While I couldn't hear it, I knew the small pool behind my cottage, which a previous owner had created by damming the brook, was slowly, steadily filling. With the spring run-off and all this rain on top of it, the pool was on the verge of flooding, which spelled trouble for my cottage's weakened foundation, and for the Fiersens and the whole village if the water wheel was damaged. But how could I stop this incessant rain? Drug everyone with happy juice?

It was worth considering.

My thoughts kept straying from my book, and more often than not, the lurid novel ended up resting on my knees as I mulled over everything going on as of late. First, I had the Van der Daarke's mysterious return to consider. Then there was the problem of Ilia and the threat of her being forced to marry someone she didn't love, and who, I suspect, was feigning attraction to her for his own benefit, whatever that might be. Ilia's possible Desolate sighting was troubling on more than one level, and to top it all off, there was all this incessant rain to worry about.

It helped that Lady Faylan had given me permission to spy on the Van der Daarkes, and I knew where I'd start—with Josepha Isola, the carriage driver. The problem was, I wasn't entirely sure I felt good about spying on them. Kyran Van der Daarke's imperious behavior this morning had set me against him, but I conceded that maybe he had a good reason for being prickly. From his sister's death to taking on the responsibility of Ilia and the castle, not to mention being threatened, he had a lot to deal with. So the jury was still out, making me uneasy about spying on him. I didn't hunt the weak—what was the fun of that?

I decided that when he came to pick up Ilia tomorrow I'd find out more about him, and what I learned would guide my future behavior. Whatever I discovered, I would be sorry to see Ilia go. I had to admit it was nice having a companion in my cottage, someone to look after, even though there wasn't that much of a difference in age. Ilia might be a Van der Daarke, and fey, but she acted like a normal girl without a hidden agenda. From what I gathered, she simply wanted to resume her old life…working on her art project, hanging out with her friend, Tiffany, and graduating. It seemed refreshingly simple, and I felt for her that she'd ended up here instead. As much as I love Hawthorn Lane, it isn't for everyone, especially someone as innocent as Ilia.

But was it for Kyran Van der Daarke? Or his cousin Renwick? I couldn't help wondering what Renwick was about, and how I could get him to spill his secrets. He seemed to fit in at Hawthorn Lane quite well already, leading me to believe he'd been here before. But wouldn't the rumor mill have churned that one out? I'd have heard that a Van der Daarke had returned; nobody could resist sharing that juicy of a tidbit. At the very least, I would have felt the breach when he arrived. I might not be fey, but even the animals felt a breach; it was like an earthquake—you just couldn't miss it.

Maybe he was one of Lady Faylan's spies, slipping back and forth between here and the Alterworld, gathering information for her. It was a good theory, as she was the only one of us who could mute the breach, unfortunately I had the feeling she was the one who'd scared him off at the village fountain.

I sighed and closed my book, my eyes flickering shut in the heat of the fire and from the warmth of the melted chocolate in my belly.

Hopefully tomorrow would bring some answers…and an end to this bloody rain.

Chapter Ten

Kyran Van der Daarke—or should I say, *Count* Van der Daarke—apparently felt no need to knock when entering other people's homes. Early the next morning, I heard the lock slide out of its latch and the door whisper open as he entered the cottage. Curse it, it was still raining out—I could hear it on the roof and smell it in his wake as he stepped inside and shut the door behind him.

Lying on the chaise, I feigned sleep, watching him from beneath my eyelashes. He stood alert and still, as though expecting to be pounced on at any moment. Like a well-trained spy, he spent a long time gazing about the cottage, taking everything in. He even sniffed the air, which was spiced with the scent of peat smoke and cinnamon. Then at last his eyes landed on me and stayed there for what felt like forever.

Finally I'd had enough of being studied and pretended to stir. I sat up drowsily, turned my eyes on him, and screamed like a banshee.

"It's all right," he soothed, holding up his hands. "It's only me, Kyran Van der Daarke." I didn't stop my bellowing. "I'm sorry to come in like this," he tried again. "Please *stop*!" Satisfied he wouldn't enter my cottage again without knocking first, I closed my mouth. He might be nobility, but that didn't make it okay for him to trespass. "I knocked, but no one answered," he explained in measured tones. "Three times, in fact." I wasn't sure I believed him, but I'd been up late, so it was possible I'd been sleeping so hard I hadn't heard anything.

"You're here early," I informed him, though I had no idea what the actual time was. It was a slippery concept here in Hawthorn Lane, ebbing and flowing like the tide. I owned a grandfather clock, but it didn't always keep time accurately, and besides, I couldn't see it from where I sat. I did get the sense that dawn hadn't shown its face all that much before now.

"I apologize for that, but there is much to be done."

I yawned and stretched. "Did you manage to secure help from the Fiersens?"

He nodded. "Two girls and a boy are coming today, which is why I showed up so early. I must get back before they arrive."

I lifted an eyebrow. "Don't you trust Renwick to handle them?"

His expression soured and I noticed his expensive haircut was looking a bit tousled today, like he'd already run his hands through it in frustration many times this morning. "I heard what happened to Ilia," he said, dodging the question.

I frowned. "What did Renwick tell you?"

"That she got spooked and ran off."

"Was that all he told you?"

"He told me that he saw your little group heading into the village and thought to follow you to check up on Ilia. Someone suggested giving him a tour and not long afterwards Ilia ran off. He wasn't exactly forthcoming with details."

Or completely honest, since he'd been the one to ask for a tour. "Did he mention that *he* got spooked and ran off?" I hadn't meant to share this bit, but I wanted to know what Kyran truly thought of his cousin.

"Funny, he left that part out." His tone was bland as he spoke, giving nothing away, though his eyes didn't meet mine. He was torn, then.

"What's the deal between him and Ilia?" I pushed. Who knew when I'd get him in this position again? "She thinks she has to marry him."

"Not that it's any of your business," he said stiffly to the fireplace mantle behind me, "but it's what her mother wanted." He sighed and ran a hand through his hair, his face suddenly weary. "I, on the other hand, am not entirely on board with the idea." His eyes, dark and deep like a passage to the Underworld, locked onto mine.

"Oh, for Grim's sake!" I cried, suddenly uncomfortable. I indicated the rocking chair. "Sit down." He paused for a moment, then crossed the room. When he passed by me, I felt a shock wave hit my chest. I remembered the odd sensation from yesterday and felt a stirring of anxiety. There was no storm today, only rain, and the power of the shock was greater than static electricity. So what was this strange phenomenon happening between us?

When he was firmly in place, I slid off the chaise and pulled on my dragon robe to cover my thin white nightgown, which was threadbare enough to be see-through in places. Kyran was doing his best not to look, a prudence I found rather tedious. "I'm making you something to eat."

He stared at me, more thrown by this innocent announcement than the provocative state of my gown. There was something very backward about that. "But you cannot serve me… I cannot take… That is, I had something earlier…"

"What did you have?" I demanded, if only to avoid hearing another half-finished sentence.

He winced. "Cold coffee. It was quite bracing."

"I'm sure it was. Stir up the fire, and I'll fix us both something. I'm hungry myself."

He opened his mouth to protest, took in my determined stance, then shut it again. Without another word, he kneeled before the fire and added some kindling and a few turves of heather peat as I went about my preparations. Nothing fancy, just limoney tea, toasted rhubarb bread left over from last night, and fried pepper eggs with a couple rashers of crisp bacon.

By the time I was done, the fire was roaring and Kyran was back in his chair, his eyes closed. I paused for a moment and returned the favor of studying him as he had studied me when he thought I was asleep. Dark circles lurked under his eyes and a hollowness in his cheeks spoke of many missed meals. What was with this family and starvation? Even sitting still, his long fingers tapped the rocking chair's smooth arm and his long, spidery eyelashes fluttered as though in a dream. I had a sudden desire to play my clariflute for him, to soothe him to sleep, if only so he could escape his troubles for a few moments.

Flustered by such sentiment, I announced, "Here we are," and set the tray down on the rowan table I'd made from a tree slab Missy Thornback had given me. Handing Kyran his plate, our fingers brushed against each other and I felt that tantalizing jolt again. He seemed to have felt it, too, his dark eyes flying up to meet mine. I quickly looked away, not wanting to appear the naïve young lass unable to cope with an innocent union of flesh, but it wasn't easy. I wanted to look at him, wanted to figure out what he was doing to me, most importantly, if he was experiencing the same effect.

I returned to the chaise and watched as he tucked into the simple meal like a beggar. As with Ilia, the food disappeared quickly. When he was done, I passed him my plate, took his empty one, and returned to the kitchen to cut myself two slices of bread. Luckily I always baked extra loaves, so there would be plenty left for Ilia when she awoke.

We ate in silence, only the sounds of the snapping fire and silverware clinking on stoneware to fill the quiet. When Kyran was done eating, he leaned back and sighed contentedly. "I am in your debt, Miss Gragan."

"Yes, well, you'd better call me Lorelle," I said, taking his empty plate from his lap. Not a spot of food remained—not even a smear of egg yolk or a tiny breadcrumb. "Someone recently told me my last name reminded him of trolls. And while I find that somewhat pleasing, I'd rather not have that image of me in your head. I am looking after your niece, after all." I set our dishes in the sink to be washed later, then returned to the chaise. Tucking my feet up under me, I leaned forward, schooling my expression to one of concern. "I'm worried about Ilia."

He stiffened. "I wouldn't ever hurt her, if that's what you're thinking…"

"I'm not thinking that at all." I did my best to sound appalled he'd suggest such a thing, even though I'd been the one to imply it in the first place. "I'm worried that with her mother's death and being wrenched from the one place she was happy that she's suffering from melancholy. Thinking she has to marry her cousin Renwick, whom she doesn't seem to care for, isn't helping matters."

Kyran's expression had darkened during my speech and I thought he was about to berate me for sticking my common nose in his high-born business. But he surprised me. "I'm worried about her, too. This has all been a bit much for her, I agree. But as for Renwick, he isn't all bad. She could do worse." He watched me carefully, assessing my response. "He pretends to love her, but I don't think he has feelings for her."

"And what makes you say that? You barely know the man."

"I don't have to know him to know his feelings for Ilia are a sham. After we were introduced, he paid more attention to me than he did to her. I must say it was all rather uncomfortable." It hadn't been, but Kyran didn't need to know that.

His fingers, one of which boasted a copper-red scab, clenched the arms of the rocking chair. "Did he now?"

"I don't think he hurt Ilia's feelings, if that's what's making you angry."

"That is *not* what's making me angry." The fire popped loudly behind him, adding a bit of theatrics to his indignant outburst. "I sent him on an errand and he spends it gallivanting after the local wenches like some sort of Lothario! We Van der Daarkes are above that sort of common behavior. It simply will not do."

I felt my own anger rising. "If you're thinking I welcomed his advances, you're sadly mistaken. I don't care for men who think they're above others simply because they have an old family name or pots of money to throw about. And you referring to me as a local *wench*? That smacks of hypocrisy if I've ever heard it, being that your sister was willing to marry off her daughter to the first taker."

He fell back in his chair, looking a bit stunned, and I had the feeling few people argued with him. "My apologies," he said stiffly. "I was not referring to you when I said wench, but at any rate, I phrased my thoughts poorly."

"Indeed you did."

"So you have no interest in Renwick?" he persisted.

"Actually, it's really none of your business whether or not I find your cousin irresistibly attractive…in a boyish sort of way, that is."

His mouth turned down. "I suppose I deserved that."

His response surprised me; it implied that my dig had made a mark. But I didn't let my feelings show, schooling my expression to one of cool dignity. "You deserved much worse than that, but I'm refraining myself for the sake of your niece." I jerked my head up at the loft.

"Of course." He rose, suddenly business-like. Our little tête-à-tête was over and I found that I wouldn't have minded it lasting longer. I liked provoking this man. "I thank you for your hospitality. You've made it easier for me to face the coming day." He dug a leather bag out of his pocket. "I hope this will suffice as payment."

I stood and took the bag from him. When I opened it, I found ten Goldenars inside, gleaming dully up at me. It was a lot of money. The Van der Daarkes must have left a good amount of their wealth behind when they'd fled Hawthorn Lane, perhaps believing they'd soon return. They'd also left clothes, judging by Kyran's cloak and Renwick's natty outfit of yesterday. So it was possible they'd meant to be back within a short time.

How curious.

"It's more than adequate," I said, trying to keep my voice calm. With this little windfall I'd finally be able to fix my foundation, hopefully before any more bad weather hit. I should also be able to buy a new dress, or at least the material to make one, some new books, as well, and stock up on Effervescence for our next cold season.

"Will you fetch Ilia?" Kyran interrupted my blissful reverie. "I must be going."

An idea occurred to me...one that would kill two birds with a single stone. "Why don't I bring Ilia to the castle when she awakens? I'll feed her first, of course, then bring her by. I'd hate to wake her when she's sleeping so well, and I think a good rest will help improve the state of affairs between you."

He didn't answer at first, instead took his time staring into my eyes as though searching for the ulterior motive he knew was there. I returned his stare with as much innocence as I could muster. It must have been enough to satisfy him, though Grim knows how I managed to dredge it up, for Kyran nodded. "That will work for me."

"Good."

"I could send the carriage."

"No need. The walk will do us good."

"It's raining out."

"I have two cloaks, and besides, this is the best time for finding Dragon Moss, which grows along the road to the castle. I use it for curing heartburn," I explained.

"You're a healer?"

"Not quite. I only make the elixirs and potions. Missy Thornback taught me a lot before she retired to Wuthering Wood a couple years back."

"Ah. Well, look after Ilia on the walk up. Take a lot of breaks. She's rather fragile, and it's a bit of a hike."

"I think she's much stronger than she looks, and she'll be less fragile when she gets some food in her."

He winced. "Food. I meant to take care of that, too. I'm afraid shopping is not my greatest strength. Can you tell me the names of some good shops in the village?"

"I'll tell you what. Before we go to the castle, I'll stop in at a few and arrange for deliveries."

He looked like I'd just handed him the moon. "You'd do that?"

"You overpaid me, and while I'm no angel, I'm also not an opportunist. I'll make sure you and your niece will be well-fed tonight, and for the week to come."

"Not Renwick?"

"Especially Renwick," I said with a suggestive smile.

"I'll take you up on your offer, Miss— That is to say, *Lorelle*. Thank you."

"We'll be there an hour or two before supper, *Count* Van der Daarke, if that will suit."

He winced at the appellation. "That will suit me admirably. And it's Kyran, if I'm to call you Lorelle."

"As you wish, Kyran."

I nodded to him and he took his leave, glancing back at me one last time, his expression inscrutable, before leaving the cottage and taking his charged presence with him.

I smiled, feeling quite satisfied with my dealings. I now had access to the castle and Count Van der Daarke in the palm of my hand.

It was a lovely sensation.

Chapter Eleven

Ilia slept through both my screaming and Kyran's visit. The tisane I'd given her had done its job. After a good twelve hours of solid sleep, she would awaken refreshed and calmed, and ready to return to the castle. Or so I hoped. If not, well then we'd cross that bridge when we came to it.

While Ilia slept, I did chores, then readied myself for the day, applying a hint of rose and sage oil to the hollows of my throat and wrists before dressing with care. My first visit to the castle (inside it, anyway—I'd peeked through the windows, of course, but despite my best efforts had never found a way in) deserved to be a special one and I wanted to look my best for such an auspicious occasion.

I was watering the plants when Ilia descended from the loft, her golden hair messy and her eyes puffy. She yawned and rubbed at her eyes. "That was the best sleep I think I've ever gotten."

I smiled at her. "Good. You needed it. No nightmares?"

She shook her head. "Only good dreams. Lovely ones, actually. I dreamed I was riding a unicorn through a dark wood and we came to a pool and looked at our reflections and I looked like a princess, Lorelle! I've never looked like a princess before, not even when I dressed up as Cinderella for Halloween."

"Do you want to look like a princess?" I asked with amusement. "They never strike me as the most self-sufficient of creatures."

She frowned, thinking this over. "Well, I guess not. But princesses look pretty and so did I, pretty enough, anyway."

"Pretty enough for what?"

"For a boyfriend!" she exclaimed, looking at me as though I were daft. "It's all me and Tiffany ever talk about. She'd love this dream, Lorelle. I could tell her about it, couldn't I?" Her hands clasped together. "It's just a dream, after all."

Should I tell her that nothing in this world is as it seems, that dreams can often mean more than one realizes? "You look pretty now," I said to distract her, "with your hair clean and out of those wet clothes. If you gained some weight that would help your looks, too."

"Do you really think so?" she asked hopefully.

"Definitely." I was starting to understand that when Ilia had replied, "What do you think?" when I'd asked her if her cousin wanted to marry her, it hadn't been spoken out of conceit. "Your cousin Renwick thinks you're pretty," I went on, determined to work out Renwick's motives for going after Ilia. I wasn't sure what kind of title she held as niece to a Count, but she couldn't be too low down on the totem pole.

"He thinks my money's pretty," she replied, showing a surprising perceptiveness.

Aha. Not a title then, but money. "So Renwick wants to marry you for your money?"

She shrugged. "It's certainly not for my looks. He knows we're rich."

"And your mother left everything to you." Ilia nodded, not looking exactly thrilled at the prospect. "But she wanted you to marry Renwick to look after you, even though you have your own money?" Something about this didn't make sense.

"I guess so. That's what Renwick said anyway, and he would know what she wanted. He spent a lot of time with her when I was at boarding school."

That's what Renwick said… And what a reliable source he was. So maybe Ilia's mother hadn't wished her to be married after all. Maybe "Cousin" Renwick was actually a shiftless bounder, looking to move in on innocent prey. Pretending to be family would make it easier for him to latch onto Kyran and Ilia, now wouldn't it?

I couldn't wait to suss out the truth, but first things first. "Your uncle stopped by this morning. To take you back to the castle."

Ilia's eyes widened with fear. "But I don't want to go back!"

"Why not? Is it so frightening there?"

"There are strange noises all over the place and it's cold as ice and there's nothing to eat."

"Well, old places are full of odd sounds. As for the cold, I think that was because there weren't any fires burning when you arrived." She gave a reluctant nod. "The food part I can remedy. I told your uncle we'd do some shopping and have everything delivered to the castle. You could help me pick things out. Trust me when I say you'll be very pleased with all the delicacies there are here. We do love our food." Ilia swallowed, torn between her appetite and her fear. "And I'll be accompanying you to the castle, so you won't have to go alone."

"You'll help me settle in?" she asked timidly, looking up at me from beneath her short, thick eyelashes.

"Of course. I'd be happy to."

She beamed, her face lighting up, and I felt my affection for her grow. "All right, I'll go." I patted her on the arm, like a child who's been good, and she smiled at me sweetly. I didn't exactly like using her this way, but accompanying her to the castle would benefit us both.

She ate breakfast with gusto, dressed in one of my nicer gowns, and after fetching her Alterworld clothes and stuffing them in an old cobweb silk sack, we departed, hoods pulled over our heads to stave off the rain.

We didn't make it far, being met by a carriage, black and gleaming as the devil's horns, right outside the gate that united the shoulder-high stone wall surrounding my little cottage and garden. Josepha sat in the driver's seat of the official Van der Daarke carriage, which he had pulled around so that it faced the village. The four-in-hand, with silver trim and dark carvings, was very grand, and the family's coat-of-arms on the door featured a lightning bolt piercing a skull, which seemed appropriate, given Kyran's electrical presence.

Seeing us, Josepha touched the rim of the green velvet top hat he always wore, underneath which sprouted a shock of unruly brown hair. Elfin ears, one tip slightly bent as though he'd slept on it that way one too many times, peeked out from under his hat's brim. His skin was pale brown and splattered with a multitude of freckles, as though someone with a mouthful of coffee had sneezed on him.

As we were long-time acquaintances, the wood elf grinned amiably at me, but when he caught sight of Ilia, his mouth dropped open for several long seconds. Shaking himself, he jumped down and opened the carriage door. "Miss," he indicated with a grand gesture, his eyes on Ilia only. She blushed and took his hand as he guided her into the coach. His clasp lingered until I cleared my throat and their two young hands parted ways. "Miss Gragan." He nodded to me and I nodded back.

"Josepha." His eyes went past me to the interior of the coach. "You know she's a Van der Daarke," I said in a low voice, "and that bodes you no good."

The joy went out of him in a dark sigh. "Nothing bodes me good in Hawthorn Lane."

"True."

"I didn't truly see her...that first night. It was too dark. But now that me eyes have perceived her, they'll never look upon the world the same again."

Oh, Josepha and his poetry. It would be the death of him. "Very romantic, Josepha, but not in the least practical. If you want to advance here, put her out of your mind."

His cat-green eyes widened. "So she really is to marry that rat cousin of hers, eh?"

I laid a calming hand on his arm, pulling him away from the carriage. "That's not set in stone. What else did you hear?"

He glanced at the carriage, then leaned toward me. "It was when they left the Alterworld to cross the border. Master Van der Daarke carried the sleeping miss into the carriage, and I was waiting by the border watching for Unwelcomes, as is protocol when a crossing is being made. That Mister Renwick hadn't crossed yet. He was talking to someone on the other side, though I'm not sure how. I couldn't see him, but I could hear him, and he said, 'We're here and nothing bad has happened, so I guess we'll be safe. For now.' And then there was a part I couldn't hear cause the blasted wind kicked up its heels at that moment. When it calmed, I heard, 'I'll take care of things on this side, don't ye worry, and then ye can come. Until then…we won't be able to speak.' After that, he crossed over, though he didn't see me, there's a bit of luck."

"How did you know to go there that night?"

"An order was made by raven."

"Whose raven?"

He shrugged. "A communal one." Communal birds were used for a small price by those of us, like myself, who didn't own one of their own. "I got paid a good price for the job, I'll tell ye that much, it being a holiday and all."

"Hmmm… I wonder who sent it." When he lifted a clueless shoulder in response, I asked, "Anything else I should know?"

A sly look crossed his face. "Master Van der Daarke might listen if ye were to tell him what a catch I am."

"Josepha, you know quite well that a Van der Daarke would put me in the same category as you—common as a mouse in a larder and just as welcome."

His mouth scrunched up. "A snob, eh?"

"Through and through. It's in his blood."

"I suppose he can't help it, then. But she's different…" He nodded at the coach.

"Yes," I replied thoughtfully. "Ilia's different."

"I like different." He grinned.

I grinned back. "Me, too. All right. I promise I'll do my best on your behalf. You and I have always had an arrangement about these sorts of things, haven't we?"

"We have indeed. There isn't much else to say, though I can tell ye this. Master Van der Daarke is a man with burdens. They weigh him down like bags of stolen goods clapped on his shoulders. I don't know what's worrying at him, but I'm keeping me eyes open."

"Good idea." I turned toward the carriage. "Now, we have much to do today, and very little time to do it in. I suppose the Count told you what we're up to?" He nodded importantly. "To *Devil's Cakes* first, then? For a little sustenance before we embark on our mission?"

His smile was wide. "Just the place I'd have started meself."

After stuffing ourselves with sweets under the watchful eye of Jacques, we spent the next few hours making the necessary arrangements. Luckily the shopkeepers were more than happy to put everything on Count Van der Daarke's bill, as my purchases were a shade on the extravagant side. They would have been happier if I'd shared a bit of gossip with them—everyone was dying to know more about the family—but I kept my mouth shut, saying only, "The last thing I'd want to do is get on his bad side," and that was enough to make them back off. That was the last thing they wanted, too.

At *Tres Pristine*, I ordered the basic necessities for housecleaning and for one's personal grooming, including some of my own concoctions for Ilia's toilette. Afterwards we moved on to *Posh Nosh*, a high-end grocer, where Ilia, after only a few moments browsing, looked like she'd died and gone to heaven. The selection was marvelous, ranging from salmon pâté and succulent sausages to chocolate cranberry syrups and lemon-cherry delights, and I could only wish I made more money to indulge my gluttonous tastes here.

Everything was to be delivered that afternoon, and with undue haste, I imagined— everyone dying to get a chance to see inside the castle. I had a feeling that on this occasion all the shop owners would be overseeing deliveries personally, "to make sure things go smoothly," of course.

I was surprised that everyone left Ilia alone, especially after her prophecy of the day before. But they were respectful toward her, perhaps wary of losing her uncle's favor...and Lady Faylan's, as well. Unlike yesterday, Ilia seemed happy being out and about, sneaking peeks at Josepha several times, asking me about him as subtly as she could, which wasn't very subtle, and sighing over a lovely dress in the window of *Fawn's Fashions*.

"Perhaps you could order a few gowns for your time here?" I told her after the fifth sigh.

She clasped her hands together. "Do you think Uncle Kyran would pay for them? I have money, but I don't have any with me."

"I'm sure he'd much rather pay for new clothes than to have you continue being seen wearing a commoner's dress," I said, perhaps a shade more tartly than was necessary.

Her eyes clouded. "What do you mean?"

"Isn't it obvious, Ilia? I'm not your sort. I'm poor, and I have no family name of any importance. For someone of your stature to be seen wearing something of mine is a disgrace to your family name. It doesn't bother me, though," I lied. "It's just how things are done."

"I don't see you that way, Lorelle," she told me earnestly, her hand clutching my arm. "I think you're awesome."

"Well, thank you, Ilia. I don't see myself that way, either, but it's how your uncle will see me and he's the Count here. The villagers will look up to him and follow his lead."

Her forehead wrinkled. "That doesn't seem right."

"It isn't right, but it's the way it is, and I've no control other than to not follow it myself."

"Then I won't buy any new dresses!" she proclaimed, leaning her forehead against my shoulder.

I smiled down at her, feeling a little hiccup right where my heart was. "That's sweet of you, Ilia, but I'm afraid that won't do me any good. Besides, I'd like to see you in a new dress, one that's better for your coloring. You look a bit washed-out in mine."

She made a face and peered up at me. "Washed-out? That's bad, isn't it?"

"But it's not bad to want a new dress, Ilia. What's bad is acting like a princess just because you have money."

"I promise I won't act like a princess with you, Lorelle." She grinned impishly. "But I might try it out on someone else."

I was really starting to like this girl.

I grabbed her shoulders and spun her about to face the bright pink doors of *Fawn's Fashions*. "I know just who that someone should be."

Chapter Twelve

Fawn's Fashions is run by two high elf sisters, Fan and Dawn Ravenna, and they are the hoitiest of the toitiest around here, which is saying a lot considering the wealth of competition. I might like their boutique, but I don't particularly like them and their puffed up snobbery. What amuses me greatly is that they have a brother, a forest wandering bibliophile and fashion faux pas, who has a bit of a hero-worship thing going on with me, probably because I don't have to answer to anyone. Luckily for the sisters, Oren is currently on a walkabout, or I'd make sure to flirt with him right in front of them.

They also didn't like how I entered their shop whenever I felt like it, searched through all their garments, then left without purchasing anything (mainly because I couldn't afford anything of theirs). For me, it was fun simply looking and fantasizing, but it was also good business. Knowing fashion and the price of clothes helped me determine who had what in Hawthorn Lane. If someone with little money was suddenly wearing a beautiful new dress from *Fawn's*, I knew something was up. As a bonus, my presence annoyed the crap out of Fan and Dawn, and because of that, I tried to visit them at least once a week.

"Here's your opportunity to play the princess," I whispered to Ilia as we stepped inside the shop. To give the Ravenna sisters their due, their store was truly splendid, with long, highly polished counters and brilliant, constantly changing displays, often with live mannequins. Gilded mirrors everywhere added to the sense that the store went on and on, and you couldn't help but look at yourself every time you passed one. The shop sold the latest feminine and masculine fashions, jewelry fine enough to bedeck a royal personage, and an assortment of style accessories—parasols, ties, cravats, gloves, and shoes. "Stand over there," I pointed to an ostentatious display, "and follow my lead." Ilia giggled and did as she was told.

Moments later, Fan and Dawn sashayed toward me, their matching expressions cold as ice. I happened to know for a fact that they'd undergone extensive facial and torso remodeling, a sort of plastic surgery but with magic, and it showed in the sharply perfect profiles they presented to the world.

"You again?" Fan sneered. She was the older of the two, about my height, and thin as a rail. Her perfectly coiffed hair, set in an elaborate hairstyle that likely took her maid at least two hours to create each morning, was a sight to see today. The amount of curling and braiding and gelling and tucking it must have taken to keep it upright was a miracle of engineering. But then, they knew the Van der Daarkes were in town and likely had expected a visit soon. They'd want to impress them and ensure their business by looking their trendiest best.

"Lovely to see you, Fan," I gave my typical greeting. I had long since discovered that acting affably toward the sisters was the best way to go about irritating them. "New hairstyle?" Her hair was a perfectly nice blond color, but not as radiant as Ilia's and I found myself feeling a possessive sort of pride in the girl. As I'd been the brave soul to brush out the mess last night, I figured I deserved to bask a little in its reflected glory.

Fan automatically reached up to pat her hair-do, then stopped, her hand dangling in mid-air. "Why are you here?" she demanded. "Fetching something for someone? Have you taken up a delivery service as a way to make ends meet? We know how you struggle, poor thing."

Dawn, the younger sister, smirked, but kept her mouth shut. Of the two, she was the least clever and whenever she tried to criticize me, it ended up biting her in the butt. Her hairstyle was equally as elaborate as her sister's, but not as tall. What she wore—a pale blue gown of Sylph Silk, was gorgeous, but not as gorgeous as her sister's golden Faerie Dust frock. Basically, she was a younger, *lesser* version of her sister.

"I'm here to look for dresses," I replied.

Dawn snickered, and unable to resist, retorted, "Like you could afford our ware!"

"Just the smell of you reduces the value of our merchandise." Fan sniffed, waving a delicate hand in front of her nose. "Really, do you bake your own bread and tend your own fires? You smell of flour and peat smoke, and I do believe it's giving me a headache."

"That's probably your hair-do," I pointed out. "That get-up could house a whole family of rats, with room to spare. Must be awfully heavy."

She glared down her nose at me. "I'll have you know this is the latest style, reserved for only the best lineages."

"And who told you that?"

"My sources in the fashion and beauty *métier*." Fan loved showing off her French.

"Well, I'm sure your sources are laughing their *derrières* off right now. You can barely hold your head straight."

Okay, so I wasn't *always* nice to them.

"I've a mind to ban you from my shop!" Fan cried.

But you won't because I'm Avice's friend, I thought to myself, and Avice spent a lot of money here.

"It's my shop, too," Dawn sulked.

"If you want me to leave then I guess Miss Van der Daarke and I will go elsewhere. Ilia?" I called.

She stepped out from behind the display, a dress in hand. "Yes?" she answered, her expression innocent, as though she hadn't heard a word.

"I'm afraid we shall have to quit this abode."

She did an excellent job of looking confused. "But why, Lorelle? We just got here!"

"I'm afraid they don't want you—"

"Oh, Lorelle," Fan broke in. "You're such a kidder." She tittered and the resulting effect made her sound like a drunken bird. "Of course we want you here!" Fan turned to Ilia confidingly. "Lorelle's a dear, isn't she?"

"I thought you said she smelled."

I almost snorted out loud.

"Oh, no. I'd never say such a thing. You misheard me!"

"Are you saying Miss Van der Daarke has inadequate hearing?" I challenged.

Fan looked horrified and Dawn could only stand frozen, her little brain likely having a stroke. "Not at all! I just mean, we do endeavor to keep all harsh odors from our establishment, the better for our clientele to enjoy the delicate atmosphere we aspire to maintain at all times."

"And I don't smell delicate?"

"You smell of home and when our customers come here, they don't want to think of home, they want to think of exotic locales."

I tilted my head to one side, letting Fan sweat—not that she actually could, having had her sweat glands removed—as I pretended to consider this. "So people who have fires in their homes shouldn't come here? Why, that would eliminate most your clientele!"

Probably not, but it wasn't done to let on that we knew perfectly well the wealthy preferred to only use Effervescence. I thought it a shame. I've always liked a good, crackling fire.

Fan gave a strangled laugh and threw up her tastefully bejeweled hands. "Everyone is welcome here, Miss Van der Daarke. Of course they are!"

"So you accept pretty much everyone as clientele?" I needled. Really, this was too easy.

Fan's sharp-boned cheeks flushed painfully, something I hadn't believed possible. I thought she'd had her blood removed at one point, too. "To a certain extent," she replied cautiously.

Ilia stuck her nose in the air. "I want only the best. I was told this place is the best!" She stomped her little foot and I mentally applauded her. *Good show, Ilia.*

"And you shall get it," Fan assured her.

"So this is the only place that sells clothes around here, Lorelle?" Ilia asked, turning to me.

"Not at all."

"It is if you want the best quality and the latest trends," Fan spoke up, her chin set at a haughty angle.

"Really?" Ilia looked doubtful as she glanced around. "Well, I suppose it will have to do."

And it did do. Under my supervision—mainly to keep the sisters from grilling the poor girl, though several sly questions were asked by Fan, and successfully parried by yours truly—Ilia tried on twenty gowns and picked out nine that she liked. Apparently she had decided to stay here for a while. She would return tomorrow to be fitted properly, and after the seamstresses made the appropriate adjustments, the dresses would be delivered. Once again, no doubt, accompanied by the proprietresses themselves, their gowns fashionably revealing, but with even taller hair-dos than today's. I hoped the messenger birds wouldn't get caught up in them.

"You must pick something out, too, Lorelle," Ilia implored.

"I'm fine, Ilia."

"That's no fun." I shrugged. "All right, if you were to pick one dress, which would it be?"

I looked around. "Oh, I don't know." I pointed. "Maybe that green one."

"That's the one she always ends with," Dawn crowed, showing more perspicacity than I'd have credited her with. I hadn't realized she'd been watching me, though likely she'd only been making sure I didn't steal anything or talk to Oren. "Probably because it's our cheapest one."

I didn't care about the price. It was a beautiful gown. Made of elfin moss, it was simply cut but entirely elegant and would bring out the green in my blue-green eyes. But even being the cheapest, sadly it was still out of my price range.

"She'll take it," Ilia determined.

"Absolutely not," I replied firmly. "I cannot take anything from your uncle, Ilia. I *won't*."

"It's not from him, it's from me!"

"He's paying for it. Now we should get going." I would not be pushed into doing something I didn't want to do. I'd learned how to handle myself quite well from dealing with the fey here. They're a sneaky, clever lot, which I've found I rather like. Life can get boring when there's no challenge to it. "We still have to get you home and it's growing late. It doesn't do to be out when darkness falls." Dawn's sour face reflected her envy at the fact that I was the one escorting Ilia, and I reveled in her bitterness for a second or two.

"I suppose," Ilia said morosely.

"I'm sure Josepha will get us there in good time," I craftily added, and she brightened at his name.

We took our leave of the sisters, whose expressions couldn't seem to decide on whether to be happy to have sold so many dresses to a peer of the realm or mad that I was the one connected to the family, and not them.

Outside, I checked the weather conditions. The rain had stopped some time during our shopping expedition, though the sky remained overcast and a wind was picking up. Ilia didn't seem to notice the gloomy weather. Her face had taken on a joyful glow and she looked rather appealing for such a skinny little pip. Happiness was a good look for her, a look that would be hard to maintain in this contrary place.

Seeing her face light up even more as she spotted Josepha waiting for us, I knew I'd have a battle to get her to leave Hawthorn Lane. Typical teenager that she was, she already had a crush on the boy. Even so, I'd have to at least try to convince her to go. There was something about her that drew trouble, and here in Hawthorn Lane that could spell disaster.

Josepha jumped down from his seat to open the door for us. "Did ye have a successful day?"

I nodded. "I believe we did. Now to the castle, and make haste. You and I will want to be off home before the gloaming."

"The castle is me home now, Lorelle," Josepha announced grandly. "I'm to be the official coachman, among other things. I shall look after the horses, drive the carriage, and be trusted with important errands." He looked quite pleased with himself.

"Congratulations, Josepha," I said. "That's good news."

"How splendid!" Ilia agreed, sounding like a young Victorian maiden. Even more so when she added, "It'll be good to have a strong *man* about the house."

I refrained from pointing out that her uncle was a strong man—he gave the appearance of being so, anyway, beneath that cloak of his. In her mind, though, her uncle didn't signify. Nor, it appeared, did Renwick. He was going to regret running off yesterday.

His chest jutting out importantly, Josepha ushered us into the carriage. The village square was busy and we had gained a lot of observers throughout the day. Josepha's name would be on everyone's lips tonight, for the first time spoken in a tone of respect, even if somewhat grudgingly given. I imagined many would fight to buy him a drink if he were to visit the pub later…in exchange for information, of course. Lucky for Kyran, Josepha knew how to keep his counsel, and hold his drink—both lessons learned the hard way.

Once seated, he urged the gleaming black horses into a smart trot. The cries of the messenger birds could be heard overhead, and I'm sure they were having a field day, seeing me, a plebeian, escorting Ilia to the castle.

As we rolled along, Ilia and I were as quiet as the birds were loud, both tired from our long day. But it was a good quiet, filled with satisfaction at a day's work well done. At least it was a good quiet on my part. About halfway through the journey, Ilia spoke up.

"Lorelle?"

"Yes?"

"Do you think that Desolates could be real?"

"I'm not sure," I answered honestly. A gust of wind battered against the carriage and I grabbed hold of the leather strap dangling from the ceiling to steady myself. "I've never seen one. As far as I know, they're just a story."

"Hmm," she murmured, her thin features doubtful. "Well, I'm afraid to tell you they aren't just a story. They're very real, and one is following us now."

At that moment, Josepha cracked the whip, crying, "Fly, ye devils. Fly!" The coach lurched forward, and the horses began to gallop at top speed up the mountainside as a horrible shriek echoed all around us.

Ilia clutched at me. "Don't let her take me, Lorelle!"

I held the girl tight as if to protect her, though what I thought mere flesh could do in the face of an immortal, heart-stealing monster was beyond me.

Chapter Thirteen

"Hang on!" Josepha cried over the panicked whinnying of the horses.

"What's happening out there?" I shouted, but he didn't answer. I could only hope it was because he was trying to concentrate and not because he was no longer there.

"She's coming for me," Ilia whimpered into my shoulder.

I pulled her away from me and looked her in the eye. "*Who* is coming, Ilia? And why do you keep saying 'she'?"

She pointed to her temple. "I see her! In my mind. She starts out beautiful…long, golden hair, her face is so pretty…and then, and then…" She hiccupped back a frightened sob. "And then she changes. She turns into a demon, and her mouth is nothing but sharp teeth in a black hole. She wants my heart, Lorelle!"

I shook her a little. "You have to stay calm, Ilia. If Josepha heard you and started worrying about you, he couldn't concentrate on keeping us on the road." We were traveling quite fast now. Too fast, and I could only hope Josepha was the one still driving us.

She gave a shuddering sigh, but was nodding, her little rabbit teeth clamped down on her lower lip. "O-okay. I'll try."

"Do more than try," I ordered her.

She gave another nod, a stronger one this time. "I'll do it. I'll stay calm."

"Good girl." I let go of her arms. "Hang onto something." She grabbed hold of a leather strap and held on tight. When she was as secure as she was going to get, I opened a window and peered out. It took a moment for my eyes to adjust, as it had grown unusually dark. Even though it was only late afternoon, it seemed as though someone had sucked most of the light out of the day.

When I could see a little better, I looked around, searching for our pursuer. There was no one that I could see, not on my side or behind us. Even the messenger birds had disappeared, leaving behind an eerie quiet, with only the crunching of the carriage wheels over gravel and horse hooves hitting stone to be heard. Leaning farther out, I looked around another few seconds to reassure myself that the coast was clear and was about to slip back inside when something grabbed my arm.

Startled, I looked up…right into a nightmarish face barely held together by rotting teeth, black holes for eyes, and cracked, oozing skin. "Give her to me!" the creature screamed, and foul air filled the air between us.

Heart pounding, I struggled to pull her hand off my arm, but her grip was insanely strong. Long, broken nails bit into my skin, sinking deeper and deeper, and waves of fear and disgust rippled through me. Whatever this monster was, it wasn't a sanctioned fey, and from what I'd heard, outlawed fey tended to be either obsessed, desperate, or mad. This one seemed to be all three.

"Get off me!" I screeched, still working to pry her decaying fingers loose. Throughout the struggle, my free hand was feeling about the top of my boot, and at last it found the hilt of my dagger. I pulled the knife free and slashed at the bony claws clutching my arm. The Desolate howled in pain, the piercing noise making my ears ring. Taking advantage of her distraction, I wrenched my arm free and pulled back inside the coach, slamming the window shut.

Ilia's horrified eyes were on my knife, which was covered in a dark viscous substance. "Is that…blood?"

"I should think so, being that I nearly took her fingers off." I pulled a handkerchief from between my breasts and wiped away the blood.

"It was her? The way I described her?"

"Oh, yes," I replied, sheathing the knife. "You think she's the one you saw at Haunted Hollow?"

She nodded. "How are we going to get free of her?" Her face went white. "And Josepha? What about him?"

"I'll take care of it." I reopened the window.

Her eyes widened. "No, Lorelle!"

"You'll be okay, Ilia."

"I don't care about me!" she cried. "We're going too fast. You'll fall."

I paused for a moment, taken aback. It had been a long time since anyone had placed my welfare above their own. In fact, I wasn't sure anyone had ever done so, completely and unselfishly. Only one person had come close, and that had turned out to be a lie.

"I'll be fine," I told her, getting a hold of myself. "This isn't the first time I've been up on top of a moving coach."

She frowned at the idea. "But it's me she wants."

"And she won't have you. Not if Josepha and I have anything to say about it."

Before she could argue further, I opened the window and peered out. Not spying the Desolate anywhere, I pulled myself up onto the window frame, where I could see the coach's roof. No one appeared to be on it, although in this world that meant nothing. Josepha sat hunched over on the driver's seat, unscathed as he urged on the horses.

Or so I thought until I saw a shadow coalescing on the seat beside him. Slowly a dark, sinewy arm stretched out and draped around his neck. He straightened up, looking around. He sensed something was there, but couldn't distinguish what it was. It was all he could do to keep the panicked horses from leaving the road and crashing into the trees.

I eased myself up onto the roof. Once there, I flattened my body and began to pull myself toward the coachman's seat. As I grew nearer, Josepha began to struggle. That *thing* had him in a death lock now, her hands wrapped tightly about his throat.

I rose to my knees, nearly losing my balance as the coach hit a rut and swayed. At the last second I grabbed hold of a post, stopping myself just before I pitched over the side. Heart pounding, I continued forward. I had to hurry. Josepha's struggles were weakening and if he lost control, the horses would plunge into the forest, killing us all.

Gathering my strength, I stood and launched myself at the Desolate. Wrapping my arm around her torso, I pulled with all my might, surprised at how solid she felt. She wavered, but kept her grip on Josepha. My face was right by hers now and the smell was awful, like rotting flesh and vomit. I barely suppressed an urge to gag, tightening my hold and jerking hard.

"Leave me be!" the Desolate shrieked.

"Let him go!" I shouted, tightening my grip on her. "He's not your enemy."

"No, but he's in my way, and I've a heart to reclaim before this day is done."

Josepha's elbow shot out, catching the horrid creature on the jaw, and at the same time I pulled my dagger and swiped. At the last second, she twisted out of my grip and I fell forward, missing my mark. The footboard slowed my descent, but didn't stop it and I ended up dangling over the board's edge. If I fell I would be crushed under the coach's wheels.

"Whoa!" Josepha urged the horses to slow, but they wouldn't be calmed. They knew what was near and believed their only escape was to run far away. Little did they know they couldn't escape this enemy.

I tried to push myself up, but the Desolate jumped on top of me, trapping me. She shoved me through the space between the carriage and the horses' flying hooves—a few more inches and my face would be smashed in by an iron-shod hoof. My heart pounded painfully in my chest as I struggled to hold myself up while slashing backward at the Desolate.

"She took my lover from me!" the ghoul screeched, though it sounded more like a sob. "She must pay for that."

My nose was an inch from getting pushed into my face when a strange sort of whistling noise sounded near my head, followed by a thud. The pressure on my back disappeared, and when I next felt a hand, it was only Josepha, grabbing my dress and pulling me upward. When I was settled next to him, he pulled hard on the reins, not letting up until the horses finally gave in and slowed down. When the carriage rolled to a stop, the elf tied off the reins and jumped down to soothe the frightened beasts.

"Are you all right, Ilia?" I called out, frantic.

She clambered out of the carriage, jumping to the ground. "I'm fine," she answered as I climbed down from the coach, legs shaking. "She's gone."

"Where did she go?" I asked, wielding my dagger.

Her eyes darted about. "I don't know, but we're safe now." The sky had lightened once more, and I thought maybe Ilia was right.

As I sheathed my knife, the sound of hooves caught my attention and I looked up to see Kyran astride a horse, galloping toward us at high speed. He pulled the black stallion to a stop and jumped down, reins in one hand, a longbow in the other.

"Ilia!" He dropped everything and grabbed hold of her arms, looking her up and down as a father would. "Are you all right?"

She nodded, her eyes wide. "I'm fine, Uncle Kyran. Josepha and Lorelle saved my life."

He straightened and faced me, his eyes traversing the length of my body, this time not as a father would. "I'm most grateful to you both. You're all right, then?"

I nodded sharply, more unnerved by the intensity of his gaze than I'd been by our attacker. "Quite well, thank you. Nearly got my teeth knocked to the back of my head, but then…" My eyes fastened on his bow and I realized what that whistling sound had been. "You shot her."

He looked down at it. "I thought it might be the thing to do being that she was about to kill you."

"Exactly the thing to do." I swallowed, thinking how easily he could have missed his intended target and hit me instead, especially shooting from such a distance. "Your arrival was quite fortuitous."

"I was outside with this beast"—he nodded at Rogue, a notoriously fractious horse that nobody wanted because they couldn't control him—"when I heard a strange cry, so I ran inside, grabbed the first thing I could find off the wall, then came as quickly as I could."

"You have excellent timing." While my statement was sincere, it galled me that I'd had to be rescued by a man, and this one in particular, who thought himself lord of all he surveyed.

He strode over to Josepha, who was seeing to the horses. "Are they settled now?" He looked around, his stance wary. "I don't wish to be out here any longer. I thought I saw whatever that thing was running off into the woods, but it could return at any time."

"They're settled enough to see us back home, milord," Josepha answered. "I'll give them a good rubdown and they'll be right as rain."

"Excellent." He clapped Josepha on the back. "You saved my niece's life. You're to be commended."

Josepha beamed. "It were me and the miss." He nodded at me. "We look after each other, eh, Lorelle?"

Kyran glanced back and forth between us. "Do you?"

"Aye. She's the sort to get herself into all sorts of trouble, milord."

"Me?" I cried indignantly.

Josepha grinned. "Ah, that got ye some color back, eh? Ye were a wee bit pasty for a moment there, Lorelle. Didn't like the looks of it."

"Oh, well." I straightened my bodice and swiped ineffectually at the skirt of my dress. "I was perfectly fine. Just not used to being attacked by a Desolate, that's all."

"Desolate?" Josepha echoed, his eyes wide. "Ye really think?"

"She said she wanted Ilia's heart."

"She were cold, weren't she?" Josepha used his free hand to pull his cloak tighter about him. "Smelled like the grave, too."

"What did she want?" Kyran demanded.

"She wanted me," Ilia replied, looking rather calm for being the target of a murderous fiend.

"Whatever for?"

She shrugged. "Revenge, I suppose."

He pulled back, his face going pale. "Revenge? For what?"

"I don't know." There was a moment's silence as this sunk in.

"So what exactly is a Desolate?" he said at last.

Josepha nodded at me to answer. "Ye tell him, Lorelle. Before today I just thought they were a story."

"Me, too." I sighed, wondering how to explain a story that had come to life. The fey here had always treated Desolates as fantasy, so I'd thought that if *they* didn't believe in Desolates, then Desolates couldn't possibly exist. How wrong I'd been about that. Which made me wonder what else I was wrong about regarding this place. "There's a myth that when a person dies from a broken heart as a result of treachery, he or she can turn into a Desolate. Desolates seek revenge by going after the heart of the person they believe wronged them. The scariest part is that they can make mistakes, so they could take anyone. Though this Desolate seems very focused on Ilia."

"So I didn't kill it?"

"I don't think so. I'm not really sure if Desolates are alive or dead, but they can be hurt. I think they can also heal themselves very quickly." Which would explain how the Desolate had recovered so rapidly from nearly losing several fingers.

"That's not very reassuring." He turned to his niece. "Are you sure it's you she seeks?"

"I do. I, well…" She drew herself up. "I sense it."

I thought maybe Kyran would take this opportunity to tell his niece the truth about her being fey, but he said nothing. He was either protecting her, as I had been, or he didn't know he was fey himself. While that seemed impossible, I knew it wasn't. It could be that his family had never told him about their fey. It wouldn't be the first time.

I looked around. The sky was darkening as dusk approached and the afternoon deliveries would soon be arriving. "You should head back to the castle," I told Kyran. "The vendors will be delivering your wares soon and you should be there to greet them. I'll see myself home." My encounter with the Desolate had shaken me more than I cared to admit and right now the idea of sitting in front of my fire with a glass of *Dark Spirits* and a good book sounded more appealing than spying on the Van der Daarkes.

"I think not," Kyran said, surprising me. "You're coming with us. You'll be safer at the castle."

"I'll be fine," I protested. "The Desolate is gone."

"I'm not taking that risk." He grabbed my arm and steered me toward the coach, a pulsating shock passing between us as we walked. I was starting to feel a little warm and fuzzy about his concern when he added, "If something happened to you, I'd be blamed, and I have enough problems as it is."

Dandy.

Not being given a choice, I ducked inside the carriage. As I sat down, Ilia grabbed my hand and squeezed it. "I'm so glad you're coming, Lorelle."

And so the decision was made. But of course, isn't that what I'd wanted all along? An invitation to enter the castle by Count Van der Daarke himself…

Huzzah for me.

Chapter Fourteen

When we stepped inside the castle I saw that the Count had been busy. The Great Hall was well-lit with torches and it actually felt warmer inside than outside, a momentous feat for such a large space. I had a feeling the warmth was because Kyran had already received a delivery of Effervescence from the Iverich family. Their motto was: *Take, or it will be taken*. I thought it should be: *We don't like being poor*.

I looked around the darkly decorated hall and took in the vibrant tapestries, which depicted either hunts or violent battle scenes. Higher up, shadowed balconies awaited cloak-and-dagger intrigue. Otherworldly carvings, which decorated the Grecian posts that supported the high ceiling, glared at me in warning, and an army of weapons commandeered any wall space not covered by tapestries or torches.

Very welcoming, the Van der Daarkes.

As my eyes continued to wander, I spotted a number of pots designed to hold and disperse Effervescence. Of the best quality, they were likely made by the McFintrick family, maestro elves who were excellent and inventive potters. I'd once traded a batch of my special black clay for a set of their mugs and bowls, and counted myself lucky to have them. One of the Count's vessels was shaped like a skull's head, another was a striking snake, yet another was a mummy. I liked his selection. It sent a definite message… *Don't mess with me*.

One of *my* mottoes.

Being from a powerful family, and likely not knowing any better, which the Iverich family had certainly taken advantage of, Kyran displayed his Effervescence with pride. Lucky him, he could get away with such ostentation. Most fey here wouldn't dare show any weakness, or even hint at it. But he was a Van der Daarke and could do what he wanted. A part of me, a part that I tried hard to repress, envied him this power.

"Do you remember where your room is, Ilia?" the Count asked.

Her face scrunched up. "I think so."

"Why don't you both go and tidy yourselves? I've numerous tasks to attend to, not to mention I need to deal with those deliveries. I'll meet up with you both later."

I had the sense I was going to be here a bit longer than I'd thought, perhaps get invited to dinner. Now that I was inside the castle, I decided that dining here would be ideal for my mission, and probably quite enjoyable, as well.

"Until later," I replied with a grin. After looking at me for a tick too long, Kyran left the foyer through an archway leading off the Great Hall. From my explorations of the castle's exterior, I knew it was a massive and convoluted building. The family had added on over the centuries, creating a sprawling estate that could serve as its own small city. I wondered if all rich and high-born families felt the need to build such immense dwellings. Maybe they did it to escape family members. That, at least, made sense to me.

There were two staircases, one on each side of the hall. Ilia paused for a moment, then headed toward the one on the left. Not that it mattered which one she took, as they both led to the same corridor. When we reached the top, she turned left and continued down a hallway lined with portraits of Van der Daarkes. It wasn't as brightly lit up here, making it hard to see any details as we hurried past.

Five doorways down, Ilia opened a beautifully carved door and entered an opulent room, complete with a balcony and two window seat nooks. Its grandeur was befitting a princess. A dark princess, but a princess all the same.

"This is nice," I said, looking about me.

"And warm!" Ilia clapped excitedly. A fire was burning in the hearth, cheering up the room with its flickering flames. Effervescence pots were spread around the perimeter, adding to the warmth.

"Do you like it better than you did last night?" I teased Ilia as she spun in circles.

"Much," she agreed.

"But it's still not your school…"

"Actually, this place is growing on me." She skipped around the room, stopping to study a series of dark Dutch landscape paintings. She quickly moved on to a toilette table, stroking the tarnished silver brushes and glass-bottled perfumes sitting on it, and finally ended her tour by pulling on the leering knobs of a wide and sturdy wardrobe. She peered inside, ruffled through the gowns hanging there, then closed the doors. Two battered suitcases sat nearby and she kicked one. "I suppose I won't be needing what's in here anymore, will I?" She looked delighted at the idea.

"You do know it's dangerous for you to stay here, Ilia," I said, deciding that the subtle approach wasn't going to work. She needed to be warned about the dangers of this place. At least then I'd feel I'd done my job.

"I know, Lorelle." She plumped up a pillow on her unmade bed, a four-poster with black curtains that resembled a mourning shroud.

"But I don't mind. I'm not scared anymore. I was at first because it was all so new and Uncle Kyran was worried about something, too, and I didn't know what it was, and then I thought I'd have to marry Renwick, but I've decided that maybe I don't."

"Well, I'm glad you realize that, but I'm still worried. That Desolate seemed particularly interested in you."

She sighed. "Yes, it did, didn't it? I wonder why?"

"Maybe your uncle knows something. He must have heard stories about your family's time here. I could ask him."

She clasped her hands together. "Oh, would you, Lorelle? I like him more now, but he's still rather scary."

"You're not scared of a Desolate, but you're afraid of your uncle?" I smiled. "You're an odd duck, Ilia."

"Oh, but I *am* scared of the Desolate," she corrected me. "It's just a different kind of scared."

"You won't consider leaving?" I tried one last time.

She shook her head. "I know it's strange, but I sort of feel like I belong here now. The villagers have been so friendly, haven't they?"

I had a feeling she was referring to one villager in particular, but I kept my mouth shut. I didn't want her getting her hopes up about a relationship Kyran would never allow to happen.

"All right. I won't bring it up again…well, unless I feel your life is in danger."

She beamed. "It's a deal."

"Why don't you go get cleaned up first?"

"You don't mind?" Her eyes flicked toward my face.

"Not at all. I'll sit by the fire and warm myself."

"I'll hurry."

"Take your time," I told her, and she left through a small side door, closing it behind her.

Instead of sitting, I wandered around the shadowy room, plotting my next move. If I hadn't known it before, I knew it now—the Van der Daarkes had a lot of money, and they'd sunk a hefty sum into this castle over the centuries. So why leave it all behind? Some terrible thing must have happened, but what had it been?

I, along with the other villagers, had assumed the family had survived whatever had happened to make them leave. Obviously we'd been right. But did Kyran know why his family had left their ancestral home in the first place? Would he tell me if he did? It wasn't likely. Ilia didn't even know she was fey, but Kyran must know *something*. He'd decided to come here, after all, which meant he knew the place existed. Renwick must know things, too. But how much did they know, and how was I going to get it out of them?

Ilia emerged from the bathroom, her hair smooth once more. "Your turn."

I stepped inside the cozy little room and peered into an ornate mirror over the old-fashioned sink. I was surprised, then annoyed, to find a dark smear slashed across my cheek. Why hadn't anyone told me I had Desolate blood on my face? It was not an image I wanted to present to the world; it smacked of carelessness. I quickly washed off the crusted blood, brushed out my hair with one of Ilia's bone combs, and re-did my bun.

I hadn't been gone all that long, but when I returned to the bedroom I found Ilia fast asleep. Sometimes the effects of a good tisane can carry over into the next day, and in this case, in combination with our hectic afternoon, its residual effects were too strong to fight. After studying her a moment to be sure she was all right, I decided to take advantage of this opportunity.

Quick as a wink, the door was shut behind me and I was out in the long, silent hallway, the thick carpet muffling my steps. I decided to start my investigation with the portraits. I began at the far end and made my way down the hall, fascinated. Unlike our stiff and rather dull human portraits, these paintings felt almost alive. All the subjects' poses were designed to show off their *sui generis*—their uniqueness and superiority over the commonplace. Women on rearing horses revealed ample cleavage and strong, bare legs. Some were posed as though to strike you dead with their outstretched fingers. All were sensual and powerful. The men demonstrated great feats of strength, lifting tree trunks or hurling heavy objects through the air. Children, wands at the ready, experimented with magic, orbs floating before their intense young faces.

I was halfway down the hall when I came to a series of black and white photographs of a ball. All were entitled, *The Danse Macabre*, and dated at the bottom. I moved closer to one particular photo. It was the last in the series, and dated a hundred years ago.

The dancers all wore enchanting costumes, but had removed their masks for the photograph. The woman who had caught my eye wore a white gown, reminiscent of a Greek goddess, and had long, blond hair and smiling eyes.

It was the Desolate.

Chapter Fifteen

I stared at the Desolate woman for a long time, a chill creeping through me like ghostly fingers down my bare back. Here she was, alive and well, and judging by her radiant smile, happy to be alive. So what had happened to her? Hawthorn Lane had its fair share of stories about the seduction and betrayal of its inhabitants, but I didn't view the lurid tales as entirely real, more like the novels I read—a story meant to entertain.

But here was the Desolate, vibrant and carefree, and definitely not a story.

What had gone wrong for her? Did it have anything to do with the Van der Daarke family fleeing Hawthorn Lane? I thought it might, as she was targeting Ilia Van der Daarke.

I was about to continue onward when I heard a door open and turned to see Ilia peek out. I wondered briefly if I should show her the picture of the Desolate, then decided not to. It was another omission I would later come to regret, but at the time I was reluctant to introduce more problems into her life. Something about the girl brought out a compassionate side to me that had been missing for a long time. I wasn't so sure becoming more empathic was a good thing—living in Hawthorn Lane requires a certain measure of selfishness to survive—but it was too late to back out. I had taken on Ilia and would have to see this through.

"Lorelle?"

"I'm right here." I met her halfway. "Are you up for exploring?"

She stretched and yawned. "Sure. I don't want to do it on my own. Not with Renwick creeping about." She looked around, her eyes wary.

I laughed. "I don't blame you."

We spent the next couple hours wandering about the maze-like castle. We discovered a music room filled with instruments, including a grand piano made of the finest walnut and still in tune. There was an expansive library that, while stocked with what must be very old books, still had the power to make me salivate. What surprised me most was the lack of dust and cobwebs, along with the pristine state everything was in. Even the bedding looked fresh, as though it had been changed only the day before. Someone must have cast a stasis spell, but whether or not it was a Van der Daarke remained to be seen.

We visited the dungeon, a cave-like room filled with hand-blown wine bottles and huge oaken casks. My mouth watered at the selection of reds and whites displayed on the racks; the wines had to be over a hundred years old and hopefully were still drinkable. Maybe I could convince Kyran to open a bottle or two for dinner…if I was invited, that is. He'd made it clear that while he was offering me protection, he wasn't doing it for my sake.

My favorite room was the ballroom. The double doors, carved from a dark, noble wood, stood at least ten feet tall and each displayed the head of a wolf carved in high relief. The beast's fanged snouts projected threateningly, and each tooth ran the length of my hand. It was an unusual entrance for a ballroom, and certainly sent a message, though I wasn't quite sure what that message was.

To reach the dance floor, one had to descend a wide staircase. Off to my left and right, a balcony encircled the ballroom, and three chandeliers, adorned with black crystals, hung from the high, domed ceiling. Tudor windows, likely very beautiful in the bright sun or flickering candlelight, and which could be opened to allow fresh air in to cool the dancers, ringed the dome.

The floor itself was crafted from the finest maple, with the family crest in the center. I could imagine the dancers twirling across the floor, and if I closed my eyes, I could see myself down there, the exhilaration of wild, spinning speed swelling my whole being with light. Ilia and I agreed, with stars in our eyes, that this was an amazing room that needed to be used, and soon.

Throughout the castle countless long hallways and stairs spread out before us, leading us back and forth and up and down. Ilia even found a couple hidden doors and passages, striding right up to them as though she knew exactly where they were.

"You seem to have a good sense of this place," I remarked as we made our way to the kitchen, drawn by the delightful smells wafting down the hall.

She preened a little. "I do, don't I?"

"But you've never been here before?"

A thoughtful look crossed her face. "No. Weird, huh?"

"A little." I wondered if she was finally making the connection that she was fey, but she remained quiet as we neared the entrance to the large, spacious room, bustling with activity.

By silent agreement we stopped where we were, staying out of sight. The two oldest Fiersen girls, Sinead and Gemma, were preparing a meal, Sinead at the immense cast-iron stove and Gemma mixing something in a bowl propped on a sturdy oak table in the middle of the room. Sinead was the most sedate of the Fiersen clan, her dark red hair pulled back into a sensible bun at the nape of her neck and a pristine white apron covering her gray gown. But while she might be the calmest, she was not one to be messed with. Her ire was fierce when roused, and it was a fool who tried to get one over on her.

Gemma, at nineteen, was two years younger, and miles apart in terms of personality. Her golden-red tresses poufed out in a wild mass of curls, with only a thin bandeau tucked behind her elfin ears to tame them. The hair band was failing in its duties, as evidenced by the number of times she blew upward to relocate a stray tress. Gemma had a quick temper, but was also quick to forgive. Not so with Sinead. Rumor had it that she forgot nothing and forgave little.

But the sisters were good workers, as were all the Fiersens. Joining them was their brother, Conor. Born between the sisters, he was the eldest male, and he strutted about like a rooster, puffed up with all the pomp attached to such a coveted position. His shock of red hair lent to the rooster image and secretly made me smile every time I saw it. He was a hard worker, but he also played hard, drinking more than was good for him.

At that moment Conor was directing workers as they carted in crate after crate of food and goods into the kitchen. He did the job well, if a little imperiously, but the workers, whose wide eyes took in everything they could, put up with it. Conor had a position at the castle, and this gave him license to act a bit puffed up.

It was a good thing there was an extensive larder and access to the cellar for cold storage, as I'd ordered far more food than I realized. I glanced over at Ilia and her eyes shone brightly. I envied her the food selection, and thought I really ought to come to tea in a day or two to make sure everything was all right.

We soon got bored of watching the Fiersens work and left them to it. After meandering down a long corridor, we ended up back in the Great Hall where we found Kyran speaking to Merceen Arie, a patrician elf and owner of *Scentsibility*. Knowing that if I skipped her perfumery I'd pay for it, I'd stopped by and purchased several bags of rosemary and marjoram for a cleansing burn. After being shut up for a hundred years, I thought the castle could benefit from a good purifying. Though it already smelled pretty fresh in here, I noted, as fresh as any ancient building can smell anyway.

Seeing Merceen, my mood soured. Where Avice could be predatory, she did it in a good-natured way (usually). It was simply who she was—a carnal creature full of a lust for life and flesh. Merceen, on the other hand, was rapacious and went after her prey with a ruthless drive stunning in its speed and destruction. Basically I, along with most of the villagers, tried not to give her a reason to go after us.

She wore her thick, glossy brown hair in coils around her head, a hairstyle that made her look more like Medusa than a temptress. Even so, she was stunningly attractive…if you like Gorgons, that is. A low-cut gown showed an expanse of olive-toned cleavage that was both provocative and tasteful at the same time. Of French blood—noble, according to her—she was irritatingly condescending, extremely rich, highly clever, and, according to the rumor mill, well-versed in the art of lovemaking. She was a very vexing person for all these reasons, but mainly because she had made me feel more than once that I didn't belong in Hawthorn Lane.

Like Fan and Dawn, Merceen didn't like me because I was poor and because I was friends with Avice, whom she considered a competitor. The feeling was mutual, but as I mentioned earlier, I don't go out of my way to show it. Not buying anything from her shop, which I suspected was a cover for something more nefarious than selling perfumes, would have brought her wrath down on my head, and I didn't need that. She might decide to do a little digging, and what she'd find out about me—that I was all too human—was simply too big a risk to take.

I put out my hand and stopped Ilia from going any farther. She glanced at me and I nodded at Merceen. She was talking animatedly and Kyran was listening intently, his expression serious, his head nodding on occasion. Every few moments, she'd touch him on the arm.

Ilia's wrinkled nose told me she got the message—this woman was trouble. So what she did next totally threw me. She left my side and approached the two, her walk determined. I sighed and hurried after her. Leaving her alone to deal with Merceen would be like sending a lamb to slaughter.

"Hello, Uncle Kyran!"

He turned to face her. "Ilia." His eyes immediately scanned the area and found me. I couldn't read the expression on his face so I wasn't sure if he was pleased to see us or annoyed. Likely the latter.

"Who's this?" she asked, all innocent blue eyes.

"This is Baroness Arie. Baroness, this is my niece, Ilia."

Merceen gave Ilia a haughty glance down her strong nose, followed by a slight nod, the movement wafting the scent of her personal perfume in my direction. It really was a work of art, capturing her essence perfectly. Which means it smelled like spoiled brat on a stick.

"How do you do, little girl?" she enquired, looking over Ilia's head at

Kyran, a patronizing half-smile on her face. Smiles were hard for Merceen.

But Ilia surprised me again and didn't correct Merceen's mistake. "I'm fine, ma'am," she answered, and Merceen winced at the form of address, which everyone knew was shorthand for 'you're ancient, lady.' I didn't know if Ilia was being polite or devious. Probably devious. It appeared that Hawthorn Lane was already corrupting the poor child. "And you, ma'am?"

"I'm well, merci."

Merceen was doing a good job of ignoring me, though I didn't mind. I had no wish to speak to the elf. Unfortunately, Kyran found it necessary to intervene. "You must know Lorelle?" He indicated me standing there and I stepped forward dutifully. His eyes swept my face and seemed relieved I'd rid it of Desolate blood. I'm not sure why he cared. Neither my behavior nor my appearance reflected on him or his precious name.

One finely plucked, perfectly arched eyebrow rose in icy acknowledgement. "Yes, I do know Miss Gragan." Subtly—or not so subtly, depending on how you looked at it—she'd corrected Kyran by calling me Miss Gragan. She might regret reproaching him; I certainly hoped so. Merceen sniffed the air, searching for her scents, none of which I was wearing. She turned to Ilia. "You really must stop by *Scentsibility* some time. I could have our perfumer, Lenay, create something just for you."

"I'd probably be allergic," Ilia said airily. "But thank you, anyway, ma'am."

Merceen sniffed again, in annoyance this time. "Suit yourself. So, Count Van der Daarke." She stepped toward Kyran and turned her back on us, effectively shutting us out. "I shall *count* on you for dinner." She gave him a pained smile, obviously finding herself quite amusing.

"I'll let you know when Ilia and I are free," he neatly sidestepped her trap. "I'm going to be terribly busy for some time, Baroness."

"Oh, yes. You and Ilia. Of course." Clearly she hadn't *counted* on Ilia being a part of the invitation. "I'm so glad your exalted family has returned at long last. We nobles do need to stick together, you know." She aimed a pointed glance at me and I wanted to clock her.

"Ah, yes," Kyran agreed and the thought came to me that I'd just found a use for the poison in the ring I always wore. *Finally*. He started to steer her toward the door. "I'll let you know," he repeated. "Thank you for coming."

She laid a hand on his arm. "It was my pleasure. I'm really looking forward to hearing all about why your family left and why you've come back now. We're all so curious."

He flung open the door. "Ah! There's your carriage." Gleaming white and decorated with gold filament, Merceen's coach was hard to miss. It wasn't tacky—Merceen didn't do tacky—but it was ostentatious. She seemed to feel the need to remind people that she was important. All it did, however, was remind people that she was a snob.

"Merci, monsieur. Until we meet again, oui?" She held out her gloved hand to be kissed and Kyran didn't quite fail her, taking her hand and bowing over it. But he did not kiss it. Keeping her hand firmly in his grip, he guided her out the door.

"How did I do?" Ilia demanded when they were gone, her eyes big and excited.

"You were perfect, Ilia."

"I guess I learned a thing or two from my mother, after all," she said with satisfaction.

"Yes, well, don't become her. I like you the way you are."

Her eyes teared up unexpectedly, and I was glad to see it. I needed her to keep her innocence, since mine had long ago been burned out of me. "You don't think I'm like her, do you?"

"I didn't know your mother, Ilia, but from what you've told me I can't see you ever being like her."

"Because I'm *not* like her." She sniffed and wiped her nose on her dress sleeve, which was *my* dress sleeve. I sighed and tried not to think about it.

"Oh, buck up," I ordered. "I just told you I like you being nice. It isn't easy being nice in Hawthorn Lane, you know. Around here, there's a constant battle between being good and being bad and one I fear I've been losing since my arrival."

"But you *are* nice," Ilia insisted. "Much nicer than Baroness Pruneface." She giggled appreciatively at her insult and my lips twitched. "I like that you don't treat me like a baby. And you looked after me when I needed help, giving up your own bed and your food, too. You even loaned me your dress." She looked at her sleeve and gave me an apologetic smile. "Which I've been using as a handkerchief."

"Yes, well, they might as well make me a saint right now." I was joking, of course. As I've said before, I'm not a saint, and I don't want to be a saint. Saintly people bore the crap out of me. Give me a devil any day.

And just as I thought this, Kyran Van der Daarke strode back inside, shutting the door behind him with a bang.

Chapter Sixteen

"I believe dinner's in order," Kyran announced, looking both hungry and a bit tired.

"With wine?" I asked, inviting myself, pride be damned. I was starving after such a long day. Where before I'd longed for the comfort of my cottage, I now simply wanted to eat, drink, and be merry. Or at least the first two.

One corner of his mouth lifted. "Wine for you, something stronger for me, I think."

"There's *Lightning* in the dungeons," I said, pleased to be officially included in the meal. "It's a spiced cognac and ice grape mix and my friend adores it, so if you want to keep some around, don't let her know you have any."

"I'll keep that in mind. And what's your poison, Lorelle?"

I laughed. "Funny you should put it that way. I prefer *Dark Spirits*. It's a sap wine, from the Blackthorn tree, mixed with cherry and lemon bitter."

"I'm not familiar with it, but it sounds delightful. Show me the way," he indicated with a wave of his arm.

Ilia took over as leader, skipping like a child down the steps. I followed her, warning Kyran to watch his head on the cellar's stone archway. Standing in front of all the wine racks and casks, I could tell that even the good Count was impressed with the selection. "You might want to keep a lock on the door," I advised. "Conor is a good worker, but has been known to enjoy a drink or two during his off-hours." I know I was sounding a bit possessive, but between Conor and Avice, they could drain this place within a fortnight.

Kyran took this in with a nod. "Duly noted." He made his selections—a bottle of *Dark Spirits*, a flask of *Lightning*, and for Ilia a strawberry-shaped bottle, filled, fittingly enough, with strawberry cordial—then led us up to the dining room, a dark chamber with a long table and fireplaces at both ends. He settled us on the end closest to the kitchen door, and where a fire burned warmly. An Effervescence pot shaped like a ghoul squatted on the table—a bizarre sort of centerpiece—and its presence made me smile. "Not too macabre?" Kyran asked.

"Not in the least. We're a dark group here."

"So I've noticed." He indicated for me to sit and Ilia took the chair opposite. She had been quite chatty down in the dungeon, prattling on about our finds while exploring the castle, and I was glad to see she was relaxing around her uncle. But now she was quiet, and I thought I could see why. There was another place setting at the table, and it was laid out next to her. "I'll go check on dinner," Kyran said, then left with an awkward sort of bow, as though while he felt the urge to do it, he wasn't quite comfortable with the antiquated gesture.

When he was gone, I reached over and pulled the place setting over to my side. Ilia gave me a grateful look. "I don't even want him looking at me, but having to sit right next to him would be torture."

I wouldn't go as far as that for myself. As Kyran had said, Renwick wasn't a bad guy and he wasn't the least bit hard on the eyes, plus I rather enjoyed playing the upright madam with him. But it behooved me to remember that there was something off about him, something hidden, and I was determined to find out what it was, especially as it seemed related to me. I could put up with his attention for the sake of gaining good information.

Kyran returned with Renwick, who was jauntily swinging his cane as he entered the dining room. When Kyran saw that I'd moved Renwick's place setting, he paused for a brief moment and frowned. His eyes met mine and I returned his gaze with a pleasant smile. The frown deepened, but he made his way to his high-backed chair, a leering skull's head at its top, and sat down without a word.

Renwick pulled out his chair and sat next to me, bringing with him the scent of musk, clove cigarettes, and whisky. Someone had been enjoying himself. "Lorelle!" he greeted me as though we'd known each other for years. "You can't imagine how pleased I am to find that you're staying for dinner. What's the grand occasion?"

I gave Kyran a sideways glance to communicate, "See how he's latched onto me?" only to find him scowling, a shadowed groove furrowing the space between his eyes.

"After an afternoon of shopping, I escorted Ilia to the castle," I explained, "and as it had gotten a bit late, Count Van der Daarke was kind enough to invite me to dine before I returned home." I wasn't sure what Kyran had shared about our encounter with the Desolate, but as he hadn't interrupted to correct my account, I figured he'd kept our little run-in to himself. Ilia had said that her uncle was loath to share much of anything with anyone, a trait we had in common.

"So we have you to thank for this fine meal."

I laughed. "I think you should reserve your gratitude for the Fiersens."

"Well, I'm glad to see you." He reached out and squeezed my arm.

Ilia's eyes widened and she covered her mouth to stifle a giggle. "I wanted to apologize to both you and Ilia about deserting you yesterday." He flicked her a glance. "Once I saw she was all right, I realized I'd been distracted from the reason I'd come to the village in the first place—to engage the Fiersens. After seeing you, I was completely diverted from my original purpose." He gave me a winning smile, and I had to concede that he really was quite handsome and charming.

"I had wondered where you'd gone, but I'm glad to know you're well. I was afraid the villagers had frightened you away."

"Oh, no!" He gave a hearty laugh and squeezed my arm again. "While I admit they looked to be a strange lot, I simply knew I had to dash. My cousin expects nothing but the best and I wasn't about to let him down. I rely on his hospitality here—that is, until I can find some useful means of supporting myself." Another smile, slightly self-deprecating this time. He was quite the actor.

But then, so was I.

"So you're planning to stay?" I looked around, including Kyran in my question.

"I like it here," Renwick replied. "It's a bit unusual, I admit, but there's something about this place that appeals to my old-fashioned nature."

While he did seem to fit in well here, I had a feeling that in the Alterworld he was as modern as modern could be. "So you're happy to give up your cell phone?" I goaded, remembering what Josepha had told me about Renwick speaking to someone at the border. How else but through a phone? "They don't work here," I added, though I didn't tell him why. In fact, since he'd told whomever he was talking to that contact wasn't possible while he was here, he must already know. I felt a tingling ignite in my bones. Renwick Van der Daarke knew a lot more than he was letting on.

"This is like one of those reenactment villages, isn't it?" he answered. "With nothing modern. Some people might hate that, but I think I'm going to enjoy being away from technology. I will miss my lattes, though." He winked at Ilia—his first real connection with her since he'd come in—and she blushed, looking a little ill.

The kitchen door opened and Conor appeared, bearing an ornate silver tray, each corner dominated by the head of a dragon. On the tray sat an assortment of uniquely designed crystal wine glasses and snifters. Without a word, he set the glasses in front of everyone, though when he set mine down, he met my gaze, his dark blue eyes curious. "Shall I serve, milord?" he asked Kyran after I stared the elf down.

Kyran nodded. "I'll try the *Lightning*. I've heard it's got quite a kick." Conor licked his lips as he reached for the silver flask. "You game, Renwick?"

Renwick picked up the gauntlet willingly. "I'm always up for trying new things." He smiled at me as he said this.

"I'll have the *Dark Spirits*," I asserted myself. I wanted Conor to tell the others about how Lorelle Gragan seemed right at home at the Count's table. "And Ilia's having the strawberry cordial. Right, Ilia?"

Her eyes lit up. "I don't get to drink back home." She giggled. "Not legally anyway."

I'd forgotten that law. Sometimes it was so easy to pretend the Alterworld didn't exist. "You'd better go slow, then. The spirits we brew here will not be kind if you overdo, and it's very easy to overdo." Down in the dungeon I'd purposely steered Kyran toward the cordial because it was pretty tame by Hawthorn Lane's standards. Still, it packed a bit of a punch. "Take sips and limit yourself to one glass or you'll feel it in the morning." She nodded, though judging by the impish look in her eyes, she wasn't taking me too seriously.

Conor went around and filled everyone's glass, once more catching my eye as he poured. I knew Conor, of course. After all, the Fiersens were my neighbors, and despite having to look at their horror of a house every day, we were on good terms. Conor was a mischievous lad and more curious than was good for him, but no different than any of the other youngsters from the long-established families of Hawthorn Lane.

Indeed I've always wondered about the fey who've settled here permanently. I figured the Iverich family had stayed so long because this was the only place they were able to get away with acting like royalty. The other families—and why they had put down such deep roots—I wasn't so sure about. Avice's family had been here a good while, though she was the only one remaining. Her parents were dead and her younger brother, Malen, had left years ago to try out the Alterworld. He returned on occasion to visit, but seemed happy to stay away. Lady Faylan was a long-termer, as were the Fiersens, and the forest dwellers tended to have multiple generations buried in Hawthorn Lane ground. Judging by the size of their castle, the Van der Daarkes had obviously been here for centuries. The rest of us were immigrants, and while some stayed on, others bolted as soon as they deemed it safe.

I could understand why people stayed here, but I could also understand why they left. For my part, even with all its problems, Hawthorn Lane would be my home until I died. I was a refugee, but this place was in my blood. Leaving it would be like dying. I wasn't sure why I felt so strongly about a world that was not truly mine, but I did, and was glad for it.

Gemma pushed a Dionysian serving cart into the dining room, ending her brother's attempts to either read my thoughts or see through my skull. "Dinner is served!" she announced saucily. As she approached, I watched Renwick watching her. She was, if not exactly pretty, a lively gal, and appealing for it. His gaze was appreciative, but noncommittal. I turned to see if Kyran was watching her, but found his dark eyes on me. I gave him a slow smile, and to my surprise, he returned it. It was small, barely lifting the corners of his mouth, but it was genuine. I found myself liking it, and my pulse, to my chagrin, reacting to it.

As Gemma set the first course in front of us, Renwick lifted his glass. "To Hawthorn Lane."

We lifted our glasses. "To Hawthorn Lane!" Ilia's toast was the most enthusiastic of us all. I took a sip and closed my eyes to savor the moment. The wine tasted amazing, dark and rich, yet crisp as fall apples. With each drink I felt as though I were swallowing life's blood. But as I'd warned Ilia, I made sure to limit myself to sips. While my tolerance was higher than hers, I was not immune to the power of this world's spirits.

"And to our guest," Renwick added. "Lorelle."

I smiled, but inwardly I thought it a bit much. Ilia toasted me happily, "To Lorelle!" and Kyran tipped his glass at me with a nod, then took a healthy swallow. "To Lorelle," he said quietly.

We tucked into our buttery acorn soup and after a few moments of silence Renwick asked me what I did here in Hawthorn Lane. Though it took some doing, I was able to describe my job without revealing overmuch. The delectables I collected were hard to find and very powerful, but I made the task sound mundane. It was a habit—to hide things—but also, in this case, good practice. This was my livelihood, and I didn't trust Renwick with its secrets.

"So you're a refugee like us?" he asked when I trailed off. I'd lost him while explaining the medicinal properties of Kutra Ivy, which, of course, had been the point.

"In a manner of speaking. But I'm not exactly like you, am I? Your family lived here for many generations, while I'm a newcomer. It does seem strange to me that your ancestors left all this behind. You must know why." My tone was light, as though the answer didn't matter one way or the other.

Renwick laughed and waved his snifter of *Lightning* at me. I had a feeling he was already a little sauced. "I'm afraid my ancestral line wasn't as fortunate as Kyran's here. We were the 'poor cousins' and if we lived here, we were likely relegated to some hovel."

"You don't know anything about this world?" I was surprised. He seemed so at home here. "It must all be rather odd for you. A land filled with strange creatures and unusual customs. Surely you knew something of it before you came."

He shrugged, his bedroom eyes focused on me, then he nodded at Kyran. "I'm sure my cousin knows much more than I do."

I turned to Kyran. "Well?"

He didn't answer right away, seeking refuge in his drink. Unlike Renwick, he seemed no different than his usual reserved self after drinking more than half the glass. Perhaps, like me, he wanted to keep his wits about him. "We were told things, of course, but very little," he answered, his words measured. "Whatever happened that forced us to leave this place, I always had the feeling it was something the family wanted to forget. But we did not forget our *exalted* position, I can tell you that." A muscle in his cheek flickered, and behind him the fire flared. "My parents—both of whom died young—and my grandparents—same fate, I'm afraid, were forever going on about tradition and the family name. They seemed to be trying to make up for something someone in the family did, and that something was pretty bad, so we had to pay the price."

I stared at him, surprised as hell. It was a lot to share for someone so reserved. Maybe Kyran was feeling the effects of the *Lightning* after all. It just wasn't as obvious as Renwick, who was pouring himself more. I thought about stopping him, then decided not to. He was a big boy and him being drunk served my purposes.

Ilia giggled, then hiccupped. "We did something very, very bad!" Her cheeks were flushed and her eyes bright. She, too, appeared to already be feeling the effects of her drink, and we hadn't even reached the main course yet. I should have been more forceful in my warnings, or more vigilant anyway.

Gemma returned and took our soup bowls, followed by Conor with the main course, which consisted of succulent ribs of beef, caramelized, spiral-shaped baby carrots, and stewed apples, with fresh potato and cheese bread and homemade garlic butter. It was standard Fiersen fare—simple. But it smelled heavenly, and tasted even better.

The Van der Daarkes were quiet for the rest of the meal and I put it down to the drink. They didn't realize its potency and were suffering the results of their ignorance. By the end of the main course, Ilia was openly yawning. Renwick had drawn into himself, as though thinking hard on something, and Kyran responded to my subtle, and sometimes less than subtle, attempts at trying to elicit answers as to why they were here and why now with mere grunts until at last I gave up and returned to enjoying my meal.

Finished with his dessert—a warm, red chocolate soufflé topped by homemade whipped cream—Renwick rose abruptly. His cheeks were flushed and he looked particularly young and handsome at that moment. "Come with me, Lorelle." He held out his hand. "I'll give you a tour."

"She'll be staying here," Kyran replied for me, which I thought was a bit high-handed, but not unappreciated. I know from experience that I don't like dealing with drunks. And they've learned from experience that they don't like dealing with me. "You can escort Ilia to her room."

It said something about Ilia's inebriated state that she didn't even flinch at this suggestion, simply stood to leave. "Let's go, Cousin," she said to Renwick. "But let's hurry. I think I'm going to be sick." She gave a little belch.

He bowed to her, swayed slightly, and caught himself on the back of his chair, one of his fingers slipping into the skull's eye socket. "It'll be my pleasure." He turned to me with a humble smile. "We should've heeded your warning, Lorelle."

"Well, now you know. We do everything more *intensely* here in Hawthorn Lane."

His grin was slightly lecherous. "How intriguing."

I felt a stirring in my loins—such an archaic phrase, but so apt. "Good night, Mr. Van der Daarke."

"Now, now, Lorelle," he slurred. "We've shared drinks. That makes us friends."

"Not in my world."

He ignored this. "I'll give you that tour another time, when we have the whole day to ourselves. I know this place top to bottom, you see."

He didn't wait for me to answer. Maneuvering around the table, he let his hand trail along my shoulders, feather-light and yet as potent as a lover's touch. Reaching Ilia, he took her arm and led her from the room, leaving me to wonder why Renwick, who'd only just arrived, was so confident that he knew the castle, 'top to bottom.'

He had to have been here before.

Chapter Seventeen

"You should probably go check on them," I said to a silent Kyran. "I'm not sure I trust a drunk Renwick with an even drunker 18-year-old."

One long finger tapped on the table as though in warning. "Don't tell me you're jealous?"

"Of which one?" I joked, but it didn't drive away his frown. "I happen to feel a bit protective of your niece. She's not very sophisticated, and your cousin strikes me as someone who's had more than his fair share of experience with the ladies."

Kyran stood abruptly, startling me. "Wait for me."

I set my crisp white linen napkin on the table, my movements deliberate. "I really should be going. I don't want to be walking the forest trails without all my wits about me." I was ready to go home, back to my fire and my warm bed, to somewhere safe and free of the tension I often felt around this family.

He gave me a clipped nod. "Of course. You can go when I return."

That's not what I had in mind, but after he left I made no move to leave. Some twenty minutes later, I'd finished the last of my drink and was feeling quite warm and pleasant from the heat of the fire. I'd purposely avoided thinking too much about anything—a lovely benefit of drinking *Dark Spirits*—and felt quite content. Gemma and Conor had cleared the table, neither of them speaking a word to me, though Gemma looked like she wanted to ask a million questions. Every time she opened her mouth, though, Conor gave her a warning look and her lips would press back into two dissatisfied lines.

When Kyran returned, he surprised me by sitting down. "I must take her back to the other side," he began. "She can't stay here. Not with that Desolate after her, and with…well, the other challenges here."

Did he include Renwick as one of the other challenges? "I agree with you. But she no longer wants to go and forcing her would only traumatize her further."

He sighed and leaned back in his chair, which barely supported his broad shoulders. "I was afraid of that. You did your job too well, though I'm glad she no longer seems as frightened by me or her cousin."

I paused, choosing my words carefully. "You're sure Renwick's a Van der Daarke?"

"Oh, he is one," Kyran replied, sounding annoyed at the man's effrontery for being related to him. "I can sense it in his blood." Well, there went that theory, though it did tell me something important. Kyran knew he was fey. "It's a distant connection, so his marrying Ilia isn't entirely disgraceful."

"You don't still think they should marry?"

"What I think doesn't matter," he said gruffly.

"Of course it does. You're her guardian now."

He grimaced. "Yes, for all my sins. For the record, I would oppose it. As you noted, she's too innocent, not to mention too young for him." He was careful not to criticize Renwick, I noticed. When I didn't say anything, he went on, his expression pained. "I must…" He paused. "Well, I must apologize to you."

This was unexpected. "For what?"

"For my cousin. His behavior tonight was not befitting a Van der Daarke."

"Which behavior? The getting drunk, or asking to give me—a commoner—a tour of the castle?"

He waved that away. "He was being awfully familiar with you. It's not how a Van der Daarke comports himself."

I laughed. "I'm a big girl, you know. I can handle myself. We commoners are good at that."

He drew himself up. "You think I'm a snob, don't you?"

"Well, you did call me a wench, and just now you implied that your cousin being nice to me was unbefitting a Van der Daarke."

He blinked. "You're making me sound like an unmitigated prat."

"*I'm* not making you sound that way." Kyran turned his dark eyes on me, the emotion in them not wounded per se, but a shade on the discomposed side. "Really, Kyran. I get that you're a snob, but what I don't understand is why you seem to be under the impression that I'm not one."

He looked taken aback. "What?"

"Has it ever occurred to you that I'm lowering my egalitarian standards being seen with a toff like you?"

He laughed. "A toff like me? You're serious?"

"Perfectly."

"You needn't look so superior about it," he said, a little peevishly I thought.

"I have so few chances to look superior, Kyran, I must take advantage of them when I can."

A small smile pushed away his annoyance. "I suppose you must." He stood abruptly. "You must be tired. I shall escort you home."

"There's no need. I know the way."

"That may as well be, but I'd be remiss in my duties if I didn't accompany you and something were to happen."

"Be remiss in your duties... Well, Grim forbid that happen."

He frowned. "Is that a yes?"

"I suppose I can't stop you following me home, so yes." I gestured with my hand. "Do your duty."

I stood, swayed a little, and joined him. Together we walked toward the Great Hall in stiff silence. I knew I was being childish, getting upset that he wanted to escort me home, but I really didn't want to feel beholden to this man for anything.

When we arrived in the hall, he held up a hand to me. "Wait here," he commanded, and I imagined it was something he often said to people before he went off and did whatever he did without their presence getting in his way. It was something one would say to a dog, and I wondered if he thought no more of me than he would a pet.

He left the room at a brisk pace, and I wandered over to study the amazingly life-like tapestries. Someone very skilled had created these masterpieces, and they must have cost a fortune. A few of the figures looked like Kyran, a couple even resembled Ilia, but none matched Renwick. Distant cousins apparently don't make the cut for expensive tapestries.

"Must have cost a fortune," came a drawl behind me, echoing my earlier sentiment, and I spun about, startled. I hadn't heard him coming, and I prided myself on hearing things coming. No doubt he'd left his cane behind. I'd have heard that for sure.

"Mr. Van der Daarke," I greeted Renwick stiffly, more to cover up my shock than to make a point.

But he took my reserve as a slight. "Still with the formalities?" He stepped close to me and reached out, his finger touching a stray lock of hair that had slipped from my bun. The spicy *Lightning* on his breath along with a hint of his cologne were enticing, and I had to work to control the shiver fighting to give me away. He tucked the lock behind my ear, then leaned in to whisper, "What can I do to make you relax around me, Lorelle? I've an idea, a very good idea, but I think I might end up losing a limb, or an even more important body part, if I were to follow through on it."

I hastily stepped away. I wasn't entirely sure what I felt about Renwick, but he was a very attractive man, and obviously skilled at the art of seduction. Try as I might to be a tough and independent woman, I was also human, and it had been a long time since I'd been intimate with a man. Too long.

Unfortunately, he followed me, trapping me against the wall by placing his hands on either side of my shoulders. He leaned forward, his golden-brown gaze intense, and I realized he no longer looked the least bit drunk. I swallowed, my senses overwhelmed by the velvet touch of the tapestry on my palms, his intoxicating scent, his nearness and his body heat.

"I told you my view on using first names," I said, turning my head slightly to avoid looking him in the eye.

"But you call my cousin by his first name."

"I do, don't I?" I responded in a flippant tone. "How odd."

"I'm not the enemy, Lorelle. I'm here to help you."

My breath hitched in my throat. "What do you mean?"

He paused, and I sensed he hadn't meant to say that. "I mean, well, that I'm here for you. If you ever need...*anything*." The way he said the word implied all sorts of sensual promises, but it didn't distract me like I'm sure he'd intended. He'd meant something else, and was trying to convince me he hadn't.

"I'll be sure to let you know if I do." I turned my gaze on him, meeting his bedroom eyes with a seductive look of my own. Then I reached up and touched his cheek, letting my fingers trail downward, into the dark, prickly stubble of hair along his jaw. I leaned toward him and when his lips parted, I ducked down and slid out from his little trap, hurrying away from him as fast as I could go.

I had reached the center of the hall when Kyran returned, and for once I was glad for his presence. I could hear Renwick pursuing me, and who knew what he would have done if he'd caught me? I shivered at the thought, then pushed it away.

"The horse is saddled—" Kyran began, then saw Renwick and stopped. "You're still awake?"

Renwick laughed. "I'm not a child, Kyran. I can handle my liquor." Steady on his feet, words clear, I saw he truly could handle his drink, though he'd led us to believe otherwise.

"I saw how you handled your liquor, Renwick. You can return to your bed now, get some sleep. I'm taking Lorelle home."

Renwick's lips thinned. "How noble of you."

Kyran smiled—a real one—and I nearly stepped backward, stunned at the sight of it. I had never seen him smile like that and its radiance pierced me. "Not noble, merely gallant."

Renwick glanced back and forth between us and I schooled my features to blankness. Even so, I felt sure he'd caught my reaction to Kyran's smile, as he looked both ill-tempered and calculating when his eye caught mine.

I turned to Kyran. "Shall we go?"

He nodded and held his arm out to me. I hesitated before taking it and he noticed my delay, his eyebrow quirked. But his expression changed when my hand touched his arm and a jolt of electricity passed between us, quick as a lightning strike. Breathless, I glanced up at him, but he said nothing in response, his eyes slightly dazed. Images flashed through my mind, but they were dark and swirling, and I couldn't make them out. I could only feel giddiness, euphoria, wonder.

"Be safe, Lorelle," Renwick said, pulling me back to reality. "I'll stop by your cottage tomorrow to see if you need *anything*."

"She'll be busy with Ilia tomorrow," Kyran spoke up, his voice slightly hoarse.

I will? "Yes," I replied, going along. "Ilia has a dress fitting tomorrow and I should be there for moral support. The Ravenna sisters can be a bit high-handed." It was a nice excuse, but unsettling. Kyran couldn't have known about the dress fitting and my promise to Ilia. Yet he had told Renwick I'd be busy with her.

"Perhaps I'll join you," Renwick said with a devious smile. "I could use a few new outfits myself."

"Tomorrow you'll be going through the stable supplies," Kyran reminded him.

Renwick frowned. "Forgot about that."

"Good night, Renwick," I said, needing to end this conversation. I was growing tired, and that was not a good state of mind around these two. "I'm sure I'll see you sooner or later. It's a small village, after all."

He looked surprised, but pleased that I'd used his first name. "I'll be watching out for you, Lorelle."

I gave a nod, then Kyran spun me toward the door and out into the cool night. The rain had let up, leaving behind a light mist. Josepha was waiting, holding the reins of Rogue, who snorted and pawed at the ground. While the elf's expression remained impassive, I knew he was taking in that the Count was escorting me home, and I was holding his arm, no less. More tightly than was warranted, I suppose, but it did feel good, tucked up under my breast as it was.

I'm getting as bad as Avice. I sighed, but I didn't let go.

Kyran took the reins and mounted the magnificent black beast, then reached down and grasped my upraised hand. This time the shock of contact nearly stopped my heart. Kyran let out a muffled groan as he pulled me up in front of him. We sat like that for several long moments, both of us needing to catch our breath.

"Ride, Rogue!" Kyran finally cried, and the horse bolted forward, leaving behind what was likely a very perplexed Josepha.

I found it a little disturbing that I didn't have to point out the path through the woods that led to my cottage. Kyran not only seemed to know it, but quite well, as though he'd traveled it many times before. Despite his confidence, I kept my eyes and ears open. Although I'd never had any close encounters with the wood fey, I'd heard of other villagers who'd made the mistake of angering the tempestuous creatures.

Within a short time, we crossed the little wooden bridge that spanned the brook behind my cottage. Over the hollow echo of horse hooves, I noted how fast the rushing water sounded beneath us. I could just make out the pool in the darkness and it did indeed look ready to spill its ink-like contents onto the grounds surrounding my home. Tomorrow I'd have to lift the mechanism for the dam or be in danger of having my cellar filled with water.

"You've a potential flood situation here," Kyran spoke, his first words since we'd left the castle.

"It's all this bloody rain. I'm going to lift the sluice gate in the morning. That should help."

"Where would you go if something happened to your cottage?"

"My friend Avice would take me in."

He was silent for a moment. "I see. I'll help you tomorrow."

"Oh, I'm sure I'll be fine. Thank you for the ride," I added as he dismounted outside my gate and held up his hand to me. I stared at it for a moment. "I've got this," I told him, not up to another jolt this night, and slid off the horse to the ground below.

I turned to face him and he gave a bow—more relaxed this time, the movement already becoming natural to him. It seemed Kyran Van der Daarke was not immune to the proprietary magic of Hawthorn Lane. "It was my pleasure. I'll see you tomorrow."

I stopped, my hand on the gate's cold wrought-iron. "You will?"

"I, too, require new clothes. Shall we meet at the shop, say around eleven?"

"Uh, y-yes," I stuttered, discomposed. "That should be fine." I turned to go, hurrying down the little cobblestone walk. After unlocking my front door, I turned back to see Kyran, mounted on Rogue, waiting. I tossed him a wave and he nodded before giving Rogue his head. Master and horse dashed off into the darkness of the night, leaving me to wonder what Kyran Van der Daarke was up to.

Like his cousin, he had questionable intentions regarding myself, and I was determined to find out why.

Chapter Eighteen

I was not to get the respite I'd been longing for. Avice, lounging on the chaise in front of my fireplace, turned at the sound of the door. Really, I'm not sure why I bothered to lock it when I was surrounded by magical creatures. She said nothing and neither did I as I hung up my cloak to dry near the fire. Taking in its dancing flames I figured she must have had her lackey, Ensign, build it up for her. Avice could simply have used magic, but she was a lazy witch and preferred to avoid casting spells, claiming conjuration tired her out. Unlocking the door was probably her limit for the day.

"So it's true," she said in a deceptively honeyed drawl I had come to know as her 'I'm royally pissed at you' tone.

"What's true?" I asked, trying to sound innocent, though it was merely a delaying tactic.

As Avice knew all too well. "Cut the crap, Lorelle. I know you went to the castle."

"I did," I admitted.

She gasped, clasping a hand to her barely contained breasts. "Without me? How could you?!"

"I was bringing Ilia back home. It's what her uncle and I decided."

"Her *uncle*!" She shook her finger at me. "I know about *him*. *Count* Van der Daarke he is, and from all reports better looking than Adonis. And he's not old!" she delivered her coup de grace, and quite vehemently.

"I never said he was," I replied calmly.

"B-but..." she sputtered helplessly, her mind casting back. "But you never denied it when Ilia called him old!" she finished her sentence triumphantly.

"Everyone knows that teenagers think anyone older than they are is practically ancient."

"Well, I'm not practically ancient," she huffed.

"Of course you aren't," I soothed.

Her eyes narrowed dangerously. "You're doing that thing again."

She was right. I was. "What thing?"

"Where you treat me like I'm a halfwit!"

"I was only agreeing with you, Avice. No need to get all puffed up over nothing. So is there something you wanted? Because it's been a long day, and spending the evening with the Van der Daarkes, while entertaining, has tired me out."

Avice's face turned so red I thought her head was going to explode.

"You *dined* with them!"

"Count Van der Daarke…Kyran…was merely thanking me for looking after Ilia and for escorting her back home. She's changed her mind about staying, by the way."

"Has she?" Avice snipped. "And that makes a difference in my life *how?*"

"You're acting like a spoiled brat, Avice. What did you expect me to do? Turn down the invitation? I hadn't anticipated it so it wasn't like I could invite you along."

"But you could've invited me to go clothes shopping with you." Her mouth twisted like a fretting child's. "You know I love shopping!"

"I wasn't expecting to do any of that," I told her truthfully. "Kyran paid me to order provisions for the castle and that's what I was doing when Ilia saw a gown in the window at *Fawn's Fashions* and wanted to go inside. I figured Kyran would be thrilled to get Ilia out of my inferior dresses and into something a bit more appropriate for the niece of a Count, so we went in."

"Oh, now who's being a brat? You're not the least bit inferior, Lorelle. In fact, you're the classiest person I know…so svelte and mysterious." She eyed me up and down, the light in her eyes brightening with arousal. It didn't take much for Avice.

"Thanks, but I felt quite inferior surrounded by such opulence. The castle was very grand."

"Oh, Lorelle!" Avice leaned against me, poking at my ribs and giggling. "You poor thing, being forced to mingle with the elite." Avice knew quite well my opinion on the haves and have-nots of this world. "Now tell me everything and leave absolutely nothing out!"

So I did tell her, though of course I left several things out, including the Desolate attack. When she found out about that, as she undoubtedly would, I'd merely claim the Count asked me not to say anything for fear of frightening the villagers. And Grim forbid a peasant such as myself go against the wishes of *milord*.

When I was done with my story, she sighed happily and gave me a sloppy kiss on the cheek, her arms wrapped tightly about me. "That was almost as good as a roll in the hay."

"Almost?"

"Yes. But a roll would make it all the nicer. You wouldn't consider…" She pulled me tighter, her breath growing rapid.

I pushed her away. "No, Avice, I wouldn't. Besides, I'm exhausted. Go home. It's getting late, and I'm not letting you sleep in my bed."

"But it's cold out there!" she pouted.

"Call your coach."

She slumped, but turned back and waved her hand at her raven, Eros. "Fine. But I'm coming to Ilia's fitting tomorrow. When is it?"

I stifled a groan. Of course she would know about the fitting. I didn't want her to meet Kyran, for a multitude of reasons, but as it was inevitable, I decided to cave in and tell her the truth. "Around eleven, if Ilia recovers from drinking too much strawberry cordial."

Little lines appeared between her eyebrows. "So early?"

"It's what the Count wanted, and eleven is not early."

"Says you." She stood abruptly, plumped up her breasts, then pulled on her cloak in a graceful twirl. "Two early days in one week. This can't be healthy. Oh, well. We mustn't keep the Count waiting." At the door, she stopped and turned about. "Is he really as gorgeous as they say?"

"Who?"

She snorted. "Now who's being the half-wit? Kyran Van der Daarke, of course. His cousin Renwick is a tempting little morsel, so I hope his looks run in the family. Though poor Ilia got passed over, didn't she?"

"I think she has potential. She's just too thin right now."

Avice nodded. "Everyone likes a girl with a bit of padding." She patted her own backside appreciatively.

"See you tomorrow, Avice."

"You didn't answer my question," she persisted and I silently cursed her. "And you can stop cursing me under your breath."

Damn her witchy eyes. "I can't really say. He's handsome, I suppose, if you like the haughty, self-important type."

"Which I do," she interrupted. "Go on."

"I imagine some people would find him good looking."

"Do you?"

I shrugged. Did I? I wasn't sure. "I don't know," I answered her.

She scanned my face. "Oh, Lorelle. Always the enigma. One of these days you're going to have to lower those impossibly high standards of yours and shag the first bloke you see. Just to get it over with."

"I'm not a virgin!"

"I should say not. But you're one here. It's been so long, you've probably grown intact again."

"Stars above, I hope not."

Avice threw back her head and laughed. "Hear, hear." She tilted her head at the door. "There's Ensign. Poor chap. I do keep him running about."

"You do."

"Luckily he's devoted to me."

"Luckily," I agreed. Hunched over and wizened as a dried apple, Ensign was the epitome of the loyal servant. I didn't feel sorry for the dwarf, being that I suspected he liked serving as Avice's whipping boy and devoted minion. When I'd first met him, I'd scolded Avice on how she was mistreating him and he'd burst out crying, fearful that Avice would make him leave her. Which she wouldn't, and didn't. She knew a good thing when she had it. Mind you, she wasn't abusive, just not exactly considerate of his wants and needs.

Co-dependency isn't pretty in any world.

"Kisses." Avice blew several at me.

"Hisses." I threw a few hisses back.

She laughed delightedly, then was gone, leaving behind her seductive scent and a whisper of emptiness.

After getting ready for bed and fixing myself a cup of melted choco, I curled up on my chaise to read. But like last night, I couldn't concentrate. Instead, I could only think of the unfortunate woman who'd become a Desolate. Who had she been, and what did she want with Ilia? I wondered if I should tell Lady Faylan about the Desolate's attack. The overseer might know who the young woman was, which could help me figure out what she wanted with Ilia. The trick was deciding how much to tell the overseer, and when.

My other concern was Renwick. How could he know the castle as well as he claimed? And why had he said he was here to help me? Did it have anything to do with the person he'd been talking to in the Alterworld, just before crossing over? I didn't like that I couldn't figure him out. Was he a fey-hunter? A private detective? And who had he been talking to?

A horrible thought occurred to me. What if the person had been my mother? Or worse... My stomach clenched painfully. What if it had been Dallen?

No, no, no. Not him. Anyone but him.

But then again... Dallen, a gregarious sort of guy, could have met Renwick in the bar where he worked part-time as a bartender. If Renwick was a fey-hunter or private detective and the two of them got to talking, Dallen might have brought up that I had disappeared. Renwick could've said, "You're in luck. I find lost people." Dallen could then have recruited Renwick to track me down, telling him some hard luck story to make Renwick believe he was helping me. Being fey, he'd know how to find me, too, even in such a strange and difficult to find place.

I heard a cracking noise and realized I was making such tight fists that my knuckles were popping. My theory was so plausible…and so horrifying.

Dallen Lemechant was the man I was meant to marry, even though we'd only known each other not quite a year, having met in a café when I was seventeen and he was twenty-one. Almost from day one, my mother looked at him as our savior. I wasn't sure how a bartender majoring in Political Science was going to save us, or what he'd actually save us from; still, I didn't care one way or the other. I loved him to an extent I'd never thought possible, wholly and deeply. Corny as it sounded, I thought he was my *soul* mate.

My mother agreed. She, who didn't love anyone other than herself, absolutely loved my boyfriend. In her eyes, he could do no wrong. In return, he showered her with charm and flowers and concerns about her day and offers to help around the house, even gave her money once in a while when my mother got fired from yet another job. He made me happy, and miracle of miracles, he made my mother happy. I thought I'd won the lottery.

Then I came home early from my job at the nearby bakery and caught him in bed with my younger sister, Eudrea. I still have dreams about it, his heaving rump, her ecstatic cries. I ran off, staying away for hours, and when I returned, I found my mother sitting at the kitchen table, smoking, an ashtray full of stubs and ash near to hand. When she saw me come in, she said in a tight voice, "Sit down."

No "You poor thing," or "I'm so sorry," or "Everything will be all right." My mother didn't do sympathy, other than when aimed at herself, that is.

When I sat down in the cheap wooden chair, sticky with years of accumulated grease and grime, I regarded my mother warily, wondering what she was up to.

"You *will* marry Dallen," she said without preamble, tapping her lighter on the table like a mad woodpecker, "and you *will* love him."

Hours earlier, before seeing him with my sister, it's what I'd wanted to do above everything else. I had loved him with all my heart, and thought he'd loved me just as much. He told me so often enough. And besides, he was going to be my ticket out of this house. Haunted by my demented mother, my equally deranged sister, and an even more insane aunt, life in the Gragan household was pretty depressing. Nobody got along, inside the family or outside it. Not one of us had ever had a relationship that lasted longer than a month. My mother and aunt serial dated at a mad rate that only made them miserable, Eudrea slept around, and until Dallen, I had avoided the whole thing altogether.

"But he ch-cheated on me!" I cried out, breaking into fresh sobs.

My mother slapped me across the cheek, hard enough to make my head jerk to one side. I immediately stopped crying, knowing that worse was coming my way if I kept it up. Mother was not the sort of person to coddle her children, or even love them. Actually, she didn't even seem to like us all that much. Except Eudrea, a little. Eudrea was her favorite, though not the one she pushed to get married. My sister apparently was no good for saving the family. Whatever that meant. That's how our mother always put it. "You must marry well, Lori. It's the only way to save this wretched family."

Which didn't make sense. This was the 21st century and we lived in America. Marriage (or the wedding, anyway) was still somewhat of a big deal, but not like it had once been. Women today could go without marrying and live a good life. So why did my mother push me so hard to tie the knot? And how could my being married save our family? It didn't add up.

"Men cheat. Get used to it," Mother went on, her voice hard. She leaned back against her chair and raked a hand through her salt and pepper hair, which she kept military short. "But Dallen is a good man, despite his weakness."

"But he cheated with Eudrea," I gasped, feeling sick. "She's only seventeen, and she's my *sister*."

"That wasn't Dallen's fault. She seduced him, of course."

"Of course," I muttered. Eudrea was always competing with me, resenting everything I had or achieved. Hell, let's just sum it all up by saying she resented me for being born in the first place.

A part of me wanted to believe my mother, wanted to blame Eudrea and forgive Dallen, but another part knew he was as much to blame, if not more, for what had happened. He was, after all, five years older than Eudrea, and supposedly madly in love with me.

"So you'll forgive him and put all this behind you." Mother's tone brooked no argument. "It's the only way. Then maybe we can finally have some peace…a real life."

For a moment my mother looked like she must have back before she'd had me and Eudrea—full of hope, yearning for a life of romance and adventure, a real person. Then her features hardened, morphing her back into the woman I knew.

"How?" I ventured. "How can I forgive him?"

She shrugged and took a drag on her cigarette, eyeing me through a haze of smoke. "You probably won't, but you'll learn to live with it."

"But I don't love him anymore."

She stood up suddenly, tipping her chair backward to land with a crash. The smoke whirled away like fleeing ghosts. "Don't say that! You do love him. You *do*." This last part came out in a fierce growl that made my blood go cold.

Hot tears ran down my cheeks and there was nothing I could do to stop them. I didn't love Dallen and there was no way she could make me. But she could make me marry him. I knew she could because I knew her ways. She and Aunt Nimair employed their scheming tricks on each other and on Eudrea and me all the time.

So I nodded. "I do love him," I said through hiccups. "I never stopped."

Her features, distorted by rage, flattened out and her next words were mechanical. "He's a good man."

"He's a good man," I parroted.

"And you will marry him."

"I will marry him."

Satisfied, she left the table, not bothering to pick up the chair. That was my job. But as I did it, pushing the chair in until its back hit the table with a dull thunk, I couldn't stop thinking about how I was going to make my escape.

Chapter Nineteen

My escape plan had started out so well. I had a fair amount of money saved up from my job, a backpack filled with necessities ranging from band-aids to deodorant, and a duffel bag stuffed with clothes. My mother thought I was heading to work for my afternoon shift, but instead I hiked to the bus station and bought a ticket to take me as far away as I could get from my family and from Dallen.

The bus left at twenty past eight, and I'd only made it a little over a half hour from home when we stopped at an out-of-the-way bus station to pick up more passengers. I got off to use the bathroom—the effects of nervously drinking two cups of coffee while I waited—and when I came back out the bus was gone. I don't know what happened. We were supposed to get ten minutes, and I wasn't even close to being gone that long. But the facts were there…I was stranded at a bus stop in the middle of nowhere, at nine o'clock at night, with only my backpack. My duffel bag was still on the bus.

I was heading for a panic attack when I saw a gray-haired, stooped over woman carefully lowering herself into a beat-up Chevrolet. She saw me staring and waved me over, peering at me through thick glasses. "Miss the bus?"

I nodded, a lump in my throat. "I thought I had plenty of time…"

"Some hotshot told the driver bad weather was coming and they needed to get going. Claimed he'd checked all the bathrooms and no one was in them."

"But I was in one!"

"Guess he missed you. You aren't very big, you know."

My stomach clenched. "The guy. What did he look like?"

She shrugged. "Don't quite recall."

"Tallish? With short blond hair?"

She squinted, thinking. "Sounds about right." She noticed me looking around in alarm. There were a few people around the station, mainly workers, but no sign of Dallen. "You need a ride?"

A gush of relief washed through me. "Could you? Maybe I could catch up to my bus."

"No problem, dear."

So I climbed into her solid car, thankful for my escape. We drove for about half an hour, heading farther and farther away from any sign of civilization. I wasn't even sure this was the right direction to be going. The woman wasn't the best driver, and after nearly going into a ditch, I was tempted to ask her to stop and let me out. But then we turned off on a side road leading into the woods, and I really began to worry. The woman hadn't said much once we started driving, and so we'd settled into silence. Now that silence was thickening with my growing unease. Something was wrong.

The woman wrenched the steering wheel to the right, nearly clipping a tree, and pulled onto a rutted road, seemingly no wider than a pathway. She accelerated and we flew along, hitting bumps at a dangerously high speed.

"Is this a shortcut?" I asked through chattering teeth, knowing full well it wasn't.

She didn't answer, and we drove until the road ended. The car shuddered to a halt. "Here's your stop." Her voice was deadly cold.

"W-what?"

"Get out and leave your bag behind."

"But that's stealing!"

Her cold smile sent chills through me. "How perceptive. Now don't make me add murder to my list of crimes. Oh, wait. Too late." She aimed a deadly looking gun at me. "Leave your bag right on the seat and scootch yourself out the door. Hurry now," she threatened when I didn't move. "I've got a long ways still to drive."

Throat blocked by a heavy lump of fear, I did as she said. I didn't know what else to do. For being an old woman, her gnarled grip on the gun was frighteningly steady.

Once outside the car, I watched as she gunned it, backing up, then somehow spinning the car around in the tight space before racing off. Folding my arms against the chill of the night, I looked around, a feeling of horror growing in me. Born and raised in a city, I knew nothing about the woods, other than that they were full of wild, meat-eating animals. My only chance was to head back the way we'd come and find a driver who would take me home. The idea of going back sickened me, but what else could I do? I had nothing to live on, no food, no money, *nothing*.

I was walking back along the overgrown road when I heard it... something big crashing through the woods, coming right at me. Terrified, I took off running. Within seconds it was right behind me and I veered off into the woods, stumbling and tripping, my heart in my throat, my mind dizzy with fear.

For what felt like hours I ran and ran before finally collapsing in exhaustion beneath a large tree. My burning lungs hurt so bad it seemed easier to die than to keep running. Lying there, gasping for air, I tried to listen for the sounds of pursuit but could hear nothing over my own labored breathing.

Finally my panting quieted down and I realized that while I no longer heard the crashing noise, I now heard footsteps, careful and soft. Dallen. He'd found me. Still struggling to breathe, I pushed myself to my feet and prepared to run. But I didn't know which way to go and I froze, hoping whoever it was wouldn't see me in the dark.

Suddenly, like magic, a tall figure appeared in front of me.

"Who's there?" I whispered, my tongue thick with fright.

"I might ask the same, trespasser." The voice was strong and commanding, the words accented.

"M-my name's Lorelle Gragan," I pushed out in trembling spurts, "and I-I'm lost."

The figure didn't respond for a moment and an ominous silence wrapped its cloak around me. At last she spoke. "I see. You'd better come with me. It isn't safe to be out along the Fernie Brae at night, especially when alone and ignorant of our ways."

Fernie Brae? Our ways? "Wh-who are you?"

"You may call me Lady Faylan. I serve as the Dynastic Overseer of a realm called Hawthorn Lane."

"What's a Dynastic Overseer?"

"A very important person," she said firmly. "Now come along."

That was my first encounter with Lady Faylan. That night she brought me across the border, which felt a bit like walking through jell-o, and took me to her mansion, a surprisingly grand affair considering her plain dress and severe expression. The next morning she offered me a gown to wear and a simple, but hearty breakfast. I told her my story as I ate, and then she told me about the village and its role as a sanctuary to fey.

Of course I thought she was cracked, until she showed me what she could do, lifting the teapot with a flourish of her hand and making it spin in lazy circles. After a few revolutions, she lowered the pot to the table, then turned it into a chicken. After the chicken squawked at me and laid an egg, Lady Faylan turned it back into a teapot. The egg stayed an egg.

"This is who we are. Who *you* are, as only our kind can find the Fernie Brae. Do you understand what I'm telling you?"

I swallowed and nodded. She thought I was like her simply because I'd gotten lost in the woods, and as I was still in shock over what I'd seen and what I'd been through, I didn't correct her. It was a decision I would later come to both be thankful for and regret.

She went on to warn me what would happen if I were ever to betray Hawthorn Lane's existence to anyone. Being drawn and quartered while still alive was only part of the punishment. But if I agreed to follow the rules, I could stay and learn from her. The village brew-maven, Missy Thornback, was growing old and an apprentice was needed to take her place. When Lady Faylan described my duties, she made it sound like I would only need to gather certain ingredients and mix them together. I thought I could do that without being magical, and so I decided to take the job.

The next morning she started me on my gathering and brewing career and within a short time and a loan from her, I was able to purchase my own cottage. It didn't take me long to figure out that by making me a gatherer and giving me a loan Lady Faylan had been training me as a sort of spy who would feel obligated to her. But that didn't especially bother me. I found it a good trade-off—a new life in exchange for gathering other people's secrets. But even though I owed Lady Faylan so much, I was careful with what I told her. I had a code that I followed, albeit a strange and sometimes seemingly arbitrary one, and it kept me from revealing too much about the villagers. I was careful with what I shared as much for the sake of my quarry as for my own. No one likes a snitch. Luckily, Lady Faylan rarely called on me to use my surveillance skills, though I kept them sharp for my own purposes. Knowing secrets gave me power, something I greatly lacked in comparison to the fey.

I did love it here, but I never quite felt safe, always fearing I'd be found out, or worse, my mother would somehow learn about this place. Being that I, a non-fey, was here, I couldn't rule out the possibility she might find it, too. And if Renwick was in league with either her or Dallen, or both, if they'd told him lies about my disappearance, then I was in trouble.

Exhausted by the day, and by reliving that awful episode six years ago, I dragged myself up to the loft and fell into a restless sleep. When I heard the knock on my door the next morning, I was actually relieved to wake up. My dreams had been nightmarish, full of floods and Desolates and being drawn and quartered, and at the end of it all, Dallen showing up at my door.

My heart hammered in my chest. Could it really be him down there?

"Gragan, I'm coming in!" a harsh voice crowed.

I relaxed only a little. It wasn't my mother or Dallen, but someone equally threatening—Berenea Battle. *Thorny Issues* was due out tomorrow and the newshound was looking for a late breaking story.

"Don't you dare!" I pulled on my robe and scurried down the ladder. But I was too late. When my feet hit the floor and I spun around, there she was in all her witchy glory, her trademark, well-worn, leather-bound notebook and ratty quill pen in hand.

Taller than me by several inches and broad as a linebacker, the old hag was an impressive sight to see, especially dressed as she was. Berenea always wore the same outfit—black knickers, square-toed shoes, a half-cloak and voluminous white collar, and a tall hat, a costume that reminded me of what the Puritans wore during the Salem witch-hunts. No doubt as a witch she was making some sort of ironic statement, though it escaped me just what that was. The style worked for her, though, which meant she looked exactly like the harridan she was.

"You're going to answer a few of my questions." She pulled out a pipe and started puffing on it. Being a witch, no matches were required... her pipe lit up at her command.

A pungently sweet smell drifted toward me, and I tightened my robe's belt as though preparing to do battle. "No, I'm not, and put that out."

She stared hard at me and I stared hard right back. "You will," she pushed out through clenched, crooked teeth, and I had the feeling she was trying to mind manage me.

I swiped at the air between us. "Knock it off, Berenea. You know how I work. Ask your questions, and I'll either answer them or I won't."

She stuck her pipe back in her pocket, where it continued to smoke, and snorted in amusement. "Worth a try."

I sighed. Berenea was a hard person to be fond of, but I had to give credit where credit was due. She was one tough cookie, and she didn't back down from anyone. Besides, I had the sneaking suspicion she rather liked me despite our clashes.

Or maybe because of them.

"I'll give you three questions, then I must get ready for the day."

She grimaced, but nodded. I knew she'd ask more, but at least this gave me some leverage. Her muddy brown eyes, slightly protuberant, roamed around the cottage. She'd never been inside before, and like any good reporter, was sniffing out clues she could use against me. I felt fairly confident she wouldn't find any. She'd only spy dried herbs, loads of books, my potion bottles, bits of wood gathered in the forest, an assortment of dark knickknacks I'd collected over the years, and that was about it. No dead bodies...at least not today. Besides, I stored all my really interesting collections in the little study next to the bathroom, its dark red door kept locked at all times.

"Nice place, this." She rubbed at a mole on her cheek. Hairs sprouted from the protrusion and she absently flicked her smoke-yellowed fingernail back and forth across them.

"Thank you."

"How'd you come about it again?"

"Is that your first question?"

She grinned. "I'll strike that one. What can you tell me about the Van der Daarke family? Rumor has it you harbored one of them for a day and that you ate dinner at the castle last night. There're three of them, ain't there? They rich? Why'd they come back after all this time? Why'd they leave in the first place?" She fired the questions at me, one right after the other, hoping to make a successful strike with at least one of them.

"I've no idea why the Van der Daarkes left Hawthorn Lane, nor why they came back. I didn't ask and they didn't offer."

Her beaky nose wrinkled in annoyance. "That ain't like you."

"It's exactly like me, Berenea. I'm an observer, not an interrogator."

She groaned dramatically, her wide shoulders slumping in frustration. "But that way's so slow!"

"I know," I agreed sympathetically. "But it works for me."

"So what *can* you tell me?" she asked shrewdly.

"Do you know their names?"

Her eyes narrowed. "Of course. Keran, Lilia, and Ben."

I laughed. "You were talking to Avice, weren't you?"

"Oh, I knew I shouldn't've! Girl's got the memory of a 500-year-old corpse."

"It's Kyran, Ilia, and Renwick." I spelled out the names for her and she scribbled them down. "Kyran is Ilia's uncle and guardian, as her mother recently died, and Renwick is their cousin. For the record, Ilia is of age, though she doesn't look it."

"That one? Looks more like a child to me. Guess that's why she still needs a guardian. She's the one who came to your place, ain't she?" She looked around, then jotted down some details. I found I was curious how she'd describe my cottage. It had better sound good, or no more interviews for the old battle-ax.

"She got scared at the castle and ran away," I told her. I was giving out information, yes, but sparingly and carefully. Truth has its place and this was one of them. I wanted to give the real reason Ilia had come to me, since the rumors would not be kind to her. "You know Hawthorn Lane can be a bit overwhelming for newcomers from the

Alterworld."

She leaned toward me, and her homely scent of pipe smoke and stale sweat followed. "I do. Remember when you came here yourself, a sweet, innocent young thing. Now look at you! Sharp as a *Desolate's* teeth and just as deadly." She waited, quill poised, hoping I'd spill it about Ilia's recent encounter. Damn Avice and her big mouth. Luckily I hadn't told her about our later adventure on the way to the castle.

"What a lovely compliment," I replied dryly.

She chuckled wickedly. "I can pay you a great deal for an exclusive on the Van der Daarkes, Miss Gragan. What say you?"

"And lose my reputation? Not worth it."

"Fine," she conceded, way too quickly, and I had a feeling the topic had only been temporarily shelved. "Tell me about the castle."

"How many questions has it been now?" I asked innocently.

"This is number two." She tried to look equally innocent, but failed miserably.

I didn't challenge her on it; this was a fairly innocuous question to answer. "It's very large, very grand inside. The Iverich family has been there already, selling their Effervescence, and you know they have an eye for detail. They could tell you much more than I could."

Her black, wooly bear eyebrows rose and her eyes sparkled greedily. Berenea knew that despite the airs Coriana Iverich put on, she wasn't nearly as close-mouthed as I was. As I didn't see any harm in Coriana sharing descriptions of the castle, gained secondhand as she would never deign to go on a business call herself, I threw her to Berenea like a nice, chewy bone. "I'll do that."

"You have one more question."

Her face wrinkled up in concentration, no doubt working out what the best one would be. "What do you think of them? The Van der Daarkes," she clarified, as though she thought I'd pick someone else to give my opinion on. Which I might have done.

"I like them," I said simply. "I think they'll make a great addition to our village."

"Did they show their fey?"

"That's another question."

"So they did?" Her face scrunched up. "And what's your fey, by the by? Not sure I've ever quite sussed it out." Her voice was quiet, but there was an aggressive undertone in it that I didn't like.

My pulse flickered and I looked away, as though checking the weather. "I'm not sure what they are," I answered, struggling to keep my voice as light as the raindrops starting to spot the windows. "But I think they brought this rain with them."

She glanced away from me to get a look herself and I took the opportunity to head toward the door. When I opened it, a rush of wind and rain blew in. The mist hit my face as I looked out at the gloomy sky. Rain again. I'd have to fix the dam soon. If I could. The sluice gate could be stubborn, and it was more than likely I'd end up in the water when I tried to lift it. I might have to fetch a Fiersen to help, and that would cost me money I didn't want to part with, not if I were to get the foundation seen to.

Behind me Berenea was still, then I heard her heavy heels as she strode toward the door. "You do like to hold your secrets close to the chest," she said, coming to stand next to me, her breath pungent from pipe tobacco and the bittersweet coffees she lived on.

I glanced up at her and smiled. "I find the idea of being an open book a bit frightening, Berenea. Once read through, I'm afraid I'll be discarded."

She grinned, revealing a prominent snaggletooth. "Don't see that happening to you, Gragan. Too wily." She elbowed me, nearly knocking me into the doorframe. "Doesn't mean I won't keep trying. There's something different about you and I aim to find out what it is." Her words made me go cold and I shivered. "Get inside and shut the door," she ordered. "Such a tiny bit of a thing, the wind blows right through you, don't it?"

Everyone was a tiny bit of a thing compared to Berenea.

"I'm less frightened of catching a chill than of your being nice to me."

She threw back her head and gave a loud guffaw. "Oh, Gragan. You and me...we really ought to join forces."

"Are we on opposing sides?"

"Some might say so."

"But I thought you and I were bosom buddies," I replied, no small measure of sarcasm in my voice.

"Ha! That'd be you and Montrose!" With that and a mighty roar of laughter, she tucked her notepad into her cloak and stomped off into the rain with a backward wave.

I watched her go, then shut the door. Leaning against it, I heaved a shaky sigh. Damn that Berenea. This wasn't the first time she'd mentioned me being different, but this was the first time she'd declared doing something about it.

If she found out I wasn't fey, that'd be the end of my time here. I'd be forced to go back to the Alterworld, back to Mother and Dallen. I'd have no choice, because I had no college degree, no experience, and no real money. I'd be reliant on them, at least in the beginning, and that would be enough for my mother to work her hoodoo on my mind.

I couldn't go back. I *wouldn't* go back.

Berenea needed a distraction from me and my *something different*, but I had no idea what that could be.

Chapter Twenty

One good thing had come out of Berenea's early morning arrival...I'd have time to attend to the dam before meeting Kyran and Ilia at *Fawn's Fashions*. I pulled my hair into a messy bun, donned my mackintosh and a pair of work trousers—I don't wear dresses *all* the time—and trudged out to the brook behind the cottage, the rain smacking my face with an intensity that seemed oddly personal.

I studied the shoulder-high stone wall that surrounded my cottage and thought it should hold back the water if it didn't reach all the way to the back gate. Something to hope for, anyway. I opened the gate and headed, slipping and sliding, down the slight slope to the brook, which looked swollen as a boa constrictor after a meal. The pool had breached its normal banks, making the grass around it squishy as a wet sponge.

Glad I'd worn my wellies, I carefully made my way to the dam, passing my favorite tree. It was an ancient, massive oak with knots the size of my head and several long, low limbs, one of which curved into a perfect seat and another that supported a swing. Before starting across, I stood for a moment on the bank, considering all my options. It took only a few moments to determine there was only one. I would have to lift the heavy, cast-iron sluice gate or risk a flooded cellar, which could be disastrous. The cottage's foundation couldn't take much more abuse.

The trouble was, the sluice gates never liked being lifted, and doing so while the water was running high and fast was going to be difficult and awkward, at best. But even though it would be easier to lift the gate while in the water I wanted to avoid that. The current was moving too swiftly, and the water, having been ice not all that long ago, would be frigid. Drowning was a distinct possibility in conditions like this, not to mention a horrible way to go.

Mentally girding myself, I took a cautious step out onto the dam, wet and slippery from the rain and moss stippling the solid stone blocks, and cautiously made my way toward the sluice gates in the middle. One was already open to keep the brook running, and the other was shut to create the pool. If I were being practical, I'd keep them both open all the time. But I liked the pool and often swam in it during hot summer evenings. So here I was...doomed by my compulsion to skinny dip.

All I had to do was lift the closed gate and the pool would empty enough to temporarily stave off the threat of flooding. It wasn't a fail-safe, but for the moment, should keep the water out of my cellar. It sounded simple, but while iron is strong and can hold against the onslaught of a heavy current, it's also heavy and it rusts—two strikes against me. Every spring and fall I squirted almond oil into all the connecting parts and it helped, but with the current so strong, I seriously doubted it would be enough. But I had to try. If I failed, I'd have to bite the bullet and pay Doolin Fiersen, or one of his sons, to help me with the job.

Not wanting to give up any Goldenars just yet, I decided to try it myself first. I kneeled down by the gate, cold water seeping through my pants, and reached into the freezing torrent. Moisture sprayed my face, making it hard to see, but I managed to grab hold of the iron. Too late, I realized I should have worn gloves for the job. But I had my grip now and I was determined to make this work. I gave a tug and the gate moved a little, allowing a bit of water to trickle through. I gave another tug, but nothing happened this time. I tried again, and then again. The gate slid a tiny ways up on my last two attempts, but I couldn't get good enough leverage to lift the gate any higher.

I let go and stood up, shaking out my already numb hands to warm them. I'd have better leverage standing, but not the best balance. The situation wasn't ideal, but I didn't think I had much choice. Teeth chattering and fingers stinging, I reached down once more and grabbed hold of the gate. When I had a good grip, I gave a hard tug and the gate rose a couple inches. Success. Thrilled to be set loose, water rushed through the opening, gushing outward in a yellow-white stream. Four more inches and the gate should be high enough. Steadying myself, I tightened my grip and jerked hard. The gate rose two more inches and more water poured through.

One more time, I promised myself. Putting all my weight into the job, I heaved upward and the gate slid up so fast that I lost my balance. As I struggled to regain my footing, water sprayed through the opening like a fire hose, hitting me right below the kneecaps, and my fight to remain on my feet was lost. Before I could react, I pitched sideways into the roaring brook and was immediately sucked underwater.

Rolling and twisting in the wild current, I fought to reach the surface as the stream carried me toward the mill. My knee cracked against a rock and I almost screamed from the pain, a potential disaster being that I was underwater. *Get a grip*, I ordered myself as water went up my nose. Blindly I fought my way upward and at last broke through the churning surface with a gasp.

"Help!" I cried out before getting dragged under once more. My wellies were basically buckets now and my mackintosh had wrapped around me like a shroud, a frighteningly apt description.

My heartbeat pounded in my head as my shoulder slammed against a larger boulder, knocking the last of the air out of my lungs. Stars filled the darkness in my mind, and I started to panic. I couldn't get back up. *I couldn't get back up!*

I didn't want to die this way. I couldn't die this way. With the last of my strength, I used my feet and pushed off from a rock to propel myself upward. I burst from the brook's tight grip and shouted for help as soon as I hit the air, though who I was crying out to I didn't know. Nobody lived near enough to hear me.

"Lorelle!" a distant voice called out, surprising me. "Hold on!"

I fought hard to stay above the surface, my arms flailing and my feet kicking. The roiling and rushing of the water was disorienting, and I felt like a plastic bottle in an ocean storm. I had to get out of the water, or die.

And then, as though snatched up by an unseen hand, I flew out of the brook and landed on the bank. Kyran reached me a few moments later and dropped to his knees beside me, his face tight with anxiety. Without a word, he rolled me over onto my side, and I coughed and retched until I'd spewed out all the water I'd swallowed. When I was finally done, I flopped onto my back, exhausted.

"Are you all right?"

I opened my eyes to see him hovering over me, his agitation sparking the air between us. "I will be," I managed to say.

"You're hurt. I'm taking you to your cottage." I tried to sit up, but he pushed me back. "I'll carry you."

"I'm fine," I mumbled. "I'm—"

"I'm carrying you, so stop talking."

I obeyed, but only because it hurt to talk. Kyran lifted me into the air and I don't remember much after that until I was inside. If a jolt had passed between us when he'd picked me up, I didn't feel it. Numb from cold and shock, I probably wouldn't have felt much of anything right then.

I must have passed out because the next thing I remembered was lying on the floor and Kyran telling me I needed to get out of my wet clothes. I wasn't sure how I was going to manage that since my arms felt like cooked noodles.

"I'll help you," he said, his voice low and hoarse.

Not a good idea. I sat up, nearly cracking my head against his. "I've got it," I pushed through chattering teeth. Everything about me was shaking and I wondered how I was going to manage the buttons on my shirt and trousers.

"I'll do that part, then I'll fill your bath while you do the rest."

I glared at him. "Did you just read my mind?"

"I made a logical deduction," he answered. "You were staring at your buttons and looking baffled. Now let me do this before you die from hypothermia."

There was no choice but to submit. I turned my head away and tried to relax as he slid my mackintosh off. Once it was gone, he undid the buttons on my shirt, his large fingers struggling with the tiny discs. I felt a tingling all throughout my body as his fingertips worked on each button. Even though he wasn't touching my skin directly, I could still feel the contact like tiny firecrackers going off.

When he reached my pants, I nearly jumped out of my skin, but these buttons were bigger and he worked quickly, as though he, too, wanted to be done.

When the last button was unfastened, he stood and spun away from me, saying quickly over his shoulder, "Strip down while I fill the bath. It won't take me long."

Once he was in the small bathroom under the loft, I pulled off my shirt and pushed down my pants with numb fingers. He must have removed my boots when I'd been unconscious and I was glad I didn't have to try and take them off myself when my hands felt like blocks of ice.

I was completely naked when a hand clutching a towel appeared from the bathroom door. "Here."

Grateful, I took it and wrapped it around my shivering frame. A minute later, Kyran came out, stepping around me so that he was closer to the kitchen than to me. His eyes picked out a spot over my head and focused on it. "There'll be tea when you come out."

"Toast, too?" Despite all my retching, or maybe because of it, I was absolutely famished.

His smile was wry. "Toast, too."

A thought occurred to me. "Do you know how to make it?"

His lips flattened out. "I'm not entirely useless."

"No. I guess not. You saved my life. That's twice now."

"Butter and honey?" he asked, ignoring what I'd said about him saving my life, even though it was true. He didn't even look pleased, simply resolute.

"Sounds delicious."

He tossed his head at the bathroom door. "Go now."

I spent a long time in the tub, only climbing out when the chill that had taken over my body reluctantly moved on. In the mirror, I gazed at my wounds…deeply bruised hip, a cut along my hairline, to which I applied my healing salve and bandaged after I dried off, a few scrapes on my hands and knees. All told, not too terrible for nearly dying.

When I came out, Kyran was kneeling in front of the fireplace, building up a good blaze. He didn't say a word, simply closed his eyes. Towel clutched firmly to my chest, I climbed one-handed to my loft to fetch a dry gown.

Ten minutes later, I was warmly dressed in my favorite blood red cashmere satin, my hair was brushed out, and I was feeling much more like myself instead of a drowned rat. I descended to find tea and toast on the coffee table and a fire roaring. The heat felt so good I wanted to wrap my arms around it and hold it tightly to my body. Kyran was sitting in the rocking chair, looking, despite his high-born status, as though he belonged there.

Without a word, he poured our tea and I drank mine down greedily, each swallow easing the pain in my throat. The toast disappeared quickly and when it was gone, I felt like a new person.

"Thank you," I said when I'd swallowed my last bite and licked the last bit of honey off my fingers. "That was just the thing."

"I told you I'd help you," was his reply.

I looked up from refilling my teacup. "What?"

"Yesterday…I told you I'd help you with the dam."

"Oh. Well, I guess I thought you were just being polite."

"I'm never just being polite," he said stiffly. "I mean what I say."

I cocked an eyebrow at him. "I'll try to remember that."

"See that you do."

I sighed. "I'm sorry to have put you out by nearly drowning." I paused a second. "Just why exactly were you at the brook?"

"I had a feeling you'd do something like this."

I glowered at him, feeling like a naughty child caught with her hand in the cookie jar. "You did, did you?"

"I would've been here earlier, but I thought I'd better check on Renwick and Ilia first. Both were fine, but sleeping like the dead."

"I'm sure I would've been fine, as well," I sniffed irritably.

He leaned forward and I forced myself to remain where I was. His presence was so strong, so electric, that I wasn't sure my heart could handle such close proximity after what I'd been through. "What I'd like to know is…how did you get yourself out of the brook? It was incredible to see."

"How did I…?" I shook my head. "I didn't do anything. I was just about to ask you the same thing."

He looked as though he didn't believe me. "Then who did it, Lorelle?"

"I don't know. A naiad perhaps? That's a river spirit," I explained. "You do understand the fey nature of this world…"

"Of course I do." Though his expression was a trifle unsure. He might know of fey, but he didn't *know* them. That knowledge only comes through experience. "But I saw nothing to indicate the presence of another creature."

"Then you must've done it yourself. With magic."

He pulled back. "That's unlikely."

"Unlikely?"

"Magic isn't exactly my forte," he reluctantly admitted.

"I find that hard to believe." I knew enough about Hawthorn Lane to know the Van der Daarkes wouldn't have gotten as far as they had, or risen so high, without being powerful fey. Magic runs through their veins as surely as blood. Even if no one had told Kyran about his fey, he must have sensed its presence.

"I'm not from this place, Lorelle."

"But you are fey."

He blinked. "As are you."

"But I didn't do anything. I was panicking. I couldn't even think straight, so it couldn't have been me." His eyes bored into mine, as though suspecting, as Berenea did, that there was something different about me, something lacking. "Didn't anyone in your family tell you about your ancestors and their abilities?" I tried again.

His face grew cold and he seemed to withdraw from me as though stepping backward. "My parents divorced when I was ten, and I really didn't see either one of them much after that, which was a good thing."

"When you were only ten?" I whispered. "What happened?"

"They fought all the time, that's what happened. Prior to the divorce, I spent much of my life at boarding school. An English one, if you can believe it." That explained the accent.

"Sending your children away seems to be a thing with your family."

"Ah, yes. Ilia. It probably was the best thing for her. Melaina, my sister, like my mother and father, was not good with children."

"And you?"

"Never having had one, I've no idea."

"I suppose I'm the same way," I confided, "though I do enjoy the antics of the young Fiersens. They're quite amusing." I paused, then asked what some might consider an intrusive question. "Do you think you'll ever reconcile with your parents?"

"I sincerely doubt it. They're both dead. They died when I was sixteen."

I pulled back from the abruptness of his news. "Oh. Even though you didn't get along, I'm sorry for your loss."

"Thank you," he said stiffly, flames reflecting off his dark eyes as he stared at the fire.

"I imagine it's hard to lose someone like that, never being given the chance to fix things."

He stood abruptly, his expression that of a trapped animal, as though he'd shared far more than he would have wished. "I came to tell you that Ilia is not up to a fitting today."

"Ah, yes," I replied, gazing up at him. "I imagine not. You seem fine, though."

"And you, despite your dunking, look to be recovered."

"I am, actually. It's good to know I'm not growing soft in my old age."

"Wait until you're as old as me."

I laughed. "I'd say I have a long time to go until I get there. You're absolutely decrepit."

One corner of his mouth tilted up in amusement, then he held out his hand, which wasn't as fine and soft as I would have thought. "So are we still on?"

"Still on?"

"For our shopping expedition."

I stared at his outstretched hand. Something inside me wanted to grab hold of it and never let go. That *something* was clearly irrational and I quickly pushed it away. Kyran had made it quite clear that he and I came from very different worlds, and I had to admit that I agreed with him on that. We would never make a good match...not that he wanted that. Nor did I.

"I'm not sure what use I'd be to you."

"I'll need your help with my selections."

He didn't look as though he needed help with anything. Everything about him conveyed poise and success. Still...

"All right," I said, surprising myself. I took hold of his hand and he pulled me up off the chaise. This time I definitely felt the strong jolt passing between us. It rippled through my body like lightning across water, but I didn't dare let go.

Our eyes met, but neither of us said a word.

Chapter Twenty-One

Kyran had ridden Rogue over, so we galloped into the village on the fine black stallion, the electric vibes pulsing low and fast between us. It didn't seem like Kyran to want to put himself on parade, but here we were. The ravens and falcons screeched overhead, heralding our arrival in the village as well as any trumpeter. For the moment, the rain had stopped and intermittent bursts of sunshine shone down upon us like a spotlight from the spirit world.

It wasn't quite eleven o'clock, yet the store's French doors were open wide, letting in fresh air and the occasional flying pixie. Fan and Dawn were 'working' in the display window, straightening the dresses on the living mannequins and, judging by the sisters' matching irate expressions, squabbling with each other. No doubt they were expecting Ilia to return today, and had opened early to be ready for her.

Boy, were they going to be surprised.

When they spotted Kyran riding up, their mouths dropped open like marionettes, and when they saw me with him, their eyes widened in horror. I felt a distinct sense of satisfaction warming the cockles of my heart. I couldn't afford their dresses, but what did that matter when I could practically feel the heat of their jealousy from ten feet away. It felt very good, very *warm*.

To avoid touching Kyran skin to skin, I slid down as soon as he dismounted, the heels of my ankle boots hitting the cobblestone with a satisfying thud. A part of me liked the electric jolt that passed between us—there was something illicit and powerful about it that I greatly enjoyed. But another part of me felt uneasy every time it happened, as though each shock was a warning to stay away. I couldn't do that, though—I had information to gather—so I would simply have to keep my hands to myself.

Kyran motioned for me to go ahead of him into the store, and I swept inside, head held high and my feet barely touching the floor, I felt so buoyant. *So this is what superiority feels like!* I could definitely see the allure of it.

"Count Van der Daarke!" Fan greeted smoothly, having recovered from her shock. From her perfect posture to her elegant walk, she was all social grace and charm as she sashayed toward him. Of course none of that charm was directed my way. "Fan Ravenna, proprietress of this fine establishment. What a pleasure to meet you at last." She held out her bejeweled hand to him and he took it and bowed over it. She positively simpered in response, fake eyelashes batting and glaring white teeth bared like a deranged rabbit.

Today her maid had outdone herself, creating a confectionary delight out of Fan's blond tresses that would rival a faerie wedding cake. Laden with jewels and styling oils and glitter galore, the hair-do was a work of art. Though the fact that Fan was able to hold her head up straight impressed me even more than the elaborate coiffure, which had to weigh a good ten pounds. The dress she wore was gauzy and practically see-through, but the cut was exquisite. The gown skirted the line between classy and wanton, with classy winning out by a hair, and therein lay the key to the sisters' success.

"A pleasure, Miss Ravenna," Kyran said, his eyes glued to her hair. I doubt he'd ever seen the likes of it outside a circus tent.

"Oh, do call me Fan." Dawn cleared her throat menacingly and Fan threw a careless hand back over her shoulder at her. "And this is my little sister."

"I'm the proprietress here, too," Dawn proclaimed, sticking out her hand. Kyran took it, and she watched him avidly as he bowed over the white lump. "I do just as much as Fan does, you know. More sometimes."

"Is that right?" Kyran let go of her hand and straightened up with a small smile, leaving Dawn almost melting in adoration.

She nodded, eyes wide. "I'm very good with the clients, especially the male ones. Males are my specialty."

Fan's nostrils flared angrily, and I thought she was about to take Dawn's head off, but she controlled herself at the last second, curling her reaching fingers into fists. Fan might be a horrid snob, but she wasn't stupid.

"Go close the doors. It's starting to rain again." Dawn reluctantly did as she was told, a pout marring her perfect features. "She's a dear little thing, isn't she?" Fan purred to Kyran, her expression a perfect study in patronization.

"I've come to purchase a few outfits," Kyran replied, refusing to be drawn into their little contest. Score one for him. "I prefer darker colors," he went on. "And double stitching, of course. I'll need several waistcoats of varying colors and a good selection of trousers. I like cuffs. Plus I'll need footwear and outerwear."

Fan looked at him with new respect. Here was a man who knew what he wanted. "Of course, Count Van der Daarke. I'm sure we'll find the perfect wardrobe for you. All will be very dignified, very noble, as befitting your elevated status." *Elevated status? What was he, a giant?* I had to stifle a giggle, earning an inquisitive look from Kyran. This was all just so surreal. I quickly straightened my features and tried to look innocent. "Why don't you come along," Fan went on, ignoring me, "and I'll show you our wide selection." Normally Royalton, a faerie who worked for them, would see to Kyran, but if he was here, Fan didn't mention it. No way was she giving up this opportunity. "We have the latest from Paris, Rome, even Stockholm, and they rarely ship overseas. Luckily I know someone, who happens to be an admirer of mine. I've done nothing to encourage it, mind you! But I won't say no when the fabulous Ingmar offers to send me his latest work."

Kyran waited patiently until she was done, then he indicated me. "I'd also like to purchase a dress for Miss Gragan." Recovering from my surprise, I aimed a smile at the sisters, more jubilant than gracious, I admit. So far they'd succeeded in ignoring me entirely.

"Uh..." Fan pushed out, her eyes distressed. The last thing she wanted was for a commoner to be seen wearing one of her dresses.

"She'd look good in that one." He pointed to the dress I'd coveted for far too long. "It matches her eyes."

Dawn and Fan gaped at me. Behind their shocked countenances flickered an uglier emotion, something that went beyond jealousy, tainted as it was by murderous intent. Someone like Count Van der Daarke shouldn't even see someone like me, much less notice the color of my eyes.

As much as I liked to see the sisters suffer, I couldn't accept the dress. It smacked of hypocrisy on my part and possible blackmail on his. Something like, *I'll buy you a dress, and you'll keep your mouth shut about us.* "Thank you, Kyran, but I don't need a dress."

"Ilia told me you liked that one. Do you not?"

I frowned. "When did she tell you that?"

"When I checked on her last night, right before I escorted you home." Dawn and Fan both gasped, and judging by the devilish gleam in Kyran's eyes, he'd said that on purpose to make them infer something had gone on between us. What was he trying to do? First he acted like he was too good for me, now he wanted his name linked with mine? Sneaky bugger. He was up to something, but damned if I could figure out what.

As I couldn't very well point out that Ilia had been drunk and didn't know what she was talking about, I could make no argument. "I couldn't possibly accept—" I tried again.

But Kyran smoothly interrupted. "You couldn't possibly accept a thank you gift from the Van der Daarkes? A little something to show our appreciation for your most gracious welcome and solicitous attention to my niece? Oh come now!" He cocked an eyebrow at me and I sensed he was enjoying my discomfiture.

"Well, put like that…"

The sisters had been watching us with the avidity of vultures gathered around a dying beast, but now Fan was tiring of the conversation. "We'll get right on that, Count Van der Daarke. We at *Fawn's Fashions* pride ourselves on being able to handle even the most difficult fashion cases." *Implying that I was one of them.* "We shall see that Miss Gragan gets the perfect dress."

Kyran pointed at my dress again. "See that she gets that one."

Fan looked like she'd just downed a lemon bitter…through her nose. "Of course."

With what looked suspiciously like a triumphant smile aimed directly at me, Kyran left with Fan to try on numerous outfits. Dawn was stuck with me, and she made no attempt to hide her annoyance, poking me with pins, pinching my skin as she pulled in the waist, making snide remarks about my weight and the bandage on my forehead, asking if I'd been in a bar fight. I put up with it all, mainly because I was about to get the dress of my dreams. So what if it was tainted by the idea that Kyran was giving it to me with some sort of extortion in mind… I sighed and tried not to think about that part.

At last we finished and Dawn took the dress to the back room for the seamstresses to alter. I was glad it was only the one dress. Ilia was going to have to do this for all nine of hers, so it was best she didn't do it with a hangover. It was hard enough without one. How did the rich do this on a constant basis?

Take the eldest Iverich girl, Enchanté (her mother, Coriana, was another Hawthornite who liked to show off her French), whom I often saw out clothes shopping. What I didn't know is if she did it because she liked it, or because she simply had nothing else to do. I suspected the latter. While she was a faerie, she wasn't a snob. I imagined she went shopping because she was bored, and maybe lonely.

Too bad the Iverich family didn't believe their females could be something more than an ornament for others to admire and envy. Only the males could do real work, even if they didn't want to. Enchanté's older brother, Charlton, for example, had been forced to be a part of the family business. At least he looked like he'd been forced, his dark, brooding expression seemingly never changing whenever we passed one another in the street. Their brother, Hanover, was the typical youngest child…into wine, women, and song, yet he too was being trained to the business. He often rebelled by sneaking off to the Alterworld whenever he could, returning looking like hell and in need of an age reversal potion. Enchanté might like business more than her brothers, yet was stuck trying on dresses.

At any rate, their world was not mine, and I was glad for it. Kyran Van der Daarke could keep his family name and dignity. All the hoity-toities could. Give me my warm, cozy cottage and comfortable, independent life any day. And maybe a pretty dress once in a while.

I am human, after all.

Kyran and Fan rejoined us, Fan positively beaming…well, as much as her tight face would allow. "Oh, Count Van der Daarke, you have such excellent taste," she said, practically spewing water she was gushing so much.

"I owe that to my mother. She was the one who knew fashion. It was her abiding love." His words were light, but I detected an undercurrent of bitterness there.

Fan, as usual, was oblivious. "I would so love to meet the Countess!"

"I'm afraid she died some years ago."

Her hands clasped together and her voice was sympathetic. "I'm so sorry, Count Van der Daarke." Yet there was a mercenary gleam in her eyes. The Count's stock had just risen for her. He was alone and unencumbered by parents who might not like her; he was the heir to the castle; and he was damaged by his loss. There was just so much for her to exploit. Nostrils flared as though scenting prey, she looked practically on the verge of jumping out of her knickers for the man.

"Thank you, Miss Ravenna." I noticed she didn't correct Kyran, asking him to call her Fan, nor did she call him by his first name. I wondered if she'd tried it out and he'd firmly, but politely, corrected her. He must have or she'd be Kyran this and Kyran that. Did avoiding being on a first-name basis indicate a desire on Kyran's part to put her in her place, or simply what he did to people he considered beneath him? Either option was equally likely, though I noted he did call me Lorelle. I preened a little, knowing full well I was being ridiculous. "You've been most helpful and gracious," he went on. "I'll return tomorrow with my niece and we'll finish our fittings at that time."

The bell on the shop door jangled importantly, and in strode Lady Faylan, looking imposing as always. When she saw Kyran, she stopped in her tracks and her face turned a sickly shade of gray. "Marekai?" she gasped. At least that's what I thought I'd heard, though I didn't know any Marekai in Hawthorn Lane.

For his part, Kyran didn't respond as dramatically to her as she had to him. His expression was watchful, yet relatively calm.

"Lady Faylan," I stepped forward to greet her. "This is Count Van der Daarke." I turned back to present him. Only now did he react, though he quickly doused the surprise widening his eyes. So he knew Lady Faylan's name well enough to react to it, but he didn't know her face. The day we'd met I'd mentioned her name as a contact for finding workers for the castle, and he'd reacted to hearing it then, as well. Question was, how did he know her name?

Kyran bowed to her. "How do you do, Lady Faylan?"

Drawing her shoulders up, Lady Faylan pulled herself together, though I was probably the only one to notice anything amiss. "I'm well, thank you. I knew your family. Before they left, that is."

"I'd love to hear your memories of them."

Her mouth twisted slightly. "You think so?"

A twitch of his left eyebrow was the only clue he'd thought, as I did, that her response was a bit strange. "I do. I know little of my family's time here."

"I see." She relaxed a little. "So they didn't speak of this place?"

"Not much. My mother and father weren't exactly big on sharing."

"You knew your grandparents?" Her tone was soft, probing.

"They died when I was young, as did my parents."

Her gray eyes glinted. "That must have been hard for you."

"It would've been if I'd known them well."

"And your great-grandfather? It was he and his family who left this place. Did you know anything about him?"

I frowned. How did Lady Faylan know what line Kyran had come from? He could have been like Renwick, a distant cousin.

"I know nothing of him," Kyran replied coolly, "beyond his gravestone."

Lady Faylan looked off to her right, as though something had caught her attention, but not before I noted a brief wave of something terrible cross her features. "His gravestone," she repeated, her voice strange. "Well, I imagine it was resplendent. Your great-grandfather liked that sort of thing."

Kyran closed his eyes for a moment, as though searching his memory for an image. "I remember it being somewhat small." He opened his eyes and I realized that's exactly what he'd been doing…remembering. "Spotted with lichen, and cracked down the middle as though struck by lightning."

She returned her gaze to him and I thought she looked both pleased and thwarted. "So what brings you to our little village, Count Van der

Daarke? We are all so curious." Her eyes found mine, but I remained still, my expression pleasant and somewhat vacuous. Something strange was going on here and I wasn't about to get myself dragged into it, not on her terms.

"Well, I guess I was curious myself. I'd heard of Hawthorn Lane, but knew very little about it, other than that my ancestors once lived here."

"But however did you find the Fernie Brae?"

"My cousin knew of it." I gave a slight cough to stifle my gasp. Renwick had known where to cross? How? And wasn't he the one to claim that Kyran knew much more than he did? What was going on with this family? "Perhaps his parents were more open to talking about Hawthorn Lane," he went on, as though trying to answer my question, but failing. "You'd have to ask him, though." Kyran's eyes left Lady Faylan and went to the door. "What luck. Here he is now."

Lady Faylan swung about, just as Renwick stumbled into the shop. "Ilia," he wheezed. "She's gone!"

Chapter Twenty-Two

A cold wave of fear swept through me. "Ilia gone? Again? Are you sure she isn't just exploring the castle? Or maybe she went to my cottage."

"I'm sure," Renwick replied. His eyes found Lady Faylan and he went still, as though if he didn't move, she wouldn't notice him. But she did, of course, and her reaction was difficult to read. She wasn't pleased to see him, but she wasn't angry, and she hadn't gone all pasty, either, not like she had with Kyran. So Renwick knew her by sight, and Kyran knew her only by name. But while she seemed to know both of them, only one had the power to disconcert her…Kyran.

"I got your note," Renwick said to Kyran, "and thought maybe she'd be up to a fitting, after all." He flicked a glance at me. "I thought I could escort her here, then return to my work at the stables. But when I went to her room, it was empty. Ilia is rather messy, but the room looked to be in more disarray than even she could be capable of creating in such a short time. I thought I'd check at Lorelle's cottage before coming here, but she wasn't there, either."

Funny that he knew where I lived.

"Disarray?" Kyran echoed. "You think there was some sort of struggle?"

"Her room wasn't messy when I saw it yesterday," I offered.

"Her suitcases had been knocked open and their contents strewn all over the place," Renwick elaborated. "On top of that, there was a strange smell in the room, a combination of dirt and death."

During this conversation, Dawn had returned to the main salon. When she heard Renwick's last words, she threw up her hands and screeched, "The Desolate must have got her!"

I turned and glared at her. "What are you talking about, Dawn?"

"I was passing through the town square while on my way to the shop the other day," she explained importantly, "when Ilia ran past me. Gorn was at the fountain and asked her what she was running from. She told him a Desolate was after her." Dawn's eyes were thrilled, her cheeks flushed. So Ilia had said something about the Desolate before I'd arrived, which meant that by now the whole village had heard about her sighting.

Lady Faylan's gray eyes fastened on me. "What's this about?"

Well, almost the whole village had heard. "Nothing, really," I replied, working to keep my voice calm. "That day you met Ilia—well she thought she'd seen a Desolate at Haunted Hollow. I didn't think that was possible since they aren't real, so I didn't bother mentioning it."

"Isn't that the creature we fought off yesterday afternoon?" Kyran asked.

Lady Faylan glared at me and I cringed. Damnit. "Lorelle?"

"On the road to the castle a woman tried to attack Ilia."

"There was something wrong with her, wasn't there?"

I remembered her sharp teeth and dead eyes. "Oh, yes. But like I said, I didn't think Desolates were real."

"And you *didn't think* to tell me about this event?"

"I meant to, but—"

"What does this Desolate creature want with my niece?" Kyran demanded, interrupting me with perfect timing. I needed a moment to come up with a plausible story for why I hadn't told Lady Faylan what had happened…twice.

She turned toward Kyran and her hard features softened a little. "Her heart, of course."

"So Desolates are real?" I asked, though I already knew the answer.

"Whyever not, Lorelle?"

"But everyone here always acts like they're made up."

"Rather ironic in a place like this, don't you think?"

"Well, yes," I admitted sheepishly. "But if Desolates are real, why pretend they aren't?"

"The reason is obvious. Desolates aren't interested in going after just anyone's heart; they go after the person who wronged them. To admit Desolates are real is to risk being exposed to gossip and possible banishment."

That made absolutely no sense. The villagers in Hawthorn Lane were always doing something they shouldn't be doing, including betraying their lovers, and no one pretended otherwise.

Something else didn't make sense. "How could Ilia have wronged a Desolate? She's never been here before."

Lady Faylan glanced out the window, her jaw tight. "Yet another mystery." She turned back and gave me a meaningful look. I wasn't sure what the look meant…that she wanted me to solve the mystery, or leave it alone.

Kyran stepped forward to stand next to me. "I propose we split up. Lorelle and I will search the woods near the castle. Renwick, you go through the village and ask if anyone has seen the girl."

Renwick nodded, his eyes on me. He cocked his head at my bandage, but I only shrugged, as though it was nothing.

"I'll organize a search party," Lady Faylan stated firmly. "There are a lot of places to cover." She wasn't exaggerating. The moors were expansive, as was Wuthering Wood. Atermorte Cemetery, a sprawling maze of mausoleums, tombstones, and statuary, presented its own special challenge, not to mention one would have to deal with Cutter Flint, the reclusive caretaker.

"I'd appreciate that, Lady Faylan," Kyran said to her with a slight bow. "I'll head to the castle first to see if she's returned."

She gave him a quick nod, then left the shop, her back straight and head held high. Her stride was unhurried, though I couldn't help but think she was fleeing from us.

"We would help search, Count Van der Daarke," Fan said, "but we cannot leave the shop."

"I'll help!" Dawn offered, earning an irritated glare from her sister. "You can handle things here, can't you? That's what you're always saying, anyway." Well, well, well. What a surprise. Dawn was such a shadow of her sister that I often viewed them as a single entity, thinking that if one did or thought something, the other (Dawn) would go along with it. Judging by Fan's expression, she was surprised, too, but not in a nice way. Before she could protest, though, Dawn grabbed a startled Renwick and pulled him out of the shop. I smiled, finding myself actually rooting for her.

Kyran and I followed them out. The sun had lost its battle, giving way to a heavy fog that would make our search much more difficult. Renwick and Dawn entered the shop next door, and I turned to Kyran. "I think the Desolate might have taken Ilia to Haunted Hollow. It's only a guess, but that smell Renwick mentioned…it's what that creature on the coach smelled like, and the Hollow is where Desolates supposedly reside."

"It's worth a try. If we don't find her there, we can head up to the castle afterward."

"You don't want to split up?"

He shook his head. "Better we stick together."

Better for whom? I wondered, but I didn't argue.

Leaving Rogue behind, we hurried down the street toward the Hollow. Even with the thick fog, the Hollow stood out as its own entity; its fog was darker and weightier somehow, as though filled with sorrow. Nearing the entrance I slowed down and turned back to warn Kyran to stay close.

But he wasn't there.

"Kyran?" I spun around. "Kyran!" A chill ran through me. Either he'd gotten lost in the fog, or he was up to something, which would explain why he wanted me with him. I called one last time, and as I stood still to listen for his response, I heard something else…frantic crying coming from the Hollow.

I didn't have time to wait. I dashed through the opening in the blackthorns, and was nearly through to the other side when a branch whipped me. The thorns gashed deep scratches down my back and I gasped in pain as I spun about, ready to defend myself. But I couldn't see anything threatening—the branches were still and nothing lurked nearby.

Reaching around to my back, I found the material whole and my skin untouched. The attack had been an illusion, meant to scare off intruders. This had never happened to me before, which meant something was different today…something I needed to be worried about. Heart beating a little faster, I made my way down the uneven stone steps, ears open to any strange sound, though they were all strange here in the Hollow.

The sobbing had stopped and the quiet was thick as pond muck as I crossed the Hollow's floor, my steps quick and soft. Here and there, looming up suddenly, the boulders seemed to be moving about, getting in my way, slowing me down. When something cool and hard bumped against me, I knew I wasn't imagining things. I was being hunted. I darted in the opposite direction, hoping that while doing so I didn't smash face-first into a boulder.

I didn't go far. "Ilia!" I called desperately, looking about. "Are you there?"

"Lorelle?" My name bounced off the stones around me, seeming to come from all directions at once. "Help me!"

I spun around, trying to figure out which way to go. If only I'd told Ilia she was fey so she could protect herself. If we made it out of this alive, I'd have to make sure she knew. To survive Hawthorn Lane, she needed to be able to defend herself against the dark forces always skulking along the borders of our little village.

"Where are you, Ilia?" I called out, the words too loud in my ears.

"I'm over here." The voice was coming from my left and I raced toward it, stumbling on a rock. I hadn't gone very far when a chill took my limbs hostage. Something about this wasn't right. But before I could figure out what it was, a large object hit me from behind, knocking me to my knees. Whatever it was jumped on my back and pressed down hard on my neck, forcing me to flatten onto the ground. Face turned sideways against the rough stone, I glimpsed the Desolate's frenzied face, her teeth bared, her eyes dark and wild. Her mouth grew closer and closer to my neck, and I swallowed hard as her fetid breath hit my cheek.

"Do not interfere," she growled, her voice raspy with fury.

"Where's Ilia?" I demanded, using my free hand to swipe at her. Her arm dug into my neck, the pain forcing me to stop.

"She's mine now. I *earned* her."

"She didn't do anything to you," I pushed out. The Desolate's weight on my back and her arm against my neck was making it hard to breathe. If only I'd pulled my dagger before entering the Hollow.

"She took my love from me!"

"How could she do that? She only just arrived in Hawthorn Lane, and it's been a hundred years since any of the Van der Daarkes lived here." I hoped that was true. I wasn't entirely sure about anything when it came to that family. "And I saw your picture at the castle, when you attended the *Danse Macabre* ball. It was dated a hundred years ago."

The arm lifted slightly, giving me a chance to suck in a shallow breath. "A century?" Her voice cracked. "It's been that long?"

"It has."

"But I'd swear she's the one!" she persisted.

"Ilia wasn't even born then. It had to have been one of her ancestors."

"Then she must serve in her ancestor's place."

I shivered. "Will that work?"

"It'll have to," the Desolate answered, though her voice was uncertain.

Sensing a weakness, I threw my head back, smashing it into her face, then bucked my body, throwing her from me. I scrambled to my feet, then spun around to face her, dagger in hand. The Desolate slowly stood, the fog wrapping around her like a heavy veil. Her dress was tattered and there was a dark hole where Kyran's arrow had struck her shoulder.

"Leave Ilia be," I warned. "She's not the one who wronged you. She's innocent."

"As was I!" She beat her chest with a ragged fist.

"What proof do you have that Ilia's ancestor betrayed you?"

"My lover told me. He said he'd been promised to another. To *her!*"

"Are you sure he was telling the truth?"

"Of course I am," she replied, though her weak tone and uncertain expression implied there was no *of course* about it. "He wouldn't lie to me."

I stiffened. "In my experience men lie."

Dallen had lied to me. He'd claimed he thought it had been me in the bedroom that day. My smell, the taste and feel, everything had told him it was me. Even though being so spontaneous wasn't like me, he'd added with a frown.

This last bit was the one touch of truth in his story and had momentarily made me doubt what I'd seen. But then I'd hardened myself. I had to go. I no longer loved him, would never love him again. Eudrea was welcome to him.

The Desolate sunk to her knees in despair. "I gave up my life for him!" Her eyes flit about like dying moths and her hands grew into crazed creatures, shaking uncontrollably.

"Your lover… Do you remember his name?" I asked softly.

She gazed up at me, her empty eyes pooling with sorrow, then she whispered the name, her voice trembling as she added, "It's burned on my soul."

And now it was burned on mine.

Chapter Twenty-Three

Oh, stars above. That was not a name I'd expected to hear. "Is he, is this man still alive? It's been a hundred years, remember."

Her bony shoulders lifted, then dropped. "I'm not sure. I only know he fled at the same time the others did."

Spiders of excitement zipped up my spine. This was it. This was the answer. "Then you must know why the Van der Daarkes left Hawthorn Lane."

She looked surprised. "Of course I do. Everyone knows."

"Not anymore. There are stories, but I don't think any of them are the truth. I think there was a cover-up."

A tear ran down her cheek, and its unexpected appearance made me see the Desolate in a new light. She'd once been a beautiful young woman, with her whole life before her, and she'd been reduced to this…this *monster*, by a man. By a faithless, lying man.

"You're sure Ilia isn't the one?" she tried one more time.

"I'm pretty sure."

She held out her hands. "I don't want to be this creature anymore. Please help me!"

I swallowed, unsure what use I could be to her when I didn't know how to do or undo magic. "I'll try my best. But first I need to know what really happened to the Van der Daarke family—why they left. I think it might be related to what happened to you."

She shuddered and looked around, a growing desperation filling her dark eyes. "I won't be able to fight it long."

The fog billowed and slithered around me, taking on a life of its own, and I shivered. "Fight what?"

"The desire to take her heart." She moaned and clutched at her dead one. "Even if she's not the one, I won't remember that when I lose control. The resemblance is too great."

"I'll try to work as quickly as I can," I hurried to assure her. "But first…you *must* tell me. Why did the Van der Daarkes leave?"

"Ilia!" a voice cried in the distance.

The Desolate's eyes widened in fright, and she sprang to her feet, ready to flee. "That voice, it sounds familiar."

"That's Ilia's uncle," I told her.

"The one who shot me?"

"Well, yes, because you were trying to get Ilia."

She clutched at her arms. "I can't help myself. Since she came, I've felt an urge for vengeance stronger than anything I've ever known."

"Ilia!" a different voice, farther away, called out imperiously.

The Desolate stepped backward, startled. "Not *her*."

"She's looking for Ilia, too," I explained, though what Lady Faylan was doing here was a mystery. "Do you know her?"

"Know her?" The Desolate gave a raspy laugh. "She's my sister."

"Lady Faylan is your *sister*?"

"*Lady* Faylan? Oh, that's rich. She's no more a lady than I am."

What? "So who are you?"

She straightened, looking dignified. "It's been a long time since anyone has called me by my name. I am Juletta Faylan."

"It's a beautiful name."

Her eyelids twitched. "But one I can no longer live up to."

"I'm sorry, Juletta."

"Don't pity me!" she hissed. "If you want to stop me from taking that girl, then you learn the truth." Her cold fingers grasped my arm, and I was to feel their presence for days to come. "Promise me you will."

"I promise, Juletta."

She pointed at a nearby boulder with a shaking finger. "Take her and go. I can't promise anything. I can only try not to seek her out. But know that I grow weaker with every passing hour."

"I'll find out the truth, Juletta," I said as I sheathed my dagger. "I will. But please, you must tell me—"

"Ilia!" Kyran called out, closer now. "Lorelle!"

Juletta grasped at her throat, as though strangling. "Go now. Quickly!"

I nodded, then sprinted toward the boulder and climbed the narrow stairs. When I reached the top, I found Ilia passed out, her face pale and her skin cold. She was wearing PJs from the Alterworld, flowered pants and a sweet button-up shirt. Not for the first time I thought how young and slight she looked. On the plus side, I was able to half carry, half drag her spare form down the steps.

When my foot touched the ground a voice whispered in my ear, "They left because of the curse."

I spun toward the sound, but like a ghost Juletta was nowhere to be seen. Frightened, I pulled Ilia along the ground, knowing she was going to be bruised and scratched at the end of our journey, but hopefully still alive. Moans echoed around the Hollow, spurring me to move faster. Juletta was fighting to keep her promise, but I had a feeling she wouldn't be able to fight for long.

We were halfway to the stairs when Ilia started to struggle. I tried to maintain my grip on her shirt, but she was thrashing about too much and I let go before she got hurt. Her eyes were closed and she was breathing hard, and I stepped back, uncertain what to do. I had to get her out of here, but I couldn't get near her with her arms and legs flailing about as though she were caught in a seizure.

"Lorelle!" Kyran's voice sounded very near. "Ilia!"

"Over here!" I cried.

Within moments, he was at my side and kneeling down next to Ilia. He looked her over, then his worried eyes peered up into mine. "What happened to her?"

"I don't know. It just started." I crossed my arms over my chest as a cold chill ran through me. "Where were you?"

"I thought I heard something back by the bridge and stopped to listen, and when I turned to continue on, you were gone."

"I was wondering what happened to you," I said aloud, while thinking to myself, *I'm not sure I believe your story.* "I would've waited, but I heard Ilia crying out and figured I'd better go quickly. I tried to get her out myself, but she started fighting me." I looked about, my stomach tight. All around us, the fog writhed and danced in the wake of Kyran's arrival, veiling everything, good and bad. "We have to get her out, Kyran. The Desolate is here."

He didn't waste a moment. Leaning over Ilia, he placed his palm against her forehead and she went still. He hefted her up into his arms and nodded, his face grim. Taking the lead, I slowly led us out of the Hollow, all the while hoping we'd get away before Juletta lost control.

When we reached the top step, a despairing howl, like the Hound of the Baskervilles, sounded behind us, only feet away. I pushed Kyran through the blackthorn archway and stumbled out after him, my heart racing.

Before us the outline of a coach appeared from out of the fog like a ghost ship. A door swung outward and Lady Faylan, her face white in the darkness of the coach, beckoned us over. "You found her," she acknowledged, barely glancing at Ilia's still form. "Quickly now. We'll take her to the castle."

"My cottage is closer," I said as I helped Kyran lift Ilia into the coach. I had no intention of going to Daarke Castle right now, not after hearing the name of Juletta's lover. "We should take her there."

Lady Faylan's left eyebrow twitched angrily. "That's not for you to decide."

"Lorelle's right, Lady Faylan," Kyran interrupted. "It's where Ilia will feel most comfortable, and after this experience, she's going to need all the nurturing we can provide."

Lady Faylan lowered her head slightly in deference, a gesture I don't think came naturally to her. "Whatever you wish, Count Van der Daarke." Her eyes on him were respectful, but there was an element of pique in them that made me curious. She seemed divided in her feelings about Kyran, a man she'd supposedly never met.

Knowing what I did about her now—that her sister was a Desolate, and that the title of lady wasn't hers to exploit—I had to wonder who she truly was. She had lied to the villagers, and had undoubtedly been the one to make us believe Desolates didn't exist. She'd also told us she'd search the other side of the village, yet here she was at Haunted Hollow, likely guessing her sister had taken Ilia. Finding us here must have been a bit of a shock, though, competent leader that she was, she hadn't shown it.

We arrived at my cottage to find Avice standing outside, damp from the heavy fog and looking full of the furies. Kyran carried Ilia past her and into my cottage, which I know I'd locked. Whatever Kyran was, he could make doors unlock and open before him, and he could calm a person with a touch, as he had with Ilia in the Hollow. He'd been evasive about his powers, but I had to think he knew more and could do more than he was letting on.

"Where were you?" Avice sputtered as I passed her. "I was only a little bit late!"

I held up a finger and turned to Lady Faylan. "You can call off the search. I'll attend to Ilia and let you know how she fares."

She drew herself up. "You're in no position to be telling me what to do, Lorelle Gragan."

"I'm sorry, your Ladyship," I apologized, even though I wasn't sorry in the least. "But time is of the essence. It's best we keep people informed, don't you think? For their safety. That Desolate did something to Ilia, and I need to see if I can undo it. Unless you know a way…"

She stared at me, her face half-shadowed inside the coach. I couldn't read her expression, which no doubt was vexed. "Like you, I didn't even know Desolates were real." *Liar.* "But also like you, I should've known better than to believe that."

"You'll tell the others?"

"Of course. I'll return here when I've finished informing the villagers of the danger. I won't ring the bell, as I'd like to avoid a panic." And avoid inciting the villagers to go after Juletta with pitchforks, no doubt.

"Why don't I send a report?"

"All right," she conceded after a moment's pause. "But I expect to hear a *full* report, and soon."

"Absolutely," I replied, planning to tell her nothing. Nothing of importance, anyway.

She gave me a gracious nod and I returned it, then she tapped the roof and the coach lurched forward.

When she was out of earshot, Avice turned on me. I thought she'd ask me about what had happened to Ilia, but I should've known better. "Who was that man?"

"Oh, Avice," I sighed. "Can't you give it a rest for two seconds?"

Her mouth puckered in annoyance. "No, I can't *give it a rest*, Lorelle. It's my curse." For a moment, she looked like she meant it. Maybe she did. "So?"

"That was Count Kyran Van der Daarke, and he's Ilia's uncle."

"That man is Ilia's uncle? You said you weren't sure if you found him attractive."

"That's what I said, and I meant it."

She regarded me as though quite sure I'd lost my mind. "Then you, my girl, either need spectacles or your head checked."

"Are you coming in or not?"

She smiled at me. "Is this your way of saying you're sorry?"

"I don't have anything to be sorry for, but yes."

She threw back her head and laughed, exposing her beautiful throat. Inwardly I felt something pierce me, like a thorn in the heart. Avice was truly irresistible.

I didn't stand a chance.

I shook myself. What was I talking about? Stand a chance with who? Kyran? Ridiculous. He wasn't interested in me, would never be interested in me, and even if he was, he'd soon find someone else. It's what men did when it came to yours truly. Avice was wrong about me. I was never the one with the high standards, so either I had a bad habit of picking the wrong sort of guy, or all men were the wrong sort of guy.

I'm pretty sure it's the latter.

Even if Kyran did like me, it didn't matter. He was a high-born, and I wanted no part of him and his kind. Besides, I'd survived this long without a man, and been quite successful at it, too. I should be proud of myself.

So why did I feel so empty inside?

"Come on, Avice," I said to my beautiful friend. "It's time you met the Count."

Chapter Twenty-Four

When I stepped inside the cottage I found Kyran kneeling on the hearth stirring up the fire and Ilia draped along the chaise, still as a corpse.

"Is she all right?" I asked him as he threw a log onto the coals. She didn't look all right, and truthfully, I had no idea how to make her all right.

Kyran glanced over his shoulder and spotted Avice. After giving her a brief nod, he turned his focus on me. "We'll have to wait and see."

"What can I do?" I asked and Avice cleared her throat. I turned toward her, heavy with defeat. "Oh, yes. Kyran, this is Avice Montrose, my friend."

Avice stepped forward and dipped a low curtsy before Kyran, revealing far more of her bust than should be legal. The thorn that had pierced me earlier wedged itself deeper into my chest. "It's an honor, Count Van der Daarke."

Kyran rose stiffly and gave her a clipped bow. "A pleasure, Miss Montrose."

"The *pleasure* is all mine," she purred. "Or it will be, once we get to know each other better." She wrinkled her nose flirtatiously at him.

Kyran glanced at me, one eyebrow raised. "I heard about you from my cousin, Renwick, Miss Montrose."

She blushed as naturally as a blooming rose, though not from modesty. Avice didn't possess a modest bone in her body. She'd once confided that when young she'd practiced the art of blushing in front of the mirror for months until she'd conquered it. *Men like it when a woman blushes*, she told me. *Makes them feel in control, even though they aren't in control at all.*

"All good, I hope?" she asked, her blue eyes sparkling.

"Would you expect anything less?" he responded diplomatically. I wondered what Renwick could have to say about Avice when he'd spent his time pretty much ignoring her, although whatever it was might be why Kyran avoided answering her question directly. I felt the thorn give way a little.

She giggled. "You Van der Daarkes are quite charming. Must be a family trait."

Kyran's lips tightened. "I'm afraid charm is one trait I didn't inherit. I think Renwick won all of that one, while I gained all the gravitas."

"You underestimate yourself, Count."

"I know myself, Miss Montrose. There is a difference."

She frowned prettily. "Miss Montrose makes me sound like a schoolmarm. Please, call me Avice."

He looked at me and I shrugged. It wasn't up to me what he called her. Actually I preferred he didn't call her anything, so I definitely wasn't going to be of any help to him. "Avice it is." He hesitated, glanced my way again. Really…what did he want from me? "And you may call me Kyran," he said after a couple beats. Avice beamed smugly, confident she was well on her way to making a conquest.

Kyran appeared to be taking in her reaction, though Avice didn't notice. If she'd been paying attention to him instead of gloating, she'd have seen a man who was not overly pleased. What an enigma he was. Did he like her or not?

Knowing the answer wasn't going to help Ilia, I made myself useful by grabbing the llama wool blanket I'd crocheted and draping it across her still form. She shifted a little, mumbled something unintelligible, then settled.

I was staring down at her when Kyran spoke up. "The Desolate did this to her, not you."

"I know. I just feel so helpless."

Avice laid a hand on Kyran's arm. "You must be so worried."

"That I am," he answered briefly, then casually turned away, leaving her hand behind as he kneeled down to reposition the burning logs and turves of peat.

Avice went on, undeterred. "What happened to her?"

She'd directed the question at Kyran, but I was the one to answer. "You know when Ilia said she saw a Desolate at Haunted Hollow the other day? Well, she really did, and one kidnapped her from the castle this morning. Fortunately we managed to find her before it could take her heart."

Avice gave a startled gasp, and only a bit of it was theatricality. Over the years she's lured so many men and women from their partners that she had good reason to be afraid of vengeful lovers. "Please tell me you're joking."

"I wish I was." I took a deep breath. "Something happened last night and I didn't tell you about it because I didn't want to scare you."

Her eyes narrowed. Avice knew quite well I hadn't kept mum because I was concerned about her feelings. "Tell me what?"

"We were heading up to the castle when a Desolate attacked us." Avice's eyelashes fluttered and she swayed. Before she could fall, Kyran was on his feet and catching her. He lifted her into his arms and set her down in the rocking chair, where she draped her arm dramatically across her forehead.

Kyran turned to me. "Some tea might be in order." A little gleam brightened his normally serious eyes and I had the sense he was amused by Avice's dramatics. I hoped that's all it was. Most men, and a few women, too, would practically kill themselves to prove they were her hero, fetching her drinks, mopping her brow, making love to her later when she clung to them in fright.

"I think you're right," I said dryly.

While Avice milked her faint, I prepared the tea and cut up slices of rhubarb bread, warming it in a pan on the stove. Avice loved my rhubarb bread and would have to give up on her 'damsel in distress' routine when I brought it to her. She couldn't resist the stuff. Most people couldn't, probably because of a few secret ingredients I added.

Between tending to the fire and silently helping me with setting out plates and cups and saucers, Kyran kept an eye on Ilia while I kept an eye on him. I think we were both asking ourselves the dreaded question, *What if she doesn't wake up?* and not liking the answer.

It wasn't until I brought the tea over to the little table that Ilia finally revived. Sitting upright, she looked around, gasping. Setting the tray down, I hurried to her side. "It's all right," I soothed, patting her back. Seeing me, she sobbed and flung herself into my arms. Unsure what to do, I threw a wild look at Kyran, who gave me an encouraging one back as he sat down on the other side of her. Following some sort of long-buried instinct, I slowly wrapped my arms around Ilia's skinny frame and held her close, stroking her soft hair and murmuring words of comfort. It was a gesture completely outside anything I'd ever received growing up, and I found myself feeling a bit envious of her. But I didn't stop. Likely Ilia hadn't ever received any kindness as a child, either.

Avice peeked at us from beneath some curls that had fallen across her face and decided to stir herself. She couldn't stand not being the center of attention. Someone could be dying on the floor right next to her, and she'd be the one demanding everyone cater to her, citing bystander trauma.

"Where am I?" she groaned pathetically.

"You know perfectly well where you are, Avice. Give her some tea, Kyran, and a slice of rhubarb bread. That should make her feel better."

Ilia pulled away from me and sniffed. "You have more rhubarb bread?"

"I baked extra," I told her as I smoothed down her hair, which had been pushed up against her face when she'd thrown herself into my arms. "I warmed it, too. Would you like some?"

"Yes! I'm *starving*."

"That's a good sign."

"I didn't eat breakfast this morning. Wasn't exactly feeling it." She frowned and pressed a hand to her stomach. "That's the last time I drink alcohol, *ever again*," she vowed with the fervor of youth.

"Don't say that!" Avice laughed. "You'll forget all about it by tomorrow, luv. Trust me." She leaned forward. "Hand me another piece of bread, Lorelle." I handed her the plate and her dainty fingers snatched two pieces. Kyran helped himself to a slice and I took one for myself.

Eating our bread and drinking tea to the sound of the crackling fire, we all sat companionably in silence. It was surprisingly peaceful, considering what had brought us together, and I found I was enjoying myself. I felt like I was part of a family, a happy one, and it was the most comforting feeling I'd ever experienced.

When the bread and tea were gone, I wished more would magically appear so that this moment in time would go on and on. It seemed everyone felt the same, being that no one moved or spoke for several minutes. Kyran glanced at me from time to time, doing so in a way that neither Ilia nor Avice would notice. The last time he did it I found myself smiling at him and his eyes seemed to lighten as he smiled back.

After a gulp of tea gone awry, Ilia was seized by a coughing fit, breaking the mood. While she recovered and Avice continued her helpless waif routine, I cleared the little table and with Kyran's help washed up. It was a rush job that I'd likely find evidence of later, with a bit of bread glued to a plate or a tea leaf stuck inside a cup, but I was feeling restless, completely opposite to my earlier mood. The time had come to ask Ilia about what had happened.

Kyran and I worked together without words, while Avice and Ilia chatted about Ilia's new purchases from *Fawn's Fashions*. Avice promised to join her tomorrow for her fitting and I breathed a sigh of relief. Towel drying a plate, Kyran glanced over at me. "Feel like you've dodged a bullet?"

I laughed. "It's not my idea of a good time."

"Nor mine. I was hoping I'd have you there for moral support."

"Avice is very good at this sort of thing, and she'll make sure everything goes well for you. Fan and Dawn know not to cross her. She's a good source of income for them."

"Then I guess I should be grateful."

I nudged him with my elbow and even that brief contact sent a tiny shock through me. "You should be."

"But won't you have to try on your dress? Make sure it fits?"

"I will, but it likely won't be ready. Fan and Dawn will make sure yours and Ilia's outfits come first."

"That doesn't seem fair."

"Ilia ordered her dresses before me, and you're the one paying for everything. You should come first. Besides, their seamstresses are overworked and underpaid. The last thing I want to do is make demands on them."

His eyes darkened. "I didn't think of that."

Of course you didn't. The rich seldom do. But I kept those words to myself, mainly because just as I was about to speak them, it occurred to me that maybe I wasn't being entirely fair to Kyran. He was helping me with the dishes, after all, something rich people don't ordinarily do, especially those with the word Count before their name. "Avice will be thrilled anyway, whereas I'd just be cranky."

"You? Cranky?"

I threw him a dirty look. "Maybe a better word would be feisty." I draped the washcloth over the faucet handle. "It's time."

He sighed. "I suppose it is."

He hung up his towel, and we joined Ilia and Avice discussing the benefits of satin. Ilia turned to us, hands clasped together nervously. "I suppose you want to know what happened."

We both nodded. Kyran grabbed the two chairs from my dining room table and set them in front of the fire. He indicated me to sit, then sat down next to me. I caught Avice watching me as I lowered myself into my chair, her expression cool and assessing. I didn't like that look; it meant she wasn't thrilled with what she was seeing. But what was she seeing exactly? Something between Kyran and me? The idea both unnerved me and set off an explosion of heat in my stomach. *We come from two different worlds, and I'm not sure I trust him*, I reminded myself. *So Avice is just being Avice—possessive and overdramatic.*

"I don't know what time it was," Ilia began, "but it was light out when I woke up. I was really thirsty and got a drink of water from the bathroom. I felt sick and needed some fresh air so I went out onto the balcony. That's when she grabbed me."

Avice's lips parted with avid interest. "She touched you?" She shivered delicately, an action that made her breasts vibrate seductively. Avice was often shivering…with cold, in delight, in anticipation, from hunger. It took very little beyond a potential suitor's presence to elicit a shiver out of her. "How did that feel?"

Ilia looked haunted. "Like being touched by death. Her hands were so cold and her eyes…" She shuddered. "I fought her and we tumbled into my room, knocking stuff about. But then she must have done something to me because I don't remember anything until I woke up here."

I let loose a sigh of relief. Ilia had been frightened, but what happened to her could have been worse. Much, much worse. "You were lucky."

"I know." Her hand fluttered up to her heart. "How did you find me?"

"Lorelle found you," Kyran told her. "In Haunted Hollow."

"But how did you get me away from her?"

"We had our own little tussle."

"You fought a Desolate?" Ilia looked impressed.

I nodded, and the cold sensation of Juletta's fingers on my arm sharpened into pain. "She jumped on my back, but then I managed to shake her off. When I was free, I demanded she tell me why she was going after you."

"You *talked* to her!" She leaned closer, eyes wide. "What did she say?"

"She said that her lover rejected her because he was promised to another. To you."

"Me?" She looked both startled and flattered. "But how's that possible?" She grinned at the very idea. "I haven't even had a boyfriend yet!"

"I think it was someone who looked like you. From long ago. One of your ancestors, maybe. The tapestries on the wall in the Great Hall… some of the figures look like you, some like Kyran."

Her eyes lit up. "Why didn't you tell me? I want to see them!"

"I only noticed them after dinner, when you were in bed sleeping it off." I gave her an affectionate smile.

She hung her head. "I'm *never* touching alcohol again."

"What are you not telling us, Lorelle?" Avice demanded.

Damnit, Avice. Why do you always do this to me? I sighed. "She told me her lover's name." I did not want to share this part. I wasn't ready to. It was my secret, mine to keep and protect. If I shared it, bad things could happen. Someone could get hurt.

I looked around at everyone, remembering our peaceful moment when I felt like I was surrounded by family. I had to trust someone, and they deserved to know. At least Ilia and Kyran did.

My eyes met Kyran's. Sitting next to him all this time hadn't been easy. This close I could sense his every movement, and once in a while his leg would touch mine, setting off sparks between us. "Tell us who it was, Lorelle," he said. "We'll keep it quiet. Right, ladies?" He looked sternly at Avice and Ilia.

"Right," they both answered, eyes glowing with anticipation.

"You're not going to like it."

He sighed. "I imagine not, but tell me anyway."

"His name is…" I paused, knowing once I said the name it couldn't be unheard. "Well, she said her lover was Renwick Van der Daarke."

Chapter Twenty-Five

"Renwick?" Avice and Ilia exclaimed at the same time. Ilia looked pleased—it meant an out for her—while Avice definitely did *not* look pleased.

"But how's that possible?" Kyran asked.

"I have no idea. Maybe it was his ancestor who spurned her. Juletta said that her lover left Hawthorn Lane at the same time your family did."

"Juletta?" Avice echoed.

"That's the Desolate's name." I didn't feel ready to share her last one, though. I needed time to think, to decide what it could mean for my relationship with Lady Faylan.

"I knew she was there," Ilia blurted out. "I mean, I sensed her. But I couldn't help myself. I went out onto the balcony anyway. I had to see her. I had to know…"

"Know what?" I asked.

She straightened up, resolute. "My enemy."

I hid a smile at her youthful bravado. "I don't think she's truly your enemy, Ilia. She promised me she'd try to stay away from you, and in exchange I told her I'd look into what happened to her." I turned to Kyran. "Are you sure you don't know anything about this?" I wanted to ask him about the curse, but being that his family might be involved in it, sensed I needed to step carefully.

His eyes shifted away. "Not about any of that." Then about what? Before I could ask, Kyran went on, "Do you think her Renwick is our Renwick?"

"Whatever happened to Juletta occurred a hundred years ago, back when the Van der Daarkes first fled Hawthorn Lane. So unless your family can live really long lives…?" He shook his head. "Then I don't think he's the one. However, I have this feeling your cousin has been here before without telling anyone, so I'm not sure what to think."

"He's been sneaking around? That snake!" Avice growled. "We should string him up." I felt quite certain she was more mad about him not showing any interest in her than the fact that he might have been playing fast and loose with young Juletta's affections.

"I can't be certain of that. So let's just make sure we have the facts straight before we start lynching people."

A loud knock sounded on the door. "Open up, Gragan!"

"Keep your pants on, Berenea!" I yelled, then turned to Ilia. "Berenea runs the paper, and she's going to want a story. I need you to tell her what happened, from the beginning."

"Hold on!" Kyran protested. "I won't be having my niece in the paper."

"You don't have a choice. She'll end up in it whether you want her to or not, but this way Ilia will have control over the story. If you don't let her tell her version, Berenea will simply make stuff up."

"It's what she does," Avice remarked. "She can't stand holes in her narrative. But I'm an old hat at dealing with Berenea. I'll help Ilia."

"Thank you, Avice," I said. "Just don't give out Juletta's name, and leave Renwick out of this, too. We don't want to tip our hand too early." She nodded, though I'm sure she wouldn't have minded throwing him to the wolves.

"I suppose you're right," Kyran reluctantly conceded. "But the Van der Daarke name is at stake here, and it falls on me to make sure it's protected."

"Which is why Avice will be a great help. Ilia will come out of this looking like a hero, won't she, Avice?"

"Just follow my lead, luv." She gave Ilia a conspiratorial smile, which Ilia returned. She might have been frightened by her experience, but she was young enough to recover quickly, and even find the excitement in it all.

I rose and went to the door, opening it wide. "Come in, Berenea. I see you got my message."

She frowned. "Your message?"

"From Lady Faylan. When you heard what happened, I knew you'd figure out that I wanted you to come here. I want the real story told, Berenea. The villagers deserve to know the truth about the Desolate, and they need to be able to take steps to protect themselves." *Because I don't trust Lady Faylan to do the right thing in this*, I didn't add. *Not when the Desolate is her sister.*

Berenea's eyes lit up. "Oh, Gragan." She punched my shoulder. "Knew I could count on you."

"And I know I can count on you to treat Ilia Van der Daarke and her family with the respect and dignity they deserve."

"The Van der Daarkes? Here?" Berenea pushed past me, then pulled up short. She wasn't an obsequious woman, but even she was impressed by Kyran, an imposing man in all situations, but especially in such a small cottage. "I didn't know *you* were here." She looked both greedily thrilled and a little gobsmacked.

"Count Van der Daarke, this is Berenea Battle, journalist, editor, and owner of *Thorny Issues*, our local paper. Berenea…Count Van der Daarke."

He bowed to her. "Miss Battle." She bowed back, putting her whole body into it, then straightened up, her face flushed.

I stifled a laugh. Berenea Battle flustered…this was a first. "You must promise to focus only on the Desolate and Ilia's experience with it. The Van der Daarkes don't know their family history, and I'm afraid Ilia is only up to a short interview, so you must make the most of it."

She nodded fervently. "Of course, of course."

"You know Avice." I gestured toward my friend.

Berenea's lips pursed. "I do."

"Hello, Berenea!" Avice greeted her with a mischievous smile. "Lovely to see you."

"Always in the thick of things, ain't you, Montrose?"

"I can't seem to help it, Berenea. Trouble follows me about like bears to honey."

"Not the only thing that follows you about," Berenea grunted, her eyes rolling.

Poor Berenea. She and Avice had an interesting relationship. Berenea knew her readers loved hearing about Avice's latest contretemps (Avice was quite aware of that, too) and so she was often featured in the paper. But Berenea hated being beholden to anyone in any way, and Avice was no exception to that rule. What made it worse is that Berenea is one of those bears attracted to Avice's honey and it irks her something fierce. To add insult to injury, I'm quite sure Avice has never attempted to seduce Berenea, which had to be even more irksome.

"Count Van der Daarke, if you will?" I indicated the door. "I want to check the dam and see what state it's in. I'm not sure lifting the sluice gate will be enough to hold back the water."

Berenea grew alert. "Think a flood's a'coming, Gragan?"

"I don't know. With all this rain, it's certainly possible."

"That'd mean your cellar gets soaked and the Fiersen's wheel gets destroyed."

I didn't add that my entire cottage could be destroyed, as well. "Yes, it would, unfortunately."

She reached for her pipe excitedly, then stopped herself. "That's big news."

"And you're getting it straight from the source," I reminded her.

Her finger touched the side of her nose, then flicked my way. "Message received, Gragan."

"I certainly hope so." I turned to Kyran. "Count Van der Daarke?"

He looked at Ilia and Avice, then at Berenea, who had already settled herself in his abandoned chair by the fire. "Are you sure?"

"Quite."

He joined me reluctantly. "Miss Battle."

She gave him a two-fingered salute. "Count. A real pleasure." Then she turned to Ilia, pulling out her notepad and quill. "Start at the beginning, would you, lass? And don't leave anything out."

Kyran joined me reluctantly and we went outside. The fog had lifted, but the sky remained overcast. For the moment our little world was holding the rain at bay, and I was grateful even if it was only a brief respite. Any more rain and I'd be able to grow mushrooms from my own ears.

Kyran followed me out to the dam and soon we were standing side by side on the bridge, watching the water roar through the opening. "If we get any more rain, you could be in trouble."

"I know. But there's not much more I can do."

"Then why'd you bring me out here?"

I turned to look up at him. "Because I wanted to talk to you about something without Ilia and Avice hearing."

I thought he'd be upset—more bad news coming his way—but he only looked intrigued, and a little *flattered*? "Go on."

"How do you know Lady Faylan?"

He didn't seem surprised by the question. "My father often mentioned the name Faylan during his rants about Hawthorn Lane. It was something about them supposedly not properly doing their job protecting the villagers from harm."

"Well, that first day we met Renwick, he recognized her and conveniently disappeared before she got too close. And then, when he saw her in *Fawn's Fashions*, he looked like he'd seen a ghost."

"So you think he could've been the same Renwick who betrayed Juletta?"

"I don't know. It might only mean he's been to Hawthorn Lane before. How well did you know him before coming here?"

"Not at all. Ilia had met him, but I don't think she knew much about him. Melaina, my sister, knew him best."

"Did she tell you he was your cousin?"

"No, he did. But like I told you, I can sense his blood connection, so he's being honest about that."

"Which brings me to my next question. Exactly how much do you know about your fey?"

He rubbed at a tiny rug of moss growing on the bridge. "Not much, but what I do know is from what Melaina showed me. When we were young, we still sort of got along, united in our hatred of our parents. It was after one of their more vicious fights…Melaina had discovered the ability in herself and wanted to share with me what she could do. More likely, she wanted to frighten me. What she didn't figure on is that I realized that if she could do it, I probably could, too."

"So you *can* do magic."

His eyes grew dark. "I wouldn't go that far. The best way to describe what I do is that I can make things happen by thinking about them. It's a rough sort of ability, and one I haven't practiced in years. Really, it was more something I did when I was young."

He shifted uncomfortably, obviously unused to sharing things about himself. He was also leaving something out of his little story. I wasn't sure what, but I let it go for the moment. "How did you come to know about this place?"

"My parents were often arguing, even after they split. They fought about everything—money, going out, friends, a book—and sometimes about Hawthorn Lane. My mother wanted to come here, but my dad always refused. Said we couldn't, that it wasn't allowed."

I wondered if maybe it had to do with the curse Juletta had mentioned. Maybe the Van der Daarkes had cursed the Faylan family for failing to do their duty, driving the Faylans to banish the Van der Daarkes. It would explain Kyran's father's anger toward them, and maybe how Juletta had come to be a Desolate.

"One day," Kyran went on in a flat voice, "while I was home from school for holiday I asked my mother about it. When she got over being mad at me for eavesdropping, she told me what she knew. Hawthorn Lane was for people who are different, *magical*. It was a safe place, she explained, and I thought she looked sad about that. She went on to say that my father's family had come from here, but she had not, though he was no better than her." He shook his head, his brow furrowed. "The whole time she was talking I had this feeling she wasn't supposed to be telling me any of this. She had this defiant look on her face, and I figured my father must have forbidden her to speak about it. For all I know she'd had this same conversation with Melaina already. I wouldn't put it past her. My mother hated my father very much." He pulled off a piece of moss and flung it into the water where it was swept away like a magic carpet.

"You must have been curious."

He shrugged. "I was at first. The next time I was home I asked my mother to tell me more about being fey and Hawthorn Lane, but she pretended she didn't know what I was talking about. Like I was mad."

"Ouch."

"That's the kind of thing she did. It took a long time for me to realize that *she* was the mad one, not me. I think her relationship with my father made her go mad."

"What did he do to her?"

"He was very good at being mean." He scraped his knuckles against the railing and I decided not to venture any further down that road.

"So you knew of Hawthorn Lane," I pieced together the facts, "but Renwick was the one who knew how to get here."

"I think maybe Melaina told him. She said something once to me about going to the Fernie Brae, just like that place Lady Faylan mentioned at the shop this morning. So either Melaina told Renwick about it or he already knew."

"His family and yours must have gone their separate ways after leaving Hawthorn Lane."

"We must have, since I had no idea he existed."

"I didn't see his likeness on the tapestries, but that could simply mean his relations weren't important enough to be included."

He grimaced. "With my family, that's quite possible."

"So why did you come here, Kyran?"

He gripped the railing of the bridge, his knuckles turning white. "I needed to get away."

"Renwick mentioned something about you being threatened."

He sighed angrily. "Of course he did. He doesn't exactly keep secrets, my cousin. Not mine, anyway."

"So he was telling the truth?"

"Things were happening back there, in the…"

"The Alterworld?"

"Yes. The Alterworld."

"What kind of things?" I pushed when he didn't continue. This is what he was holding back, and as I sensed it was important to figuring out the mystery surrounding his family, I wasn't about to relent.

"Strange things. Accidents." He turned toward me. "Look. This isn't something I want getting around, but several weeks ago, I started feeling like someone was following me. Then a month ago someone nearly ran me over with a car. I dismissed it as an accident until I was shot at a week later, two different times, the second time the following day. The first time I could tell myself it was a car backfiring. The second time, after numerous shots, I couldn't fool myself any longer."

My stomach churned. "You think someone was trying to *kill* you? But why?"

"I'm not so naïve to imagine I've never made an enemy. The business world thrives on rivalries. But I've never done anything underhanded to anyone, so I'm not sure who would hate me so much they wanted me dead."

"So you decided to get away."

"When my sister died under suspicious circumstances, I knew I had to. Poison would be my guess. Her death was quick and the coroner diagnosed a heart attack, but she was only thirty-six and relatively healthy."

"So you think someone was targeting your whole family?"

"I do."

"And now Ilia is being chased by a Desolate who claims a Van der Daarke betrayed her... Coincidence?"

"If so, it's a strange one. What's the connection?"

Other than your cousin Renwick? "I don't know, especially when so much time has passed."

His eyes roamed the nearby forest. "You think we're in danger here?"

"You could be. Hawthorn Lane may be a sanctuary, but it can't protect you against everything." I stared at the white water racing downstream. "There is one thing we can do."

"What's that?"

"Tell Ilia she's fey. If she learns a little magic, she'd be better able to protect herself."

"You can train us?" He sounded excited at the idea and I glanced over at him, oddly disappointed that I had to say no.

"Not me. I have a feeling you're mage fey. That means you're a wizard and Ilia would be a witch. No," I went on reluctantly, "Avice is better suited to teach you sorcery." I clutched the railing tight, knowing what this would mean. Hour upon hour together, private lessons, testing out love spells. A shudder went through me.

"You're cold," Kyran said in a quiet voice.

"I think someone just walked over my grave."

Someone by the name of Avice.

And she wasn't walking, she was dancing with glee.

Chapter Twenty-Six

Kyran and I poked around the dam for the next half hour, which was oddly entertaining as we let the falling water pummel our hands, skipped stones in the pool, and talked about our unexpected shared enthusiasm for pop rocks. In the end we decided there was really nothing more to be done for the dam. Kyran mentioned using sandbags, and while I thought it a good idea, sand wasn't exactly plentiful in Hawthorn Lane. We had loads of dark soil, rocks galore, and peat that covered miles on the moor, but sand wasn't a readily available commodity. I couldn't ask anyone to use magic to whip it up, either, fearing they'd question why I couldn't do it myself. Re-routing the water was a possibility, but as overheard from numerous fey, magic can't fix everything, especially if it involves an element—earth, air, water, and fire—all of which are notoriously tricky to handle. I wasn't giving up, though. If someone could make Fan and Dawn look like ice models, it stood to reason that conjuring up sand should be doable.

We were quiet as we headed back to the cottage, the ground squishy beneath our feet. I was silent because I knew Avice would be taking over the Van der Daarkes as soon as she could get her horny little hands on them. Kyran…well, I didn't know why he was so quiet, though maybe he sensed my inner seething and decided, wisely, not to get involved.

I wasn't sure why I was so angry, though maybe I'd come to see Ilia as *mine*. A wee bit on the possessive side, I know, but I liked the little imp and hated seeing her turn into another Avice. Avice has a habit of picking up and encouraging wannabes, and one Avice was enough, thank you very much.

When we reached the cottage, Kyran held the door open for me. Avice and Ilia had made more tea and were talking excitedly when we came in. Berenea was nowhere to be seen.

"Did she get her story?" I asked as I pulled off my cloak and hung it on a hook near the door.

Avice beamed at me. "By the time we were done I thought she was going to experience the big 'O' right in front of us. Naughty girl." She saw my face. "Don't worry, Lorelle. I guided the interview, as I always do, and made Ilia look like both an angel and a fierce heroine."

Ilia laughed. "She did, and I liked it."

Kyran and I took our chairs by the fire and I was glad for its warmth on my back. I was shivering, and not entirely from the cold. "Your uncle has something to tell you, Ilia," I said slowly as I poured Kyran a cup of tea. When I handed it to him, our fingertips touched, igniting a sensuous shock that nearly made me drop his teacup into his lap. "It's something I wish I'd pointed out to you earlier," I went on a bit unsteadily, "but you've had to deal with so much already, I didn't want to overwhelm you." I turned to Kyran, indicating it was his turn to talk.

"You do understand, Ilia, about our family?" he began stiffly, then cleared his throat. "That there's something different about us?"

"Other than that we're stinking rich and own a castle?"

He allowed himself a small smile. Ilia, it seemed, was growing on him, too. "Other than that."

"Well, I know we have ancestors who lived here, and that this place is for mythical, I mean, fey creatures, and…" She stopped, her eyes wide. "I'm fey, aren't I?" He nodded, watching her carefully. But he needn't have worried; she was ecstatic. "I can't believe it! I thought maybe it was possible since we once lived here, but I wasn't sure because nobody said anything and I can't just ask about something like that!" She clasped her hands together. "What kind are we? I'd love to be a faerie. I'd wear beautiful dresses all the time and flutter about granting wishes!"

"You're thinking of the human version of faeries," I told her. "Here in Hawthorn Lane they're a bit different, though they do like beautiful dresses, I'll give you that. In addition to being vain and nitpicky, they don't like humans, or what they call humdrumans. They think they're stupid and a blight on this planet."

She blinked uncertainly. "You mean, they're humanists?"

I laughed. "Not quite. I'm not sure what you'd call faeries who hate humans. Feyists? They're not all that big on other fey, either, so I think the word could fit."

"Well, I think that's silly. Tiffany's a human, and I like her very much. And I won't stop liking her just because I'm a *faerie*." She added a little flourish to the word that would have made the faeries proud.

"But maybe you aren't a faerie, after all," I said. "Maybe you're a witch."

She tilted her head to one side. "I guess I wouldn't mind that, either. Hey!" She brightened. "Couldn't I use my powers to fight the Desolate?"

"Well, that's why I wish I'd told you earlier, so you could protect yourself. Avice is a witch"—Avice gave her a lazy wink, and I thought she'd probably added a little *Lightning* to her tea—"and if she's up to it, she could teach you both a few things."

Avice sat up faster than you could say the word *sproing*. "You know

I'm always up for a good time, Lorelle!" She laughed charmingly. "I mean, I'm always up for helping others." She placed a soft hand on her bosom. "Helping others is my raison d'être."

I barely refrained from throwing my teacup at her. "What do you think?" I asked Ilia in as calm a voice as I could muster.

"I think that would be brilliant!"

"We'd pay you, of course," Kyran added, his expression a bit more reserved. Actually, if his knitted brow was any indication of his feelings about the idea, he wasn't all that keen on it. I wanted to believe his reaction was because of Avice, but it was more likely that he didn't want the world to know he wasn't very skilled at magic. It had to hurt his Van der Daarke pride something awful to admit he wasn't perfect at everything one could possibly do on this planet.

"Pay me?" Avice looked delighted. "I don't think I could..." she demurred.

"I insist," he said quickly. "I'd hate to take advantage of you."

"What makes you think I don't like being taken advantage of?" By the end of the sentence Avice's voice had grown quite husky.

"I can't imagine you allowing anything so trite to happen to you."

Her lips parted seductively. "How perceptive you are."

"So it's a deal?"

Avice didn't try to dissemble any longer. "It's a deal." She stuck out her hand and they shook on it. I watched them both closely, but neither one reacted to the contact. Avice looked her typical smug self, and Kyran appeared satisfied when he met my curious gaze.

I quickly looked away. Once again Avice had gotten her way, and I had lost out on the chance to make friends of my own. They'd soon become her slaves, and I would become a distant memory, if remembered at all.

"I'm a witch!" Ilia sighed happily and hugged herself, her skinny elbows sticking out. "I can't believe it."

"We should start your lessons at once!" Avice stood abruptly and swayed a little, clutching at Kyran's shoulder.

He reached out and righted her. "I cannot start today, I'm afraid, but I can accompany you both into the village. I left Rogue there and must fetch him before he chews through his reins." He looked at me. "What do you think we should do about Renwick?"

I was a little surprised that he wanted my opinion. "Just be careful around him. I don't sense he's a big threat, but I do think he's up to something."

"I'll keep an eye on him."

"You'll watch out for Ilia when she's with you?" I said to Avice as she headed for the door. "You know how you can be." A bit of a low blow, I suppose, but Avice wasn't known for her maternal instincts, and I was mad.

"Better than you," she huffed. "While under your supervision Ilia was attacked by a Desolate, got hit on by her good-for-nothing cousin, and drank too much, causing her to miss her appointment for her fittings!" Of the three, Avice was obviously most put out by the last bit. To her, missing a fitting was akin to missing your child's funeral. She had a warped sense of what was important.

"Be nice, Avice," Ilia gently scolded her. "Lorelle has been very kind to me."

I blinked back tears. "Thank you, Ilia. I enjoyed our time together, and I'll miss you."

"Oh, we'll see each other again, silly! Of course we will."

"Of course," I said around a lump in my throat, bending over to clean up their teacups. "Now go on, all of you." I shooed at them with my head as I stood with the tray in my hands. "With all the goings-on, I've been putting off my work, and I've gotten behind."

Kyran stood and took the tray from me. "We'll help you clean up first, Lorelle."

"No!" I pulled in a deep breath. "I mean, I'll be fine."

"Oh, leave her be!" Avice cried, her hand on the door handle. "Lorelle likes being alone, don't you?"

"I just, I just have so much to do." Trembling, I turned my back on them and started filling the sink with hot water. What was wrong with me? I'd known them for two days, not two years!

Kyran set the tray beside me. "We shall leave you, then," he said, his tone formal.

"Yes," I replied without looking at him. "Thank you for getting the tray," I added.

"Goodbye, Lorelle!" Ilia gave me a hug from behind, which I now luxuriated in, where before I would have shook her off. She was like the sister I'd always wanted or the daughter I might never have. It was quite frightening how close I'd grown to her in such a short time. How weak I was becoming! "Next time you see me, I'll be a practicing witch!"

"My coach is waiting and the horses are growing restless, Ilia," Avice spoke up. "We should go."

I patted Ilia on the arm, not turning around. "You're going to make a great witch."

"I hope so." Ilia let go of me and I heard her skipping away, young and innocent as a child heading out to recess.

The door opened and I listened as Ilia and Avice's voices faded away. When a few moments passed and I didn't hear the door close, I turned around, nearly jumping out of my skin. Kyran hadn't left yet and I found him still standing in the doorway, his eyes roaming over the cottage as though memorizing it.

When his eyes met mine, the look in them was so intense I grew lightheaded. I sensed he was memorizing me, too. Then, with a brief nod, he was gone and I was left alone.

Chapter Twenty-Seven

For the next week, an uneasy quiet settled over the village. Berenea's article on Ilia's experience with the Desolate had frightened the villagers into staying indoors, frequenting only the closest shops, cafés, and pubs. Avice had made sure to portray Juletta in the worst light, so to the inhabitants of Hawthorn Lane Juletta held no name beyond monster. But that was probably just as well. I didn't want people to know who she was until we solved this mystery, as the person who'd done this to her, if still alive, might want to make her disappear. Berenea's earlier interview with me didn't make the issue, other than that she got everyone's names spelled correctly, and I was grateful. The less I appeared in the paper, the better.

It didn't help the village mood any that the skies remained overcast, and the clouds hung low and menacing, nearly on the verge of bursting open like an overripe plum. Snow was still melting up on the mountain, so the water level in the brook didn't drop. I checked the dam every day, but nothing changed. I knew I should look into making sandbags, but I kept finding other things to do. I seemed to have taken a fateful view of the flooding, of everything, actually.

My life returned to its old routine—collecting delectables, baking, concocting potions, and selling and bartering my goods in the village. Everyone thought I was brave to venture out. It wasn't long, though, before their awe turned to suspicion. *What does Lorelle Gragan know,* they whispered to each other, *that allows her to wander about freely while the rest of us hide inside?*

After sensing their mood change I made sure to keep my transactions short, and even started pretending I was as scared as everyone else, but I had to make a living somehow, didn't I? My act helped somewhat, but the suspicion remained. Actually, the villagers have always been a little suspicious of me. As Berenea had pointed out, there was something different about me, and if she sensed it, surely they did, too.

Luckily I didn't have to spend too much time in the village, devoting myself to clearing the outdoor herb and flower gardens of dead plants, mucking out the chicken coop, and picking up fallen limbs. I spent time trimming branches on the peach, apple, and cherry trees and removing the witches' brooms from the blueberry bushes for later use. I also inventoried my canned goods, scrubbed the cottage from top to bottom, and aired out my rugs. All this work kept me at home and cut down on my chances of seeing Avice and any of the Van der Daarkes, or Lady Faylan. I was supposed to update her on what I knew, but I didn't want to seek her out. Nevertheless, she'd eventually come to me, and the suspense was setting me on edge.

Adding to my dark mood, I felt certain Ilia and Avice were becoming fast friends, and I felt left out and painfully alone. I could have gone to them, joined them—I knew this—but something held me back. I wasn't one of them, and besides that, participating in their training sessions would give me away. Sooner or later one of them would ask me to show what I could do and I would no longer be able to hide my embarrassing lack of fey.

So I stayed away and my misery grew.

As I worked on my elixirs, a number of questions kept running through my mind. With each repetition I came no closer to an answer, but wracking my brains helped distract me a bit from my loneliness, and to be frank, from my jealousy. I kept picturing Avice and Kyran together, their naked limbs entwined just like when I had caught Dallen and Eudrea going at it, and my whole body burned with humiliation. I had to think about something else or go mad, and the questions helped ease my tension a little.

The biggest mystery involved Juletta. I tried to work out what could have happened to her, but as the villagers were staying indoors and keeping to themselves, I didn't have access to their gossip like I usually would. I was hopelessly stuck, though my mind kept returning to the curse she had mentioned. What was it exactly, and who had cast it?

After a few days of mulling it over, I came to the disturbing conclusion that maybe Juletta had cast the spell herself. Spurned by Renwick, she could have cursed the Van der Daarke family all those years ago, making them flee Hawthorn Lane, and thus inciting their longstanding anger toward the Faylan family. Then, when her beloved never came back and made amends to her, her heartbreak changed her into a monster. When the family at last returned, she sought revenge on her lover by going after Ilia, the girl she thought he'd married. Being that her sense of time was messed up, the mistaken identity made sense.

But if my theory was true, it meant we couldn't trust Juletta, not if she was still bent on vengeance. I had told her Ilia couldn't be the one who'd wronged her, but she might not have believed me, or still thought Ilia could serve in her ancestor's place. Juletta might even have told me she wouldn't hurt Ilia simply to put me off my guard.

And it had worked.

With that worrisome thought in mind, I sent a note to Kyran via Josepha, who'd stopped by for a tisane, warning him to stay alert and briefly explaining why. While I was terribly worried about Ilia, I had a sneaking suspicion this wasn't the entire reason I was reaching out to Kyran. For some strange reason, I wanted to see him. But I also wanted to avoid him. If I met him and he looked besotted, then I'd know for sure Avice had won him over, and I just wasn't ready to have another one of her conquests shoved in my face.

Josepha remained mum on the affairs at the castle, and while I admired his loyalty, it also annoyed me. He did, however, expound at great length about Ilia's beauty and graciousness and the lovely way she wore her hair. Tiring of his effusions I soon sent him off, but not before handing him his tisane, the note, and a pot of clover honey cream.

He looked sheepish when he took the pot from me. "I didn't earn this, Lorelle," he said, and tried to hand it back.

"Just take it, Josepha. You can give it to Ilia."

His eyes brightened. "I will!" He rode off to deliver my message and the honey cream to Ilia. The tisane was for him. The lovesick fool wasn't sleeping well. *I wonder why…*

To my surprise, Kyran showed up the next day, and his knock shook the entire cottage, the reverberations vibrating in the hollow of my chest as I listened. "Lorelle?" he called, sounding his usual lordly self. "Are you there?"

I was, of course, but I stayed quiet as I ducked low behind the chaise. I'd started putting a chair under the door handle to keep out unwanted visitors and was glad for its presence. Some time soon I was going to have to come up with a permanent system if I wanted to keep the fey from entering my cottage whenever the hell they felt like it.

"I got your note," he persisted, and I realized I wasn't fooling him. "I warned Ilia and she's taking the threat seriously. Her lessons are progressing, though I think the two of them spend more time talking about fashions than magic. I went for my fitting, but it was challenging without you there. The Ravenna sisters are very persistent."

I stifled an amused snort. Persistent? They made Sisyphus look like a slacker.

"I've been busy with the castle, so I haven't gone to any lessons." My head popped up. Did that mean Avice hadn't had her way with him? "I suppose I should, but maybe one day when I've all my wits about me. I've been watching Renwick, but he's been out a lot and has made no further overtures toward Ilia. In fact, he seems to be avoiding her." A few seconds passed. "Well, I guess you're not here. But if you were, I'd hope that you were well."

More time passed and eventually I crept into the conservatory from where I could see around to the front door through a gap in the thick foliage. Kyran was gone, and I felt both relieved and wretched. My hands clenched into frustrated fists. What was wrong with me? I wasn't even sure I trusted him, and what's more, he was rich, condescending, and entitled. In short, he was exactly the sort of person I despised.

So why did I want to see him so badly my chest ached?

Whatever the reason, it was a feeling I was going to have to suppress. Count Kyran Van der Daarke and Miss Lorelle Gragan came from two very disparate worlds, not just in terms of social standing, but also in terms of fey. In Hawthorn Lane, where pedigree rules, these two differences cleaved a divide between us greater than the Grand Canyon.

He visited twice more, and both times I was at home, though for all I knew he could have come while I was out gathering in Fell Forest. I had the feeling he hadn't, though. It was like he knew when I was home and came only then. Both times, he arrived on horseback, and both times he spent a few minutes updating me on what was going on in his life and in Ilia's. He told me that Renwick vacillated between working diligently and sneaking off to the village, or at least that's where he told Kyran he'd been when he returned to the castle. I wondered where Renwick was actually going on his little excursions, and judging by Kyran's tone when he spoke of him, he was wondering, too.

The castle, he reported, was nearly restored to its former glory—here pride deepened his voice—and he would soon be free to pursue other interests. He placed a special emphasis on *other interests*, and I had to believe he meant making magic with Avice. I winced. What a telling and painful Freudian slip that had been.

Kyran made one last visit, but this time, he didn't knock. Hands covered in bone dust, I watched with curiosity as he slid an envelope through the crack beneath my door. Afterwards, hands aloft, I ran to the conservatory and watched him ride away, his new cloak flapping in the wind like a bird of prey. When he was gone, I wiped my hands on my work apron and hurried over to the door.

The envelope was pale gray and made from heavy card stock, with a black etching of Daarke Castle on it, and I knew immediately that Ilia had drawn it. Wanting to keep the envelope, I breathed hot air along the seal and slowly worked it open. I pulled out a single sheet of paper, thick and luxurious, and set the envelope aside. As I read, my heart began to pound with excitement and dread…

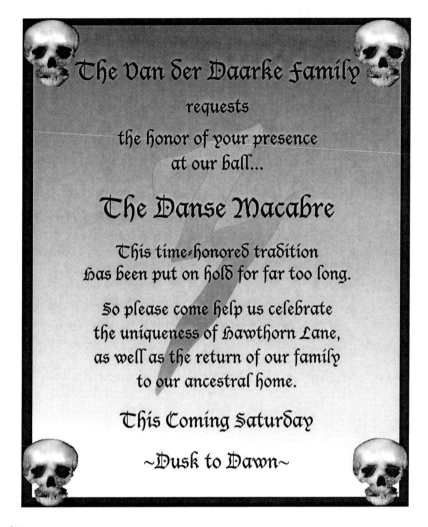

Please come was scrawled at the bottom.

I stood for several long minutes, reading and re-reading the invitation. With each new perusal waves of hot and cold swept over me. I couldn't go. I wanted to, desperately, if only out of sheer curiosity, but I couldn't. It wasn't right. I didn't belong there. Add to that the temptation of libations while mingling with fey and my risk of being discovered increased ten-fold. All it would take is one slip, one poorly chosen word, and I'd be found out.

But stars above, I wanted to go! I thought longingly of my new dress, still waiting at *Fawn's*. It would be perfect for the ball, and I still had a stunning mask I'd used when I'd agreed to be Poe's raven for a play a few years back. The black and green would look amazing together.

But going was out of the question.

Flinging the invitation onto my cluttered table, I returned to work, my hands shaking and my mind in a fog.

For days afterward, Kyran didn't come to the cottage, likely preparing for the ball. I had a feeling Avice had come up with the idea. She'd been wanting a ball in Hawthorn Lane for as long as I'd known her, but of the houses that had ballrooms, Lady Faylan was too private and the Iverich family too cheap to give one. Their excuse was the constantly ongoing construction at their estate, and while the changes and additions seemed a never-ending exercise (rumor had it that Coriana Iverich was perpetually dissatisfied with everything), you'd think they could find one space in their monstrosity to hold a dance.

They would attend the ball, though, no doubt about that. The Iverich family was rich, but while high-born, they held no title, so Coriana Iverich would love to hitch her daughter, Enchanté, to Kyran Van der Daarke. At last she'd have the title she craved, though not the happiness, neither for her nor her daughter. She would use Enchanté as a pawn in her quest for status, whether it was what her daughter wanted or not.

Unfortunately for Coriana's plans, while Enchanté was beautifully turned out and talented in many arts, she was a bit of a mouse. Kyran, I felt quite confident in saying, wouldn't be interested in someone like that. Not enough fire for him, I'd warrant. Besides, the jury was out on the Van der Daarke's fey. If they weren't faerie, all bets were off. Coriana might be tempted to try to buy her way around the faerie law of purity, but she wouldn't succeed.

Kyran wouldn't be hurting for fey prospects at the ball anyway. Numerous non-faeries would be attending—Avice, Fan and Dawn Ravenna, Baroness Arie, not to mention a myriad of fey debutantes, all angling for a chance to marry a Van der Daarke. Connecting one's name to the Van der Daarke family, still respected and admired even after their inauspicious departure, would be considered a great triumph. Plus, they were new, and new is always alluring.

In attending the *Danse Macabre*, the fey would be at their best and most predatory in their hunt to snag their quarry. If I hadn't stood a chance before, being surrounded by beautiful, powerful fey, some of them with titles of their own, my chances plummeted. Not that Kyran Van der Daarke would consider being with a commoner like myself anyway.

But what did it matter? I wondered, as I went about my work, my hands red from the hot water needed for my potions, my eyes and nose running from working with dried smoke peppers. No man, fey or otherwise, would want me.

Not that I wanted, or needed, a man, I told myself, a bit wearily now, having repeated it too many times to count this last week. I had made a vow to myself after what had happened with Dallen. I wasn't going to get married. But a man of Kyran's standing would need to marry to carry on the family name; it's what his kind did.

Not, I reminded myself, *that I'm even interested in him.*

To sum up, he didn't want me, and I didn't want him.

And that's exactly how it should be.

Chapter Twenty-Eight

I should have known I wouldn't get off so easily. Two days before the big event, an irate Dawn showed up at my door.

"Let me in, Lorelle!" she shouted noisily.

I set down my mixing bowl and went to open the door. Dawn pushed past me, a garment bag draped over her arm. She wasn't dressed in her usual elaborate costume, but wore a simple shift and hair-do that looked better on her than her usual over-the-top look. She glanced around the cottage and her nose wrinkled up as though she smelled something bad, even though only yesterday I'd polished all the wood with lemon and lavender beeswax polish and today I'd baked several batches of whipped chocolate and rose petal confections.

"What are *you* doing here, Dawn?" I asked as I removed my apron.

"Slumming, apparently." She held up the bag. "I brought your dress."

"Why?"

"So you can attend the ball, you ninny!"

"But I'm not going to the ball."

Her jaw dropped and her mouth worked as though chewing cud, but no words came out. Finally she forced herself to speak. "Have you lost your mind? It's *the* event of the season. Of the *year*!" She paused. "Really, it's the biggest thing ever to happen to me."

"That's kind of sad, Dawn."

"No, it's not, you twit!" She pulled out my dress and held it up for me to admire. It looked as magnificent as I remembered, and I felt a brief tug knowing I wouldn't be wearing it any time soon. "It's just that nothing good ever happens to me."

"Which is really kind of sad," I persisted.

She shrugged. "I suppose." Her eyes darted over to me. "Renwick Van der Daarke is a perfect gentleman, don't you think? Though I've heard tell he's going to marry that drip, Ilia." She clapped a hand over her mouth. "Don't tell Fan I said that about the girl! She'll murder me."

She probably would. "I won't say a thing, Dawn."

"Oh, you wouldn't, Miss Perfect," she snipped, then stomped her foot. "Oh, bust! I can't seem to help myself sometimes. It's just that I don't think Ilia really likes him. She certainly didn't act like it when she came for her fitting the other day. He was there, you know, picking out his own wardrobe, and she kept trying to sneak away from him even though he hardly seemed to notice her." The corners of her mouth twitched upward into a satisfied smile. "Anyway, I helped him immensely, and he was perfectly lovely to *me*." She sighed. "Why can't I be the one men flock to?"

"Maybe if you stopped acting like your sister's reflection, people would see you for who you truly are and like you more." The words were out of my mouth before I could stop them. What was I thinking? I was an observer, not a commentator. Observers stay safe. Commentators, never thanked for their words of wisdom, don't.

Dawn's expression was, to put it nicely, dumbfounded. "How dare you, lame girl!"

"Am I wrong?" I asked, deciding that I'd already put my foot in it, might as well follow through.

She stamped the floor. "No, you're not!"

"So what are you going to do about it?"

Her face was stricken. "Does everyone in the village think this about me?"

"I'm afraid it seems to be the general consensus. In fact, I think a lot of people don't even know your real name. Fan always refers to you as *my little sister*, doesn't she?"

Comprehension spread over her face. "She does!" Her shoulders slumped. "But what can I do? I'm not very smart, you know. I hide it well, but there it is." I heroically refrained from rolling my eyes. "And I don't know how to do anything else, really."

This seemed to be a recurring theme for the young females of Hawthorn Lane. First Ilia, now Dawn. Sad to say, but I imagined there were a lot more like them in this archaic place.

"Maybe you could start simple…like with finding your own style."

"You think that would help?" She didn't seem convinced.

"It might help people see you as someone separate from Fan."

"I don't know. I'll have to think about it."

"Start small," I suggested.

Her eyes darted away from mine and I noticed her hands were trembling. "Maybe."

For the first time since I'd met Dawn, I actually felt sorry for her. Perhaps someday she'd break free of her sister's tyrannical rule, but for now even the thought of defiance was too much for her. Change was frightening. Rebellion, horrifying. And in the end, Fan would only try to make her sister change back.

"How much do I owe you?" I asked, reaching for the dress.

"Lucky you," she sneered, her mouth a jealous twist. "Count Van der Daarke already took care of it." She pulled the dress out of my reach. "We have to make sure it fits first. He's paying us to see that you're perfectly satisfied. Fan is thrilled with the extra money, but she doesn't like me being gone. We're overrun with orders right now and spending every spare second filling them. The Count really should've given people more time to get ready for the ball." She made a face. "Don't tell him I said that!"

"I won't, and I agree. But I guess he wanted the dance to be held on the day it's always been on…the second Saturday after Beltane."

"How do you know about that?" she asked suspiciously. "Were you alive back then?"

"No. I read that book Professor Ballylee wrote on the history of Hawthorn Lane," I replied calmly, mentally patting myself on the back for being so nice.

"You read that snoozefest? Yawn." She glanced at my bookshelves, stuffed with all my beloved books, distaste wrinkling her perfect face. "Fan says women who read are destined to live a life alone."

"Fan's wrong." Dawn didn't look convinced, and I sighed, knowing I was fighting a losing battle, especially being that I was currently proving Fan right. "Just give me the dress, and I'll try it on."

She handed it over. "It's very tight. I'm not sure you'll manage alone."

"I'll manage." No way was I letting Dawn see my undergarments, which were growing a bit shabby.

I did manage alone, though only through sheer determination. Form fitting didn't even begin to cover this dress. Though strangely enough, despite its lack of give, it was quite comfortable. I had to hand it to the Ravenna sisters. They knew their stuff.

I emerged from the bathroom and did a pirouette. Dawn clapped her hands. "Stunning. Not you particularly, Lorelle. But the dress." She kissed her fingers. "We are geniuses, aren't we?"

Considering they'd only ordered the dress, not made it, I wouldn't go that far, but I agreed anyway since Dawn had been the one to fit me. "It's certainly snug."

Dawn grabbed the garment bag and draped it over her arm. "It's perfect as it is, and I'm not changing a thing." Her lips split into a wicked smile. "Good luck getting out of it, Lorelle."

The door slammed behind her and the sound of carriage wheels followed. I looked down at my dress in dismay. How was I going to manage? Damn that Dawn. And here I'd been so nice to her. Served me right for trying to help her out.

I stood there for a few moments, fuming about my situation, when there was a knock on the door. I rushed over and swung it open. Thank my lucky stars! Dawn had just been messing with me.

"You came back—"

Oh, bust.

I gaped at Kyran and he gaped at me. "You look, you look…"

"Stuck?"

He blinked. "What?"

"I'm stuck. I won't be able to get out of this on my own. It's too tight."

His hooded eyes flickered. "You need my help getting out of your dress?"

"Nice try. I need help, but not yours. I'll have to summon Avice. She's had a lot of experience getting out of tight dresses."

Kyran's eyebrows flew up, no doubt imagining such a scenario. "Avice is in the middle of a spa treatment. I know, because Ilia is doing it with her. They both tried to get me to join them, but I bolted."

I laughed, though on the inside I felt a twinge of jealousy. "Coward."

"I accept that title. It's a small price to pay for avoiding mud masks and pixies filing my nails."

"Most people love going to spas."

"Do you?" Strange bloke, he looked genuinely interested in my answer.

"I can't afford them, though I'm quite sure I'd like the massages and the hot baths and the sauna, too." I hugged myself. It sounded so lovely right now. "I do like being warm. Rumor has it there's a hot spring beneath Savage Mountain. The dwarves found it, but won't tell anyone where it is. They're either using it for themselves—doesn't that make a pretty picture?—or getting it ready to charge money, which is more likely. I don't blame them for keeping it a secret. Someone—okay, the Iverich family—would try to take it over and the fighting would be endless." I realized I was babbling, but I couldn't help myself. Kyran wouldn't stop staring at me, the look in his eyes almost covetous.

"I think I'd like that myself. I like being warm, too. Hot, actually." He cleared his throat suddenly. "You'll be at the ball?"

I shook my head, trying to look regretful. "Dances aren't really my thing."

"What?"

"I said, dances—"

"No, I heard you, but I can't believe you won't come. Ilia has talked of nothing since the announcements went out."

"Ilia? *She* wants me to come?" *Not you?* I barely managed to keep from saying out loud.

"As do I, of course," he added smoothly. "But Ilia needs you there. Your friend Avice… Well, she's a lovely woman, I'm sure, but I don't think she's the best influence on my niece."

This only made me feel slightly better. It shouldn't, because Avice is my friend. But I felt so horribly jealous and alone at that moment that the pettiness just snuck in through the cracks. "But Avice is of high blood. I'm only a commoner."

"Only a commoner." He shook his head. "You're still hung up on that?"

"It's not a hang-up, it's the truth. Your kind sticks to its kind. That's the way it's been for centuries, both for humans and fey. *Especially* fey. Hawthorn Lane might be a sanctuary, but it's also very backwards here." My words sped up as I realized how true this was. "Don't get me wrong, I love chivalry and wearing long dresses. I like pomp and circumstance. I love beautiful things, too. But Hawthornites haven't caught up with the Alterworld in treating people equally, and from what I remember, the Alterworld was never all that good at it, either."

"Then we should change that."

"We?" I gave a wry laugh. "Are you willing to give up your title? Your power and position here? Are you willing to sully the family name, a name that has existed, according to Professor Ballylee, for millennia? Are you willing to do all that?"

His jaw tightened. "You're overreacting. I don't think it needs to go as far as that."

"I think it's the only way."

"Well, I don't." He stood straighter, his stubbornness carving his body into tight lines.

"What makes your family so special anyway?" I demanded. "Why is your blood so much better than mine?"

"I never said it was," he huffed.

"You don't have to say it, it's clear in your every word and gesture. You think yourself superior because you're a Van der Daarke. I'll bet your father drilled that into you and your sister's heads from the moment you were born."

From the look on his face I knew I was right. "That's not fair."

"But it's true."

"My father and mother were not people I'd wish to model myself after. I've told you about them. They were very unhappy, and they took their misery out on me and my sister."

"And yet you can't escape what they taught you, can you?" I said sadly. "You can't help but be a product of their beliefs."

"I don't know what you want from me, Lorelle." His tone was weary. "I want to do right by this village. I want to fit in. It's the first time in my life where I felt like I belonged somewhere. What's so wrong with that?"

"Nothing. I think it's lovely what you're doing." I meant it. "But you're still a Van der Daarke, and here that means you're the one at the top, and you can't change that. A person can't suddenly become something they're not."

"Is that so?" Judging by the amused light in his eyes, he found this humorous. "All right then, how about over time? Why does change have to happen all at once anyway? I prefer evolution to revolution. Far fewer deaths."

"Oh, stars above! There's a reason why we have revolutions…because sometimes people refuse to understand anything but force." I was being a bit hypocritical now, as I'd just advised Dawn to start small in rebelling against her sister. But the point needed to be made.

His hooded eyes sparkled even more. "So you're staging a revolution, is that what this is?" The way he put it made me sound like a petulant child.

"I guess so," I replied coolly.

"Sounds like a strange cause to take a stand on."

"Equality? I think it's a very good cause." And would serve to hide the real reason I couldn't go to the ball.

"But I invited everyone in the village. How can I be more egalitarian than that?"

"Everyone?" Well, crap.

He leaned closer and smiled, knowing he'd won. "Everyone." He paused a second before delivering the killing blow. "So if you don't go, you'd be the only one, and that's a rather superior position to take, isn't it?"

Well, that was below the belt. "Maybe I'm busy that day," I huffed. "Did you ever think of that?"

"Doing what?"

"Some people have to make a living, you know."

"Many people here have to make a living and yet they managed to clear their busy schedules to come and welcome my family to Hawthorn Lane."

"They're doing it for the free food and a chance to gawp!"

"Now, now," he chided. "That isn't very charitable, is it?"

My response was to step back and slam the door in his face. As I stood there fuming, I could hear his laughter for what seemed like an agonizingly long time.

And I was still stuck in my stupid dress.

Chapter Twenty-Nine

I'm not sure how I managed to wiggle myself out of my gown without ripping it in half, but I did, eventually. Afterwards, I hung the dress in the wardrobe in my loft, out of sight, but unfortunately not out of mind.

I'm still not going, I told myself resolutely as I ground fungi into powder, using my mortar and pestle with ferocious intensity. Kyran could make of it what he would, but I wouldn't be pressured into attending a ball I had absolutely no interest in attending.

Small lie.

Okay, *big* lie.

My problem, and I very well knew it, was that I really, really wanted to go…even after Kyran's verbal smackdown. Plain and simple, I was lonely, and I was tired of feeling left out. Dawn was right. It would be the most interesting thing to happen to this place in a long time, and I was going to miss it for a reason I was no longer sure I agreed with.

I spent the next day moping around, struggling to settle down to anything worthwhile and productive. To avoid dwelling on my worries, I started to prepare the garden for spring planting only to find myself leaning on the hoe, staring off into the distance, the roar of the brook and my traitorous thoughts distracting me from my work. Luckily I'd already done a lot of spring prep—weeding, raking, starting seedlings in my conservatory, planting the peas—or I'd be getting behind. The growing season waits for no one.

I put concocting elixirs on hold for the simple fact that I couldn't trust myself to concentrate. Getting a potion wrong could mean someone's death, and I certainly didn't want to be responsible for that. Not unless I meant it, anyway.

I visited the cellar numerous times via a trapdoor in my floor, checking and re-checking the foundation for leaks. The walls were damp and the floor moist, but so far, no major problems had arisen. I had called on the Fiersens last week to get an estimate on the work that needed to be done and Doolin Fiersen had given me a fair quote. Unfortunately, he couldn't start work until after the ball. Apparently Kyran had hired the whole family to help out with the preparations. Which made me wonder who would be serving the food and drinks if everyone had been invited as guests. I smiled wickedly. There was no way Kyran could wiggle out of that…he had to have people to serve, which meant not everyone would be treated equally.

Oh, if only I was going so I could rub that in his face!

The morning of the ball brought a slight change in weather. Overnight the fog had lifted somewhat, only to reveal towering clouds, darkened to the color of slate, lurking overhead. The wind was gusty, tossing about dead leaves and howling through the labyrinthine streets of the village like the cries of the recently dead. It seemed more like a fall day than a spring one, except for the smell. The air, perfumed by the musky scent of budding hawthorn flowers, was springy, carrying with it a touch of the wild and expectant.

As I walked into the village to pick up more bottles and vials, I was surprised to see how busy it was. The villagers bustled to and fro, from one shop to another, all preparing for the celebration to beat all celebrations. Once again I felt a misgiving over my decision. What, after all, would it harm for me to go?

Only my pride, which is all I have, that's what, I told myself sharply. Straightening my shoulders, I marched down Vildrey Boulevard, past the statue of our elfin hero, Arius, toward *Crystalline Vessels*, determined to make my purchase, then flee home to hide.

I received numerous nods and greetings, all oddly buoyant in this crotchety place, and I was rather glad for them. A respite from the petty bickering and spiteful dramas was what we all needed, and this ball might mark a new beginning for the villagers of Hawthorn Lane.

Except I wasn't to be a part of it.

Silly fool, I cursed myself, then entered the perilously stocked store, filled with an assortment of beautiful and unusual crystal bottles in all shapes, sizes, and colors, and stacked and shoved into nooks and crannies that looked ready to overflow at any minute. I made my selections quickly, as today most people weren't looking for what I sought. They were focused solely on this evening's event. Atlene, the store proprietor and designer, chatted with me as she wrapped my purchases, obviously thrilled to be going to the ball. She was closing at noon, I learned, so she could get ready for the festivities. I listened to her talk with only half an ear—conversations with Atlene were rather circuitous. I often felt like she was taking me for a walk around the lake, when in fact the destination was only a few feet from where we'd started. Most days I enjoyed the journey, but today I had too much on my mind.

"See you there, Lorelle!" Atlene cried with enthusiasm as I turned to go. Grateful she hadn't noticed my inattention, or been offended by it, anyway, I gave her a wave and left the shop in a hurry.

Only to run right into Ilia.

"There you are!" she cried.

"Here I am," I said, catching her.

Her happy smile at seeing me flipped into a frown. "Where have you been, Lorelle? I thought you'd come visit me at the castle. I sent tons of messages. Didn't you get any? I wanted to get away and come visit you, but Avice…" She grimaced. "Well, she's rather hard to break away from."

"Messages? I didn't get any messages."

Another grimace. "Oh, damn that bird! I purchased a raven from Mr. Wicklow at *Wicklow's Bric-a-Brac* only to find out afterward that he's not exactly trustworthy. He told me the bird was well-trained, but it won't do anything I ask! When I complained to the old turd he said I was probably doing something wrong. I told Avice and she said I should've gone through her, but I wanted to do something for myself for once, and I screwed it up!"

I laughed. "First off, Geordie Wicklow is very good at tricking people. When I first came here, he got me not once, but twice, so I'm a bigger fool by far. Your 'raven' is probably a crow, which is why it won't listen. Crows are very smart and will do what they want, when they want. The trick is to use lots of blatant flattery. It'll turn around soon enough. Try training it to food, then only give it treats after it's done its job."

Her eyes widened appreciatively and she threw her arms around me. "Oh, I missed you, Lorelle!"

It was the most gratifying thing I'd heard in a long time. Before the Van der Daarkes had arrived, I'd been starting to wonder, in a morbidly self-pitying sort of way, if anyone would miss me if I went away, or died.

"I missed you, too, Ilia. I wanted to come see you, but I thought you'd be busy with lessons. I know Avice is quite demanding, especially when she has a new friend."

Ilia nodded enthusiastically. "Boy, is she! The thing is, I'm not really sure I've learned any magic from her. We always get distracted, talking about fashion and boys and food. She has a lot of visitors, too. We get interrupted like twenty times an hour! At first it was exciting, all that coming and going, but now I think I'd rather spend more time at home helping Uncle Kyran. She's hard to say no to, though." She frowned, but despite her frustration, I noticed she had gained some weight over the past two weeks and was looking quite pretty.

"Avice is very hard to say no to," I agreed.

"I was wondering if you could talk to her about maybe spending less time with me? Though it will have to be in a way that flatters her, won't it? I've learned that much. You could do it at the ball. Aren't you excited about it? I'm so excited I can hardly see straight!"

"I'll talk to Avice, but not at the ball. I'm not going."

The excitement in Ilia's eyes faded away. "What?" She glanced frantically about. "But why not? I don't understand. Uncle Kyran has been in such a great mood, asking me if I thought you'd like this or that."

A delicious, and traitorous, warmth spread through me. "He has?"

"Oh, yes, and it's growing tedious." Her eyes widened. "No offense! You're not tedious, but when someone does something over and over, well, it gets old. Like Avice and her visitors. They're all alike and she doesn't seem to see it." She paused. "Well, maybe she does since she likes you so much and you're different. You don't kiss up to her like those others. The Damnay twins are the *worst*."

"Probably because they're new to town. They don't know any better."

"Well, I'm new, and I know better." Her nose wrinkled. "But wait… you've gotten me off track." Damn, she'd noticed. "You have to come, Lorelle! I need you there."

"Look, Ilia. I understand you're worried about the ball. It's your first big event here in Hawthorn Lane, but you'll be fine."

"I won't be because you won't be there," she said mulishly. "I'll be thinking about you all night."

"No, you won't. Not when you're getting asked to dance by all the young men. Probably some women, too."

She dimpled prettily. "Do you think?"

"I do. You've grown prettier since I last saw you."

"Really? I'm eating more. I think that's helping, like you said it would." She frowned. "Wait. You're doing it again."

I smiled. "You know when your mother told you that you weren't bright? Well, she was wrong."

"I don't know about that, but you're doing it *again* and I'm not falling for it." She pushed out her chin. "If you don't go to the ball, Lorelle, then I won't go."

Oh, balls. "Don't be daft. Your uncle needs you there. You're the hostess."

She crossed her arms stubbornly. "I don't care." A gust of wind battered us, ruffling our clothes and hair. Ilia's eyes flicked toward the Hollow and she shuddered, her face growing pale.

I followed her gaze. "What is it, Ilia?"

"I keep dreaming about her, Lorelle. I keep thinking she's going to find me."

"Truly?"

She swung back to look at me, her arms dropping to her sides. "I'm not making this up to get you to come to the ball, Lorelle. I promise on my mother's grave." She crossed her chest. "Every night I dream of her and every morning I wake up in a cold sweat. But this morning, the dream ended differently. Usually I wake up right before she can catch me. But this time, I don't get away. I wasn't fast enough, and I couldn't do any magic because I couldn't remember any of it—though there wasn't much to remember."

Damnit Avice. Self-involved, as usual. If Ilia was telling the truth, and judging by the sweat beading over her top lip, she was, then she was in trouble. Fey sense these things. I'd heard enough stories to know that. But while sometimes the second sight helped the seer, sometimes it didn't.

"Have you told your uncle?"

She shook her head. "He's been so busy. I didn't want to bother him. Besides, they're only dreams. Aren't they?" Her look was pleading.

I grabbed her hands and held them tight. "I've learned to listen to my dreams, Ilia. If you feel that the Desolate is coming, then you should be on the lookout. You must be careful." I looked around, suddenly realizing something. "In fact, you shouldn't be alone right now."

"It happens at the ball," she said softly.

"The ball?"

"She comes to me at the ball. I didn't want to tell you because you'd think that's why I wanted you to come. But that's not it at all. I want you to come because I like you and you make me feel safe and good and no one has ever made me feel that way."

"Oh, Ilia. I like you, too. And that's why I think you should leave Hawthorn Lane." Her eyes widened in dismay. "I told you I wouldn't say anything more about you leaving unless I thought you were in danger," I rushed to say, "but this is about as bad as it gets. You could *die*."

She straightened her shoulders. "I'm not leaving, Lorelle."

"Just until this blows over," I begged.

"It won't blow over and you know it. I have to face this head on."

"I can't stand by and watch you get hurt, Ilia."

"You won't have to. You're not going to the ball, remember?" She began to tear up, then sniffed resolutely. "You're right, you know. I must do my duty as a Van der Daarke. I shouldn't get all the benefits of being a member of this family without having to earn them. Goodbye, Lorelle." She squeezed my hands and let go, turning away.

My heart wrenched at her words, so brave and adult. "Ilia, wait!" She spun around, expression hopeful. "I'll go. I'll be there at the ball."

She burst into tears and raced toward me, throwing her arms around me and nearly knocking me off my feet. For better or worse, this girl was my responsibility. Damned if I was going to let her get hurt because of my foolish pride.

Chapter Thirty

When Ilia had calmed down, I held her away from me at arm's length. "Don't tell anyone, okay? I'm not sure how much I want to be seen, but I'll be close by, keeping an eye on you."

She sniffed. "That doesn't sound very fun."

"Well, I'm not going to the ball to have fun. I'm going to look after you."

"But I want you to have fun, Lorelle! Avice says you're too serious all the time, that you have to loosen up a bit."

Probably true, but I had my reasons. "What else did she say about me?" I couldn't resist asking.

Ilia shrugged. "That was pretty much it."

"Oh, well, that's good." I knew how merciless Avice could be, so I'm glad she hadn't aimed her barbs at me. On the other hand, it would've been nice for her to have said something along the lines of "I sure do miss Lorelle, that wonder of all wonders."

Ilia reached up and pushed back a strand of my hair. "I think she misses you."

"Really?" I tried not to look too interested. "Why do you think that?"

"Because every time Ensign announced a visitor, she perked up, all excited. But then when she saw who it was she'd look all sad, like she'd been expecting someone else."

"Maybe she was expecting your uncle."

"He did come by to fetch me a few times and she was happy to see him, but I could tell he wasn't quite who she wanted."

I felt a warm glow in my chest and was sorry I'd called Avice—if only in my head—self-involved. Even though it was true. "I'll seek her out at the ball and say hello. Will that suffice?"

"No." Ilia took on a stern, adult face. "But I guess it's the best I'm going to get out of you. I'm not giving up, though." She wagged a finger at me. "You will have some fun at the ball even if it kills me, Lorelle."

"It just might."

She frowned. "Not funny."

"I wasn't trying to be. This is serious, Ilia. I'm coming to make sure nothing bad happens to you. If I screw that up, I won't forgive myself."

She teared up again, her newly adopted adult persona dropping away. "You're the first adult in my life to ever really care about me, Lorelle. I mean, my best friend, Tiffany, cares, but it's somehow different because you're older, like you know more."

"I don't know about that, but I do know what it's like to grow up like you did. I guess that makes me more sympathetic with your plight. Now," I said brusquely, before I started getting all mushy, "how did you get here?"

She waved a careless hand at *Faer Hair*. "Renwick's inside getting a trim. He should be ready to go any time now. I know we're supposed to be careful around him, but I was so desperate for something to do, I gave in and came along for the ride. He's actually been good lately and hasn't been trying anything."

"Does your uncle know you're here?" I didn't like how she'd been left alone like this.

She looked at the ground. "Not really."

"I see." I felt a little better knowing Kyran didn't realize Ilia had snuck off and put herself in danger.

"I'll be fine, Lorelle. I feel it. And besides, Josepha drove us."

I looked around. "Where is he, then?"

"Picking up some supplies for Uncle Kyran."

"Ilia! You shouldn't be by yourself. It's too dangerous."

"But I was going mad at the castle! There's nothing to do. I wanted to help out with preparations for the ball, but the Fiersens kicked me out of the kitchen, then the ballroom, then the Great Hall, basically telling me I wasn't needed."

"They think it's beneath you," I explained. "Doing work like that."

"Beneath me? At boarding school we had to take turns scrubbing the toilets…with a toothbrush! I think I can hang a few decorations."

I laughed. "Well, look at you being all feisty!"

She joined in my laughter. "I know. It's not really like me. But I don't like being treated differently just because I'm a *Van der Daarke*. It's wrong, and kinda weird, too."

"Well, don't let your uncle hear that. He's going to think I've turned your head with my subversive ideas about equality."

"You feel the same way? Of course you do. You're an *independent* woman." She said this in the same reverent tone one would reserve for speaking of kings and queens. It was quite flattering.

"So you understand I'd look like a hypocrite if I attended something put on by the aristocracy I'm supposed to be rebelling against." I was almost starting to believe this excuse for my not going. Maybe Ilia would believe it, too. "But I guess going to one ball isn't going to turn me into one of *them*."

"Of course it won't." She giggled happily. "I'm so glad you're coming! It was my idea for the ball, you know. I saw how you looked when we found the ballroom, like you'd never seen anything so wonderful. And after you were so brave with the Desolate and saving my life *twice*, I wanted to do something special for you."

"It was your idea? I thought it was Avice's."

Ilia beamed. "Nope. All mine. I heard about the *Danse Macabre* from Josepha and realized we should have one, too. Uncle Kyran agreed, and here we are."

"Well, I think you've done a good thing for the village, and thank you for thinking of me. That means a lot. More than you know." I turned away to hide my tears. *Really, Lorelle*, I admonished myself, *Hawthorn Lane doesn't need any more liquid in it*. When I had myself under control, I said, "I'll wait out of sight until I see you and Renwick get in the carriage. When I know you're safe, I'm going home to get ready." I felt almost giddy at the thought. I was going to a ball!

For once Ilia didn't protest. "Okay. He should be here soon." She hugged herself happily. "I can't wait!" She leaned toward me and whispered, "Do you think Josepha will be there?"

"He wouldn't miss it for the world," I assured her, finally understanding why she wasn't exactly embracing the aristocratic world and its exclusive attitude. Dating the 'help' was a big no-no amongst the gentry, but having sex with them was tolerated. Hypocrites.

I squeezed Ilia's arm, then slipped around a corner and waited as she went inside the salon. It didn't take long for her to emerge with Renwick following after. He ran a hand over his new haircut, which didn't look all that different than before. Then, side by side, they strolled, for all the world to see, toward the carriage Josepha had just brought around.

For all the world to see…

Something about that seemed a bad omen to me, but I shook it off, and waited to see them safely inside the coach before hurrying home with my purchase.

⚡

I spent the rest of the day finishing up an order, grinding, mixing, and stirring like a good little brewer. It was getting late, so I cleaned up the kitchen then went to take a long, hot bath. When I was done soaking, I rubbed a mixture of bergamot and geranium oil—both protective essences—into my pliant skin, luxuriating in the heady scent as my fingers kneaded my sore muscles. I would've preferred that someone rub the oil in for me, but beggars can't be choosers. A few spritzes of sage, lavender, and lemon oil body spray, and I was ready to get dressed. Maybe getting into my gown would be easier now that I was all slicked up.

It wasn't, but I didn't mind. I wasn't in a big hurry. I certainly didn't want to arrive at the castle too early and have to be announced. I wanted to remain hidden, at least from Kyran. My pride couldn't stand witnessing his satisfaction at winning, nor did I particularly want to see him surrounded by beautiful, seductive fey. When I finished dressing, I piled my hair high, leaving a few dangling curls, then donned my crystal skull necklace and matching earrings.

Costume complete, I took a look at myself in the ancient cheval mirror tucked into the corner of my bathroom and blinked twice in surprise. I hadn't really looked at myself the first time I'd tried the dress on, being that Dawn kept telling me to hurry it up. But now…well, I had to admit I looked rather daring, the neckline of my dress cut low enough to show my breasts off to their best advantage, while still covering my birthmark. The dark green of my gown went perfectly with my creamy skin and brought out the ever-changing hue of my blue-green eyes, like an ocean in the sunlight. My seemingly altered appearance was a lovely illusion that I happily allowed myself to be taken in by.

Satisfied with my attire, I headed out into the living area and grabbed my cloak and mask. The cloak I pulled on right away, and the mask I would don just before I entered the castle. Fell Forest was not the place to pretend to be someone I wasn't. I had tried on the mask earlier to make sure everything was in working order, and only needed to fix the strap a little and straighten out the feathers before spritzing them with a light oil to bring out their sheen. I was going to be the most fetching raven ever, though the ravens might not agree.

A glance at the clock told me I still had plenty of time. But if I left now, I could set up watch outside the castle to observe all the carriages arriving and see everyone's costumes without anyone noticing me. The idea filled me with pleasure. Lately I'd been too noticeable, and it felt good to return to my normal, unobtrusive, rather sneaky, self.

When I stepped outside, the air was crackling with electricity. It was still light out and I could see dark clouds racing across the sky, so low I could lasso them if I wanted. Thunder rumbled in the distance, sounding like an army of horses galloping toward Hawthorn Lane. An occasional flash of lightning lit up the sky and the wind blew in mighty gusts, bending the trees as easily as feather grass. The rain that had been holding off seemed destined to show itself tonight, though I could only hope it would pass us by—for the sake of my cottage, as well as for the party-goers and their costumes.

To protect my hair from the wind, I pulled up my hood and made my way through the forest at a good pace. My night vision has always been excellent, and I was glad for it on this wild evening. The forest was dark and forbidding, and I felt as though I were being watched. While I usually didn't feel unwelcome here, tonight a crackle of suspense burdened the air, making me jumpy.

The feeling of danger reminded me of Juletta, and I realized with a guilty start that I hadn't been fair to her. Caught up in my own woes, I'd not only failed to figure out what had happened, I'd sort of already assumed she was the villain in the story, despite no evidence to support this theory. I pledged then and there to track down the truth, no matter the cost to myself. I could only hope I wasn't too late.

It wasn't long before I was on the trail that ran parallel with the road, and glad for it, as the way to the castle was jammed with carriages and horses. Overhead flew some of the lesser mages on linden brooms, joined by hordes of pixies and a griffin. A few of the villagers came on foot, not having the money for horse or carriage, and I sympathized with them as they scurried along, anxious to be indoors and out of this gale. The wind was mischievous tonight and plucked at them like the fingers of a demanding child. A band of young centaurs and fauns joined the procession, and I wondered how Kyran had known about them. The residents of the woods were an elusive lot.

The gentry's horses wore their own costumes, which came in a variety of colors and designs, with matching hoods, like what you'd see in a medieval jousting tournament. I recognized the Iverich family's large silver coach, their blood-red coat of arms prominent on the door. Their horses, a long, spike projecting from between their eyes, wore silver armor, and looked like warrior unicorns as they tossed their heads in protest at the constraint of their reins.

Seeing them coming, lanterns alight, voices loud with excitement, was thrilling, and I was glad I'd come. Even if I did meet up with Kyran and had to eat crow, I no longer cared. This was all so wonderful, and despite a growing feeling of uneasiness, I knew I'd remember this magical night for years to come.

I followed the procession up to the castle, then watched again as the villagers entered the lit-up building, leaving their horses for the Fiersens to attend to. It seemed to me that tonight the Fiersen family, in not being able to enjoy the festivities, was getting the short end of the stick. But knowing Doolin Fiersen, he couldn't pass up an opportunity to make money. He had a lot of mouths to feed. Kyran might have invited them to attend as guests, but employees won't say no to their new employer, especially not one of such high standing and with such deep pockets.

When the crowd trickled away, I decided now was the time to head inside. Making sure no one was around to see me, I was about to step into view when a young woman in a white dress and mask hurried across the courtyard and rushed up the steps to the castle, her heels clicking on the stone.

There was something familiar about her, but as she was wearing her mask and her hood was up, I couldn't quite pin down who it was. Donning my own mask, I followed her inside with a little bounce to my step. It was time I found Ilia and made sure she was safe. I had filled an amulet with the protective herbs of cinquefoil, sage, and fennel for her to wear, and needed to give it to her.

If Juletta did come tonight, I wanted us both to be ready for her.

Chapter Thirty-One

The Great Hall and its offshoots were filled with villagers, chatting amongst themselves while openly appraising the castle interior, and less openly, the other party-goers. I passed by a plague doctor, his bird-like mask successfully hiding his identity. He nodded to me and my raven's beak nodded back. I met Medusa, numerous fanged beasts, and Death. One young faerie modeled a spider web veil, complete with live spiders. Some of the young fey wore crowns adorned by insects, animal skulls, deadly flowers, or spikes; there were even a couple vampire and werewolf masks. I was glad to see that youthful defiance and rebellion were alive and well in Hawthorn Lane.

I was making my way toward a nearby hall, which I knew would bypass the majority of the villagers, when someone called my name. Damn. I hadn't wanted to be recognized. Fighting an urge to pick up my skirts and skedaddle, I spun around. "Yes?"

A young man stood before me, and when I didn't immediately recognize him, he took off his mask—a simple affair of black silk. "It's me. Charlton."

Well, well, well. Charlton Iverich, the oldest of the Iverich brood, and the heir apparent, had just addressed me, low-born Lorelle. This was a first. "Oh, hello, Charlton. I didn't recognize you."

His brow furrowed, as though he didn't know how to handle not being automatically known. However, I'm not sure why I should have recognized him with his mask on; I'd hardly know him with it off. Any interaction we'd had in my six years here at Hawthorn Lane had been limited to brief encounters on the street. Families like the Iveriches don't mix with common folk like me. "You're looking well."

I laughed. "What an effusive compliment, Charlton. I'm simply undone by it!" I fluttered my hand over my artificially heaving chest.

His patrician lips pursed in consternation. "I'm sorry. That was poorly done."

"Oh, no worries. You could try again, though."

His silver-colored eyes roamed about, looking everywhere but directly at me for inspiration. "You are looking *quite* well," he said at last, then paused, his expression pained. "I'm afraid I'm not adept at complimenting women, Miss Gragan."

"*Miss* Gragan? I just called you Charlton twice now, so you'll have to call me Lorelle. To do otherwise would be an insult," I added, simply for the fun of it. Charlton was an even bigger stiff than I thought.

Gripping his mask in his hands, he looked like he was trying to strangle it. "Ah, yes. Of course, *Lorelle*. My apologies."

"Is there something you needed, Charlton?" I prompted, wanting to find Ilia and get myself settled into a private nook to keep an eye on her.

"I thought that maybe I could escort you into the ballroom."

I glanced around the room, disturbed by the number of watchful eyes on us. Was this a joke? Charlton Iverich was a big catch in Hawthorn Lane, and not just for his money. Standing at six feet tall, his slender build exuded sophistication in the finely tailored tailcoat he wore, and his light brown hair was styled perfectly—not long, but not overly short, either. He looked like someone who would be a wonderful dance partner, his graceful form twirling across the floor while dancing the Phantom Waltz. He was quite good looking, too, if one could get past his serious countenance—I'm not sure I've ever seen him smile. He looked like a man who carried the weight of the world on his shoulders, and perhaps he did…the world of the Iverich family. As heir to the business, he was responsible for a lot of people, and rumor had it that his father, Wexford Iverich, was not in good health. Charlton's mother, Coriana, on the other hand, would likely live forever. That, and her excessive spending, was another burden he would have to bear.

It sounded as though I should feel sorry for Charlton Iverich, and I found I did. As everyone was watching us, and most of them obviously displeased with what they were seeing, I decided to give the poor guy a break. No doubt he was simply looking for an excuse to escape the Great Hall, which was full of eager debutantes, and I'd be doing him a kindness, short-lived though it may be, since they'd just follow.

"All right," I agreed. "Let's go."

He gave a stiff nod, as though we'd completed a business transaction, then pulled on his mask. When he held out his arm to me, I took it with a small smile. Together we made our way through the packed halls toward the ballroom. Since I knew where it was located, I did the leading, pulling us along at a fast clip. I didn't like being surrounded by so many bodies, all of which created a stifling warmth that added to my sense of unease.

We arrived at the ballroom to find the wolf doors flung open wide, allowing the enticing throb of music and the glow of bright, glittering lights to greet us. We stood for a moment on the landing, taking in the splendor all around us. Several of the diamond-patterned windows set in the dome ceiling were open, letting in a lovely breeze that cooled the air and made the candle flames flicker. Along the balcony, I took note of a spot behind a Grecian column where I might hide out after I found Ilia.

Down on the dance floor I quickly spied Dawn and Fan, their massive hair-dos giving them away. I also saw Lady Faylan, whose ramrod stance couldn't be mistaken for that of anyone else, though her ball gown appeared to be more elaborate than her usual prison-warden ensemble. Other standouts were Killew, her expansive girth spilling over the sides of an elaborate and well-cushioned chair, with Jacques near to hand. Judging by the wide eyes and gaping mouths of the villagers as they passed by the couple, this was a sight many thought they'd never see. How had Kyran convinced Killew to leave her lair?

Grizzled dwarves gripping mugs of *Agababa Ale* in their meaty fists stood around talking and laughing, pungent smoke curling up from their pipes. Flitting pixies zipped in and out amongst the dancers, while most of the faeries congregated together in one corner. Berenea hadn't bothered with a mask, but she wore a top hat in honor of the occasion. She was, of course, watching everyone closely and happily jotting down notes. I recognized Renwick from his ever-present cane; he was standing quite closely to some woman I didn't recognize. Merceen was also easy to spot, surrounded as she was by her perfumery minions. Avice stood at the edge of the dance floor, barely visible amidst her bevy of beaus, but resplendent in a white swan dress and mask. She looked to be having a good time, laughing and touching each one of them in turn. The beaus didn't look as happy, competing as they were for her attention with an air of desperation that only made them look foolish. The Damnay twins were the worst of the lot, but I knew they'd mellow out with time. The sort of energy needed to revolve around Avice's sun was too much to maintain for long. Everyone with any sense of survival learned to treat vying for Avice's attention as a marathon, not a sprint.

Couples were already dancing, though numerous others helped themselves to the buffet tables lining one entire wall. Kyran, I realized, wouldn't need anyone to serve, only to refresh the tables. The Fiersens, working in shifts, would get to enjoy some of the ball's festivities after all. In fact, there was Gemma, chatting up a fray elf. I both applauded Kyran and mildly cursed him, as he'd taken away my best argument against him. Ah, well. I wasn't in the mood to argue with him anymore. I was here, and I'd made my choice, so I might as well enjoy it. Besides, I wasn't really sure what I was trying to prove anyway. That he was gentry and I was not? That was already a given. That my view of the world was more acceptable than his? Maybe.

"Would you care to dance?" Charlton unexpectedly asked when we were halfway down the stairs.

I peered sideways at him, though it was hard to read his expression behind the mask. "You want to dance with me? I thought I was merely a decoy to help you escape all those young girls circling you like a pack of wolves." I remembered the wolf heads on the ballroom doors and smiled inwardly. A message to the single, perhaps? Or a warning? Either way, someone in the Van der Daarke family had possessed a wicked sense of humor.

Charlton's ear tips turned bright red, surprising me. I hadn't thought of Charlton Iverich, or any faerie, as a blusher. It seemed there was more depth beneath his austere exterior than I'd realized. "You noticed?"

"If it makes you feel any better, I don't think anyone caught on that escape was your intention."

"But you caught on. You're a very good observer, Lorelle."

"I was taught well, I suppose, though I'm even better at protecting what I observe."

He relaxed slightly. "That's refreshing."

"Especially in this village."

He gave a wry chuckle. "Hear, hear."

The musical ensemble, *Mad Hatter*, made up of an elf flautist, two mages, one of which played the lute and the other the bone drums, a dwarf fiddler, and a pixie singer, ended their song with a dramatic flourish and prepared to start another. The music was enticing and I found myself drawn in.

"I'd love to dance with you, Charlton."

At the edge of the dance floor, Charlton took me in his arms, and while I didn't experience the same jolt I did with Kyran, it was a nice feeling to be held by him. As I'd guessed, when the music began, Charlton was a wonderful partner, and I knew he made me look better than I was. Numerous eyes were upon us as we twirled around and around. I felt breathless and light and the music was like champagne to my ears.

After three dances, Charlton took me aside. "That was rather fun," he said, slightly breathless.

"It was," I agreed, slightly breathless myself. We had ended up by the buffet, and I found myself looking it over, wondering where to start. Seeing the elaborate spread reminded me of the ever-hungry Ilia and I guiltily remembered my mission in coming here. I found it strange that

I hadn't yet seen her or Kyran. Where were they? A surge of alarm shot through me, and my mouth went dry. What if Ilia was in trouble, and I'd missed it?

"Do you know Ilia Van der Daarke?" I asked Charlton, who was helping himself to a drink from the punchbowl. When he offered the black crystal cup of *Sinful Cider* to me, I started to shake my head, then realized I was parched.

Just one cup, I told myself firmly as I took the goblet and cautiously sipped from it. *I'll be fine with only one cup.*

He poured himself a glass. "Only by sight." From those three words, marred by a sullen edge, I guessed that his mother had urged him to make Ilia's acquaintance. If Ilia were faerie, she'd be a good social catch.

"I was wondering if you saw her anywhere. I was going to meet up with her, but I've yet to find her."

"I haven't seen her at all, actually."

"Could you look? You've got quite a few inches on me and all I can see right now are twirling bodies."

"Oh, yes. Of course. You and she are friends, I take it? I think someone mentioned that you helped her adjust to our strange little world when she first arrived."

"We are friends," I agreed. "I feel rather responsible for her now."

"Ah, I see." His expression was thoughtful. "How good of you, taking her under your wing. Give me a moment and I'll look about."

He scanned the room from left to right. "Ah, there she is." He pointed across the floor, and I felt a rush of relief. "Dancing with an elf." His brow furrowed slightly, and I could tell what he was thinking—that the niece of a Count shouldn't be dancing with a lowly wood elf, who could only be Josepha. "I see her uncle, too, and he's—" He stopped. "Well, it would appear he's making his way towards us."

I stood on my tiptoes to see. "Towards us? Are you sure? Why would he be coming this way?"

But Charlton didn't have a chance to answer, not that he would have any more idea than I did why Kyran was marching toward us like a tank with legs, narrowly avoiding the dancers whipping by him. Before I could react, Kyran was standing before us, his broad form next to Charlton making him look like a schoolboy. Kyran was yet another person here tonight who couldn't disguise himself wearing only a mask. I'd know him anywhere.

"Lorelle." He gave a short, sharp bow. He was wearing a finely woven gray and black tailcoat over a forest green waistcoat that matched the color of my dress. His mask, designed to look like a panther, was cleverly done. "You came."

"I wouldn't dare say no to you, milord." I gave him a saucy smile. He didn't return it, his expression strained. I cocked a questioning eyebrow at him. "Is something wrong?"

"That dress really does suit you. It's very, um…"

"Tight? Yes, well, I had a hell of a time getting it off after my fitting. Get another glass of cider in me, and I'm not sure how I'll manage it tonight."

Charlton choked on his drink, and as I clapped him on the back, Kyran rounded on him. "Charlton Iverich, yes?" Kyran's expression was thunderous and I started to feel a little jumpy. Was there something I was missing?

Recovered from his coughing spell, Charlton regarded him stoically. "At your service, Count Van der Daarke. Is something wrong with the Effervescence?"

Kyran looked momentarily thrown. "Effervescence? Oh. No. Everything's fine."

"Glad to hear it," Charlton replied smoothly. "Actually, I was hoping to discuss your other energy needs at a later date." Ah, the Iveriches. Always the businessmen.

"Oh? Yes, yes." Kyran nodded distractedly. "Fine. But could you excuse us for a moment? I wish to speak to Miss Gragan alone." He must have sensed that he was acting strangely, since he tried to smile after he was done talking. He didn't succeed though, still looking vexed. "Something has come up and I need her opinion."

"I hope all is well?" Charlton asked, and my estimation of him rose. He wasn't the sort to kowtow, and I respected him for it.

"Yes, yes." Kyran waved his hand. "I simply need to speak to Lorelle privately."

"As you wish." Charlton turned to me, his tone bland, "Save a dance for me, Lorelle?"

"Of course, Charlton," I replied in an equally blasé tone. When he was gone, I turned to Kyran. "What was that about?"

"Ilia told me you'd decided to come, but only to keep an eye on her, and here I find you fraternizing with an Iverich!"

My heart, which had been beating rapidly, me thinking something was wrong, sped up in protest at such a strange and unexpected attack. "Fraternizing with an Iverich? Are they the enemy?"

Kyran's hands bunched into frustrated fists and his jaw went tight. "I've heard that you like to keep to yourself and thought maybe it was shyness holding you back, even though you ridiculously kept insisting it was the difference in our status. But here you are, dancing with an Iverich, who is high-born, when you avoid me like the plague for the same reason. Explain yourself."

"Wait a second. You *heard*...?" I was incensed, and not just about being ordered to explain myself. "Have you been *gossiping* about me?"

His eyes widened in affront. "Me? Gossip? Absolutely not. One of the fitters at *Fawn's Fashions* said something about you when he was doing my fitting...just in passing."

Just in passing, my arse. "You were discussing me with Royalton, weren't you?" Royalton is a faerie who works part-time at *Fawn's Fashions*, and the only reason he does it is to earn a discount on clothes. He spends the rest of his time carousing and getting up to no good. The other faeries like to pretend he doesn't exist because he gives them a bad name. I rather like him, maybe because he's always nice to me. He can be catty, yes, but he also has a sweet side, meaning he'd lend a hand or a coin to anyone who needed help. I think it's this part of him the faeries hate so much.

"Your name came up," Kyran said vaguely. "He said you weren't what he'd call a socialite."

I narrowed my eyes at him. "Well, that's true. I typically don't like to mingle, but since you asked me so nicely, I decided to come to your ball only to be told I should be on watch duty for your niece!"

He blinked at me, looking quite sorry he'd opened his mouth in the first place. Good. "I didn't mean it that way, Lorelle. I invited you as a guest, not as a nanny."

"Well, it's what I wanted to do, anyway," I admitted reluctantly, "but I got waylaid by Charlton and went along with the charade because he was desperate."

"Desperate?"

"There are a lot of matchmaking mums here tonight, Kyran. I'm sure you've held your fair share of scintillating conversations with said mothers regarding all the charms their lovely, unattached daughters possess?"

His frown flew off, swift as a bird taking flight, to be replaced by a small smile. "I see. I thought—" He broke off, not elaborating on what he thought, holding out his hand instead. "Dance with me, Lorelle."

I stared at his outstretched palm, which was not nearly as soft as it should be for a blue blood, then met his dark eyes. "Dance with you?"

"Yes, you know. Where I hold you tightly in my arms and we spin in circles, tripping the light fantastic."

My head felt as though it was tripping the light fantastic, and I wasn't sure if it was the cider or all the blood rushing away from my brain in shock. Either way, it was a dangerous state to be in. "What about Ilia?"

"She's already dancing with someone." So he knew about Josepha and was okay with it? I wasn't sure what to make of that.

"I thought you wanted me to watch her."

"What I truly want is to dance with you, Lorelle. Stop being so dense. You know very well that's why I wanted you to come. Why do you think I hand-delivered your invitation? And pathetically scribbled, *Please come*, on it?"

"Because you're a sadist?" I managed to push out.

"Maybe. But more likely it's that I'm very selfish and when I want something I go after it. You're the only person I've ever met who's helped me forget my troubles. You made the death of my sister feel less awful. You even made me forget that my life is in danger, and with you around I feel less worried about Ilia. You're wonderfully distracting."

My heart both swelled with pleasure and melted in pity. Poor Kyran. He'd experienced a lot of bad luck lately. Not just him, but his whole family had. His sister had lost her life, he'd nearly lost his own, and Ilia had lost her mother. I wondered, could it be from the curse? I shuddered at what this might mean.

Kyran gave me a concerned look. "More footsteps treading upon your grave?"

"I'm a little chilly," I deflected his concern. "I think a dance would be just the thing to warm me up." I needed time to think, time to work through everything. Something connected all this, but I couldn't figure out what it was.

Before I could zero in on it, Kyran took my hand, sending a shock wave through me, and pulled me onto the dance floor.

If only I'd had the time to think I might have figured everything out before disaster struck. If only…

Chapter Thirty-Two

Kyran was not as smooth a dancer as Charlton, but he made me feel like we were the only two people on the floor. He held me so tightly against him that I could see nothing else, feel nothing else, but *him*. Unlike Charlton, his arms about me were anything but comforting, especially with the sparks crackling between us. Dancing with Kyran, I felt like I was walking along a precipice and one false move would send me pitching over the edge.

And yet I didn't care.

The mood in the room pulsed with pleasure. The villagers were obviously having a good time, their faces alight with bliss as they danced, as they bit into a spicy jam tart or sipped from a glass of *Sinful Cider*, as they talked and laughed with one another. This is what the villagers of Hawthorn Lane needed, a chance to come together in harmony. No one was fighting or bickering, not even Jacques and Killew. Everyone had left their troubles behind with the intention of enjoying the soirée of the century.

Well, maybe not everyone...

Between the first and second dance, I spotted Avice with Charlton, and her eyes when she saw me with Kyran widened in surprise. Just as quickly, the laughing blue turned a fiery red, and I felt quite sure she wished she could shoot flaming orbs at me. Maybe she could, being a witch and all, and I was glad when we whirled away from her. Kyran seemed to sense my anxiety, maneuvering us so that we never seemed to cross Avice's path after that.

With each pass around the floor my confidence rose. Kyran was dancing with me, and he was avoiding Avice. Even though he and I weren't meant to be together on a permanent basis, I didn't care. I would savor this moment, this night, for the rest of my life, hugging the memory to my chest like a warm, soft pillow, most especially on those nights when my loneliness hit me hardest.

During the next pause, I caught the Ravenna sisters and Merceen Arie, all watching from the sidelines, eyeing me with malice. Their anger didn't bother me, though preferably they'd find their own partners and stop shooting daggers at my eyeballs. Tonight I wanted everyone to be happy, including my enemies. *Especially* my enemies. When they had their own happiness, they'd be less likely to want to ruin mine.

With each dance, the music grew more vibrant, becoming almost frenetic as we spun around the dance floor like leaves in a wind devil. I soon forgot about Avice and the Ravenna sisters and Merceen, about Ilia and Renwick, about all my troubles, and simply reveled in the moment. Gusts of cool air swept across the ballroom, refreshingly welcome yet ominous reminders of the coming storm. The songs, played in a minor key, were darkly romantic and tragic and tantalizing all at the same time, and the beguiling notes slipped into my mind where they took root, lifting me up to the windows to dance in the breeze. Add to the haunting music the enticing sensations of Kyran's soft wool coat on my cheek, the feel of his hand low down on my back cupping a curve possessively, his warm breath on my neck as he bent to whisper something in my ear…

I didn't want it to end.

But of course it had to. The band announced a short break, and Kyran and I reluctantly stopped dancing. Our arms still firmly in place, we stared at each other in a daze, Kyran's eyes dark with an emotion I'd never thought to elicit in another person again. Yet I couldn't look away, knowing full well my eyes held that same intense longing. A covetous heat sped through my body and my mind grew dizzy with desire.

What's going on? a distant part of my mind demanded. How had I gone from deeming Kyran Van der Daarke a pretentious toff to wanting him more than anyone I'd ever wanted?

It was only when I heard a cough that I pulled my eyes from Kyran's to see that the other dancers had cleared the floor. At some point they'd made way for us to dance alone, and were now staring at us like an audience waiting for the next act to begin. No one said a word and somehow their silence was worse than their censure. My cheeks grew hot and I pulled away from Kyran.

I wanted to flee, but stopped myself when I saw Renwick step forward from the crowd. A woman followed after him, her hand on his arm possessive, her mask gone. She was very thin, and the blond highlights in her hair expertly reflected the glow from the chandeliers. Her painted nails, red as spilled blood, brought to mind eagle talons, and around her neck, and on her wrists and ears, diamonds sparkled. She wore a red dress, covered in sparkles, modern-looking and slit along one long leg. Her shoes were black stilettos, the sort that could be used as a weapon if need be. The overall effect was both beautiful and deadly.

Letting go of Renwick's arm, she came to stand directly in front of me. "You're Lorelle Gragan?" She spoke loudly, addressing not just me, but the whole room.

I nodded uncertainly, suddenly wary. "I am."

Her expression grew triumphant. "You're the one who must break the curse."

A wave of whispers rode through the crowd and up the stairs, sending a shiver along my spine. I had no doubt that anyone lingering out in the hallways would soon be here to watch the spectacle.

"What are you talking about?" I demanded angrily as I pushed up my mask. She was ruining my glorious night. The heady feeling that had vanquished the bitter loneliness growing inside me had fled. She had obliterated the romantic delirium I'd been reveling in as surely as lobbing a grenade at me.

One plucked eyebrow rose in gratification, as though I'd delivered my line perfectly. "Your blood started this…" She waved her hand around the room. "And only you have the power to end it."

"Started what? End what?" I glanced over at Kyran, whose mask dangled from one hand, but he looked as clueless as I felt. Wait, no. He didn't look clueless. He looked sick, and he was staring at the woman as though he knew her.

A stirring in the crowd up on the balcony caught my eye, and I spotted Ilia as she pushed her way toward the railing. When she saw the woman, she reared back as though struck. "It can't be!" she cried out, her voice mimicking the remorseful tolling of a funeral bell.

The woman laughed. "Oh, yes it can, darling."

"Melaina," Kyran breathed out from behind me, and when I turned to look at him, I found his face etched with grief and confusion. "It really is you."

"Hello, Brother." Melaina's whole being inflated with exultation. "I've returned from the dead."

Kyran shook his head as though to deny what he was seeing and hearing. "But how, Melaina? Why?"

"Oh, I never really was dead." She turned and motioned for Renwick to join her. He had removed his mask, and I expected him to look surprised, but he only looked distant, as though he wasn't really here with us. "Tell them, Rennie darling."

Rennie darling? So she was the one Renwick had been talking to at the border. Melaina Van der Daarke. *I'll take care of things on this side, don't you worry,* he'd said to her. *And then you can come.* And now here she was…

Renwick looked at me, his eyes flat—lost was the roguish spark I'd grown used to seeing. "We need you to end your family's curse, Lorelle."

"My *family's* curse? But they aren't—" I broke off, realizing I couldn't continue down this road or I'd give away that I wasn't fey. "They aren't from here," I ended feebly.

"Au contraire!" Melaina sang out, her eyes bright, and the thought occurred to me that she was either high or had lost her mind. Maybe both. "Go on, Rennie."

He cleared his throat. "Your great-grandmother once lived here and she cursed the village. You're the only one who can break it." He gestured at Melaina, as though making sure I knew he wasn't the one asking me to do this. "We're tired of fighting it." So he and Melaina must be lovers, meaning he'd tried to marry the daughter of the woman he was sleeping with.

Now there's talk show gold for you.

"I have no idea what you're talking about," I tried again. Which was entirely true. Even though Juletta had mentioned a curse, I knew nothing about it, and certainly nothing about a great-grandmother who'd lived here. "None of this makes any sense to me."

Melaina rolled her heavily made-up eyes. "Just my luck that the person responsible for my happiness, for the happiness of this entire village, is a half-wit."

"Hey now!" I glanced back at Kyran for support, but his stunned eyes were still on his sister and he remained mute. I turned back to her. "Maybe if you explained everything, I might be able to help you. But I can't do anything if I have no idea what you're talking about."

She closed her eyes, as though searching for patience, then opened them again. "Your great-grandmother, Elowina Gragan, cursed the Van der Daarke family and the whole village because Marekai Van der Daarke, our great-grandfather"—she indicated herself and Kyran—"wouldn't marry her."

I felt a cold shock, strong as an earthquake, buckle through me. Marekai was the name Lady Faylan had called out when she'd first met Kyran, making his existence a possibility. But to have a great-grandmother I'd never heard of? How could that be? Granted, my mother and grandmother hadn't married anyone to elicit a name change, so we might be related to this Elowina, if she truly existed. But I felt sure we hadn't come from Hawthorn Lane, and we definitely weren't magical. The only curses we could drop were of the F-bomb persuasion.

"I'm afraid you've got the wrong person," I announced, trying to sound confident.

Melaina reached out and used one long, red fingernail to slowly pull down the neckline of my gown to reveal my broken heart birthmark.

"Then how did you get that?"

Gasps went off like bombs around the room. "A curse's mark!" someone shouted over a crack of thunder.

I pushed Melaina's hand, which lingered longer than necessary, away. "It's just a birthmark. Nothing more."

Her ice blue eyes glinted dangerously. "Don't deny it, Lorelle. This birthmark is the key to solving everything. It means that you're the only one who can remove the curse that has haunted this place and our families for a century."

Kyran, who had remained silent through all this, finally spoke. "Is it true, Lorelle?"

I spun about to face him, surprised at how forbidding he looked. "I have no idea. I know nothing about this curse or how it's haunted anyone."

"It's why we fight so much," Renwick explained, sounding more animated now. "Why the people in our families can't get along with anyone for any length of time. It's why the villagers are always quarrelling. Surely you've noticed that?"

"Lots of people fight," I protested, though his words made a chilling sort of sense. "That doesn't mean I'm the cause...or the cure."

"Fix this, Gragan!" Wexford Iverich shouted from the crowd, his voice filled with authority even as he leaned on a cane for support. "You have the power to stop our misery, so do it!" His outburst ignited an uproar from the crowd, the villagers jeering and pointing at me as though I were the devil.

Unnerved, I was about to tell them the truth—that I couldn't curse anyone because I had no powers—when Lady Faylan stepped out from the crowd. I was surprised, no, *stunned*, to see that in addition to her sensual gown, she'd braided a pale blue ribbon into her brown hair and sprinkled sparkles on her eyelashes.

Sparkles.

Had the whole world gone mad?

"It's not that simple," she said, her voice strong and carrying, and the crowd quieted.

"Why not?" Melaina demanded. "She's the key. She simply has to take away the curse and we can all be happy again. Including you, Lady Faylan."

If Lady Faylan was surprised that Melaina knew her name, she didn't show it.

"But how am I to do that?" I asked, careless of what others might deduce from my question. I was weary of this back and forth argument that was getting us nowhere. Never had my little cottage seemed so appealing to me as right now. Kyran and I could slip away and meet up there. He would shut the door behind us, our eyes would meet, then we'd move toward each other, each step agonizingly slow—

"You must marry my brother, you simpleton!" Melaina spat, interrupting my fantasy.

This time the crowd really went wild, the sound rising and rising until the whole room was filled with their scandalized roar.

Chapter Thirty-Three

Not realizing what I was doing, I took a step away from Kyran, distancing myself from the man who had given me so much pleasure only minutes earlier, and which now seemed like a lifetime ago.

"You can't be serious!" I shouted at Melaina over the noise. "We can't get *married*." Not wanting to miss a word, everyone suddenly stopped talking and the room fell silent, only the sound of the wind whistling mournfully through the windows could be heard. "We're not even from the same social class," I went on, my voice shaking a little. "Your family is known and revered. Mine isn't. We don't even live here. We're from the Alterworld, and I'm quite sure we've never—"

I'd been about to say, lived here, but Lady Faylan interrupted me again. "Your great-grandmother Elowina fell in love with Marekai, Lorelle," she explained, "but his family disdained her because they thought she wasn't good enough for them. It was a view held by others, too…that such a common creature as a Gragan wasn't good enough for a Van der Daarke.

"But we all underestimated Elowina," she went on. "None of us realized that she was an Omni-Fey." A few people in the crowd screeched in fright, others bellowed like angry bulls, most just stood wide-mouthed in awe. I was one of the wide-mouthed ones. Not only was I not fey, I certainly wasn't an Omni-Fey. Omni-Feys are the rarest of creatures. When they're born, they pull powers from every fey in existence, making them the most powerful fey of all. They are both revered and feared in equal measure. Like a genetic anomaly, the phenomenon runs in families, but even then it only happens once or twice in a millennium. So even if my great-grandmother had been an Omni-Fey, the chances were astronomically against me being one, too.

"The Van der Daarkes thought she was a lowly commoner," Lady Faylan continued, "when in fact her family is more ancient and powerful than theirs by far. Unlike the Van der Daarkes, Elowina never flaunted her power, preferring to keep a low profile…until that fateful day when she made her curse."

"Explain yourself, Witch," Melaina hissed. "If Lorelle's high-born, then why can't she marry my brother and be done with it?"

High-born? Ancient and powerful? Impossible. Melaina and Lady Faylan couldn't be more wrong about my family. If they saw my mom taking a drag on her cigarette, her hair a wild, oily mess, or my Aunt

Nimair after a two-week drinking binge, they'd change their tune. But I couldn't argue that they had the wrong person because then I'd give myself away. I'd almost done it earlier, just to get them off my back, but now I realized I had to keep my mouth shut. I wanted so desperately to stay in Hawthorn Lane, now more than ever, and if the villagers found out I'd been pretending all this time they'd never trust me again.

"I was there when Elowina made the curse," Lady Faylan said, her eyes distant. "I remember what she said very clearly and will share it with you so you'll understand what we are up against." She took a deep breath and began what sounded like an incantation. "'I have loved a man dearly and was unfairly spurned. This man that I loved'"—here, Lady Faylan's face soured—"'loved me in return, but his family tore us asunder, believing I wasn't good enough for him. Until this wrong is righted, those of this world will never be at peace with another soul. Love will come hard, and all the powers I summon now will fight against unions with all their might. Misery shall be your destiny, as it will be mine. When the world senses that amends have been made, when two souls from two different worlds unite, we shall all be freed from this curse.'"

Melaina groaned. "Oh, lovely. So what exactly does that mean for us, Witch?"

Lady Faylan's expression tightened, but her voice remained calm as she explained, "It means that to remove the curse, marriage won't be enough. The two key players must first love each other deeply and unequivocally. You can't force love to happen, just as you cannot force it to end. The latter is why the curse was brought about in the first place."

Melaina looked disgusted. "So you're saying she and my brother must *love* each other, too? But how? They barely know each other, and as you said the curse will fight them at every step."

It already did fight us. Whenever Kyran and I touched, an opposing force sprung up between us, as when two magnets repel each other. And yet I didn't entirely dislike the sensation, seeing it as a challenge. I supposed I could live with it if it brought about an end to the curse.

But it wouldn't make any difference whether I could live with it or not if I didn't love Kyran deeply and unequivocally, and that I could not do when I hardly knew the man.

"There's no other way?" I asked. "Can't someone just do a countercurse?" Someone with real power, I didn't add.

Lady Faylan gave me a contemptuous look. "You think I haven't tried? The curse is too strong. I did manage to blunt the spell, so we have that to be grateful for. But I cannot break it."

"So how come you're the only one who knows about the curse?" I wondered aloud.

"After the Van der Daarkes fled, Elowina cast a blank-out spell to keep the villagers from trying to counteract her curse. I somehow managed to regain my memory, though it wasn't easy. I tried to help the others remember, too, but I didn't succeed." Lady Faylan closed her eyes, drew in a deep breath, then opened them again. "Knowledge of the curse is a burden I've carried alone for far too long."

"But why Kyran?" I persisted, not sure I believed Lady Faylan's story. Something about it didn't make sense. "Like Melaina said, I don't even really know him."

Melaina's snort was disdainful. "Because he's Marekai's descendant, you stupid girl. He not only inherited this castle, but the curse, too. In this family, you can't have the good without the bad." If Kyran was the heir, then I must be one, too. Mother and grandmother as the oldest had failed to find love, so they'd passed along the burden to me, also the oldest. But unlike Kyran and his inheritance, my being an heir hadn't come with any perks, like a castle and boatloads of money. At least if I had his money, I might be miserable, but I'd be miserable in style.

"You want to fix it so that you can be with *Rennie darling*, is that what this is all about?" I challenged Melaina. I glanced at Renwick, but he avoided my eyes, his own gaze fixed firmly on his feet. It was strange how different he was around Melaina, though I had a feeling she had that effect on people. "So why did he pretend to want to marry Ilia? What was that all about?"

Her expression grew proud. "That's where the genius of my plan begins. My parents were always fighting, you see, and lucky me, being stuck at home while Kyran, the male and heir, was sent away to school, I got to hear their mindless arguments, day after day, month after tedious month. At first I tried to block them out, but then one day I was so bored I decided to listen. I'm glad I did. I learned all sorts of things about our family, about this place and the curse. After they died, and after numerous relationships of my own had gone bad, I knew the curse was real, and I knew it had to be undone or I'd go mad like my parents." *I think the ship has already sailed on that one, sister.* "So I began to make plans. I started searching for other Van der Daarkes, and eventually I tracked down Rennie's line. As it turns out, that side of the family lived not all that far from our hometown. I invited Rennie to come stay with me and help me with my plan. It wasn't long before we became lovers."

"But aren't you related to each other?" I glanced up at Ilia, but I couldn't read her expression even though she, along with most of the other party-goers, had removed her mask. If I were to guess, I'd say she was probably in shock. Her mother was still alive, and her mother's lover had been pursuing her daughter's hand in marriage. Yikes.

Melaina gave me a patronizing look. "Barely, and besides, it's what the high-born do. Marry like to like to keep the bloodline pure and strong." She took my silence for assent, when it was anything but, and went on, "When I told Rennie everything, he completely understood, as I knew only someone of our blood would. We love each other, but we fight constantly. It was too much like my parents to be borne, so I decided to fix things once and for all. First we had to find this place, which was easier than I thought. I simply followed the pull—I'd felt it all my life without realizing what it was, and when I stopped fighting against it, it brought me to the border like a homing pigeon. Once I knew where Hawthorn Lane was, I sent Rennie in on a reconnaissance mission to learn everything he could about the village and about Lorelle."

Well, that explained his knowledge of the castle, his fear of Lady Faylan, and his ease in going about the village. It also explained how he'd known where I lived. Though it didn't explain how he'd gotten into Hawthorn Lane without setting off the breach.

"But how did you know about my part in this?"

"I tracked down your family, of course. During my parent's fights the name Gragan came up more times than I could count. My father was like a broken record." She lowered her voice. "'Elowina Gragan's the one who started this! She's the only one who can end it.' Of course, by that time she was dead," she went on in a normal tone, "so it would have to be her ancestor, wouldn't it? That's what my father decided, but he never did anything about it, never tried to fix things." This was said in disgust. "But I'm not the sort to sit back and wait for the world to come to me. I went looking and easily found you. Like Rennie, your family didn't live all that far from mine. It was as though none of us could totally escape the pull of Hawthorn Lane." She gave a bitter laugh.

"When I met your mother, she told me you'd run away—which I could well understand; that woman is repulsive." Pride made me want to defend my mother, but I quickly gave it up for a lost cause. "She said you were probably dead, but I refused to believe that and I began my search again. Then it occurred to me that with Hawthorn Lane so close by there was a chance you'd been pulled here, too. When Renwick found you here, I knew I was on the right track, that we had a chance to make my plan work. That's when I faked my death. It sounds extreme"—her eyes briefly flicked toward her brother—"but it was the only way I could get Kyran to come to Hawthorn Lane. Mother told me she'd shared a few things with him, and so I made sure he saw this place as a sanctuary. I figured if we scared him enough, he'd come here. So Rennie made a few attempts on Kyran's life, and my brother did exactly what we thought he'd do—he bolted straight for Hawthorn Lane."

"You did that, Renwick?" Kyran said in a strangled voice. "You let me think someone was trying to kill me?"

"She made me," Renwick said quietly, his face reddening.

"Oh, you wanted to do it," Melaina snapped. "You thought it'd be funny. At any rate, he got you here, Kyran, easily as herding sheep. Then he pretended to want to marry Ilia to get her to flee to Lorelle. I know my daughter, and I know she found Rennie frightening. Too manly for her, I imagine. It was the perfect way to pull Lorelle in and connect her to the family. Brilliant, hm?" She looked quite pleased with herself. "When Ilia showed a little pluck for once in her life and tried to run away, Rennie followed her and made sure she went to Lorelle's cottage. Not being the sharpest tool in the box, she went right where we wanted her to go."

"I think Ilia's very smart," I spoke up, disliking this woman immensely.

Her lips pursed. "Coming from you, that's not exactly a compliment."

Change that to hate. I *hated* this woman immensely. "So why did Renwick act like he was attracted to me?" I asked, my expression innocent. "I could see him befriending me for your plan, but why proposition me when I was supposed to be meant for Kyran?"

Sorry, Renwick, but I'm throwing you to the dog...no, make that bitch.

Melaina's nostrils flared. "He was simply playing a part, weren't you, Rennie?"

"Yes," he agreed, his eyes on me wounded. I felt a little guilty, but not much. He'd made Kyran fear for his life, he'd used Ilia, and he'd tricked me. "I was playing a part so that we could end this curse. For all of us." He looked at me meaningfully.

"See?" Melaina gestured with an outflung hand, as though trying to knock some sense into me.

"Oh, I see," I replied, my tone implying my disbelief.

Her lips parted to argue, but closed again as she gave me a thin-lipped smile. "So now that you know what role you play in all this, Lorelle, what are you going to do about it?"

"Do?"

"To end the curse, of course." It was her turn to be triumphant. "Lady Faylan said your family's high-born, so there's no impediment to your marriage to my brother, and no impediment to you ending this curse once and for all."

I felt hot and prickly inside. This was like with my mother and Dallen all over again. "I can't marry someone because you want me to. Lady Faylan said we had to be in love, and you yourself said the curse would fight it."

"Everyone here saw you two dancing together. I think we have enough evidence of love right there."

"That's not love. We've only just met each other." I turned to Kyran. "Say something or we're going to end up married!"

"You're high-born," he said in a low voice, his expression inscrutable. "Just like me."

"I'm not high-born, and I'm not *just like* you. Your sister's wrong. She's got the wrong person!"

"Melaina isn't wrong, Lorelle." Lady Faylan followed her assertion with a wry quirk of her lips. "You really are the true descendant of the woman who cursed us all."

"She *is* wrong!" I cried. But I knew my protest was in vain. Lady Faylan had no good reason to lie—my being a high-born put us on equal footing, which is the last thing she'd want.

I wanted to strike out, wanted to deny everything, but I could only clench my fists and stand there in mute disbelief. My whole life was a lie. Believing myself a fighter for the oppressed, for the poor and the lower classes, seemed ridiculous now, and all the high-minded principles I'd held so dearly had become a cruel joke on me.

I was one of *them*.

"Not in the least," Lady Faylan corrected me, seeming to relish in my discomfiture. "Now I understand why when I first saw you, I felt that I knew you. In countenance you don't greatly resemble Elowina, but now I see you have her aura. I wonder that I didn't see it before."

I turned to Kyran, looking for an ally. He reached out and touched my arm, and I nearly fainted, the shock was so strong. As the throbbing sensation pulsed through me, I could no longer deny the connection between us, and to my past. "We could end this, Lorelle."

I pulled away from him. As pressured as I felt to do the right thing, as much as I thought I desired him, I couldn't marry him simply because people wanted me to. It was the same thing that had happened to Elowina. Someone had dictated how her life should go, and look at how that had turned out.

"There's one problem, Count Van der Daarke," I said, keeping my voice cool and level. "I'm not in love with you, nor would I ever be." Several hisses issued from the crowd, along with a few cries of *Liar!*, but I ignored them, my heart beating painfully in my chest. "I was pretending to like you, so I could gather information." I gestured to the crowd. "You all know that's what I do. I'm a gatherer. It's what I do," I repeated, my voice breaking slightly as I watched the effects of my words on Kyran. He looked like I'd kicked him.

Before he could challenge my lie, a frightened scream rang out from the balcony. I looked up to see Ilia struggling in the arms of a woman dressed like an avenging angel. I knew that woman. She was the one I thought I'd recognized earlier as she entered the castle. I couldn't place her then, but I could now. It was Juletta, and she had a dagger pointed right at Ilia's heart.

Chapter Thirty-Four

"No!" I cried out, staying Juletta's hand. "Please don't!"

She looked down at me, then bared her teeth in a hiss. "I *must*. She took Renwick from me. It's because of her that I'm this monster!"

For his part, Renwick only looked confused as he watched the drama unfold, his hands rising up as though to fend off her accusations.

"No! Please listen to me," I begged her. I'd promised Ilia I would look after her, and I'd failed. I'd gotten too caught up in my own pleasure and had forgotten she was in danger. "Renwick doesn't want Ilia, and she doesn't want him."

Juletta pressed the knife harder against Ilia's chest and the girl gasped in fear. But other than that one sound, she stayed unnervingly quiet and still, her face pale and drawn. "You're lying, Lorelle. I saw them together in the village today. They looked very much in love."

For all the world to see…

Oh, hell's bells. "But didn't you hear? He doesn't love her. It was all a trick, Juletta."

"Juletta?" Lady Faylan clapped a hand to her chest. "How can this be?" It was a good acting job, as Lady Faylan knew very well that Juletta was the Desolate.

"What trick?" Juletta demanded, ignoring her sister.

"He used Ilia," I explained, rushing to get my words out. "He pretended to want to marry her so she'd run to me, and force Kyran Van der Daarke to follow after so that he and I would meet. They wanted to use us to lift the curse."

"But he didn't want to marry *me*!" she groaned.

"He did," Lady Faylan said firmly, stepping forward. "He did, Juletta. But his family made him betroth himself to his cousin. You know how the Van der Daarkes are. They rejected Elowina, Lorelle's great-grandmother, for the same reason…not good enough."

Juletta's wild eyes found mine. "You're *Elowina's* kin?"

I felt hot inside. "I don't know. That's what everyone's telling me."

"She's the one responsible for the curse on the Van der Daarkes," Juletta went on, as though I hadn't spoken.

"I guess so," I replied hesitantly.

Juletta looked pleased. "Good. They deserved it."

"Not all of them," I argued. "Ilia didn't do this to you. She's innocent of any wrongdoing. I can't say the same about Renwick, though."

"Me?" he protested, his expression hurt. "What did I do?"

Juletta glared down at him. "You swine. You promised me you'd marry me!"

He blinked at her. "But I've never seen you before in my life."

Her eyes widened. "Never? I'm the *love* of your life!"

"This is not the same man, Juletta," Lady Faylan intervened. "It was his ancestor who was going to marry you. But then his family took him away. They thought they could flee the curse, but it followed them. It follows us all."

Juletta's face went soft. "So Renwick really did love me?"

Lady Faylan gave a stiff nod. "When he came back for you, it was too late."

"He came back for me?"

"He searched for you, and when he couldn't find you, he returned to the Alterworld. This man," she pointed at Renwick, "is his ancestor. The first Renwick must have wed his parents' choice for him, after all, although I imagine it wasn't a good marriage, not with the curse."

"So he paid a price," Juletta said thoughtfully, the arm holding the dagger relaxing.

At that moment, a dark blur streaked across the floor, and Juletta's body jerked backward as though she'd been grabbed from behind. She cried out and dropped her dagger, and it hit the floor, making a hollow clatter that echoed throughout the deathly still room. Released, Ilia fell to her knees with a startled yelp. Bellowing a war-like whoop, Josepha rushed forward and swung her up into his arms. Then, with great speed, he carried her away from danger, the dark figure following after them.

The nearby spectators, emboldened now that Juletta was no longer armed, lunged at her. With angry shouts they lifted her struggling body into the air, and in her fragile white dress, she looked like a handkerchief about to be torn apart.

"Leave her be!" I called out, but they either didn't hear me, or didn't care about my opinion on the matter.

"Bring her to me," Lady Faylan commanded, and they heard *her*. The crowd dragged Juletta, kicking and screaming, down the stairs. She shrieked and cursed like a demon, but could not escape the many hands holding her fast.

I turned to Kyran for help, but he was no longer there. Stunned, I spun around, searching for him in the crowd. But I couldn't see him anywhere. I would have to deal with this on my own. It was not a new situation for me, but this time I felt the burden of my aloneness like a spike through my heart.

"What are you going to do?" I asked Lady Faylan, but she ignored me, her expressionless eyes on her struggling sister.

When the crowd reached us, they dumped Juletta at Lady Faylan's feet, then backed away. The overseer stared down at her sister, and Juletta stared back with loathing in her ferocious black eyes.

"I don't want to make this judgment, Juletta," Lady Faylan said, her voice low but steady, "however, I cannot let you walk amongst us. Either leave Hawthorn Lane or forfeit your life."

"Kill me," Juletta spat in defiance. "I don't want to live anywhere else, and I certainly don't want to live like this anymore."

"I cannot do that."

"Then someone fetch my dagger and I'll do it myself."

Lady Faylan held up her hand. "No. I will do as you ask, Juletta. As Dynast Overseer, you know it is my duty."

"Wait!" I cried. "There's got to be another way."

"If there were a cure for this blight," Lady Faylan said, her tone scathing, "I would know it." *I would have found it...*echoed in my head.

"I couldn't live with myself if we didn't try," I persisted. "Maybe together we can do something."

She shook her head. "You don't know what you're saying, Lorelle. You understand nothing."

Swallowing hard, I faced the crowd. "If you don't try to help her, I'll leave Hawthorn Lane and the curse will continue. You'll never be free of it."

"Oh no, you don't!" Melaina shouted. "Grab her, Renwick!"

"If you touch me, Renwick," I growled as I turned to face him, "I will curse you."

"Oh, Lorelle," Lady Faylan admonished grimly. "You know that isn't going to happen." I froze. She hadn't given me away, but basically had stated she was willing to if I didn't back off. "Fetch me the dagger," she ordered a nearby dwarf and he ran off, returning quickly with the deadly weapon. He handed it to her and she took it expertly in hand. "Hold her still," she ordered two of her apprentice mages. After a moment's hesitation, they dropped to the floor and grabbed Juletta's arms.

Going against Lady Faylan could mean the end of my life here in Hawthorn Lane, but what would it matter if I didn't stand up for a helpless creature about to be executed for something for which she was not responsible? I couldn't be that person, hiding behind others my whole life. Besides, I had promised Juletta I'd help her, and I'd done nothing. I had to make up for my failure, even if it meant losing everything.

As Lady Faylan raised the dagger into the air, I raced forward and shoved the mages away from Juletta, then threw myself on top of her, covering her body with my own. Her hollow eyes widened in surprise and her mouth, full of horrible fangs, dropped open.

"What are you doing, Lorelle?" she hissed at me. "You're going to get killed!"

"I'm the key to ending the curse," I whispered. "She won't kill me."

"Oh, yes, she would!"

"Okay, she probably would, but I can't sit by and watch you die."

"Get off her immediately, Lorelle!" Lady Faylan roared. "Or curse or not, I'll run you both through."

"Don't you touch her, Witch," Melaina growled. "She's the only one who can remove the curse."

"Don't you tell me what to do, Melaina Van der Daarke," Lady Faylan warned. "You are not my liege. And besides, we do not know for sure that Lorelle is the answer to the curse, do we?"

Melaina threw back her head in annoyance. "Who else could it be?"

But Lady Faylan didn't answer, only lifted the dagger higher into the air.

"I won't leave you," I told Juletta, though standing fast wasn't as easily done as said. Her sharp fangs were right by my throat and the fetid smell coming from her decaying body was growing more and more difficult to bear, the odor like a live thing crawling down my throat, threatening to cut off my air.

"I could take your heart," she rasped in my ear. "I could take it right now."

"Do your worst. I'm not leaving you." I braced myself, but she made no move.

"You have been warned, Lorelle Gragan!" Lady Faylan cried.

Holding onto Juletta with both arms, I summoned up all my concentration, all my emotion, and readied myself to roll away at the last possible second. Lady Faylan would catch us soon enough, but it was worth a try.

I strained to make out any sound of movement above us, but heard only the rush of footsteps, followed by a few angry grunts. I attempted to peer over my shoulder, but could only catch blurs of motion. I couldn't tell what was happening above me, but something strange was happening below me. Juletta, cold as a corpse, began to warm like morning air in the rising sun. Her labored breathing relaxed and the foul odor faded away.

I turned away from trying to keep an eye on Lady Faylan and spared Juletta a glance. Her rotting flesh had turned pink and whole, her eyes transformed into a bright, twinkling blue. She looked as she did in her photo a century ago—full of life, young and beautiful.

"Stop!" I yelled, then pushed myself off Juletta and onto my knees, holding up a hand to ward off any blows. "Juletta has been cured!" When nothing happened, I turned my head to see Lady Faylan held back by Renwick, her face emotionless. He had come to our rescue, assuredly for selfish reasons, but all the same we were alive because of him.

As Juletta looked herself over her eyes widened in awe. "I'm well again!"

I stood and faced Lady Faylan, my own dagger in hand, daring her to attack. The overseer easily shook off Renwick, but made no move toward me. She straightened her gown, her cool eyes on Juletta. "Even when the task is horrific, we Faylans must carry out our obligations. But I am glad another way was found."

Juletta looked up at her sister. "Father would be proud of you, Vira."

I held out my hand, not sure I could be as forgiving as Juletta. "Come. Let's get you cleaned up." Juletta nodded, and I helped her to her feet, her hand soft and warm in mine. I turned back to Lady Faylan, outwardly adopting Juletta's attitude. "Can you see that the festivities continue while I see to your sister? It seems our host is otherwise occupied, and as Dynast Overseer you are the most suitable candidate to stand in his place."

She gave me a regal nod, not looking the least bit guilty for nearly murdering us both. "Of course."

I pulled Juletta away and the crowd parted before us. When Juletta passed the villagers, their faces expressed their wonder and amazement at seeing her returned from the dead. When I passed, their expressions turned to awe and fear. I wasn't sure I liked that. But then, it was somewhat preferable to being ignored.

I quickly found a quiet room and shut the door behind us. Juletta was looking at her hands as though she'd never seen hands before. Her eyes were full of joy and I hated challenging her right now, but it had to be done.

"She was going to kill you, Juletta."

She waved this away. "Oh, she didn't really want to. I know that… she's had many opportunities over the years to make me disappear and she didn't take them. She was willing to risk keeping me around, but once others found out about me, she had to choose. I put her in that position by showing myself. Really, it's my fault."

I wasn't buying it. "Did she truly try to fix you?"

"Oh, yes. The problem was that I was angry and hurt, and I didn't want to be fixed, so I worked against her. It was my own selfishness that landed me in this position, which isn't easy to admit, I can tell you. Vira finally gave up trying to fix me and looked after me in her own way, setting me up in Haunted Hollow and starting the rumors about Desolates to keep me safe." She found a mirror over the fireplace and gazed at herself in wonder, touching her youthful face, turning her head from side to side. She caught my eye. "You were the only one who'd go in there, you know. Well, other than young ones on a dare. I watched you when you came, got to know you in a way, even though I never knew your name. Fancy you're Elowina's progeny." She studied me in the mirror. "Seeing you unafraid made me feel normal again. I think it's why I was able to fight against tearing you apart and taking your heart. Because there were many times when I wanted to."

I shivered. "I'm glad you held back."

"As you weren't the cause of my sorrow, your heart wouldn't have sufficed anyway. Though my mind was rather crazed so I wouldn't have understood the difference until it was too late." She cocked at an eyebrow at me in the mirror.

"How comforting," I drawled, and she laughed delightedly. "So what are you going to do now?"

"Stay at the family estate with my sister, of course."

I stared at her. "There are other places in the village, you know. You could stay with me."

She smiled, showing dimples. "Is that to be your new calling, Lorelle? Saving others from themselves?" She shook her head. "Thank you, but I think I'd prefer the manor. It's where I grew up, after all." And much nicer than my cottage, as I recalled.

"You think you could get along with your sister? Even though she kept your secret, I'm not entirely sure she has your best interests at heart. No pun intended."

Juletta laughed. "I agree. But that's nothing new. She's always been more interested in maintaining her image than in being my friend. But I'm a pretty strong witch, and I had to live as a monster for a century, so I think I'll be all right living with *Lady* Faylan." She raised an inquiring eyebrow. "Are you going to tell the others she's not really a lady?"

"No."

"Because you certainly have good reason to strike back at her," she went on, watching me carefully. "I wouldn't blame you."

"Oh, I'll have my revenge, Juletta. Don't you worry about that." I pretended to twist my evil moustache. "Besides, it'll be something you and I can hold over her head."

She clapped her hands and giggled. "Oh, goodie! I love having things to hold over Vira's head, and besides, I've always fancied myself a lady."

I laughed. "Your secret is safe with me."

"Brilliant. Lady Juletta has such a nice ring to it."

I went and joined her at the mirror. "You know, Juletta...I'm glad you're getting a second chance. I think you dodged a bullet with that other Renwick. His story—that his parents made him do it—sounds plausible, especially for a high-born, but I'm not sure I buy it. Not completely, anyway. He was old enough to stand up for what he wanted."

She sighed. "I think you're right. I feel a fool, letting myself practically die for him. What a waste."

"So you're giving up on men now?" I teased.

She gave me a horrified look. "Are you kidding? I adore men! I just need to find the right one. I rather fancy Hanover Iverich. He's the youngest in the family, isn't he? I've seen glimpses of him over the years. Really, men with money are so attractive, and he seems like he knows how to have fun." She waggled her eyebrows at me. "And I have a lot of fun to catch up on."

"He's capricious, Juletta, and always flitting off to the Alterworld."

She frowned. "I could make him want to stay home."

"Famous last words. But you can't change the fact that he's a faerie and you're a mage."

She sighed. "Maybe it's my burden in life...to always be attracted to men I can't have."

"Maybe, but for your sake, I hope not."

She fussed with her hair, keeping her focus on her locks. "I was wondering, Lorelle. What happened in there? How did I change back to my old self?"

Before I could respond, not that I had an answer for her, the door swung open and Lady Faylan strode in. We both spun around to face her. "Leave us, Juletta. Everyone's dying to talk to you." Juletta smiled widely, straightening her gown. "You look beautiful as always, so go on now. Enjoy your moment." Anyone would think Lady Faylan was fond of her sister, but I knew better. Judging by the glint in Juletta's eye, she did, too. This would not end here.

Before leaving, Juletta turned to me. "Thank you, Lorelle, for believing in me."

"Thank you for not taking my heart."

With a little wave and a laugh, she left us, and I turned to face the woman who had rescued me, who had given me a second chance at life, and who had turned out to be a complete fraud.

Chapter Thirty-Five

The pieces were starting to fall into place, and as soon as Juletta shut the door behind her, I made my attack. "You always knew who I was from the beginning, didn't you? That old lady in the car...that was you, wasn't it?"

Lady Faylan's smile was smug, and any satisfaction I might have felt at being right was blown away. "Rather convincing, wasn't I? Though driving that car was a challenge. I remember clutching the steering wheel so hard my knuckles ached for ages after that."

"But why did you do it, and why didn't you tell me who I was?"

She arched a coy eyebrow at me. "Why do you think?"

"You wanted power over me."

"Of course I did." Her tone was matter-of-fact. "I knew at some point someone would put the pieces together about the curse and come after you, and I wanted to keep you close." *As one does with their enemies.* "To make sure things happened the way I wanted them to happen. I gave you something fairly innocuous to do so I wouldn't have to worry you'd get into too much trouble, and I could also check in on you from time to time without arousing your suspicion. You made keeping tabs on you very easy, Lorelle." She looked annoyingly satisfied with herself, and I wanted to wipe off her patronizing expression with my fist. "When Renwick Van der Daarke came to Hawthorn Lane I felt his presence long before he arrived. Knowing who he was I let him cross, dampening the breach so no one would be alerted." That explained how he'd gotten in without the rest of us knowing. "At first I didn't let on to him that I knew he was here, sniffing around. Instead I watched him, waiting to see what he was up to, and he led me to you." Knowing Renwick had been stalking me, and I'd had no idea, sent a shiver up my spine.

But did his actions make him a bad guy? He'd claimed he'd done what he'd done because he wanted to end the curse. But was that true? Had he meant it when he'd offered me his help, or had that all been part of the scheme?

"That's when I was certain the unraveling of years of subterfuge had begun," Lady Faylan went on. "So I let him know I'd seen him, which scared him more than a little. He's very good at blending in, staying hidden; his side of the family always had that power." Which explained why I hadn't known he was stalking me. "But I saw him, and he knew I'd seen him. I made sure of that."

"So why didn't you confront him?"

Her smile was self-congratulatory, and it occurred to me who had ordered the carriage to pick up the Van der Daarkes on the night of Beltane, who had allowed the breach to be felt when they arrived…Lady Faylan. It was her way of keeping Renwick on his toes. How nervous he would have been feeling the breach for the first time, how he must have sweated knowing that someone was on to him, that he was at this person's mercy. And then Lady Faylan had let Melaina enter Hawthorn Lane without so much as a whimper to be heard. Why? To lower Renwick's guard? To keep things under her control? Probably both. Such constant maneuvering…Lady Faylan was like a predator, circling her prey, waiting for the right moment to pounce, or not to, whichever would better serve her purpose.

"I didn't confront him because while at that point I knew mostly what he was about, I didn't know the why of it. I thought all of them were in on Melaina's scheme, but I had to know if my—" She stopped herself, though I had the feeling she'd been about to say, *my Marekai*. "I had to know if Kyran was, too. But he wasn't. I see that now." So that's why she'd let Melaina enter secretly…to test Kyran, who, unless he was an incredible actor, obviously hadn't known what his sister was up to.

"Yes, it seems as though he's innocent in all this."

She regarded me steadily. "Are you in love with him?"

I laughed. "Hardly. I only just met him."

"His sister thinks you two should marry, to end the curse."

"I'm not going to marry anyone. Not right now, anyway. Besides, I don't think our being in love will remove the curse. I think it will take more than that."

Something fierce glinted in Lady Faylan's eye. "So what do you plan to do?"

"Go on as I have."

"But if you're of Omni-Fey blood, that changes things," she said with a triumphant *you can't win* look.

"Something you've known all along and neglected to tell me. Why?"

"It wasn't neglect. I wanted to protect the village from you."

"I don't believe that."

"I don't care what you believe, Lorelle, but it's true. If you're Omni-Fey and your powers had been allowed to manifest themselves, you might have done us real damage."

"I love this place," I protested. "I'd never do it harm."

"Is that so? Your great-grandmother claimed the same, and look at what she did. *Elowina*," she spoke the name with such malice I was immediately suspicious, "tried to destroy this village."

"What did she ever do to you?"

"She was a threat," she answered vaguely, "as are you. Your kind has always been. Though, actually, I don't think you're a true Omni-Fey, Lorelle. You simply don't have that spark. I took an unnecessary risk allowing you into Hawthorn Lane. I should never have brought you here."

"Which you did under false pretenses, Lady Faylan. You tricked me, and you stole from me. I wonder what everyone would think hearing that their irreproachable leader is capable of such deceit?"

"Don't you dare do anything to sully my name, Lorelle," she threatened, seemingly growing in size right before me. "Or I'll be sure to return the favor."

"Return the favor?" I echoed, refusing to cower. "What have *I* done wrong?"

Her upper lip curled into a sneer. "Wouldn't the villagers be surprised to learn that you've spent the last six years pretending to be one of them?"

I tried to swallow the lump building in my throat, knowing they'd be more than surprised. "But I am one of them."

"That doesn't change the fact that all this time you believed you weren't fey yet acted as though you were. You lied to us, just as Elowina did."

"Marekai knew the truth about her."

"Marekai was under her spell. He didn't truly love her. If it weren't for his parents, he'd have chosen—" She stopped, her lips clamping together.

But it was too late, she'd said too much. With her words, the truth of the matter suddenly clarified for me, and I wondered I hadn't seen it before. If my great-grandmother had been in love with Marekai Van der Daarke, it was also true of Lady Faylan. It explained her reaction to Kyran at *Fawn's Fashions* and her unusual outfit now. She saw her old flame in his great-grandson. She saw a second chance at love.

"Wouldn't they also be surprised to find out that you were in love with Marekai Van der Daarke?" I hit back. "That you never stopped loving him?"

She looked startled before quickly recovering, drawing her shoulders up haughtily. "Loving someone is not a crime."

"No, it's not," I replied. "But accusing someone of doing something they didn't do should be. What if the villagers found out that you were the one to curse the village, not my great-grandmother as you so cleverly implied?" I snapped my fingers. "That's why the curse was so lacking in detail, why no names were mentioned! You wanted the villagers to think it had been Elowina who'd done it, forcing her to flee Hawthorn Lane to avoid persecution. Then, over the years, you changed the story or put some kind of spell on the villagers so that eventually none of them knew the truth behind why the Van der Daarkes had left."

But something about that didn't make sense. Why had Lady Faylan wanted people to forget about the curse when she'd firmly placed the blame on someone who'd already fled and couldn't dispute her lies?

"I'd love to see you prove it," she challenged, one eyebrow cocked.

I couldn't. Not entirely, and she knew it. She need only make up some story about how if she had set up my great-grandmother to take the blame for the curse, why would she then make people forget about it? I was missing something, but I couldn't quite put my finger on what that something was.

I tried another tactic. "Around here one doesn't have to prove anything for others to think it true. Imagine how Berenea would spin this story."

Lady Faylan gave a careless shrug and I knew I was on to something. She was not careless about anything. "Do your worst, Lorelle. No one will believe you. Being of Omni-Fey stock, you're neither here nor there, and therefore without allies. You've great potential for power, and the other fey will respect that, I grant you. But no fey will accept you. Really, it would be best for all if you were to leave Hawthorn Lane."

"I've never been accepted here, Lady Faylan, something you made sure of, but I don't plan on leaving." I paused. "Wait a second...I know why you took me in. You didn't want the Van der Daarkes to find me, did you? You didn't want me to be in a position to undo the curse because you still hate the whole family. It's why you took away people's memories—in case someone figured out a way to reverse the curse. You wanted to punish Marekai and his family for their vanity and conceit."

At last, it had all come together.

Her fingers, claw-like, clutched at her chest. "No. Not anymore!" she cried, surprising me. "You don't understand. For ages, I'd been in love with Marekai, and at last I had gathered up my courage and professed my love for him. But he rejected me, saying he loved another." Her eyes blinked from the remembered pain. "I might have come to terms with it in time, but then he had to keep *talking*. He told me that even if he did love me, he couldn't be with me because I'm not gentry. Me! An upstanding member of a respected family! So I went to your great-grandmother, who'd been a friend of sorts, and told her what had happened, begged her for a potion to help me. That's when she confessed that she was the one Marekai loved. I was stunned. 'How can you be together?' I demanded. 'You're like me.' That's when Elowina shared her precious secret about her family."

Lady Faylan's jaw hardened. "I was furious. First for being rejected by the man I loved more than life itself, and then from realizing I'd lost out because the Van der Daarkes didn't see me as good enough for them. When they did the exact same thing to Juletta, it was the last straw. I went a little mad after that, I think. I locked myself in my room, and I concocted a curse. I cursed the Van der Daarkes and the Gragans, and then, sick of the ways of this village, I cursed the villagers, too. Perhaps I had it in my mind to blame Elowina, but the vague nature of the curse was simply the result of a young mage not knowing what she was doing."

Her lips trembled slightly as she recalled that time. "The next morning I woke to a very different world. Tempers flared over inconsequentials, fights broke out, relationships and marriages began to implode. There was even a suicide. Frightened by what I'd done, and afraid I'd get blamed, I pointed the finger at Elowina."

"So you did blame my great-grandmother."

She shrugged. "We were supposed to be friends. She should've known I liked Marekai, and yet she went after him. She deserved it." I kept my mouth shut, understanding that I was dealing with a very unstable mind right now. "Cursed and faced with an angry mob, her family fled. I was happy about that, thinking that I'd finally win Marekai. But then his family left Hawthorn Lane, hoping to outrun the curse. I thought they'd return, but they didn't. Months passed, and still no sign of them. I started to grow desperate, especially when Juletta began to sicken. The curse worsened the effects on her, eventually turning her into a Desolate."

Her fingers curled into fists. "I certainly hadn't counted on that happening, and I did what I could to help her. Thinking she was dead, my parents mourned her passing, and with the poisonous effects of the curse working on them, they died soon after, leaving me alone to face the horror.

"Day after day, week after week, I worked tirelessly to stop the curse, but in the end succeeded only in blunting its effects. I'd made a spell so powerful that I couldn't undo it. It's a point of pride in the witch world," she couldn't help adding with a hint of smugness. "But my efforts came too late. My sister was a monster, my parents dead, and the man I loved was gone. I searched for him, of course, but I could never find him. Years passed and I began to think bad things. I began to hate Marekai. I'd punished Elowina, but I wanted to punish him, too. I wanted to see him suffer. But he had disappeared as though never having existed, and you can't punish a ghost."

She gave a tired sigh. "The blunting I managed to do must never have reached those who left Hawthorn Lane. Not only did they still remember the curse, I think it drove them to an early death. Well, the ones who knew about it, that is. Somewhere along the way your families tried to cover it up, maybe in hopes of staying alive longer." She shook her head ruefully, as though at their foolishness. "Those of us remaining in Hawthorn Lane adapted to our new life, but we were never the same. My sister had it the worst, I suppose. Thanks to the Van der Daarkes, she was doomed to living a nightmare without even the palliative effects of repression to alleviate her suffering." She gave a bitter laugh. "How ironic this all is. Until you introduced me to Kyran I never even knew Marekai had died." She turned and met my eyes. "But things have changed, haven't they? I have a chance to make things right. I can break the curse."

"By being with Kyran Van der Daarke?" I said, feeling suddenly cold.

She stared at me. "Why not? I couldn't break the curse through magic, but I can through love. It makes so much sense." Her face relaxed for a moment, the change softening her features and returning her to the young woman she'd once been, full of love and hope. "And since Kyran and I come from two different worlds—as the curse states—I can fulfill the requirements perfectly. You, on the other hand, cannot. You're both high-born, both from the same world, Lorelle. Just like Elowina and Marekai." Her lips quivered with triumph. So this was why she'd let on that I was high-born... Well, originally she'd done it because she'd wanted me to take the blame for the curse. But now, my being high-born worked in a different way—it showed that a relationship between myself and Kyran wasn't the answer to ending the curse.

"You're not a lady, then?" I hadn't meant to use this information against her so soon, but she'd slipped up, and I was furious with all her scheming and manipulations.

Her eyes flashed warily. "What do you mean?"

"You said you and Kyran come from two different worlds, which means you aren't high-born and therefore can't be a lady. After all, it's why Marekai didn't want to be with you, isn't it?" The color rose in her cheeks, and I pressed home my advantage. "I suppose you also wouldn't want your sister to know you made the curse that drove away her lover and helped turn her into a monster. She'd probably kill you if she knew what you'd done. That's if the villagers don't get to you first when they hear you cursed them to a living hell."

Lady Faylan took a step backward. At last I'd managed to knock a heavy dent in her iron façade. She might better fit the requirements for the curse, but to be with Kyran she'd have to admit her low-born status, something she absolutely would not want to do. So we were both stuck. "So what are you going to do?"

I folded my arms. "For starters, I'm going to stop being afraid of you."

The tiny flicker of one eyelid told me I'd struck another blow. Her type of power thrived on fear. "You won't tell anyone what I've done, that I'm not high-born?" she asked after a moment.

"As long as you don't force my hand."

Her nostrils flared. "I see."

"Though the villagers might figure it out on their own."

She gave a contemptuous snort. "That will be the day. Just as long as you don't talk."

"I won't. Just as you won't let on about my pretense for all those years." She gave a reluctant nod. "So, are we clear on where we stand?"

"We are." I didn't try to get her to shake on it. I had a feeling neither of us would like the touch of each other's flesh.

"Someone still has to break this curse," she said quietly.

"Yes, and may the best fey win."

Lips pursed, she spun on her heel and marched out of the room. When she was gone, I leaned against the wall, exhausted.

Had I really just challenged a madwoman and witch, to boot, to a contest?

I think I had.

Chapter Thirty-Six

The door banged open and Avice scurried in, giving me no time to process what had just happened.

"Lorelle!" She flung her arms around me and held me tight, her bosom heaving dramatically. "I was looking for you, but my gallant boys wouldn't let me come until they saw I was all right. All that drama made me feel faint. I was rushing to your aid when they grabbed me and held me back. Naughty things!"

"Thanks for thinking of me," I said dryly, pulling away.

"Of course, luv." Her eyes scanned my face, gauging my mood. "I also came to warn you about Berenea. She's looking for you. She's interviewing Juletta right now, but you're next on her hit list. This is the story of the century, and she'll do whatever it takes to get the facts."

"Hell's bells." The last thing I wanted to do right now was explain to Berenea what had happened out there. She'd want to talk about Kyran and the curse, and she'd be itching to learn more about my great-grandmother being an Omni-Fey, something I couldn't tell her anything about. Which meant I had to think of a story to explain my lack of knowledge, and quick. "Thanks for the warning."

Avice's eyes continued to study me, almost warily. "You know, Lorelle,"—she ran a finger down my arm—"I've always wondered what your fey is. You're always so elusive about everything, so I thought this was just one more thing you were being secretive about. But we're best friends, so how come you never told me you're an *Omni-Fey*?" She looked more than a little hurt, and this time she wasn't acting. "I mean, you never even hinted at it!"

"Actually, Avice," I began, thinking fast, "I never really knew myself. My family didn't talk about our fey and we certainly didn't practice magic. I don't think I'm an actual Omni-Fey, anyway. Lady Faylan doesn't think so."

Avice's face brightened. "So that's why I've never seen you do magic. I simply thought you weren't very powerful and that's why you never did anything beyond gathering."

"Oh, well, I was kept in the dark. For the most part," I added.

"That's why you keep to yourself so much, to hide your weakness." She placed her palms on her chest. "But you still became my friend."

"Who could resist you, Avice?"

She giggled, all forgiven. Probably not forgotten, which meant I was only off the hook temporarily, but I'd take it. "I was worried when you didn't come to visit me all week."

"I thought you'd be busy with Ilia, and then, well…there were the lessons. Like I said, I'm not very knowledgeable about my powers, and I was too embarrassed to let on. I did miss you, though."

She patted my arm, her face aglow. "Of course you did, as did I you. But never mind all that. We've things to discuss. Can you believe Lady Faylan and Juletta are sisters? Do you think she knew all this time about Juletta being a Desolate? I'll bet she did," she went on, not giving me a chance to answer. "What a comeuppance for Miss High and Mighty!" She clapped her hands gleefully. "And speaking of snooties, I can't believe Renwick is with that witch, Melaina. Why, she's old enough to be his mother!"

"Hardly, Avice. She isn't all that much older than you."

"She looks it!" Avice cried, affronted. I nodded supportively, and appeased, she went on. "At any rate, it isn't right. Not after he pretended to like you to end a curse I'm not sure I even believe in. I, of course, saw through him, but you're so innocent, like a child, really, and the scoundrel took advantage of you." She reached out and stroked my cheek. "Poor Lorelle."

"Poor Lorelle, indeed," I agreed.

"And now they want to force you to marry Kyran!" She looked put out and her caresses grew a little rough.

I grabbed her hand and held it tight. "Nobody's forcing me to do anything, Avice."

"Are you sure about that? You're not like me, Lorelle. You're special and deserve the best." I squeezed her hand gratefully. "The men here aren't good enough for you, you know. They just aren't. Not even Kyran Van der Daarke! After you left the ballroom, he didn't even go after you. In fact, no one knows where he disappeared to, the coward. I'd always heard the Van der Daarke men weren't all they were made out to be, but now I know. I tried to lead him away from you, I really did. But he's a stubborn one." Which meant he hadn't gone for her like she'd wanted him to. My heart lightened a little. "Stay away from him, Lorelle," she went on earnestly. "He's trouble."

Maybe she was right, but I wasn't giving in so easily. "Shouldn't that be for me to decide?"

She pouted. "I'm only trying to look after you."

"Avice, I'm beginning to think that despite your disparaging remarks you want Kyran for yourself."

She lifted one shoulder, not meeting my eye. "Maybe. He's quite a catch, and that smoldering look he does—irresistible." She closed her eyes and made yummy sounds.

"I thought you just said he isn't good enough for me."

Her eyes flew open. "He isn't, Lorelle. Not for you! You're better somehow. I've always thought that, even before knowing you were high-born." Her eyes were wistful and I sensed she really meant what she said, and wasn't just being her usual selfish self. "You're the only person here that knows me for who I am and still puts up with me."

"Lots of people here more than put up with you, Avice."

"Oh, Lorelle. They like me because of my lovely assets, and who can blame them." She peered down at her lovely assets and an affectionate smile spread across her face. "But none of them know the true me. Only you do, and you still like me for who I am."

"Oh, Avice. I more than like you. I love you. You're my best friend."

She squealed and lunged forward, grabbing me in a hug and planting multiple kisses on my cheek. "I love you, too, Lorelle! Really and truly, not like what I tell the others. Oh, darling, I'd do anything for you!"

I smiled inwardly. "So you're saying that if I decided to be with Kyran, you wouldn't stand in my way?"

She didn't respond for a moment. "I wouldn't go that far," she finally said, her words measured. "I always say a little healthy competition won't hurt any relationship truly meant to be. This way, if the Count chooses you over me, then you'll know he really wants you."

"So picking me over you is the ultimate sign of his fidelity?"

"Naturally." She giggled, then sobered. "No matter what, Lorelle," she whispered fiercely in my ear, "we'll be friends forever, right?"

"Friends forever, Avice."

She hugged me tighter and I hugged her back, hoping fervently that our friendship really would weather such a storm.

Not that I really had to worry. If Kyran had cared about me, he wouldn't have abandoned me to his sister and Lady Faylan the way he had. I'd been right all along—he couldn't be trusted. No, we were better off going our own way, even if it meant that the curse would remain unbroken.

Chapter Thirty-Seven

As soon as Avice and I returned to the ballroom, her admiring suitors swarmed her and she left me behind to join them in a whirligig. Despite the dramatic events earlier, everyone seemed to have settled back into enjoying the ball—eating and drinking, dancing and gossiping, basically acting like they thought they'd never get to do any of it again. It wasn't a bad way to spend the evening.

I relished watching the festivities from the balcony, nibbling on the Octavian caviar and savory crackers I'd helped myself to while keeping an eye out for Berenea. A half hour passed this way when I finally spotted Ilia in the crowd. She was making her way through the revelers, Josepha trailing discretely behind her. Everyone greeted her with exclamations of concern, then peppered her with questions about her "horrifying" and "creepy" experience. All the attention had brought a flush to her cheeks, but despite her discomfort, she smiled and responded kindly to each villager, even Dawn Ravenna, who quickly joined the entourage. Was this Dawn's first step toward rebellion? For her sake, I hoped so.

Ilia didn't know it yet, but in a very short time her status had grown exponentially. She'd predicted something bad was coming, in front of witnesses, and she'd been right, proving herself a fey of great potential. She'd been rescued in dramatic fashion, looked stunning in a new Gossam gown, and had the last name Van der Daarke, which didn't hurt her in the least. Her shining star was on the rise.

Melaina and Renwick made no move to join her, though Renwick gave her an apologetic wave. She returned it with a happy grin, obviously relieved she'd no longer have to worry about marrying him. In response, her mother turned away, and Ilia's face crumpled, but she soon pulled back her shoulders and put on a smile as she responded to her well-wishers. Eventually her little crowd bumped into the crowd around Juletta, which consisted mostly of the darker, more rebellious young fey, and the two of them met up. The ballroom went silent and the air grew hot and dry until Ilia held out her hand to Juletta, who took it and shook it heartily.

"Can you ever forgive me?" Juletta lamented.

Ilia placed an earnest hand on her chest. "Being that it was my ancestor who spurned you, I'm the one who should be asking for your forgiveness."

"Oh, stuff and nonsense!" Juletta pulled Ilia into a hug. "No apologies from you, my girl, and I promise I'll never try to take your heart again."

Ilia laughed and hugged her back and the room relaxed, many even clapped, then everyone returned to their dancing, eating, and gossiping with great gusto. Nothing was going to derail this night for them.

It was good to see Ilia recovered and even blooming as she chatted with Juletta. They were about the same age and might even make good friends. Both had a lot to catch up on here in Hawthorn Lane and could face the growing process together. I'd no longer be needed, and that pained me more than I'd ever have expected it to. I wondered if I should even bother going to Ilia, then decided I must, even though we undoubtedly would go our separate ways after this. I had promised to look after her and had failed. I needed to say *something*.

As I made my way down to the dance floor, I couldn't help looking about, searching for Kyran. Where had he gone? At the very least, as host he should be here amongst his guests, but it was like he'd sunk into a hole in the ground, leaving us to fend for ourselves.

What a toff.

When the crowd around Ilia and Juletta saw me coming, they made way for me, eyeing me warily, unsure how to deal with my newly elevated status. I couldn't blame them. I didn't know how to deal with it, either. Ilia and Juletta were talking and laughing together, but when Ilia saw me, her expression grew solemn and I felt my stomach drop to my toes. She came to stand in front of me, her face long and terrible.

"Oh, Ilia," I rasped. This was more awful than I'd ever imagined. "I'm so sorry."

"You're sorry? It should be me apologizing to you, Lorelle. My mother was horrid to you and she and Renwick used you terribly and you got me dumped on you and my Uncle Kyran wasn't always very nice to you. How can you stand us?"

I blinked, not expecting any of this. "No, no, Ilia! I told you I'd watch out for you, but then I couldn't find you, and I got distracted—"

Her eyes sparkled mischievously. "By my uncle?"

She'd noticed. "Well, yes. He wanted to dance with me. But I didn't mean to forget about you, it's just that the music was so seductive and I'd had a glass of *Sinful Cider*, and then you were grabbed…"

"By me," Juletta interrupted, looking smug.

"And I let it happen!"

Ilia clapped her hands and laughed, surprising me. "Why do you think you couldn't find me, Lorelle? Guess!"

"There were a lot of people around, and—"

"I was laying low so you could have some fun, silly! I didn't want you to see me. I wanted you to dance, to enjoy life a little. You're too young to be so serious all the time, you know."

"Oh," was all I could say. It wasn't easy being chastised by someone six years younger than myself, and to be told I was *too young* was quite irritating.

"Look at her!" crowed Juletta, pointing at me. "Absolutely gobsmacked!"

"It's just that I promised...and well, I didn't follow through and..." I trailed away as they started to laugh.

"You don't have to save the world, Lorelle," Juletta pointed out. "You took Ilia in, you saved my life, you defended me from my sister, and you still look delightful."

I did? I do? "But I didn't save Ilia," I protested.

"Josepha and Uncle Kyran rescued me," Ilia said. "While you kept Juletta distracted long enough for them to make their move. So in a way you did save me."

I shook my head. "Wait. Kyran was there? I saw Josepha..." Standing behind Ilia, he gave me a broad grin and a finger wave. "But not your uncle." Then I remembered the dark figure. Ah. "How did he do it? And where is he now?"

Their laughter grew louder. "Oh, you should see your face!" Ilia giggled. "I can't believe you told him you didn't love him." She pointed at me. "Liar!"

"I don't... Well, I'm not sure, but I wasn't about to make him marry me for the sake of a curse. That's no way to start a marriage."

That set them off even worse. I stood there watching, taking my due, but not feeling too happy about it. No one likes to find themselves amusing to others when one wasn't trying to amuse them in the first place.

Finally Ilia took mercy on me. "He's working in the kitchen so the Fiersens could join the party. He wouldn't let me help because he said I should be enjoying myself after my *incident*." Ilia pushed me. "Go on. Go see him. You know you want to."

"But you heard what I said to him, Ilia! I told him I didn't want him."

"I don't think he believed you, and if he did, then he's not as smart as I thought he was. We all saw you two dancing, Lorelle. It was like the romance of the century." She sighed and clasped her hands together. "Oh, I wish Tiffany could've been here to see it." She turned and began to tell Juletta about her friend back at boarding school, my presence no longer needed. When she saw me still standing there, she shooed at me. "Go on! He's all by himself." Josepha lifted a peremptory eyebrow and pointed in the direction of the kitchen. I made a note to myself to make sure the elf didn't get too big for his britches after this.

I pulled myself together, then made my way out of the ballroom with as much dignity as I could muster. No one spoke to me, though they all looked like they wanted to at least try to ingratiate themselves with me, a potential Omni-Fey. But they held back, leaving me to my thoughts, and I was grateful for that. I didn't want to talk to anyone about my great-grandmother or the curse or Juletta's miraculous recovery. My plan was to be sure Kyran was all right, then I'd sneak home to lick my wounds, or at least figure out what those wounds actually were.

Close to the kitchen now, I slowly approached the doorway, not entirely sure I wanted to talk to him. I was feeling strangely fragile and what we had to talk about was serious. I'd need all my wits about me, and frankly, I felt like I'd left the whole basket of them back in the ballroom.

I peeked around the corner into the kitchen, then swiftly pulled back, heart pounding. Kyran was with someone...a woman. Slowly, cautiously, I peeked again. He was facing the doorway, working at the island table, jacket off and white sleeves rolled up. He looked rather handsome in the warm, flickering torchlight, his hair slightly tousled, a slight sheen of sweat on his brow from the heat of the room. His dark eyes were focused intently on the woman standing by the table only a few feet from him and I wished for a moment that I were the one on the receiving end of such a look.

"I'm honored you came to the ball, Lady Faylan."

"Lady Faylan. That sounds so formal. Call me Vira." She was a clever girl, all right, giving him no choice in the matter.

Kyran nodded, but didn't verbally concede to her request. Two could play that game. "Is there something I could get you?" he asked, playing the gracious host. "Something to eat, perhaps? Or a drink?"

"Oh, no. I'm fine. Really, I came here to see how you were doing. That was quite a traumatic experience for us all." She paused, waiting for him to agree, but he merely stared at her, his dark eyes giving away nothing. "But it's over, and for that I'm grateful."

"You have your sister back, too," he said. "That's a good thing."

Her responding laugh was surprisingly girlish. "Oh, I'm not so sure about that. You have *your* sister back, too. Are you grateful for that?"

Kyran looked down at the table, then back up at her. "Touché." He returned to his work setting hors de oeuvres on a tray and Lady Faylan reached out and touched his arm, stilling it.

"I'd like for us to be on the same side, Kyran. I knew your family and considered them my friends. When Elowina Gragan cursed them and this entire village, I lost a lot. It's taken me a long time to get my life back together and I don't think I could survive another shake-up like that one. After my sister disappeared, my parents withered away from grief at her loss and died not long after, leaving me entirely alone." Her voice wobbled a little. "I took my place as overseer and have had my work cut out for me over the years, trying to keep this place safe while fighting a curse that was not of my doing."

Lies upon lies. Really, her whole dress should be on fire by now. It would almost be funny if I weren't so angry with her.

"You suffered a lot," he acknowledged.

"As have you, if your sister is anything to judge by. Like Juletta, Melaina sounds the type to sacrifice anyone and anything to get her way, leaving the rest of us to pick up after her mess. We have much in common when it comes to our family and our roles here in Hawthorn Lane."

"What are you suggesting?" he asked, shooting right to the heart of the matter.

Lady Faylan's shoulders stiffened a fraction. "Truthfully I'd like someone to consult with on matters concerning the village. I know you're new here, but the longer you stay, the more you'll understand Hawthorn Lane and what a special place it is."

"What if I don't want to stay?"

I couldn't help myself. I gasped, quickly clapping a hand over my mouth. Neither Lady Faylan nor Kyran reacted and I slowly lowered my hand, stunned. The Van der Daarkes couldn't leave now. They were needed here.

"I wouldn't blame you for going," she said in a gentle tone I remembered her using with me at various times throughout our acquaintanceship, typically when she wanted something from me that I didn't want to give her. "You came here believing your life was in danger, but now that you know it was your cousin trying to trick you, you're free to return to your old life. A life that was likely much safer and more predictable than what you'd find in this place."

More predictable. Nice touch.

"I'm going to think about it," he said as he gently pulled his arm away from her hand and returned to work. "That's all I can promise at this point."

"I understand. There are times when I think of leaving myself. But Hawthorn Lane is my home and the villagers need me. So I'll stay and do my best to protect them and their interests, no matter the cost. It's my duty."

"I heard that you told your sister to leave Hawthorn Lane or forfeit her life," he said bluntly. "Is that true?"

She bowed her head. "It is. When I found out that Juletta was still alive and had taken up residence in the Hollow, I started rumors to keep people away, for their protection and for hers. I had my duty, but I would not punish my own sister if I could help it. Unfortunately, that Lorelle Gragan interfered, forcing Juletta to show herself. Lorelle's a troublemaker, isn't she? Just like her great-grandmother."

"Troublemaker?" Kyran repeated, still working, but his eyes no longer on his task.

Lady Faylan lifted one shoulder. "I took her in, years ago, not knowing who she was or what her history was. It was only when I learned her last name that I realized what I'd done. Somehow she had found Hawthorn Lane, but I didn't know why she'd come, and I must admit I was curious after her family had stayed away so long. So I let her in, thinking maybe she'd come to take away the curse. But she never even mentioned it, and now she refuses to do anything." She wrung her hands. "And to treat you, such an important and esteemed personage in our community, the way she did? Abominable."

"Abominable," he repeated in a stony voice and my heart skipped a beat.

"I think that if we work together, Count Van der Daarke," Lady Faylan continued in a soft, measured voice, though I could detect flickers of excitement in it, "we could beat this curse and return Hawthorn Lane to the way it was when your family reigned supreme."

"You and I? Work together?"

"As partners."

"I see. And you know for certain that Lorelle's family is responsible for this curse?"

"I do." It wasn't a complete lie. In Lady Faylan's mind Elowina had stolen Marekai from her, and she'd likely convinced herself that if it hadn't been for my great-grandmother, she wouldn't have needed to make the curse.

"Yet you allowed Lorelle back into Hawthorn Lane?"

"Like I said, I didn't realize who she was until it was too late. Then I felt sorry for her, and that blinded me when normally I would've been much more cautious. Thinking back, she must have put a spell on me.

Lorelle Gragan is a dark one, and perhaps an unwise addition to our little community."

"Perhaps," Kyran concurred, and I froze inside.

"I'm so glad we agree," Lady Faylan purred, her hand creeping back to touch him.

That's when I tiptoed away, making it only ten feet before I broke into a run, fleeing down the hall and out into the stormy night.

Chapter Thirty-Eight

The sky was bright with flashes of lightning and thunder cracked hard overhead as I stepped outside, viewing the deluge before me with a frown. Rain fell in sheets, and before I'd gone twenty steps, I was soaked through. The downpour had turned the road to mud, and I nearly fell several times before making it to the forest.

Once within the shelter of the trees, the rain and wind lessened and I was able to make better progress. Then the toe of my shoe connected with a tree root and my ankle twisted sharply. Stumbling, I pitched face forward, cracking my forehead on a flat stone. Dazed, I lay on my stomach for several moments, winded and unable to move.

"Help!" I eventually called out, though my voice was weak. No one responded, and I didn't know whether to be grateful or worried.

After pulling in a few steadying breaths, I managed to turn over and sit up. Head spinning, I called out again, more loudly this time. Bringing attention to myself in Fell Forest was a risk, but one I had to take. In my current state, I wasn't sure I could make it home on my own, and staying here in the cold rain brought with it the danger of exposure.

Over the patter of rain, the staccato pulse of hooves filled the air. Thanks be to Grim, someone must have heard me from the road. The pounding grew louder and louder, and then suddenly stopped. My head whipped over to the left, and my mouth went dry as I watched a large creature push its way through the thick branches of the dark pine trees growing along the trail. Even in the dark I could see it was a centaur, and a massive one at that. This one had not attended the ball—I would have remembered him.

He came close to me, each step slow and measured, and I sat very still, waiting for whatever was coming next and hoping it wouldn't be my death. His feral scent—a combination of fresh air and animal musk—reached my nostrils, and they quivered slightly in response to the exotic smell.

"You're in need of assistance, Mistress Gragan," the centaur spoke, his voice low and sure, with a burr strong enough to make me wonder if I'd somehow ended up in the Scottish Highlands.

"Sadly, yes," I gasped, wondering how he knew my name. "I'm not sure I can walk. I twisted my ankle."

"That is unfortunate."

I laughed a little. "Yes, well, it seems that this night is determined to be unkind to me."

A low, rumbling chuckle rose from deep within his chest. "I've heard of your struggles on this eve."

I blinked up at him, the rain pelting my face like pebbles. "You have? But how?" Had the other centaurs at the ball already spread the news? "And how do you know my name? I don't know yours. I'm afraid I haven't spent any more time in the forest than necessary. The villagers have always been wary of this place and I guess that rubbed off on me."

"They should be wary." *Not comforting.* "But you are always welcome here, Mistress Gragan. We of the forest knew your family before they left. They were always good to us."

They were? "That's heartening to hear, and frankly, a bit surprising. If they were anything like my mother, I can't see them being good to anyone."

"Your mother lost her way a long time ago."

"Is that a nice way of saying she lost her mind?" I asked, curious how he knew anything about my mother to make such a statement.

His deep laugh came again and I found myself relaxing a little. "I'll take you home, and in future, if you need anything, call out to the winds. They'll carry your voice to me, and I will come."

"That's very kind of you, um…"

"Rialban of the Fell," he filled in my questioning reply. His name sounded Gaelic and probably meant something regal and amazing.

"It's a pleasure to meet you Rialban of the Fell." I gave him a respectful nod. "And the offer goes both ways. You already know where I live, don't you?"

"Of course," he answered with a certainty that sent a shiver up my spine. "I'll be sure to call upon you when I need you." *When*, not if. He reached down, and I grabbed hold of his powerful hand. "Up you go." He swung me onto his wide, sleek back without effort. "Grab on," he ordered. "I don't know how to run slowly."

I laughed, then realized he might not be kidding, so I wrapped my arms around his wet, muscular, and might I add, *naked*, torso, and hung on tight. The night was improving by leaps and bounds and the urge to throw myself in the brook was fading.

"I'm ready," I told him, and he took off, galloping along the trail faster than any horse I'd ever ridden. We made it to the bridge near my cottage so quickly I'd swear I hadn't had time to draw breath, though it was quite possible I'd been holding it the entire ride. The sensation of Rialban's powerful muscles tensing beneath my palms with each stride was hypnotic, and unexpectedly arousing, especially when my hand slipped down and accidentally grazed the point where skin turned to fur. For that brief span of time, I forgot about my problems and simply enjoyed an escapade I was unlikely ever to experience again.

Rialban leaped over the expanding brook, sending a thrill shooting through my core, and landed on the other side with barely a thud. He had the grace of a ballet dancer, the strength of a bull, and the bearing of a king, and I felt flattered he'd chosen to help me. We neared the gate to my cottage, and with one quick movement, he plucked me from his back and set me down in front of him. Outside the forest there was a little more light, a distant glow from the streetlamps, and I could see his face now. A strong Roman nose, slightly crooked, perched above full lips, and where I thought he'd have flowing locks, he surprised me with a smooth skull, which suited his strong jaw and deep-set eyes.

Still holding my arms, he bent down to peer into my face. "We shall meet again, Mistress Gragan, and we shall talk."

"Y-yes," I stuttered, suddenly shy. "I'd like that," I managed to add, glad for the darkness hiding my hot cheeks. To be close to such wildness and power was a bit overwhelming.

He let go of me and straightened up, his head turning toward the forest as though hearing a call. "You must attend to your home. The water is rising." Then, with a courtly bow, he turned and galloped off, his thudding hooves matching the throbbing pulse taking over my body. I took several deep, steadying breaths to calm down or risk passing out only yards from my front door.

At last I could walk without my head spinning, though my ankle protested each step as I hobbled toward the cottage. The closer I grew to my home, the more worried I became about its well-being. Once inside, I lit a lantern and hopped down the wooden stairs descending into the cellar, stunned to see over a foot of water covering the floor.

My mind whirled with fear. This cottage was my sanctuary, my whole world. I couldn't lose it. *You must attend to your home*, Rialban had said, but what did he think I could do? Even if I was of Omni-Fey blood and possessed of great powers, I still had no idea how to use them, especially to hold back a flood.

A crack of thunder shook the house, and I swiftly headed back upstairs and out into the storm. Standing for a moment in the backyard, the rain and wind battered at me like attacking soldiers. All around me thunder exploded like cannon fire and lightning lit up the sky, startling me into movement. My shoes sunk into the mushy ground, each step descending deeper as I neared the angry brook. The downpour grew heavier, as did the weight on my shoulders. I was sick to death of rain, tired of worrying about my cottage caving in on top of me, fed up with feeling like an outsider in this place.

I shook my fist at the sky. "*Stop it*. Stop it this instant!"

Nature's response was to throw a gust of wind at me so hard it knocked me over. Forgetting my sore ankle, I leaped to my feet, furious. "Leave us, you bloody depressing blight! You've outstayed your welcome."

A bolt of lightning darted out of the sky and hit the ground only a few yards from where I stood, blowing me off my feet. Heart pounding erratically, I jumped back up, staggered and dazed, but more determined than ever. It was time to fight back.

The lightning bolt had left behind a crackling electric force that filled the air around me, giving me an idea. A crazy idea. I had no clue what I was doing, no sense of the danger of what I was about to attempt, but I didn't care. If I were truly fey, I could do this. If I failed, I was no worse off than before… that is, unless I managed to electrocute myself and melt all my internal organs.

With this less than comforting thought in mind, I closed my eyes and imagined drawing to me the electrically charged ions saturating the air, pictured them filling my body with heat and energy, envisioned my entire heart and soul bidding nature to bend to my will. It all sounded impossible, but I had to make this work, had to believe I could do it, both for myself and for my future here in Hawthorn Lane.

Just when I thought nothing was going to happen, a hot liquid force surged through me, shooting from my toes up through my torso and all the way to the tips of my trembling fingers. I'd never felt so alive in my life. My eyes opened wide and I pointed my fingers at the sky. "Begone!" I cried, and blue bolts flew out of my fingertips straight upward, swift as arrows, to blow the malevolent storm clouds hovering over the village into shreds.

"Again!" I shouted, throwing more bolts. The dark clouds ruptured into black ribbons, which quickly disintegrated in the wind. With each blast, the rain lightened, until finally it stopped. Moments later, a warm wind picked up and blew away the remaining clouds.

At last the storm was over.

But the danger was not. There was more to be done. I marched over to the dam and gathered together the remaining sparks still swirling and dancing inside me. I pulled in a deep breath, then released it, blasting the water with the heat that had built up in my body like a furnace.

When the hot, white light hit the brook, massive clouds of steam rose up like a magic trick. I repeated the process over and over, making sure to only hit the top layer to avoid steaming the aquatic inhabitants alive, until finally the water level dropped and the ground around me grew firm.

The last of the energy flew from me, and I sunk to my knees, exhausted. I'd saved my cottage, and I had done it entirely on my own. And I would continue to do so.

Curse or no curse, I would not buckle under and marry Kyran. The villagers could not force me, just as my mother couldn't force me to be with Dallen. I might be tempting fate with my rebellion, but so be it.

And with that promise to myself firmly entrenched in my mind and in my heart, I returned to my cottage.

Chapter Thirty-Nine

Dry now, I lay on my chaise in front of the fire, melted choco in hand and spiked with a well-earned dash of *Dark Spirits*, pondering with wonder what I'd learned about myself tonight. By stopping the rain and pushing back the water, I'd controlled the elements, the most difficult of all magic. I might even have saved myself from drowning when I'd fallen in the brook while trying to raise the sluice gate. It hadn't been Kyran. It had been *me*.

I could no longer deny I was fey. Not only fey, but a fey of great power, possibly even an Omni-Fey like my great-grandmother. Vacillating between elation and alarm at the idea, it occurred to me that if I were fey, then my whole family must be fey. At this realization, the alarm quickly smothered my elation. Mother with magical powers? Aunt Nimair and Eudrea, too? Sounded like a horror movie in the making.

But our being fey wasn't the worst part. It came back to me what Dallen had said after I'd found him with Eudrea. When I wouldn't return his phone calls, he'd shown up at the house to confront me. His voice was pleading, his eyes wounded as he stood on the porch, baseball cap in hand and begged me to reconsider.

"I don't remember any of that, Lorelle," he'd protested when I had to actually say out loud what had happened, since he refused to admit to anything. For once his typical charming, if a bit cocky, demeanor was gone, replaced by a desperation I hadn't thought him capable of feeling. "You *have* to believe me." And I hadn't. I'd caught them red-handed. Both he and Eudrea had seen me. How could he even pretend I hadn't seen them?

But he'd been telling the truth, after all. Eudrea had done exactly what Mother had claimed she'd done. She'd seduced Dallen, but she must have done it with magic, turning herself into me, or at least giving the illusion that she was me. How she knew about her abilities, I couldn't fathom. Perhaps Mother had told her, or possibly Aunt Nimair while drunk. Or maybe Eudrea had figured it out on her own. She was always on the lookout for ways to manipulate people, and what better way than magic? And if she'd known about magic back then, I could only imagine how good she must be at it now.

Mother and Aunt Nimair had to know something about the curse, too—maybe not the truth of how it came about, but its existence. It was why Mother was so set on my marrying Dallen, why she had emphasized that I *must* love him. But why hadn't she told me about my fey? About the curse? If I'd known, I might have been more amenable to staying with Dallen.

I shivered convulsively. If Mother knew about us being fey, then maybe she also knew about Hawthorn Lane. The centaur, Rialban, had seemed to know about her, maybe because she'd come here before. I downed a large gulp of choco, my hands trembling. The possibility that my mother might know where I was hiding was almost too frightening to contemplate.

What was I going to do? I'd done Dallen a terrible wrong, blaming him for what had happened when he'd been entirely innocent. Maybe if he'd found someone else in the years I'd been gone, then it would be all right. But if he were still looking for me? Still struggling to come to terms with my disappearance? It meant I owed him something. An explanation, at the very least. At the most, well, possibly a return to my commitment to him, to make up for what my sister and I had put him through.

The thought of returning made my stomach heave. I didn't want to go home, back to a life where a miasma of foreboding always hovered over me like a storm cloud…Mother brooding, her anger sending off poisonous waves, Aunt Nimair's endless 'woe is me' complaining, Eudrea's cruel taunts. But how could I turn my back on a guy who'd treated me kindly, who'd managed to please my mother, even, and who'd been manipulated and tricked by my sister? One way or another I had to make things right with him.

I groaned aloud. I didn't want to think about my family or Dallen or what I was going to do. I simply wanted to drink my choco and relive the memory of dancing with Kyran. I wanted to blot everything out and pretend I lived in a world of my own making, where everything was as I wanted it to be.

But that wasn't going to happen.

An imperious knock rattled the door, startling me, and I nearly spilled my drink when I realized I'd forgotten to put a chair under the handle.

"Lorelle?"

Kyran. I leaned toward the door as though drawn to him. "What do you want?"

"I came to talk to you." At the sound of his voice my heart fluttered in my chest. "I want to come in."

"Right now? I'm…" What? Indisposed? Tired? Afraid of throwing myself at you despite all my protestations?

"You've done magic, haven't you?"

I sat up straight. "How did you know?"

"Just give me permission to enter." His voice sounded as tired as my own.

"Yes. All right." I watched as the lock bar rose upward, then the door handle lifted. Kyran, looking windblown, stepped inside, bringing with him the scent of warm air and spring.

"There's a hook by the fire." I indicated the spot, hardly able to look at him. "You can hang your cloak there."

When he passed me, the shock wave between us was so strong I fell back against the chaise, heart racing. Kyran stumbled, then righted himself, hanging up his cloak and taking the rocking chair in a rush of movement.

Then everything slowed down as he warmed his hands in front of the fire, giving himself time, I suspected, to steady his pounding heart.

When he was ready, he lifted his eyes to meet mine. "You heard our conversation," he began.

"I did," I admitted. "I'd come to find you. Ilia said you were working alone in the kitchen and I wanted to see if you needed help."

"But instead you found me with Lady Faylan and listened in."

"Yes." My voice was small. "I've been gathering information for years, and it's a habit now. I shouldn't have done it, but I couldn't make myself walk away. Didn't want to, actually."

"I knew you were there."

"You did?"

"Of course. I always know when you're near."

He did? I wasn't so sure I liked that. And yet…to be *known* like that. It was a tantalizing notion.

"Lady Faylan might have taken you in," he went on, "and she might have taught you how to gather, but she's not your friend."

"No. She's not my friend."

"Nor is she mine."

My breath caught in my throat. "You seemed pretty friendly with her."

His eyes darkened. "I've learned that with people like Lady Faylan one must tread carefully."

"So you don't trust her?"

"Not a bit." The relief I felt at hearing those words was like sinking into a hot bath after a long day.

But I couldn't show my hand yet. First I needed to know why he'd come here. "I see," I said coolly. "Is that what you've come to tell me?"

He leaned forward and grabbed my hand, setting off a shockwave that traveled through my entire body in a pulsing rhythm. But I weathered it better this time, left only slightly breathless. "I'm sorry you thought I'd abandoned you, Lorelle. I had to go help Ilia and you were giving me the perfect opportunity to do so. I didn't realize that Lady Faylan was so ruthless, or I'd have come back immediately after seeing Ilia was safe. I only heard the real story while I was refreshing the tables—I'd promised the Fiersens they would be done at midnight and would not break that promise." He squeezed my hand tightly. "What she'd nearly done to you made me want to throttle the woman, but as there were numerous witnesses I held back. Next time she might not be so lucky."

At his words, a frisson of excitement welled up inside me. I had always sensed Kyran could be fierce, but this anger was something greater and more powerful, like the wrath of an angry god.

"No need for murder. Everything turned out all right, especially as Juletta was able to change herself back to normal."

"Juletta didn't do that. That was you."

I sat up straighter and my blanket shawl slipped off my shoulders. "Me? I don't think so."

"Oh?" He lifted a superior eyebrow at me. "And how do you propose it was done?"

"Like I said, Juletta did it herself."

"That's not what people are saying."

"I don't know how it happened, then, but it wasn't me. I wouldn't even know how—" What I'd done only an hour ago flashed through my mind and I changed tactics. "I've only just found out that I'm Omni-Fey, you know."

"Yes, rumor has it that you're also high-born." His eyes sparkled with amusement.

I went hot, pulling my hand from his grip. "I don't think I can be called high-born when I grew up in a neighborhood more known for its flashers than its gentry."

"It doesn't matter where you grew up, Lorelle. It's in your blood. You can't help it, nor can you escape it. Just as I can't."

I gripped my cup tight enough to crush it and quickly set it on the floor. "You're just saying that because I called you a snob!"

He smirked. "Maybe, and it feels really good, especially after being told by a certain someone that a person can't suddenly become something they're not."

I bit my lip, vexed. "Lady Faylan thinks the two of you would be good together," I counterattacked. "Maybe she's right."

"Disregarding the fact that I want to murder her, she's not high-born."

"How do you know she's not?"

"I can tell these things, remember? When she touched my arm I could feel her true nature."

"But then... Wait a second." I swallowed hard, unable to believe it. "Then you always knew I was fey."

"Of course I did. That's one reason why I can sense your presence." I wondered what the other reasons were. "But I would've assumed you were fey anyway. You live here. Hawthorn Lane won't allow the feyless to enter. The border keeps them out, or at the very least, sounds an alarm." The look in his eyes was amused, and I realized with annoyance that I'd just given away my secret.

"I've never heard that."

"I imagine Lady Faylan neglected to tell you that when you first came."

My fingers twisted the fringes on my shawl. "Yes, she did."

He leaned forward and grabbed both my hands, reigniting the sparks flying between us. "I also knew all along that you were high-born."

"All along?" I whispered. No wonder he'd left Ilia with me when he hadn't known me from Adam. No wonder he'd deigned to dance with me, to spend time with me. I was his sort...the right sort.

His eyes sparkled. "All along."

"Hell's bells, Kyran! Why didn't you say anything?"

"Because I liked watching you climb up on your high horse. It amused me."

Bastard. "You were laughing at me!" I tried to pull my hands away, but this time he wouldn't let go, his eyes growing serious.

"Not at you. Never at you, Lorelle. You make me feel as though there's hope in the world. I've never felt that way before. Ever. I want to be with you. I *need* to be with you." His last words came out hoarsely and a warm liquid heat filled all the hopeless little cracks in my heart.

"Be with me?" *What did that mean exactly?*

"I want to marry you," he answered my unspoken question.

"But we don't even know each other!"

"Then we shall take all the time we need to get to know each other." The hidden promise behind his words made my insides quiver expectantly.

"You're doing this to remove the curse."

"I'm doing this because I want you so badly I can't think of anything else."

The breath went out of me. "Ah," I gulped, wishing I had poured more than a dash of *Dark Spirits* into my melted choco. "I see. But marriage?"

"What can I say? I'm an old-fashioned guy."

"But I can't marry you," I protested feebly, no longer certain of the reason why.

"Let's not worry about that right now," he replied smoothly, before I could say anything more. "I won't push you. Not too hard. Not yet." My mind spun dizzily, his provocative words muddling my ability to think. "Though I believe it would be in your best interests to at least pretend you're considering being with me."

My brain suddenly cleared. "Why?"

"The villagers aren't going to be very forgiving if it came out that you're not trying to remove the curse. My sister won't back down, you know. She'll keep at you, and she'll do it by inciting the villagers against you. That's how she works. So if you and I made a show of getting along, they won't be so hard on you."

Ah. How clever. My wits sharpened even more. So this was to be a game. "You're saying that you're willing to pretend, too."

"I told you. I want you. I don't need to pretend."

My breath hitched in my chest. Not a game. Not for him. "But the curse says we must be from different worlds. If we're both high-born, then our love can't undo anything."

He waved this away. "We'll figure it out. I'm sure there's more than one way to break this curse."

He sounded so confident when I was feeling anything but. "If I spend time with you, it won't be to save my own skin or to undo the curse. I'll do it because I want to."

"And do you want to?"

"A part of me does."

"What about the other part?"

"There are things I have to work through…" I was thinking of Dallen, of being suddenly high-born when I'd gone on and on about being a commoner, about Lady Faylan and the secrets between us, about whether or not to reveal that my great-grandmother didn't make the curse. There was a lot at stake.

"So if I wanted to kiss you"—he leaned forward, so close I could feel his breath on my cheek—"that part of you would protest?"

"I-I don't know. I—"

His lips were on mine so fast and hard they cut off any words I might have wanted to say. I kept expecting to feel the jolt between us, but this time it didn't come. This time I felt only a hot, whirling sensation that started at my heart and reached down to my belly, descending south at a rapid pace. Kyran's arms wrapped around me, pulling me tighter, and his kiss grew more passionate, his hands more frenzied as they stroked my back. I almost couldn't breathe, and I didn't care.

When he pulled back, I was past the point of caring about anything.

Slowly I opened my eyes to see Kyran staring at me, his expression triumphant.

"Why are you looking at me like that?"

"Let's count tonight as our first date, shall we?"

"What?"

He stood and cupped my cheek with his large hand, warm and reassuring, and yet maddeningly erotic. "I'll be dreaming of you, Lorelle," he whispered in my ear, then kissed me on the cheek.

My skin was still tingling as he grabbed his cloak and was gone.

Chapter Forty

Judging by all the talk, the *Danse Macabre* ball was destined to become the event of the century. Everyone agreed. The Van der Daarke soirée had everything in abundance—excellent food and drink, a curse uncovered, a woman returned from the dead, a monster transformed back into her former self, and a potential Omni-Fey discovered.

Absolute perfection.

As everyone recovered from their hangovers and loss of sleep, the messenger birds were kept busy, flying back and forth, spreading rumors about the night's happenings, rumors that grew bigger and more elaborate with each passing day. The villagers had never enjoyed themselves more.

I kept to myself.

Berenea showed up the day after the ball and got her interview, but there wasn't much I could tell her beyond what she had already heard. Melaina and Lady Faylan knew more than I did about the curse and our families' involvement in it, which annoyed Berenea to no end to hear. I also couldn't tell her how Juletta had turned back into her former self, though I hinted that maybe Juletta had done it with her own magic. Berenea was skeptical (if Juletta had done it, why hadn't she fixed herself before now, then, eh?), but that was the version in the paper the following day. After her interrogation, she spent a good amount of time gloating about being right—that there was something different about me, she'd known it all along. I let her gloat, then showed her the door, pointing out she had a deadline to meet.

In the days after the ball, my life went on much the same as before, except it felt different. *I* felt different. I couldn't stop thinking about Kyran and our kiss, and I also couldn't stop thinking about Dallen and what I owed him.

I didn't know what to do about either one of them.

By mid-week, the villagers were starting to look at me funny when I came to the village to deliver my delectables. I knew what they were thinking. I knew what they wanted from me. To break the curse. It was finally starting to sink in just what the curse had done and was still doing to them. Not only was it killing love and ruining relationships, speculation was growing that the curse, or the dampener Lady Faylan had used on it, had also diminished the villagers' magic.

It explained why, in a village full of magical creatures, I rarely saw magic being done. Spells were made, yes, but they were of elementary quality only. Lady Faylan's turning a teapot into a chicken, while impressive at the time, I soon learned was equivalent to a parlor trick. It seemed the curse had made it impossible to do anything more than simple magic. The villagers weren't hiding their powers; as it turned out, there was nothing to hide. It came to me that this was why I was able to pass as a non-fey. No one was going to question my magic deficiency when they were deficient themselves. No wonder Avice hadn't taught Ilia much magic…she could barely do it herself.

Breaking the curse would be the saving of this village and make the villagers view me in a more favorable light. Unfortunately, while I supposedly bore the mark of the curse, Kyran and I as a couple didn't meet the curse's major requirement. We didn't come from two different worlds.

But he and Lady Faylan did.

And she wanted him.

Desperately.

He'd told me he didn't want her, and I mostly believed him, but was he strong enough to fight her? Much like myself, Kyran was a newcomer to the magic scene. Lady Faylan could easily spell him and make him her lover. *Just like that.* By the time she undid the spell he might truly be in love with her. Then she'd tell the villagers that she'd remembered the curse wrong, or make some excuse for why two highborns could be together and still break the curse, and that'd be that.

So I was stuck.

I couldn't undo the curse, I couldn't figure out what to do about Dallen, and I didn't know how to let go of Kyran. All I could do was go about my business, avoid the Van der Daarkes, and hope the villagers would turn to other topics.

But they didn't, and I knew they wouldn't.

Why should they? They were cursed. We all were, and until the curse was lifted, we'd be miserable. When it came to relationships, none of us would have more than a moment's happiness. We were doomed to endless fighting, bickering, and squabbling with our loved ones. And when it came to magic—well, that defined our village's very soul. We needed it back.

I spent the following week doing chores and playing mournful dirges on my clariflute. Doolin Fiersen and two of his younger sons came over and fixed the cellar's foundation. They worked quickly and competently, finishing the job in a mere three days. Our interaction each morning when they arrived was painfully formal; gone was the easygoing atmosphere between us, and I had no idea how to make things go back to the way they'd been. So I kept out of their way, spending my time outside working. I sowed the garden and transplanted all my seedlings, gathered wood by the barrow, and cleaned out the chicken coop.

Kyran stopped by a total of fourteen times—twice a day and never when anyone else was about. He didn't come in. He couldn't make it past the bar I'd had Doolin install, though he did make an attempt after the third day when I didn't respond. The bar held, even against his magic.

At each visit, he never knocked more than three times, merely stood outside the door waiting for me to answer. Yet he seemed to accept that I wasn't going to say a word, remaining silent himself. Each day, I sensed him growing more restless and knew it was only a matter of time before he caught me unawares.

And then what?

On the seventh day, I found myself pressing my body against the door as though to will myself through it and to the other side, into his arms. I was growing weak.

After a long week and many sleepless nights, I finally determined I had only one option…follow Lady Faylan's advice and leave Hawthorn Lane.

It was something I never thought I'd do, but it was the only way to save my home. I loved my bewitching Hawthorn Lane; my whole being was connected to this place. But I couldn't stay here knowing that doing so would keep the misery alive. Kyran would not go to Lady Faylan if I were still in the picture.

It took some time, but I finally had it all figured out. I would go back to Dallen—if he would have me—and try to make a life for myself in the Alterworld while Lady Faylan worked her magic on Kyran and undid the curse. I couldn't live in Hawthorn Lane, but I could save it. It would have to be enough. And if Dallen was with somebody already, then maybe someday I could come back here.

The trick was to get away without anyone finding out. Especially Kyran. I knew in my heart that he wouldn't let me go, and if he tried to stop me, he'd succeed in keeping me from leaving. I understood that as well as I knew my own heart. And if I stayed, that would be the downfall of Hawthorn Lane, something I could never allow to happen.

I'd rather die.

So I would leave on the morrow, at night, when all of Hawthorn Lane would be fast asleep.

And I would hope against hopes that I could find a way to be happy and stop the tears already sliding down my cheeks.

About the Author

Feeling Witchy

When author, Kristina Schram, was growing up she wanted to be a star. When that didn't turn out quite like she expected, she turned her mind to achieving other goals: Earning her Ph.D. in Counseling Psychology, working as an Artist-in-Residence at local schools, being a free-lance editor and reader, coaching parks & rec basketball, protecting the earth through recycling and using green products, and publishing her first novel, a YA fantasy called The Chronicles of Anaedor: The Prophecies.

Knowing what it's like to struggle with self-doubt and lack of confidence, her biggest dream (in addition to owning a castle) is to stamp out low self-esteem for everyone, especially young people. She lives in beautiful, wooded New Hampshire with her husband, three boys, and various pets, and can also throw a tomahawk, if need be. One of her favorite things to do is walk with her dog in the woods, where she searches for the impossible around every corner. Sometimes she finds it.

For more information on Kristina Schram, feel free to make a trip to her website: www.kristinaschram.com. She's also on Facebook, Twitter, and Pinterest.

Other Works by Kristina Schram

Paranormal Gothic Romances

The Pandora Belfry Adventure Series

Other Works by Kristina Schram

Fantasy Adventure Trilogy

  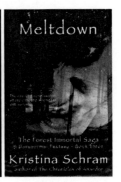

Fantasy Adventure Quartet

CPSIA information can be obtained
at www.ICGtesting.com
Printed in the USA
LVOW11s1637150218
566740LV00002B/455/P